MILENA
& Other Social Reforms

Olja Knezevic

2011.

MILENA was inspired by the real events.
The characters, however, are fictional.

Olja Knezevic
MILENA & Other Social Reforms

Edition "Savremeni roman"

Editor
Željko Ivanović

Publisher
Daily Press - Podgorica
Željko Ivanović

Prepress
Blažo Milić

Print
"Elvod Print" - Lazarevac
3000 copies.

CIP - Каталогизација у публикацији
Централна народна бибилиотека Црне Горе, Цетиње

ISBN 978-86-7706-326-9
COBISS.CG-ID 18262544

To my parents,
Ljilja and Loco

About MILENA

Dubravka Ugresic, a Croatian and international writer (Mechanic Institute Review): 'Olja Knezevic brings us a uniquely penetrating voice of female narrator. Her writing is harsh, funny and frightening. Shockingly brutal world of post-communist mafia in Podgorica she describes in her story feels fully believable.'

Jagna Pogačnik, (Jutarnji List, Croatia): 'Olja Knežević's novel 'Milena & Other Social Reforms' is a resistance movement novel. In Montenegro, it was sold out two weeks after its first publication. It takes a lot of courage to write a novel like this, because it is based around a true story, and in Montenegro, it could be considered as 'roman a clef', with thriller and love story elements; with two dimensions: 'public' and 'intimate' – all of which contributes to this novel's fantastic dynamics. 'Milena' has an authentic female voice. Olja Knežević's fiction has tremendous power, perhaps also because it is based in truth.

Balša Brković, a Montenegrin writer (Monitor, Montenegrin independent weekly review): 'Olja Knežević's novel, 'Milena & Other Social Reforms' is the most important culture event in Montenegro in 2011. It is a small masterpiece.'

Marinko Vorgić, a literary critic (Vijesti, Montenegro): 'MILENA is a wonderful first novel about the stubbornness of patriarchate and machismo of a totalitarian rule and society, where the destruction of female principle has become an ideology.'

Roman Simić-Bodrožić, a Croatian writer and columnist (Meet the Author, Croatian Book Festival): 'Crime, orgies and corrupt politicians, the generations raised on the rhythms of war hysteria and after-war depression . . . Olja Knežević's novel can be read as thriller, but what was after Milena – could have been after us as well. Whether we admit it or not, the world as shown to us by Milena is our world, too, while she – tough and vulnerable, spiteful and vivid – is the bitter fruit of that world, the heroine of our times.'

Say this city has ten million souls
Some are living in mansions, some are living in holes:
Yet there's no place for us, my dear, there's no place
    For us.
Once we had a country and we thought it fair,
Look in the atlas and you'll find it there:
We cannot go there now, my dear, we cannot go there
    Now.

                    (W.H. Auden: Refugee blues)

On the roof

I have no sleeping pills, or any kind of pills here, in London. I still don't have a GP, no registered NHS number; but I don't get sick, not even a common cold, for some reason. Now, though, I'd love some sleeping pills. At least up on the roof of my Battersea tower block, I can smoke and be left alone, not bother anyone. Down below me only the Thames, swallowing her Friday-night portion of the metropolis madness. The river is like a black trash-bag wrapped around the waist of the city.

Back home, in Montenegro, I also lived near the river, Moracha. It wasn't indifferent. It was more like a dancer-river. Mora-cha-cha-cha. A skinny, cold bitch, rushing wild over the rocks it had polished, streaks of vein-green beneath her crystal clear waters. It's beautiful and crazy, and I left it behind.

Three years ago, I landed at Gatwick. It was April but I arrived in London wearing my shaved mink coat, the colour of champagne. Already there and then, I knew I'd have to, sooner rather than later, trade that mink for a pile of GBP notes. I was as broke as a yawn in the world I'd arrived in. At school, we were taught that capitalism was death for one's soul. A sweet death, I thought at the gates of Gatwick. And anyway: was my soul alive? The Sterling musical notes (£££!) looked so solid, happy and safe to me. Much more important than a fur coat.

Later on, when I became 'Millie', when the music of Sterling persuaded me that I was London's middle-class - I did what the middle-class do: I gave the champagne mink to Oxfam.

I gave it away! My warm, illegal fur! And now, I even think in English; well, Milena-kind-of-English, but still.

I could do with that mink now, in the small hours of the night — November 16 – when the eastern wind is so sharp up here, on my roof, that my teeth hurt.

1

Yola, my flat-mate, comes to the roof to see if I'm all right. She's wrapped in a thin kimono decorated with pink kittens, purchased in the children's department of Gap on Kings Road. She's wearing no socks, only a pair of plastic slippers with two-inch heels on her soft, neat feet. She's just standing there, next to the iron staircase, like a small monument to insanity, her kimono fluttering in the breeze from the river. Her hair is short and so bleached that I could probably read by it.

'Don't worry,' I smile at my tiny Polish flat-mate from the 'picnic-corner' of our roof. 'Go back to bed.'

'You go back to bed,' she says. 'Or at least buy mobile phone, would you please? I do not need more stress in my life, little Miss Rooflady.'

'Everything is fine here, Jolly.'

'Ah, stop it.' She hates when I call her Jolly.

Yola is a good girl, but 'jolly' she is not. In fact, she believes that the people of London will only take her seriously if they consider her difficult and scary.

'Want to join me?' I ask.

'I am not tempting,' she says, meaning she is not tempted.

I have curled myself into a waterproof silver-coloured beanie. I probably look like an overgrown foetus, holding a cigarette instead of umbilical cord. Not tempting indeed.

I say: 'Well, I'll stay here for a while. I need to -'

'You need to talk with spirits. I know, I been there. One day you will understand it's better to talk with -' she makes a quick, poking gesture with her small hand – 'with me,' she whispers. 'With Yola. Remember Yola, your friend indeed?'

'You know it's Misha's birthday today?' I ask. 'His fake birthday anyway.'

'What do we do? Organise party, buy presents? You say it, Millie.'

'No, Jolly,' I say. 'I will probably never see him again. Or his family.'

'Ah,' she says. 'This is always case with Misha. Something always happened with Misha. I warned you about him. Don't take it like serious stuff. You must be strong. You must! In London everything must wear a mask. So. It's freezing here. You want to smoke in kitchen? I will let you smoke in kitchen tonight.'

'No, thanks. Go to sleep, please. I'll be fine. We'll talk tomorrow.'

Misha, my latest greatest love is 45 today. Forty-five or something. The fact is, no one — Misha included — no one knows exactly how old his body of unsolicited genes is. *Unsolicited genes*—that's how he once described himself. Misha has beautiful, wavy hair with more silver in it every day, which adds maturity to a quite oriental face. Most of the time, his eyes are jade-coloured; but when he has anger gathering inside him, some alchemy happens and the jade turns to onyx. His eyes darken, and that's it: the air around him stands still, like before a storm, and then there is only thunder in the distance, and the storm passes. Good self-control for an Eastern European man.

'Tomorrow you tell me everything,' Yola says. 'No *censura*. Tonight, no jumping off the roof, ok? Remember, life opens a window.'

'Hope it's not a tiny window. We already have those, on our skyscraper, and they drive me crazy.'

'Hope it's fucking French window for you, my friend,' Yola says, and then leaves, as abruptly as she appeared.

Could she take the uncensored version of my 'everything', and keep it to herself? Yola has learned to value privacy after her five-year London stint, but still, I'm not sure it's enough.

2

Privacy. In my homeland, much more so than in Yola's Poland, privacy is considered perverted, irreverent, sometimes even illegal. We like living anybody else's life more than our own. So we actively interfere with each other, as soon as we open our eyes. We immerse ourselves in each other's depths, each other's lungs, hearts, livers; we inquire about the breakups, we give lessons, we share praise, laughter, tears, and sweat. The country has subsequently become a colourful madhouse, where everyone is at the same time a patient and a psychiatrist. Our president is no exception. Vukas the Boss, the super-shrink; or the major patient.

In Montenegro everyone can see the President every day, even if they don't work for him or for the government. We all know our Boss's favourite bars, clubs and restaurants, and if we want to find him, all we have to do is visit those places. Reliable as he is, a true subscriber to a benign dictator's manual, the president will be sitting in one of the clubs, surrounded by bodyguards and friends that he and his wife have chosen to be their stage props for that evening; he'll be crossing and uncrossing his long legs, squeezing a glass of whiskey in his hand, observing the young women and, occasionally, other, less attractive, voters. Like a true leader, Vukas always smiles, and his smile has a hypnotic tranquility. It says: 'I'll take care of you.' It is hard to leave a motherland - or, should I say, a Fatherland? – like mine, where it's easy to find your place in some peaceful corner, while the outside world, according to the Montenegrin daily press, is getting more mad, bad and silly every day.

The Notorious Nineties in ex-Yugoslavia were my high school and University years. Montenegro was under the influence of the much larger neighbour, Serbia, and the two states shared Christian Orthodox faith, nearly extinct during communism, but revived by the warmongers.

War and genocide that began in 1991 really happened *around* Montenegro, but the smoke of war from the frontlines did reach our small republic. Our Communist conception of morality - that people are not just born equal, but they must remain equal - surrendered to the invasion of street crime, under the auspices of the state. Borders became blurred, blown back and forth by the winds of war.

For us, the young, war represented the first bite into the juicy apple of disobedience. I woke up with a fresh taste of rebellion in my mouth, against the leaders who tried to hijack our future. We did everything like a herd, in noisy groups and everyone in love with everybody else.

Every single night I went out with my girlfriends. We wore mini skirts and tight fake-leather jackets, under which we smelled of thick Nivea body milk. We met around eight in the evening on the corner of the bakery and newspaper-selling kiosks, crossed the swinging bridge on the wild, skinny river and laughed loudly while running to the town center, the main square - the Freedom Square - to bars and nightclubs. The blurred borders had let cocaine in. With it, we discovered vodka and the right to fuck just like that, without pre or post-anything. Diligent students, who used to read lots of books and date nice young men and discuss with them the good reads and the avant-garde culture, while sipping cocktails as obsolete as spritzer and bamboo, suddenly fell in love with muscular young criminals, who drove fast luxury cars, previously stolen in Western Europe. These young men carried guns and sometimes, when the police stopped us, they handed us their guns, and we hid them in our knickers or bras. New passion kept us up late into the nights full of bluish smoke, or early into the mornings, as clear and bright as our young skins. We had a lot of sex in the wild, no man's orchards of pomegranates, figs or hackberries. Or we would, half-naked and excited by the proximity to death, dance in silence in front of car headlights. Over the tops of high mountains, beyond which we were considered enemies, barbarians, tragicomic and blind, the new divisions were being made. And we were celebrating our national defeat firing hysterical gunshots into the pink sky, until another day fully reigned over us, the ethnic trash of Balkan. The least of the least, our starting point in life was minus hundred. We wanted to stay forever out: out of touch, and out on the street, like renegades.

At home, my parents spent time devouring pills they referred to as 'aspirins' and endlessly studying black chronicle and the obituaries in state newspaper. My laughter terrified them. When I wanted to punish them, I phoned a friend and just laughed into the receiver. It usually happened during a TV News broadcast. My father then made little, obsessive movements pressing the TV remote control, trying to up the volume above the sound of my laughter, and then, defeated, he cursed and threw the remote at me, like a rock. My mother hurried to close the windows and draw the curtains, her precious curtains, which she had knitted with delight, and with equal, generous quantity of thread and tears.

There had been an older brother I never knew. He was their firstborn, their little genius. When he was only four years old, a yellow Škoda killed him, at the time, long ago, when our street witnessed approximately one vehicle per hour. Mother used to work at a nearby post office, and on the unfortunate day, she was at work, bored, smoking behind the counter during the slow, afternoon shift. My father was at home, but he took his after-lunch nap, and Miloš, my brother, who'd had his suspending wheels removed from his bike at the unbelievable age of two, and who, at the age of four, was an accomplished biker already, took out his Pony bike for a ride around the neighbourhood. When the car hit him, it wasn't his fault. The speeding driver lost control and slid into the curve, his yellow Škoda propelling onto the sidewalk. Neighbours said they'd heard my brother cry out: 'Slow down, please, Sir!' before he was hit by the Škoda, and they had to scrape him off the sidewalk.

'Only four years old', said the neighbours long afterwards, even to me, when I grew up to be old enough for the story, 'only four years old, and already such perfect manners.'

Mother immediately blamed herself: why was she at work, why had she ever worked, why wasn't she a housewife? They sent her on a long, paid vacation. She dedicated herself to knitting: pillowcases and table-cloths at first, then scarves, sweaters, until, finally, she moved on to curtains.

Five years later, she was pregnant again, and the pregnancy fueled her heart and bones as she pulled the needle through the ever-widening loops of her cur-tains, fantasising about the blessed, happy life that her second child, me, was bound to have.

* * *

The civil war united my parents more firmly than anything else before, maybe even more than Miloš, their perfect child, who nevertheless let them down as a bond, after only four blissful years. The war provided a reliable daily pastime: watching war propaganda on the news. Huddled together, often with another pair of equally patriotic-minded neighbours, they sat on the red sofa in the living room, watching the news about 'war for peace'. I hated being stuck - involuntarily, and with some old, lost generation - in that absurd, loud microcosm of brainwashing TV. I became impatient with everyone that wasn't young.

Even with my Mama.

I don't know how much of the news my mother actually saw and heard. Above the TV, on a glass shelf, a black-and-white photo of my brother was placed. That was his last photograph, the one from the obitu-ary. It had been taken on the day of his fourth birthday.

He was a beautiful boy, with a glow in his eye and the already seductive smile. I think my mother just stared at the photo, pretended to follow the news. I never asked her anything. Often in summer nights, when she thought she was alone in our flat, I found her sitting on the balcony with a cigarette in her hand, and a photograph of Miloš in her lap, as she recounted to him the recent events in the world, the country, and the neighbourhood. I still didn't ask anything. From the moment I became conscious about my mum, she seemed more fragile than that glass shelf above the TV, and I was afraid that the questions about Miloš would break her to pieces, that she would fall apart and die in front of my eyes.

After the death of Miloš, my father became an insomniac. Also, he became chronically constipated. I remember his noisy, frequent, but futile, stays in the toilet, newspapers on his knees, and the door always only half-closed.

'I'm sick of the stinking Ustaša's atrocities,' Father shouted, from his toilet throne, like some Wizard of Oz. 'Trying to destroy our Serbian brothers.'

I had to laugh.

'Everything is funny to you, isn't it?' he yelled. 'I don't understand you, I just don't.'

'But it's hilarious.'

'What is? Jokes are the thing of your generation. You never want to grow up, take responsibility. You think we are so primitive, we're peasants, because we want to protect our Serbian brothers.'

I think that my father truly enjoyed speaking only

like that: from the toilet, through the half-opened door. It must have made him feel like an unapproachable wartime leader, speaking to his people from the transistor radio.

'Instead of raising children, you play the pretend-opposition. I know what you're doing. I have my sources. I weep for the future of this country.'

I waited for this, his dramatic pause, and I was quick to use it.

'Please hurry,' I said. 'I need to take a shower.'

My father groaned and cursed, but eventually, he unglued himself from the throne, if only to take a few steps to the living-room and watch the latest news, before he went to the corner of the bakery and kiosks, where he gathered and entertained a group of elderly people who also could not sleep, and together they addressed the political and health issues. They were his famous 'sources'.

'You're going out? With some nice man?' Mother asked through the loud noises of Gangsta's Paradise or Runaway Train, or some similar song that I used to listen to while applying make-up in front of the bathroom mirror.

I could see my mother in the mirror. Not her face. I saw the smoke cloud in the place of her head, and below that, her arms folded across her chest as if to protect the heart from the inevitable blow that happened after my every hasty departure.

She always acted like the family's scapegoat, the one who paid for all the music and joy once the notorious baddie, *moi*, had left our Tower of Boredom. I did distantly feel that I could have made things easier for her if only I'd winked, smiled or kissed her. Or, if I told her: 'I'm on your side, Mama.'

But I was always too busy preparing my own escape through the front door.

'No, I don't have a nice man,' I replied. 'I'm just going out with my girlfriends.'

'Well, please don't go dancing to the Ustaša songs. I'm begging you. You'll be arrested, beaten by the police. And that skirt, or whatever it is you're wearing? No one serious would marry you if they saw you in that.'

In two steps I was out of the apartment. In the building's hall, behind my back, behind the door, I heard my father shouting: 'Where are you going? When are you coming back? Why are you dressed like a street-walker?'

Yet, in my memory now, those years were the happy, sleepless and non-boring times when I always, somehow, probably just because I was so young, chose the path of freedom and truth, whenever I could choose. Which was something.

While the Civil War drew to a close, the UN sanctions were imposed on Montenegro and Serbia. The war had made the young people wild and rebellious, and now we felt strangely proud because of the unfairness of sanctions. We lived our young lives in the Balkan hellhole without bitterness, because we didn't know any better. Under those sanctions, we lived like under a new roof. Maybe the old roof had more room and light, but the new one, with its low ceiling, was a kind of refuge, where we continued to coexist with more unity and equality than ever before. We began to appreciate the art of survival in spite of having been singled out in foreign media as some kind of aggressive lepers of humanity, living down there, on the edge of their hole. But it had freed us more than any revolution.

My parents grew divided in their views.

'Vukas kept the war out of Montenegro,' my Mother repeated before almost every meal, as a kind of Balkan prayer. 'Bless him. Now, he keeps us alive in spite of these sanctions. He's a great leader.'

Father wouldn't let her get away with it. He didn't understand that it was her way of saying that every mother should be spared the unnecessary loss of a child, something she had experienced. He always contradicted her, saying that her 'great leader' Vukas and his Government simply used those sanctions to profit a lot from cigarette smuggling, and that therefore hers were the words of acceptance, of justification of the fact that we became the nation of cigarette smugglers, and their employees.

'Vukas saved us from serious bombing,' she said after the so-called Lewinski bombings by the Clinton administration, after which the UN sanctions were lifted. 'Look at Belgrade - destroyed by uranium bombs! This shows that our president is certainly backed by the Americans.'

'They're all criminals,' my father replied and hid his angry face behind newspaper.

I now know that he was right, but back then I hated

him for belittling my mother's attempts at finding something positive in our existence on this planet.

As soon as I could afford it, I put down a payment for a one-bedroom flat, and moved out, painted the walls of my apartment in lavender shade and kept my new nest uncluttered by furniture, and by heated political debates. But not for long.

3

On another November day, in 2002, in Montenegro, Chris the American and I were sitting in a pizzeria, not far from the Freedom Square in Podgorica.

'Rain again in this adulterous town,' I said to Chris.

No reply from the American. His head bowed to the Menu, he just inhaled, twice, sharply, as if unblocking his nose. I knew that he was calculating the best value for money, even in a cheap pizza-place.

'This adulterous town,' I repeated, looking at his mossy, white fringe.

Another sharp inhale. I got it. It was my smoking that bothered him, *took his breath away*.

Chris was a typical American 'dumb-fox', a lobbying specialist for the murky regions of the world, at the time engaged by the government of Montenegro to iron their image for the influential Westerners. A short man, with an inflated torso - in fact, a man, who somehow, when dressed, managed to present his belly as a strong-looking chest - he was much older than me, but still a tolerable lunch-mate even though our previous meeting in the Presidential suite at the nearby hotel had ended violently. Despite the violence, when

22

he called me and asked to see me again, I said yes. He'd acquired a considerable audacity to fit in with us, South Slavs. Undoubtedly, his fitting in had to have an ugly downside, exercised only on the safe ground: among local women. Whatever. His occasional outbursts did not shock me. Men like Chris - I could gobble them up for dessert. Though somehow I never did. Food poisoning alert.

'Why should we have a lunch?' I'd asked him over the phone.

'Business and politics,' he said. 'Your favorite combination.'

Business and politics. A phrase that covered a wide range of social initiatives. He only wanted to be seen with a young woman, I thought.

But now Chris was focused on the menu. Oh well. It wasn't like I needed his attention. I just needed some money. So, between looking at him and looking through the clouded window of that pizza-place, I chose the window.

Outside, in the pedestrian zone, there were no pedestrians. There was nobody looking to buy anything in the cluster of mushroom-roofed kiosks that displayed and sold everything from pirate-discs to original, stolen, Faberge eggs and crosses. On the pitted, crooked street nearby, empty taxis were parked. The drivers were probably on to more lucrative jobs, like smuggling; driving from point A to point B in Podgorica would put no more than 2 Euros into their pockets.

'Pizza Corleone looks good,' Chris finally spoke.

'Served with a salad on top. Let's just keep it simple, order two Corleones and two Diet Cokes, okay?'

It would take me a week to digest a Corleone.

A young waiter approached our table, yawning.

I ordered a vodka cranberry, double, and bowl of peanuts. The waiter winked at me, condoned, and I lit another cigarette. Chris's eyes were hard as cash. I looked to the side and exhaled a long trail of smoke.

'What's up?' he asked.

'All good. What about you? '

'Relax first, talk later,' he said.

My vodka arrived, my bowl of peanuts, a Diet Coke for Chris.

'Anyone else joining us for lunch?' I asked.

'Like, who?'

'I do not know. Like, our boss, maybe?'

I hadn't seen Vukas the Boss since the previous summer. He owed me a few paycheques, the Boss did, and I really needed that money.

Chris raised his white eyebrows. 'Our *boss*?' he said. 'You mean Vukas? He's not my boss, baby. I'm a freelancer.'

I laughed, but Chris didn't.

'Milena,' he said, 'when we first met, I thought you were exceptional. You were clever, so charming, yet kind of sad, which only showed that you thought about things, you cared. Seriously. It was refreshing, I'd never met such a melodramatic beauty -'

'Is that a compliment?'

'Well. Yes, it is, but it doesn't matter, because you have changed. Like, there's this irony now, jumping out

24

whenever you open your mouth. Irony and anger. And in my world irony equals pessimism. Pessimism equals no initiative, no caring. I know, it's November, and, everyone is feeling the blues, but, you know. . .'

'Go ahead.'

'Yeah, thanks. So - to quote Mark Twain, a great man, FYI killed by cigarettes. Anyway, Twain said something like how there was nothing sadder in the world than a young pessimist. You should consider his words. Because here, for a girl like you, it's not only sad. It's dangerous.'

'You see me as a young pessimist?' I extinguished my cigarette and pressed down the stick on the revolving top of the ashtray. The top swirled and opened enough to suck the dead cigarette into the mass cigarette grave.

'That part was less relevant,' Chris said. 'We need to talk about something important.'

'Well, in fact, I'm the opposite. I'm an old optimist. '

'Great.'

I *was* an optimist. Chris couldn't know it, because he wasn't supposed to know about my plans to leave the country. My passport was already in one travel agency, where I knew the directors. I was able to get a UK tourist visa without an invitation letter or the bank statements. Many years ago, when that agency was founded, and when they hired people, I wrote fake referrals for most of its current managers.

Chris and Bella, his wife, an Englishwoman, were moving in the opposite direction from me. They decided to fly south, from Belgrade to Montenegro, and buy a house on one of the beaches in the vicinity of Budva or Perast, to permanently leave their previous base in Serbia. In the region of ex-Yugoslavia, Chris was known as the 'ambassador', though officially he was never in that position. In Belgrade, he had worked for almost four years as a political and business consultant. He occasionally poked into Herceg-Bosna. He still went to Zagreb for his medical checks. Bella and Chris only trusted Croatian doctors. They knew their region of influence very well. Chris loved to move freely through the newly formed countries, chasing the best deal for his services. He understood our language, and knew how to speak it, but he felt that Americans sounded 'invasive' when trying to speak any foreign language, so he used a translator, like me, borrowed directly from the Boss.

The waiter brought one pizza Corleone. He asked me if I had changed my mind about eating. I shook my head and averted my eyes from the melted cheese in which a handful of mixed green salad was dying a slow, fat death.

Again, I looked through the fogged glass, trying to daydream, to summon the images of my happy future in London. I couldn't, not really. Chris decided to continue the conversation.

'When I say you don't know what you're saying, I'm being serious, Milena,' he said. 'Can't you tell?'

'Can't I tell what, Chris?'

'People don't like you very much anymore. They don't trust you.'

'Have they ever?' I tried to smile.

'Yes, they have. They loved you. They recommended

26

you highly, at least to me, when I first came here. But then you had to boil over, all over the place, didn't you? You can't fight them.'

'You mean someone else could, but not me?' I asked.

'Exactly.'

'And you invited me here to tell me why.'

'Well. Yes.'

'I don't really care.'

'Why?' he asked.

'Because, what information can you give me that I haven't already sniffed coming my way? Unless they're planning to kill me. But that wouldn't be useful. It wouldn't be 'value for money', right?

'Milena,' Chris started again, taking my cigarette-less hand in his. 'Milena, listen. If you just could -'

I could let him hold my hand, but I couldn't look at him. So I looked away. And then I saw her.

I saw Sonja. She was the Russian dancer used for the parties of the Montenegrin ruling clique. Sonja was always stunning but spaced out. Now, alone on the street, in the pouring rain and limping in black flannel sweatpants, she seemed only spaced out, a half-dead, mutated insect.

'Oh, my God!' I cried and jumped up from my chair. 'Look, Chris, there, it's Sonja! There. On the street!'

Chris threw a quick glance through the window glass showered in rain, and even more quickly he grabbed my elbow, pulling me back into the chair.

'You shouldn't make Sonja your business. You are not in the position to help her. Now listen carefully. That's what I've been trying - '

'Chris,' I said, 'we in the Balkans. We are never in a position. We are always between the positions. All of us. You included.'

'I just wanted to help, you, little fool,' he hissed.

I pulled my elbow out of his grip, got up again, grabbed my leather jacket from the chair and ran out of the pizzeria. I reached Sonja just as she bent and squatted on the street, under the pouring rain. I knelt down beside her.

'Sonja,' I said. 'Sonja.' I touched the top of her head.

She didn't look up or say anything.

'Come on, Sonja, get up,' I said. 'I'm going to take you somewhere safe. You need rest and care. Come, let's go.'

'Please, no police. No police,' she said, her 'L' pronounced softly, the Russian way. I heard her speak before. But that was the first time I saw her real hair, thin and brown and dull. She always wore brightly coloured wigs for the parties, before.

'I know, believe me. No police' I took her arms and pulled her up, to her feet. 'No police, I promise.'

'I'm tired. I'm so tired,' she said, her eyes closed.

I decided to take Sonja to the Shelter for women and children. It was the only fortress of safety in my town, at the time at least. It was mostly for the victims of domestic abuse, but I was sure they were not going to reject Sonja, especially after I informed them about her situation. The Shelter was just about two hundred meters from the pizza-place in which I had not had my lunch. As I was pulling Sonja past the pizzeria Chris was just leaving it, in a great hurry, with a worrisome face beneath his bushy, white eyebrows, and below the familiar, yellow umbrella.

'Hey, that's my umbrella!' I shouted after him, but he just picked up his pace, not looking back.

Sonja opened her eyes and looked at me.

'Can you believe this?' I told her. 'He just took off with my umbrella! Americans and their me-first, right?'

'You,' she said, and quickly looked away, trying to tear her tiny palm out of my hand. 'You work for them.'

'I'm only helping you now.'

She jerked her hand again. I held her more firmly.

'This is a trap,' she said and licked her chapped lips. 'They warned me.'

'Please come with me,' I said. 'I'm a good guy here.'

A young woman opened the door to the Shelter's office as soon as I rang the bell. I told her that I found Sonja in the square. Sonja, pale and near fainting, was breathing through her mouth open, like a newly hatched bird.

The young woman called another woman and they took care of Sonja immediately. They entered some room and closed the door behind them. I sat down on the massive couch, crowded with pillows with price tags on them. Pillows were - as it was written under the price that ranged between seven and fifteen Euros - made by the women who had stayed, or were now staying, in the Shelter.

'No more pills!' I heard Sonja shout from behind the door.

'It's okay, you're safe, you're safe, don't worry,' repeated the two volunteers. Sonja might believe it one day.

I was sitting tucked away among the handmade pillows when yet another woman appeared carrying two cups of coffee.

'Do you want one?' she asked me. 'Both are totally bitter.'

'I'll take one,' I said. 'Where's your manager, Mrs Vera?'

'Oh, she's right here.'

One of the doors in the Shelter-office opened and Vera came out, accompanied by a big, obviously-foreign woman with a sweaty face and bare feet that were spilling over a pair of Birkenstok sandals: Elke Konelke.

I knew Elke. Several times in the past, I'd translated for her. She was the head of the Anti-Corruption Team of the European Union; or 'that Scandinavia lesbian' as she was called in the Cabinet. They proclaimed her a lesbian because she could never be forgiven her laid back attitude to clothes, or, more to the point, her total opposition to the dress code of the Balkan female population, a dress-code most warmly applauded by men. The local female humanitarian workers hovered around in pencil skirts and high heels even when they visited the most neglected refugee camps. For the members of the Montenegrin Government that was a real humanitarian work, while Elke's style was just lesbian arrogance.

'Have we met before?' Vera, the Shelter manager, asked me. 'I'm Vera.'

We shook hands. Vera's handshake was strong. She was in her fifties and an inspirational woman; with Legionnaires' sangfroid she helped the least desirable and most disdained of creatures, while keeping the impeccable personal look and fashion style.

'Milena' I said.

Then I smiled to Elke, who told me: 'It has been a while, Milena, since last time I saw you. You still work for the President?'

A difficult question. For many reasons I wasn't sure what the correct answer was, but I nodded affirmatively.

I told them some of what I knew about Sonja. They were aware of how little chance of surviving on the streets she had. Vera and Elke went into the room to see her. I looked around and grabbed one of the embroidered pillows. Ten Euros, it said on it. I took a ten-Euro-note out of my jacket, left it in the pillow's place, and, finally, I was gone without saying goodbye to anyone.

The rain had stopped and the evening swelled in the distance, behind the jagged mountain peaks covered with snow. Some people had come out to take a walk, stretch their legs. In the elusive, sepia-coloured twilight, I saw them as faceless human contours. They said 'Hello' to me, they asked how I was, how my parents were. I answered politely, but quickly. I kept the conversation short between two outbursts of rain.

My stomach made a sad, whining sound when I reached my apartment and unlocked it.

Chris and his lunch. No proper food, and no information, just more expenses for me: the ten Euros for the pillow I was still holding in my hands. The pillow that represented Sonja and what had just happened.

Sonja was free now, but I wasn't, and both of us needed to hold on to something. A cushioned support. And
that was all – I blocked all further pathways of thought
- maybe because I was starving.

As usual, in my kitchen there was nothing decent to
eat. A square of butter in the fridge; a half empty bottle
of 'Pushkin blues' in the freezer. Vodka-blueberry mixture looking like frozen purple sick. I had moved there
three years earlier, and still the small door of my oven
was covered with cellophane. I spotted the remains of
coke, staling out on the shelves of the kitchen cabinets.
How did they even get there? I rubbed some into my
gums. It tasted more like dust. I snorted most of it anyway. And I went out on the balcony.

The girls that worked in the grocery shop below
my apartment were listening, very loudly, to the Hit
of the Month on the radio. They wouldn't hear me if
I called out to them and asked for some easy but real
food, like eggs, Argeta chicken pâté, bread and yogurt,
to be brought to me. I had to go back outside, down
to the shop. I didn't feel like leaving my flat again. All
I could see from my balcony was a sad, empty street.
That night, for some reason, everyone decided to stay
indoors. November had already skimmed everyone's
energy reserves. Only the girls' screams echoed around,
at the hour when the neighbors usually gathered under
my balcony before the main TV News, to air and beat
out the life's injustices, like old rugs. Here and there,
the lights flickered behind the tattered storey houses,
squeezed between new-money mansions and small
modern buildings, like the one I lived in. Dark rims

of Gorica hill presided over my part of town - a giant throne of a self-deluded ruler.

Well, that snortful of dusty coke had tempered my hunger a bit anyway. I squeezed the pillow tighter against my chest. It felt like still holding Sonja; or anyone, anyone that would let me hold them. Sonja was safe now. Was I safe? Well, at least I was in my own apartment. Did I lock the door? I used to never lock my front door. I should have. I thought I heard something, someone move. No. It was probably nothing, but it was starting to be scary out on the balcony, with no people outside, just loud turbo-folk voices. *Put your pretty head in my lap, swear to it you didn't cheat.* Was that turbo-folk music and life phase ever going to fade away? Better go back in, turn the TV on, turn all the lights on, and snort more dusty coke and drink *Pushkin's Blues*, and hug my new pillow, and tomorrow would be a different kind of day. What a lost cause I was, twenty-seven years old, and nothing in the fridge or in the oven. I pushed the balcony door and through the near-total darkness of my flat, I walked to the front door, to lock it.

A silhouette moved in my hallway. My heart jumped, I opened my mouth, and then the lights were switched on.

A man was in my hallway.

'Fuck you!' I screamed. 'Fuck you!'

'Did we ever actually fuck, Milena?' asked the man. 'Remind me, please.'

'Oh, you -' I was going to say 'asshole' but I thought better of it. 'No, we never did,' I said instead. If sex was the reason why Smeško Berković had broken into my flat, searched it in an attempt to find something to blackmail me with in order to sleep with me – well, five minutes of his dick inside me was not going to kill me, and I would be able to live with myself – if he was going to leave me alone afterwards. So I smiled back at him.

Smeško means 'Smiley'. Nobody really knew his real first name. Our State security's General of darkness was just 'Smeško' to everyone. Even to his soldiers, his closest collaborators. Even to the President. And 'Smiley' he was, only because of his sick, uncontrollable grin, a spasm or a deformity he couldn't or wouldn't fix. His grin was now jerking higher – he was actually smiling, for real, for once.

'Well,' he said, 'you're definitely fucked now, Milli Vanilli. Look what I've found in your laundry,' he raised his hand that held a freezer bag with a gun in it. 'First place I checked. Bottom of the laundry basket. Not very imaginative.' He had obviously let himself into my place before I came back. Of course, the passe-partouts of the government men. 'And put that pillow down, what's that now, I'm not going to shoot you or anything. Just give me your mobile phone please.'

He extended his arm to me, the one that wasn't holding the freezer bag with the gun in it. So, yes, I knew the gun. It was a limited-edition specimen of a Jericho gun, with a decorative silver handle, carved with symbols of power and respect: stars, fists, obelisks. It was so obviously made as a gift for a special person, for someone who had deserved it by contributing to the never-ending battles of State Security. Not me. It didn't belong to me. But Smeško Berković was going to pretend it did.

'You know about that gun,' I said. 'You know how it ended up here. And no way I'm giving you my mobile phone.'

'Oh yes you are. Yes way. In fact, give me your phone right now, together with your passport please. I couldn't find the passport. You have no ID crap in here, at all. Where were you all day anyway?'

I wasn't going to answer that. Chances were, he already knew.

'You make it almost too easy for me to turn you into a ghost,' Smeško went on. 'Hurry up now. I called ambulance from your landline. They'll be here in a minute.'

'What did you call the ambulance for?' I asked. 'What's wrong with good old police? Or an ambush? '

The sick grin jerked higher, to his left eye. 'The little shop sluts from downstairs saw me enter the building. But even if they didn't, nowadays it's very hip, the ambulance. More effective than police. Nobody left behind wondering why. Who could deny a diagnosis? You were listed as a dangerous, hysterical, possibly suicidal woman. There's a gun. You're a threat to this whole neighbourhood. Nobody's going to miss you, at least not for some time. Maybe just your Santa Claus Bernard, but he'll get over it. Give me the damn phone, now, and your picture documents. '

'No.'

'And put that fucking pillow away,' Smeško shouted, and he grabbed my hand.

'Let me go, you fucked-up creep!' I screamed and broke away from his grip, turned around and ran to the balcony where I screamed some more, for any kind of help.

But the Ambulance siren out-screamed me, already wailing through the silence of my street.

4

Yola reappears on the roof just to hand me a blanket and a large cup of peppermint tea, her magic drink that, she believes, chases away any darkness.

'Thank you,' I say.

'You are not alone,' Yola whispers.

I smile in the direction of her light-bulb hair as she climbs down the stairs to our flat.

I met Yola during my first year in London, at my first refuge, a dilapidated bed-and-breakfast.

'Not cheap but safe,' someone had said recommending this 'motel' that overlooked Princess Diana's Memorial Playground in Hyde Park.

Definitely not cheap. And safe? Well, it felt good not to know anyone around me, for a change. I loved the anonymity of London; I liked the monotonous skies above, with no mountains to decorate the horizon. I started dressing to blend in with the sky, with the tarmac; I crossed the streets only when the green light flashed; lived in the world of absolutely-no-incidents, please.

Yola worked as a part-time cleaner in that B&B. She came to make up my room one morning. She asked me why I had so many unpacked suitcases but always wore the same clothes. I didn't answer – hadn't even noticed that it was the case before she asked - but Yola ignored my silence and kept asking me questions. Soon, the two of us were sharing cups of peppermint tea on the days she worked, like we knew each other all our lives. She told me about her daughter she'd left in Poland with her parents; and about a husband who had gone to America to make money and bring it back home, but disappeared instead. So here she was, cleaning up 'shit without face', as she described it, for six pounds per hour.

One morning she said she was quitting the bed-and-breakfast because she'd found 'several stable Chelsea families who paid ten pounds per hour' (did the 'stability' of the families guarantee their shit would now have 'a face', I wondered) – and she suggested I moved out of that B&B as well, and moved in with her, her boyfriend Isztvan and another tenant, Rafi.

I said I needed to think about it. She then sighed and informed me that a man had died in that same room I came to occupy, that: 'A hermit-man died here and next time I come to clean – I find you in this death room. I go mad. Paying so much to sleep in deathbed. I wanted to help you. You never know what history you get with bed-and-breakfast.'

She convinced me.

Later in the day we crossed Battersea Bridge on the bus 49 and got off on the first stop after the bridge. We each pulled two suitcases, all mine. Four suitcases. What was in them? I had no idea. Yola seemed happy and proud while pulling my suitcases.

'See? Between park and river, but only one stop from Chelsea. This is centre of London. Doesn't get better than this.'

We were standing in front of the most disgusting looking skyscraper I'd ever seen. And we entered it.

The building's entrance was stuffy, as if all the tenants agreed to snub the washing machines and disinfected their bed sheets and underwear by cooking them on hobs, in tall pots full of boiling, grey water. In front of the lift, Yola kept throwing insecure side glances at me, and at one point, she told me that I'd be all right living there; I only needed to learn to put on 'the face' whenever coming home late and sharing the lift with strangers. 'No melancholy in this situations,' she said. 'You must make face of toughness but *solidarnosc*, you know. Like this,' and she demonstrated it, pulling her expression until she resembled a piranha with indigestion.

The lift arrived and when we entered it Yola pushed the small top button that looked different from other buttons, as if added more recently. Number 21.

The flat was just beneath the roof of the tower block. Yola and her boyfriend Isztvan were paying for the living room, where they shared a sofa bed. This gave them the right to 'manage' the kitchen – a perfect arrangement since Isztvan was a celebrity-chef-in-waiting, currently employed as *rotisserie* specialist in Waitrose on King's Road.

'Baked animals,' Yola said. 'Ducks, ribs, Prince Charles sausages, corn-fed chickens. The best quality. When he comes home he will bring some. He always does. See, you get your dinners free.'

'That's fine,' I said. 'I only have craving for crisps.'

'See, this is not good,' Yola said. 'Craving specific food means anemia. I read this in book for babies when my daughter was baby. You need meat. You will have meat.'

Rafi, the third flat-mate, was home. He came out of his room to greet me. Yola introduced him as 'Rafi, barman from Rome'. He corrected her: he was from *Fregene*, a fishermen's village near Rome; in London, he worked as a bar-*manager*, but he was an artist.

'Rafi thinks he's bigger man if he says he comes from fishermen village,' Yola said. 'But he's good artist, look.'

We were all standing in the tiny, crooked hallway now, additionally cramped by my four suitcases and Rafi's paintings that were everywhere, hanging on the walls or leaning against them.

'Wonderful works,' I said. The paintings were filled with faces, and all I wanted was to be alone in my new room. I was starting to sweat; I felt the sick headache rising again.

Rafi had been paying for two rooms: his own tiny bedroom, and the empty one that would be mine. He was waiting for his married paramour to divorce her husband and join him in London.

Yola told him to forget about the Italian lady.

'Show me woman who will leave palazzo in *Monte Barilla* to come to *this trolownia*,' she screamed and kicked the door of my new room open. The heavy smell of wall-to-wall carpet slithered out of it. 'And I'll show you mental case!'

'*Parioli*,' Rafi said. '*Monte Parioli*. Barilla is pasta. And she would come to me. To *me*!'

'No. Not anymore. Your *regina* for sure found herself another art student. And here's Mila from *Monte Negro*,' Yola gently pushed me toward the room. 'That's good surrogate.'

Rafi straightened his broad shoulders and raised his eyebrows at my expensive-looking suitcases and shoes. As an Italian, he must have liked and respected the sight of high-quality accessories. Then he kissed me twice on the cheeks. '*Auguri*, Mila,' he shook my hand. 'I help you with the bags.'

'*Grazie*,' I said as he pulled my luggage into the room.

There was a king-size bed in the middle, several white shelves in the corners, a cupboard - not bad, but the room was dominated by the smell of that carpet. Anything could have been hidden in that carpet. It was probably better than a *pensione* where a hermitman died, but, that thread pulled out, the whole world became a space occupied by unknown miseries, the unlucky traces of DNA.

I looked up and caught Rafi staring at me. He managed to hold my eye for longer than I wanted, or needed.

'I'd like to paint you,' he said. 'But maybe you're not ready?'

'I'm not ready,' I said.

'One day," he said and left, closing the door behind him. Then I realised that, again, I could use my suitcases as tables or chairs, and so they remained mostly unpacked, but useful.

40

My London flat-mates, it turned out, worked long hours and I slept a lot. I hardly saw them that year. My days were dull and slow, a procession of endless Sundays. I had no one to call, no one to meet. I used to wake up expecting nothing, feeling sick and tired for no obvious reason. It was probably my liver trying to rest and refresh itself, but I had darkness and pain in me. Whenever I gathered enough strength, I went out, kept walking, getting lost, turning right instead of left and left instead of right. At some point I stopped taxis and gave my address. Sometimes, a driver said: "S righ' b'ind you, love."

'What?' I cried, convinced that I'd ended up in a completely different part of town, but the cabbie would sharply point past me with his forefinger and drive off.

And then, from around a street corner a gust of salty urban wind would hit me, rising like a mad ghost from the slow-moving river.

My Battersea flat, like all other flats in that building, had no balconies, only the so-called 'butterfly', suicide-unfriendly windows. So, up on the roof, I organized a corner for me to smoke and stare down at Albert Bridge. And after the roof ritual, which varied in duration according to the weather conditions, I went back to the flat, to my room and I fell into an empty sleep.

Only now do I realise, and it makes me smile into the cold mist of this night as Yola is climbing down the iron stairs, on her way back to Isztvan and their sofa bed, that I must be one of the few people on the planet, who came to *London* to rest and make up for the major lack of sleep.

5

One Friday around noon, after almost a year of my jobless London existence had gone by, Yola stormed into my room.

'Ah, *kurwa*!' she yelled. 'I can't see this anymore. Get up now!'

'Not now, please,' I mumbled into my pillow.

But Yola was on a roll. 'You must know this: lying in bed without sleeping is passive-aggressive behavior to other members of household. And it's so dark and stuffy in this room,' she added, parting my black-out curtains and pushing the butterfly window open. 'It's like in some giant's asshole. You take shower while I make tea. Then you come to the kitchen and we talk. I found you job.'

'I don't have to work for a couple of more months, Yola,' I said, still buried in my pillow. 'Let me rest.'

She lifted the duvet and pinched my butt so hard that I sat up.

'This lifestyle is not resting,' Yola said into my face. 'This lifestyle is cross between lost tourist and illegal immigrant. I hate your bags standing like gravestones in this room! Is dangerous, that image. Please take shower.' And she left my room.

I did take a shower. Even though the shower in my London flat was the thing I hated most about my new life – the fixed, above-the-head unit that made me think of concentration camps and forced me to bend into unthinkable positions in order to wash myself properly – still it was less time-consuming than arguing with Yola, who, before she came to London, had worked as *prawnik*, a lawyer, in her native Jaworzno.

When I joined Yola in the kitchen, she was sitting behind the dining table, reading Tony Robbins in Polish. Her magic drink, peppermint tea, was spreading its soul, its refreshing aroma, from two cups placed on the scarred Formica in front of her.

'Yola,' I said before sitting down myself. 'Please let me be depressed for a bit longer. I know what I'm doing.'

'I know depressed, and you're not. You need lecture,' she replied over her book, whose title looked like an eye test and read something like *Nieograniczona Mocz*. 'Sit down, I tell you something.'

I sat down and she put her palm on my hand and moved her face closer to mine. The motivational guru in Yola shone through her green eyes.

'Is fine, you have income from apartment in Montenegro,' she said. 'But, don't you want to work? I would never stop my cleaner job until I find better one. I would never let my *garconiere* I own in Krakow to students and sleep all day in London. This is first advice we Polish girls tell each other: in London, walk around like you have good job. But you, Milena, you walk with your eyes empty. I don't know. Like you tell people: 'Take me, I have nobody and nothing here.' That's not true. You have me. And Isztvan, and Rafi. Now you can have job.'

'So what is it?' I said.

'Well, first of all, you don't expect glamour. You take it step by step -'

'And the first step is?'

'They need nanny for children.'

'Oh . . . I don't think . . .'

'Step by step.'

'Okay, who needs a nanny?'

'My Russian bosses in Chelsea,' she replied. 'Easy-peasy. Two children, both go to school, so you dress them for school, prepare lunch boxes, drop them, and then your mornings are like free. Afternoon, you pick them, go through homework, intellectual stuff. Saturday, you take them to movies and funfairs. Sundays off. I negotiate four hundred per week for you, cash. Sometimes there is tip and sometimes the woman gives clothes, bags, perfumes, all kinds of stuff. It doesn't get better than that, trust me. They asked me to do it but I said no. Work with children is for your brain to be used, you know, talking, listening, explaining. *Gushy-mushy-bushy*. I have problems with that. But you...'

'I'll think about it.'

'No time. They want to meet you at five-thirty. I told them fairy tales about you this morning so they send me home early to talk to you. The father goes on a business trip tomorrow. Oh, yes, and I told them your name is Millie. It's more easy, don't worry, I changed my name a little for this country.'

'Not Millie, please. I have a reason to hate *Millie*.'

'Well, one day you tell me reason, and I'm sure this reason will soon be silly also to you. For now, Millie is good.'

* * *

My employers, the Misha and Dina Grishin, were

44

Russians who moved to London from Ukraine. They lived in Oakley Gardens in Chelsea. Their children, born in Kiev as Alexei and Anastasya, came to London when they were five and two, and here they became Alex and Nensi.

During my interview, we all sat in the Grishins' totally dust-free, walnut-floored, split-level, double reception. Yola and I were on white-leather chairs dragged from the dining room, and, facing us, our employers and their children lounged on a large corner sofa furnished in chic patches of black velvet and black leather and adorned with a dozen of puffy, rosehip-coloured cushions. A Steinway piano, painted pink, was parked in front of the mirrored wall on the upper level of the room.

All four of the Grishins were smartly dressed. Later, I realized that the children had their school clothes on: Alex, the older one, now aged nine, was clad in a navy blazer, white shirt and navy corduroy shorts and Nensi, aged six, wore a white dress with blue stripes in which she resembled Alice in Wonderland.

The coffee tables around us were numerous and identical: marble topped, with mirrors for legs. Everywhere, thick vases, made of creamy, lacquered (probably) ivory (or was it jade?), held profuse bouquets of jasmine, white roses and other white flowers in opulent bloom. The ceilings were extra high. A tall fireplace of black marble with green streaks throughout, like veins, gaped with infinity. It reminded me of an empty family grave. It was surrounded by more mirrors in heavy frames, more white flowers and tall, fat, scented candles.

The paintings on the walls seemed like a series of disturbing takes on the battle of Borodin: instead of his famous tripod hat, Napoleon was wearing a red, curly wig of a Cabaret performer; three canvases on, General Kutuzov stood gazing at his ankles, shackled by two chopped off human heads. In between these two figures, the surviving soldiers gathered together for a drink, wearing medals around their pitiful folds of their scrawny necks. In the background, blue hills and green skies – very bright and populated by furry birds and flying rabbits – provided a sardonic illustration of chaos produced by warfare.

'I love Slavonic Naïve Art,' Misha Grishin announced as I stared at the paintings. I nodded. 'Unbelievably, I found this artist in London, and he found a way to my heart. Zhenya Orr is his name now, a tiny, nervous Russian Jew. Like him, I believe that life is combination of struggle and dream. Zhenya's time is coming, you'll see. I had to have his Borodinskaya trio. And now he has this huge painting of moors covered in dead trout. Beautiful."

Dina Grishin rolled her eyes and crossed herself behind her husband. The children looked pale and sleepy on the sofa but they seemed well behaved. In general, I considered children to be superior creatures, with sharp senses, intuition and manipulation skills. I expected Alex and Nensi to see me through immediately and conclude that I was completely unreliable, whine about it to their parents or something. But they didn't.

Misha read through my biography: a one and a half

page file that I'd quickly put together just an hour or so before meeting the Grishins. In it, I lied about my previous job, saying that it had been the Official translator for the EU Anti-Corruption Team. Misha started asking me questions about Montenegro, the prices of property there, both on the coast and in the mountains, and the condition of the infrastructure. I had all the answers. Dina observed me with a frozen smile on her face.

'Your biography is quite impressive,' Misha said. 'And so is your English. But you came to London to try out this nanny-role. Why?'

'I don't know,' I replied and everyone laughed.

'Broken heart, nasty boyfriend,' Yola jumped in.

Dina widened her smoky-blue eyes, completely and skillfully made-up: black eyeliner, black mascara and grey shades. 'How old are you?' she asked me. 'I can't tell your age.'

'Twenty-nine,' I said.

'*Twenty-nine*? A spiritual number *and* Saturn's return! Now it's your time to help others. I like you,' Dina concluded. The job was mine.

I was to start working for them on the following Monday. Misha thought this enough of a reason to celebrate, I suppose, for he opened a bottle of champagne, filled up the glasses and distributed them.

'Alex, Nensi, did you get that?' he asked the children. 'Millie will be your nanny. Happy?' They nodded.

I had no chance to say that I'd like to think about it, so I drank the champagne and decided to give the job a try for a couple of weeks. The champagne was my first drink in maybe a year. I drank it like water, in consecutive gulps, and, together with the strong scent of jasmine, roses and candles, it quickly made me tipsy. As the room blurred around me, I understood how drinking alcohol might be necessary to make living in that house of sharp edges, sharp colours and surreal images a little more bearable.

I felt like I should do something nanny-like, so I opened my arms and smiled to the children.

'Come, let me hug you,' I said.

'Mama,' Alex turned to his mother, ignoring me, '*mozhno pashli v nashim*' –

'English, please!' Dina said. 'We have guests.'

I folded my arms back in and grabbed the glass that still had several drops of champagne in it.

'Can we go to our rooms, please?'

'What's the rush?' Dina asked. 'Nintendo DS won't run away.'

'We want to change into home clothes.'

'Okay then,' Dina said and waved to her departing children as if seeing them off on a journey to America.

After they left, Yola made a small cough of announcement and wiggled in her seat. We all turned to her.

'Thank you for your offer to work here full time, but I prefer to have different clients,' she said. 'I am really sorry if this is inconvenience.'

Nobody said anything. To me it sounded as if she was buying her way out of hell by bringing another soul (me) as a replacement.

'I can still come and clean here for couple of hours several days in week,' Yola added. 'But I understand if

48

you look for someone full-time and don't want me any-more.'

'Oh,' Dina said. 'Oh. Not good news. We got used to you, Yola. Do you have anyone else, quick and honest like you? You can share two part-times, no?'

'I can ask around.'

'Please. Our nanny shouldn't also clean, should she, Misha?' Dina fixed her wide stare, that spelled XANAX to me, on her husband and I froze. I shouldn't have drunk that champagne before the job description had been clarified.

Misha got up and walked towards me carrying the bottle in his hand.

'No,' I cried. 'No more alcohol.' I could swear that Napoleon winked from the wall and mouthed: '*La femme stupide*,' and pointed at me, the old Bonaparte.

Misha laughed. 'Don't worry,' he said. 'With a biography like that I wouldn't make you go down on your hands and knees.'

A Russian devil, glowing in the setting sun. He wasn't very tall, but he looked strong, broad, with generous bone structure. His hair and his skin were of a darker shade than what I normally expected a Russian to have; as if he'd fallen asleep in a barrel of bourbon the night before. There must have been a hint of Armenia, or perhaps a touch of some more Oriental provenance, perhaps one of the distant '*stans*' of the eastern ex-USSR, in his background.

'Ay, Misha!' Dina, blond and slim, a perfect illustration for a new-age Russka *djevushka*, giggled behind his back. 'Don't start your dirty jokes now!'

'We'll keep Yola,' Misha said, refilling my glass. 'And we'll find a cleaner who can also cook.' Then he turned to his wife. 'Everything will be taken care of, Dinochka *maya*.'

Later, as we were walking back home, I asked Yola why she preferred to work for different clients and not stay with one family. Staying with one family meant she would at least avoid the drag of wasting her life on public transport.

'Full time is scam,' she answered. 'If anything in house is missing and you're full-time cleaner there, guess what: everyone makes of you their primary suspect and – bang!- you have dossier with police even if missing things are *finded* like they usually are. Dina is type who forgets where she puts things.'

'Oh, now you tell me.'

'Also,' Yola went on, 'I need my freedom. I make hours when I work or no work. I like to be able to go to Poland whenever I want to see my daughter.'

'Maybe I should've just offered myself as a baby-sitter to various families then?' I said.

'What for?' Yola said. 'You said you can't go back to Montenegro and I don't see you travelling in soon future. Time to work and save. If I was you, I keep myself busy with two jobs . . .'

'Enough now. Anyway, are the roses and all always there? The smell was . . .'

'Yeah they are. Of course this time of year, lilacs are imitation. Oh, *sheet*, I'll have to bin the real flowers on Monday and get fresh bunch. Dina must have flowers in house but when they lose their perfect white and become older – *masakra*!'

'Is Dina on some prescription medication?'

'I don't know. For me, she's just on cash.'

6

My last job, before the Grishins, had been coordinating the social reforms of President Tomović, the Boss of Montenegro.

I first met the President in May 2001. A meeting was held at the restaurant 'Mareza', a round terrace above the stale fishpond at the fringes of Podgorica. Really, that meeting, like most meetings, was just another opportunity for the local and European politicians to enjoy lunch on a sunny day. The warm spring breeze swayed the smell of pond around us. The foreigners thought it all 'so organic', or at least they kept saying it, in addition to the endless string of meaningless sentences that demanded my full focus. All of them, foreigners and locals, trusted my translations, and knew I would throw away the excess crap from the conversation; that I'd aptly handle the incomprehensible jokes. I was good at it.

Vukas Tomović suddenly appeared, surprising all of us by dragging a chair and placing himself next to me. With his long fingers, he signaled to everyone to continue with conversation. He let others speak, occasionally nodding his head and staring at the only thing that was constantly moving in that day's stagnant air: my interpreting mouth, my tool. I thought that the President didn't want to add burden to the discussion I would then had to translate. What a wonderful man.

When everything finally ended, when nobody paid the bill and everyone got up ready to go back to town, Vukas simply said to me that he wanted to see me in two days in his Cabinet, around 10 a.m. I smiled and waved my hand at him, like a real girly-girl-voter I never was: 'Sure thing, Mr President,' I said.

I guess I sensed that I'd finally get a regularly paid job. Job description? I couldn't care less about that. He probably expected from me something along the lines of my youth, looks and availability. I was obviously ambitious and happy to travel and flirt overtime. And I could always translate any story told by any foreigner.

I felt fully qualified for the job.

* * *

'Milena, my favorite name!' The president said when I sat down on silky and a bit slippery red sofa in Boss's Cabinet, otherwise dominated by mahogany. 'A proper Montenegrin name -' he sighed. His sighs were familiar to me and everyone else in the country, at least from his TV interviews.

'Everyone calls me Mila,' I replied.

'Very nice, very nice,' Vukas said, and he looked to the side, through the thick glass of his office windows. Bulletproof, I guessed.

Vukas was dressed in one of his beautiful, expensive-looking suits. He's a very tall man. Yet he looked so vulnerable; so moved by a proper Monte name. He was now staring at the high mosaic ceiling, as if noticing it for the first time. I had no idea what his 'very nice' stood for, but I felt that there must have been some kind of code in it. I didn't know what to respond to that; or if I were to respond at all. I only kept thinking that his desk was a king-size desk if ever there was one.

He cleared his throat and continued.

'Milena' he said, 'this is the thing. I need you. I need people like you. You're an intelligent young woman, and your time is now, here, with me. I want to turn this country into a kind of Monaco. Without the royals, for now,' he smiled, suddenly, quickly, as if some invisible puppeteer had pulled the strings and a smile spread across the Boss-puppet's milky-like teeth, exposing the shy boy the Boss must have been, once. 'As you know, I saved Montenegro from bloodshed, and now I want it to become a modern country, first, and then a wealthy one,' he sighed again and lifted her chin, proudly. 'I'm sure you know that there is an indisputable moral crisis in some of my closest colleagues and advisors.'

Whom was he really addressing? I looked around to see whether we were on candid camera or something.

'My political agenda,' he continued, while I fidgeted on the sofa, convinced that someone was secretly filming the meeting, maybe in order to check and analyze the responses of young population to the President's monologues, 'my plans, my reputation - all fell victim to the widespread cleptocracy, according to the opposition, who, as I'm sure you've heard, use this term a lot when describing my leadership. Frankly, I plan to get rid of that *clepto*-nonsense before I start my next mission: the in-depth social reforms in this country, which will take us into the new millennium proud of our independent and prosperous Montenegro. Yes, independent. You heard me correctly.' (I wasn't wondering.)

'But independence doesn't happen overnight,' he went on. 'America, for example, and their Republican government, they don't seem to care much about Europe, let alone the Balkans. So different from the Clinton administration. But at least, from the times of Clinton, I have a good team that has lobbied for me in Washington, and I will wait for the Republican government's full support as well. I hope you will help me in the domestic part of the job. You will have a good salary, and the title of coordinator of the social reforms.' He stopped there.

'Well,' I finally said. 'Okay. I mean - awesome. It all sounds serious, and so political. Thank you. But what do I really need to do?'

He said nothing for a while. I was shaking with the air-con's cold. It must have been set on 18 degrees - great for the Boss clad in his beautiful shirt and suit. But it was May and hot outside. I came to the meeting wearing only a light floral dress, and now I was freezing in his office.

'Please don't get me wrong,' I continued. 'Not that I don't want to do it. I'm afraid I'm just not that caliber you take me for.'

'Yes,' he said, 'your honesty is what I've immediately noticed and liked about you. So - thank you for that - I will be honest with you. I know about your youthful defiance of the Government and I understand it completely. For example, you and Mirko Petrović, our unusual so-called opposition leader, share some character trades, some, shall I say - artistic inclinations.

54

Etcetera. That's just fine. Petrović argues that he's not a politician, he's a poet, an intellectual who detests political kitsch. There is a connection.'

'What's the connection? Sorry if I seem too stupid now.'

Vukas didn't reply, again, so I continued.

'I mean, thank you for considering me artistic, but I failed to connect the dots after that.'

He finally averted his eyes from the ceiling and looked at me.

'Milena, think about our conversation when you're relaxing at home. When you're in your bathtub, when you put some music on, while watching a film, day-dreaming, whatever it is you do when relaxing – and think about this, about us working together on social reforms, visualise it for me, will you? And, you know what? Write me a report, a conclusion you will have reached. What is the segment of society in which your help would be most appreciated? What is your passion that you can turn into a job? You have to know yourself to inspire others. Make a list of possibilities for a new, fresh and prosperous country such as Montenegro. Think about what a new country like that could mean, could offer to young people, such as you. Then, pro-mote those ideas in newspapers, on TV, in meetings with your friends and colleagues, in cafes, restaurants. Make a plan, attractive enough, around which to unite the similarly artistic intellectuals. Believe that you can do that. I, myself, already believe in you.'

So was I supposed to found a movement? Artistic intellectuals, unite! I thought I'd come and meet Vukas

for a job, yes, flirt a bit, giggle a bit, get a job, go celebrate with friends. Now I was embarrassed by his
speech that sounded like the beginning of a serious
political campaign. Up to that point I never had any
political ambitions. I'd translated too many political
speeches and their repetitive phrases always wore my
spirit out, made my blood thicken. I didn't want that.
I wanted to work and earn money, but to also keep
my spirit alive. Some ambitious and beautiful young
women were already fierce activists, but I never considered myself cut out for that.

'You just caught me off guard,' I said. 'I don't know
what to say.'

Vukas gazed through the tinted windows, as if looking for an answer, written for him somewhere in the
coded game of sunrays dancing through the branches
of wild almond trees. Heavy silk curtains muted some
of those sunrays into a warm shade of old gold. I was
yearning for the outside heat. The president looked
at my legs and probably noticed the Goosebumps. He
uncrossed his legs, reached for the air-con's remote,
pressed a button and the cooling died out with a sad
moan.

'You don't have to say anything,' he said. 'Just keep
that frankness, Milena. I like it. And feel free to inter-
pret the social democratic reforms your own way. I
think it's always best, most useful, when I'm armed
with a written report about something. Then I make
sure I read it, I make my notes and I try my best to get
involved. I appreciate everyone's efforts. Respect,' he
said, and paused.

'Respect,' I repeated after a beat. *Respect*? What was that? The official salute of Montenegrin government?

He opened a leather journal in front of him.

'How much time do you need before we meet again and comment on your report?' he asked. 'Don't worry, it doesn't have to be PhD material.'

'I don't know. Give me a deadline.'

'Great, then, see you on Thursday, same time, same place. Congratulations.' He got up and came to me offering his right hand to confirm our deal with a handshake. Respect.

'See you on Thursday, Mr. President,' I said standing up. His palm was warm and dry. 'Have a nice day,' I added.

'The day has started well, thanks to you. And, call me Vukas, please. After all, everyone else does.'

He put his palm on the top of my head, as if baptising me. I wanted to melt into one of the *poids* on his tie. They all seemed so comfortable and safe there. We smiled at each other, and then I turned around and walked towards the door, trying to walk quietly, but my stilettos picked on the shiny wooden floor, like chickens. When I closed the heavy door behind me, Vukas was sitting behind his huge desk again, and he was writing something in that leather journal of his. His profile was Napoleonic.

And, suddenly, like a really good daughter, I wanted to run to my parents and tell them about my new job. I had neglected that old, retired couple for some time, the whole spring, and finally I could share some good news with them. They always claimed I was too irresponsible to provide for myself a nice state pension for a rainy day, which was how they called the present phase of their lives, although, in my opinion, it wasn't at all different than any of their earlier phases.

I went to see them.

My mother opened the door. She immediately put her hand over her mouth and muttered: 'Emaciated before the eyes of God. No food in your fridge, I bet.'

'Yes, hello to you too, Mother,' I said. 'How are you?'

My father appeared from behind the bathroom door, looked up, breathed in deeply, and exhaled so hard that the ceiling-lamp dangling above his head swayed.

Immediately, we sat down to eat.

Chicken soup, boiled chicken meat? Father always despised 'birds,' as he called such meals. Now he poured himself another helping of soup. I observed their faces with more attention, and saw they both looked tired, jaundiced.

'Are you two sick or something?' I asked.

They sighed.

'Sure we're sick. Sick of this life,' Father said.

'Most people enjoy their retirement years. It becomes their second honeymoon,' I said.

'Most people are idiots,' Father said. 'The mother of idiots is forever pregnant. And it's usually twins she carries.'

He continued to slurp the soup, exhaling angrily after each slurp. I knew his thought pattern. That soup was an enemy. That soup was deliberately hot; it too was the part of a global conspiracy against him. Always hungry like a beast, but angry even while enjoying and devouring his food; always grim-faced – that was daddy.

'We did some blood tests,' Mother finally revealed. 'Turned out we both had pathological levels of triglycerides. Ha ha ha.' Father and I looked at her. 'It's just that,' she was trying not to laugh. 'God forgive me, but it sounded as if the doctor informed us we were a couple of aliens. A couple of pathological triglycerides.'

Father snorted, then sneezed. Soup leaked from his nostrils.

'Yes,' continued Mother, 'we have high cholesterol, the bad kind, poor blood coagulation. Our livers are fat and tired and. Whatever bad there is, we have it. Our systems have completely pathologised.' She coughed weakly, as if apologising for that. 'One of the doctors, your father's old classmate, told us if we wanted to live to see our grandchildren, we could no longer smoke, drink coffee, drink red wine,' she glanced at father's wide-rimmed glass filled with thick, dark-red wine.

'That doctor's always had dry figs for balls,' Father growled. 'Red wine is healthy.'

'Not for your liver,' Mother said.

Father stopped eating. 'Listen, both of you,' he said. 'I'm not stupid. Red wine is more like food than drink. It cleanses our blood by using some sort of phenols, which it derives from grapes. It is an anti-a-engio-genetic substance. Or something. I know it. I researched it. And I have my sources.'

Mother stared at the nice tablecloth she had knitted long ago. I knew she was gathering courage. She gently placed her spoon into her plate. 'Why not drink grape juice then?' she almost whispered.

Father pushed his plate away from him, shouting: 'Fermentation, woman! Disinfection!' Then he kicked the table and stood up.

A moment later he shouted from the living room: 'And now I'm going to smoke and drink coffee! Not brown sherbet, you hear me? I want real coffee!'

'Why don't you just let him die?' I asked my mother.

'Don't say that,' she said, getting up from the dining table, to boil water for some real coffee.

In the living room, over the coffee, I told them the news of my employment.

Mother put her palms together, kissed me and said: 'Ah, God bless the President. I've heard that he helped many people personally, and that he doesn't do it for publicity. Now I see it's true.'

'Yes, sure,' my father said. 'Why would our President publicise every petty sum he throws to his hungry cattle from time to time, when his dick rises good morning?'

'Can't you ever be happy for me, daddy?' I asked. 'Can't you first say 'Congratulations, Mila,' or something like that, and then you could go on and list all the bad sides to my good news?'

'Life is too short,' he said. 'Life is too short, Milena, to play pretend-happy, but also to list all the bad sides to something so dirty and low as the coordinator for the social reforms of the Montenegrin government. It makes me - '

'What?' I shouted. 'You voted for them every time!'

'I voted for them before they started using the small

60

sums of big money they'd stolen to pay the servants they call reformers, coordinators, marketing managers. My tongue hurts now from those stinking titles. You're all only jesters and spies, that's what you are.'

'You just can't accept the progress and flow of life, can you?'

'What do you call progress? Is progress being pissed on by the self-proclaimed social reformers?' My father raised his hand in which he was clutching a cup of coffee. 'I wish I could piss on those reformers' graves. But I'm afraid this will never happen.' His hand with the cup in it fell on the table. Some coffee spilled over. He looked at it sadly. 'They've become indestructible, those Vukas clones, like cockroaches. They'd survive the Judgment Day. But I'm not so sure about you. You're not of the same material. But perhaps working for them will toughen you up, huh?'

It occurred to me that the President of Montenegro respected me far more than my own father. Was that good or bad news? Whatever it was, I decided at that moment to become a loyal and trusted employee of Vukas. I was glad that at least Mother seemed proud and relieved: to her, my full-time employment meant, most of all, that I would not be left alone, on the street, if the two of them were to die soon.

In the kitchen, as she was putting away the dishes, I whispered to her not to worry, I was not going to become either a jester or a spy. Vukas had a really high opinion of me. She nodded her head.

When I left their flat, as I was walking towards my apartment, I suddenly remembered Mamma's sunken cheeks, her trembling fingers, her thin hair, her dry hands invaded by what looked like eczema. She didn't look well at all, and seemed much more ill than my father, and I realised it only after I'd left. I let her do everything - cook and tidy up, listen to us quarrelling. I never did anything for her. I was going to visit her much more often, I promised myself; at least twice a week, after work.

7

I nodded a greeting to the security men standing at the entrance of the building of the Montenegrin presidency, and climbed the stairs leading to the first floor.

The entire first floor belonged to Vukas and Anka, his secretary. Again, like every time I came to the first floor, I felt dizzy from the strong magnolia-scented air-freshener that Anka kept regularly refilled. Anka's office was annexed to the President's Cabinet. All the visitors had to first go past Anka to get to the President, and Anka was well trained in subjecting the visitors to her cold-eye scrutiny. It was quiet on the floor; I could hear my own hair tapping at my back as I moved towards Anka's door.

I knocked and heard her 'Come on in,' muffled by what was probably her second triangle of cheese or jam pastry – Anka allowed breakfast to be her me-time during work hours. I smiled at her and proceeded to the magnificent, smooth and lacquered door behind which Vukas usually sat at that hour, munching on his greatness instead of pastry, gulping some freshly squeezed juice, reading reports, raising his chin to the ceiling from time to time, and sighing.

'You're early,' Anka said behind my back.

I turned toward her desk. 'Early?' I asked. 'What, the Boss is late, you mean?'

'The president is on his way. He had an important meeting last night.'

'He did? So who was translating?'

'I didn't say that the meeting was with foreigners.'

'Why was it important then?'

Anka rolled her eyes; of course she wasn't going to answer that.

'Do you want some breakfast?' she asked instead. 'A glass of freshly squeezed grapefruit?'

'No, thanks.'

'Sit here with me then,' Anka said, and continued with her work.

That morning, her job seemed to consist mostly of her silently destroying, terminating, a lot of irrelevant mail received during the previous days. Anka would study a letter for a few seconds and wrinkle her nose before crumpling the letter in her hand.

'Hand-written letters,' I said. 'Some effort invested. Don't you feel at least a little bit sorry for the senders?'

'Sure, honey,' she said. 'Fan mail. Obviously not for me. People have no dignity anymore. Asking for money from the President, every single one of them.'

Anka. Loyal as a mastiff, somewhat gentler looking, one of those classic secretaries with the old-fashioned, super-high hair-do's; one of those women who suddenly found themselves in a position to take care of a globally acknowledged great man, and, who, consequently, developed the ego and the hairstyle that grew in height and volume year after year. I knew she despised the gender-team of Boss's coordinators for this and that. 'Ha. Coordinators, my tit,' she must have thought.

Some of us, the coordinators, were the working bees indeed; some were the mistresses, and some mixed business and pleasure, I'd heard.

Mistresses or working bees, we all visited Vukas in his Cabinet, as part of our jobs. And we all giggled as we passed by Anka and her working desk. She was never on a break. She always sat there, proud and upright, behind the pile of letters and documents to be signed, looking somewhat like a mentor surpassed by her students – but a mentor, still, with a desk and a title.

She knew that neither one of us had the potential to become a lifetime partner of Vukas. Shouldn't then our failure, our mediocrity, make her feel more special? The coordinators came to the Cabinet, to meet with the Boss, and then they went outside, to continue their work at home, on the street, in restaurants, schools or other people's offices. The coordinators had no roots. Anka had roots; she was the only one with the office next to the Holy Cabinet, and she coordinated the coordinators. She made sure we never met each other. It was a good thing because, as I'd heard, most coordinators were the high-maintenance, serious women, who, after years of raising children and serving their husbands, committed themselves to coordinating various aspects of Vukas's rule with such zeal and competitiveness, that to them, an unmarried, young, willing and free girl like me, most certainly represented a threatening intruder, a New Age little bitch about whose actions they had every right to demur. So, in a way, I was grateful that Anka made sure I never met my coordinating colleagues. She was the one to look down on each of us individually; we shouldn't share that right with her.

Vukas entered, leaving the bodyguards behind the doors of Ms Anka's. Instinctively, I got up from the chair. His secretary did not get up. She just pointed in my direction with her head.

The president smiled at me.

'Look at these bright eyes, Anka,' he said. 'Now, did we ever have a prettier coordinator?'

'No, boss, never,' she murmured and looked down into the death-sentenced papers she held between her fingers crowded by large rings.

Vukas looked good. He had traces of a sleepless night all over his face, but he wore them well. The dimples of his youth had turned into deep lines, and when he smiled, they added vulnerability to his otherwise non-distinct features. He was not a beautiful man; but there was a lovely boyishness in his smile.

He opened the door to his Cabinet, which was still in the darkness, under the rule of heavy curtains severely drawn together.

Summer had come and gone; it had aged into October, its air that smelled of blueberries, its deceiving, gauzy sunrays, completely vanished after Michaelmas, turned into sheets of rain that cut through the days.

'This autumn humidity kills people like me,' Vukas said, removing his jacket. He lay on his back on the Cabinet's wooden floor and bent his knees. He moaned while moving his knees from side to side. I heard his spine crack. 'Damn it,' he said, 'Play sport in youth - end up on a floor in your forties. I need an Ibuprofen the size of a cheese reel. What will you have?'

'Cranberry juice.'

'Push the button, please,' Vukas said. 'I wish I could stay here. This is the best parquet flooring in town. Ha. This floor rules. Get it?'

'So funny,' I said.

Several phones were placed on the smooth mahogany surface of his king-size table. Each phone had a button on it marked 'A.' I pressed one of them.

'Anka, save us!' Vukas shouted from the floor when his secretary answered.

The phone was completely unnecessary for Anka to hear him.

Not a minute later, Anka floated in, like a good Genie from the Kingdom of Mastiffs, laden with huge bosom trapped in a sharply cupped bra, over which she only wore a tight, apricot-coloured cardigan with buttons just about to give up and burst open. She was carrying a silver tray, and on it, in front of her boobs, stood two tall glasses of juice. With a few mysterious sighs and sideway glances, she placed the drinks on the table and floated out.

'Can I get a backrub sometime during the day?' Vukas shouted after her.

'Sure, boss' came the reply.

'She has no life outside of this building,' I said. 'The magnolia-scented floor shared only by you two. The merciless destruction of fan mail. Submissive backrubs in pastel colours. Tread carefully, boss.'

Vukas laughed, and moaning, he slowly got up from the floor.

'Anka has been here forever,' he said. 'And she will be the last one to leave. On her own terms. Do you know why?'

I drew the curtains open and organised the paper cards for the president's meetings on his desk. He sat behind the desk and took his long pink pills, swallowed them with juice.

'Why?' I asked.

But he was just humming now, staring into dense clouds, so low they seemed stuck in the bare branches of almond trees. The moment for his reply had passed.

At that time of year, on an autumn day in Podgorica, with hovering, thick clouds of sulphure-dioxide from the aluminum combine and diesel from old cars, with endless sheets of rain, anyone, I bet even the Boss, could feel as though constantly trying to commit suicide, but, every time, narrowly failing to end it.

'Seems like you didn't get much sleep last night,' I said.

'Who cares? Sleep is good for growing children. Or for those who don't want to grow up, right?' he said. 'I could probably sleep on a horse if I had to, like the soldiers of Peter the Great. Do you always get your eight hours of sleep, Milena?'

'Never,' I said.

'See?' Vukas concluded and started checking the paper cards. 'We're having visitors in five minutes, right? Some foreign delegation with nothing better to do, I bet.'

'Kind of,' I said. 'I scheduled it. So don't worry, it's not really in five minutes. I always hide about fifteen minutes from the official schedule so that you have extra time to prepare and freshen up. Just in case.'

'Pierson Paterson,' he read the visitor's name aloud. 'Who are these people? They sound like a law firm.'

'It's just one guy,' I said. 'Quite young and ambitious. A new man for the OEBS office. No importance – as such men go.'

'Ha. Good. That's very good. You know that I fast on Fridays. Only small fish on the menu, please.'

'Sure. Pierson Paterson is doing his apprenticeship in OEBS. His father was in the UK's Foreign Office, Pierson may end up there soon. For now though, he is a supervisor of sorts in OEBS Montenegro. Meanwhile, rumour has it, the OEBS Ambassador doesn't much like the presence of these supervisors.'

'Ah, sure, they're sending new British blood to uncorrupt the corrupt. Replacing the Cookies.'

'With Straws.'

'With Straws. You're good, Milena, you're good.'

'Anyway, young Pierson closely collaborates with Elke Konelke whom we both know very well, but some sources say that too is not a vibrant cooperation. So. As I said, Pierson is ambitious, but fed by FT and Economist sources. The showbiz-investigators. My guess is he will bring up the cigarette smuggling.'

68

'Wake me up when he leaves, please.'

'Don't worry, boss,' I smiled. 'All I need is your authorisation. This one is mine. You can relax.'

This British guy was a man of pleasant features, with a likeable cluster of freckles thrown over his straight, nice nose, and with a tidy parting in his sand-coloured hair. He had sparkles of determination in his eyes. Easy-breezy for me; I already knew the type.

Like: he would be proud of his education; super-proud of his father – a distinguished employee of the Foreign Office; and humbly-proud of his rich Resume, dominated by his voluntary missions in tough places, like Kashmir, or-Some-stan, Sub-Sahara, Colombian villages, or Bosnian ruins.

Fine. Perfect, actually. I was going to keep him there, both in the zones of conflict and in his self-admiration, while ever-so-slowly translating it all to my president.

Vukas was doing a wonderful job, nodding in appreciation, pretending to be all ears for the achievement stories of young Pierson Peterson, and his dad. Vukas was, in fact, taking a nap with his eyes open. Without a horse, but still.

Something I discovered rather early on in my job: all English men stutter when they talk during the business or political meetings (was there a difference between 'business and political'?)

Why do they stutter? It must be a trick, a secret weapon they share in their Etons and Westminsters, to get other people to relax in front of them, and talk about the unspeakable truths.

I noticed it in the elderly 'Cookies' I worked with;

and now this young 'Straw' was doing it, as well. I couldn't help it: because of that stutter, I liked Pierson more than I'd intended to; I felt a bit sorry for him, and I wanted him on our side, but for his own good, kind of. I wanted him to have a successfully accomplished Montenegrin mission. He was probably still in the 'good observer' stage, which meant that he had seen cigarettes sold on every street corner. Maybe he talked to some vendors, or the customers who seemed very poor, but were still buying boxes of Davidoff, because, as they had certainly informed him, at least a box of Davidoffs could not be falsified. So they were really smoking Davidoffs, and not someone's tobacco that grew wildly in the Zeta region and was contaminated by the leaks from the Aluminum Combine.

Yes, he'd done his first homework. But, so what? In the bigger picture, come-on – so what? I loved using 'the bigger picture' phrase. It was so new back then, even for the Anglo-Saxon visitors, and it differentiated me from other translators.

Pierson kept on addressing the President. I translated the questions and immediately gave the answers.

'Are you sure that's what President Tomović said?' Piers asked me at one point, because Presdent Tomović had actually said nothing at all.

'The President has authorised me to give his usual statements whenever I judge appropriate,' I said.

'I'm sorry,' Piers said. 'And you are?'

'I am his coordinator for social reforms.'

'I see,' Piers looked at Vukas. Vukas nodded.

Oh, and, *by-the-way* – I was unstoppable now -

might I add that Vukas had had the UN sanctions imposed on his country, for no reason, really. He had Milošević, the super-villain, as his terrifying, mistrustful first-door neighbor. He had to make the transition from one political system via the imposed civil war – Montenegro was neither aggressor, nor the secessionist - to another political system. And the transition . . .oh, the transition. Who was the transition leader in the UK? Churchill? Thatcher? Yes. And they were the ones that would be remembered forever, right? Time and place. Time and place. But, Vukas also had the American support, as well as an opposition so weak and pathetic, really, that they still nagged about the World War II, and the divisions it had created. Some of the opposition leaders perceived 'opposition' as a business opportunity, their ultimate goal being to become *the vezir instead of the vezir,* i.e. get rich by controlling the cigarette trade. Well, they could not. That money, the cigarette-money, was for Montenegro, our motherland. Why would only the imperialistic nations nurture and love their great motherlands? Montenegro was our great motherland. So, the opposition became bitter like an old maid. Spitting on the president's name was their way to relieve their excess bile. But, it was democracy, right? Our young democracy had to get its childhood illnesses too, in order to build up its immune system.

Vukas was nodding through all that, backing my words with deep sighs of controlled emotion. It was his way of confirming that my speech represented his vision.

Thirty minutes later, as if pre-coordinated, just when

I needed a change of subject, Anka came in with cookies and tea on a tray. Pierson's face lit up, and, seizing the opportunity to make him feel more relaxed, I started talking about tea. I wanted to know everything about the culture and benefits of drinking tea, which certainly had everything to do with the creation of the famous British endurance, both on land and at sea, did it not?

Young Pierson knew his tea. He enjoyed any cup of tea – was a fan of Montenegrin rosehip that Anka had chosen, but his favourites of the moment were Japanese green teas. He talked about subtle differences between Gyokuro and Macha, and recommended Macha to me, and to Anka, who was standing next to me, her thin eyebrows raised, clearly understanding only what we were talking about (Japanese teas), but not sure whether we approved or disapproved of her rosehip choice. I knew that she took it as an insult; she brought the best tea she had in her secret cupboards, and here we were, immersed in the impossible names of Japanese teas – why? What went wrong? Pierson darted looks in her direction, and I stopped to explain to everyone the benefits of Macha for women like Anka and myself.

Anka finally smiled, raised her arm as if in surrender, and left. The rest of us drank tea in silence.

When Pierson got up to leave, I gave a sign to Vukas to pat his shoulder as we made arrangements to meet again soon, for lunch. I shook Pierson's lovely hand, and stroked it, almost imperceptibly, with my left palm.

'I thought you were going to say 'God bless you', to our young visitor,' Vukas said to me, when we heard Anka close the door after Mr. Paterson.

'God bless is reserved for the Americans only,' I replied.

'Speaking of which,' Vukas said, 'tonight I will be on a meeting with one of them. 'Ambassador' Chris and I agreed to meet in private, with whiskey and snacks while his wife, my wife and you are having fun in the Blue Club.'

'Who will be interpreting for you and Chris?'

'Chris understands our language,' Vukas said. 'Even speaks it a little. But there will also be a good friend of mine with us, and that guy speaks everything from English to Hebrew. '

'Who is it?'

Vukas didn't answer.

'Report back to me your thoughts on Chris's wife, will you? She tries too hard to be sweet. Whatever her name was? Something saccharine. *Baby*, right? '

'Bella,' I said.

8

At that time I hadn't yet met Chris Bernard, although I knew of him as 'you know Chris, the Ambassador', and, somehow, everyone was aware that Chris was never really an Ambassador, only the most widely known American lobbyist in the region of ex-Yugoslavia. His wife, Bella, was openly trying to seduce our First lady, Darinka, into becoming her new best friend, her mentor, a confidante-benefactor of a kind – something like that, kitschy but functional. She also wanted to turn Darinka into the First lady of the 21st century, who would no longer be intimidated by politics and economy, but would, on the contrary, become directly involved in it. The first lady did not speak English, so again I was interpreting their socialising. That included having lunch and dinner with the two of them at least once a week. It was another part of my famous coordination of social reforms in Montenegro.

We met about 8 p.m. in the Blue Club, the official restaurant of El Presidente and his clique, where nothing was really Blue - but the blue was the color of the ruling party - and where no one paid any bills. I wondered if someone ever regulated the accounts, whether there existed a 'coordinator for petty expenses'. Probably did.

Bella was the first one to arrive for our little Friday Blue Club dinner. She was an Englishwoman, in her fifties, with quite a sexy, curvaceous body, born in South London, of which she spoke with some nostalgia. Her South London wasn't posh; it was poor, sketchy and dangerous, with blackouts and small shops like the custom-made umbrella shop near 'the junction'; oh, it was just wonderful - and here she sighed, again, and her curves fluttered, swam and swayed - how everyone, no matter how poor they were, walked around with bespoke umbrellas, up the junction, *there*. But now, her part of London became fashionable, and she could never live there again, she couldn't bear to see the bloody wrong kind of changes 'they' were pursuing, those judgmental nobodies, all of 'them' so b*oh*ring, and condescending to the outsiders; so she bought an apartment in Pimlico, which was next to the river, and next to most of the London Russkies, as her husband

74

called them. She liked the London Russkies; why did everyone else think they had no sense of humour, just hunger, hunger, hunger in their eyes, in their blood, in their genes? Well, in London, she now lived North of the river, not on the South side, and it was a decent living space, a newly built complex with spacious rooms and parquet flooring, with reception, gym, swimming-pool, and a garage. Bella absolutely insisted that Darinka had to come and stay with her in London.

Darinka, with her perfect Italian-blonde highlights, her always bare arms, toned by 2-kilo-weights, and her regular AHA peels, was only interested if Bella's London apartment was situated 'very very close to Harrods'. Bella explained that of course it was close to Harrods; that Pimlico was practically 'Knightsbridge-upon-Thames', and far less polluted. They agreed to go to London together in January, right after the New Year party, to be organised at the Blue Club's Party Salon. That way, they would still arrive in London in time for the big sales. They would use the best of both worlds. Giggle-wow-wow. They even high-fived each other. It was the lowest high-five I ever witnessed. A moment for me to inhale; or exhale. I couldn't tell anymore.

That night, Bella also started a serious discussion with Darinka about a humanitarian action, 'heavenly designed to, in a very relaxing manner, engage Darinka in the humanitarian activities, which would make her a popular First lady'.

Of course, in translation, I could have added an 'even-more' to Bella's 'popular', but I hadn't. Bella needed to sweat it out a little bit more, in order to become the First Lady's new-best-friend and mentor-confidante.

Darinka predictably frowned at (just) 'popular'.

Bella noticed that.

'Tell our Di,' Bella added, 'that of course I meant 'more popular even among the opposition.''

'Tell Bella to call me Darinka,' the First lady replied. 'I don't have a problem with my name. But I do have a problem with 'Di'. It sounds like death.'

My brain suffered in their company. It turned into a throbbing mushroom. High risk of brain tumour: those Blue Club hen meetings always kind of amputated the most likeable parts of me.

I lit a cigarette and ordered a double vodka-cranberry.

Bella hated smoking indoors, and she despised smoking during meetings. That was her cancer-alert. No second-hand smoke in her superbly organised life. Didn't she know that I would turn into something even nastier if someone put a ban on my petty vice in public? Without a cigarette and a drink, I was likely to jump up on the table and shout: 'Vukas, my love, come save me!' Or: 'Martin Luther King, my love, come save my soul! I too have a dream!'

No. Bella really believed it was a privilege for me to translate for Di and her.

It turned out that the receiving ends of the latest humanitarian project Bella was proposing were to be the orphaned children from the home in Bijela, a village on the Montenegrin coast. Not only them. The project included the sick and vulnerable children from

76

the Central Children's Hospital in Podgorica. Bella was excited about the development of her idea, and while she knitted on and on about it, she neglected to mention the serious funds needed to start and maintain it, so I added that detail in my translation.

'So who does she think is going to finance these humanitarian missions?' Darinka asked me. 'They're supposed to go on, like, forever, no?'

I translated the question to Bella, who leaned back a little and gasped ever so slightly, momentarily shocked by the indecency of Darinka's question. But she composed herself quickly. Nobody – except me, and I didn't count - noticed her genuine reaction.

'I would be the first person to put some of my own funds down,' Bella said. 'And it would be my pleasure.'

Darinka remained silent.

'As an anon contributor, of course,' Bella continued.

'Sure,' Darinka said coolly.

Bella wasn't happy. She needed at least a spark of Di's enthusiasm.

'To start the piggy bank going,' Bella added. 'To attract the benefactors.'

Darinka laughed when I translated the 'piggy bank'.

Bella looked at me sternly, convinced that I was the one creating feedback problems. I was, in fact, hoping that she would complain about me to Chris, who would complain to Vukas, and then Vukas would talk to me about the whole Bella situation, and I'd tell him that I would rather lick hairspray from Anka's hair-do's, night after night, than eat another meal with Bella.

'What does this woman want from me?' Darinka

asked me through her teeth.

'Your money,' I answered in slang.

'She should just say so.'

'Darinka will start the piggy bank going,' I said to Bella in the way of translation.

'What a magnificent gesture!' Bella said. 'Bra-vo!' She gently applauded.

'We call champagne now,' Darinka said in English, and I joined Bella in applauding.

The two ladies could then proceed to Darinka's favourite topics: how there's no trinity holier than the trinity of good hair, bag and shoes; the top five cafes in town; and the latest fitness must-do's.

It was obvious that Darinka only accepted socialising with Bella because it also included me. I was becoming her latest new best friend. She wanted to impress me, not Bella, whose Western mentality was too elusive for our First lady. For Darinka, Bella was no more than her 'Washington-supports-my-husband' beard.

Lord oh Lord – I was praying through my vodka - send me someone now, someone to enter the Club, sit with us and speak English, any kind of English. Anyone.

And, so, the Lord, in his forever-mysterious ways, fulfilled my short but intense prayer. The Lord sent us someone.

As I was finishing my second vodka cranberry, half-heartedly mixing it with seafood pasta, into the Club walked Darinka's brother, Branko.

'Branko, what a coincidence!' Darinka said, moving her eyes fast from me to Branko and vice versa. 'I had no idea you ever came to the Club.'

It was an almost sweet attempt to fake a surprise at Branko's arrival. Her brother didn't even bother to reply.

She introduced us to each other, and Branko sat next to me, immediately placing his long arm around the back of my chair. I realized that I was on a partially blind date, i.e. I was the only 'blind' person there. I pushed my seafood pasta plate in a tepid rebellion. I was never going to pray again.

As soon as I drew another cigarette from my pack and placed it between my lips, Branko's right hand with a flame from a lighter appeared in front of my face. At the same time, his left arm moved from the backrest of my chair to hug my shoulders.

'Thanks, but I really enjoy lighting my own cigarettes,' I said. 'It's my little ritual.'

'You're so childish,' Branko said.

'You don't know me,' I said, blowing the smoke into his face. 'I don't know you. Let's keep it that way, please.'

Bella and Darinka smirked at each other in the style of: weren't Branko and Milena so cute together, even when, like, arguing?

The waiter approached our table carrying a bottle of champagne.

'Oh-la-la,' Bella exclaimed. 'Nothing but the Krug for this little party!' She had eaten only a quarter of her long veal escalope, which still stretched over the edges of her plate. Her eyes were filled with pink bubbles now.

'Shall we all order the famous Blue Club tiramisu

with this champagne?' Darinka asked, placing her fork over her unfinished plate of risotto.

'No tiramisu,' Branko answered, even though his sister wasn't really addressing him. 'You and Milena need some kind of protein now. Otherwise, you will be boiled up by all the sugar intake.' Then he turned towards me. 'Believe me, beautiful, forget tiramisu. Order some young cheese. Low-fat proteins rule. See this British woman? She knows, she's been trained what to eat where. Learn from her. Our veal is the best veal in Europe. No hormones, and the Westerners damn well know it. In Europe, they put hormones in meat and they all become homosexuals.'

I could see that Bella had hard time dividing her attention between the bottle of Krug and the bits of Branko's monologue that contained some illogically paired words she could understand, like tiramisu, hormones and homosexuals.

The waiter was still hovering above our heads, waiting for us to decide what next.

'Relax, brother,' Darinka said. Then she looked at me. 'You know, Branko is the youngest in our family,' she said. 'And the only son, so our mother spoiled him. For her, every word Branko says is the law. But, at least, he is honest, tolerant, and a quick learner, right?' She winked at the two of us. 'Three times tiramisu,' she said to the waiter.

'What's going on?' Bella asked.

'We are all going to have tiramisu with this bottle,' I said.

'Marvelous!' cried the indestructible English woman.

Branko lit up my every following cigarette, he drank champagne from my flute as well as from his, he touched me a lot, and he proudly touched himself on the chest a lot. He was not an ugly man, but he had a big gap between his short, sharp nose and his pursed upper lip, and it looked like a slide and it caused him to rustle when he *szsz*poke. I figured he was an ideal man to grow a mustache, because somehow that detail would not only make his slide less visible, but it would also put him in the right place with women; he would then attract the right kind of girls for him; the *musta-chio*-girls.

I also knew I was going to be the first one to get up and go . . . go to my Innisfree. Suddenly, I loved my little life with unprecedented intensity. I wanted to protect it from too much exposure. It had many positive sides that not many other lives had. The boss of all bosses was my only boss, and he trusted my judgment on the topics of vital interest for him, and for that light-hearted judgment he paid me two thousand Euros per month, tax-free. Plus I felt the time was ripe to ask for a raise. I didn't have to date anyone; I didn't want to date anyone; I didn't need to have sex with anyone - especially not anyone from the ruling clique. That was why I could just finish my drink, get up and say to my dinner companions: 'Good night, I have a meeting tomorrow morning,' - even though the next day was a Saturday - and when Branko jumped up and said he'd drive me home, I was able to just put my palm in front of his long, un-mustached face say: 'No,' and even add: 'Thank you.'

I decided that adding the coldblooded 'Thank you' was to be my new favourite reaction to everything. That was what I learnt from Bella - not about what kind of protein to order where.

9

'Branko?' I said to Vukas when I next met with him in his Cabinet. 'Really?'

Vukas laughed. 'He likes you a lot. Darinka told me.'

'Don't insult me, please. The retarded younger brother.'

'Not a bad catch,' Vukas said. 'His future looks bright. I'm sending him to Washington, to Georgetown University.'

'Why?'

'He'll do master studies in diplomacy. He may be appointed as the first Ambassador of independent Montenegro in the United States.'

'You'll appoint him? The little hormone-free first brother-in-law? Isn't that a bit too transparent nepotism? I mean, wasn't he the one that smuggled weapons to all the warring sides in the Bosnian war? Once a smuggler -' I bit my tongue there. 'Well, what I want to say is: why not send *me*, for example?'

'But you're my sweet coordinator, and I need you here. We have social reforms to work on together. Calm down now, there'll be plenty of opportunities for you. You already know how to talk to foreigners. Why would you lose two years of your life in boring Washington D.C. to learn the skill you already have? Tell me, why? See, no answer. So tell me this: how's Baby?'

'You mean Bella?'

'Yeah, the woman with expensive ideas. But, Darinka seems to like her ideas now. How did that happen?'

'You know, Boss,' I said, 'actually, at first I was not particularly impressed by Bella. But then I thought – why not use her to teach us something? About image. Abroad, they now call it PR. Of course, I'll have to translate all the lessons. So first of all, I'd like a raise, please.'

Vukas gave me a raise of his eyebrows.

'You want a raise for socialising with Darinka and Baby?'

I nodded my head. 'Bella,' I whispered.

'I spoil everyone,' Vukas said.

'I'm not spoiled. I work overtime.'

'You're not spoiled? A raise in salary already too big for lunching and dining with people already on my side – if that's not spoiled, then . . . How about a raise for – what did you call it? – for spreading good PR of me to my enemies?'

'What do you mean?'

'You should be able to know what I mean.'

One of the telephones from his mahogany desk rang. The letter 'A' was twinkling. Vukas pressed it.

'Your visitors are downstairs with security,' Anka's voice informed.

'We'll continue our discussion later,' Vukas said to me.

The visitor was Elke Konelke, and two additional members of her EU anti-corruption team.

'These are my personal assistants,' Elke said of the two men.

Anka, who walked the visitors into the Cabinet, sent a meaningful glance to Vukas. I knew what that was for. She wanted to replace her 'secretary' title with a 'personal assistant'. Even Anka had surrendered to the influence of too many visitors from the West. Vukas told me about Anka's new-title request. I told him that to me a 'secretary' sounded better: it meant a keeper of secrets, didn't it? On the other hand, a 'personal assistant' could even be a car-mechanic, who took care of Vukas's many cars. Nothing special, PA.

But the keeper of secrets . . . Special!

Vukas winked at Anka's meaningful gaze, and two days after that meeting, it happened: the new plate on her door said 'Anka Čukić, Personal Assistant to the President of Montenegro' in tall, gold-plated letters. It was another proof for me that all one had to do for one's dreams to come true, was to ask the President. Vukas was very tolerant of the small personal victories of his loyal employees.

Anyway, after the President's wink of approval, Anka was all melting in front of Elke and her assistants. She led them to their chairs, she swiped something invisible from two men's suits, she curtsied slightly, and then, in her hard-boiled English, her breasts heaving, she asked everyone, what they would like to drink.   G u e s t s asked for plain water only, because as they said, they found that Montenegrin tap water tasted better than anything else.

'Ee-t,' Anka said in English, with no intonation.

They looked at her not understanding the naked word thrown at them, like a bone.

'Ee-t,' she repeated, directing her three knuckled fingers into her mouth.

'Would you like to eat something while we talk?' I translated Anka for them, and they responded that no, thanks, not really, and then smiled at her. Anka let out a deep sigh of concern, as if they were a dying trio of anorexics. Finally, she left the stage and closed the door behind her.

Then Vukas suddenly roared in English: 'You are very velcome to me,' he said. 'My old friends.'

Elke's cold smile showed that she hated being called 'an old friend' by any politician.

'Congratulations on your English,' Elke replied, and she smiled at me with more warmth, undoubtedly hoping I would be translating for the rest of the meeting. She already knew, from a couple of meetings we had, that I would ignore the straying sentences about our sunny climate, joyful freedom, about the beauty of Montenegro and its happy, happy people.

Vukas caught the vibe. 'My vanderful Milena,' he announced. 'Koordinatoressa for my social reform.'

Everyone looked at me.

'How can we help you today, Ms Konelke?' I asked.

'Well . . .' Elke started and then paused because Anka reappeared with tall jug of tap water and five glasses. 'Thank you, Anka,' Elke said.

Anka nodded and left again.

'Mr President,' Elke continued, 'I must say that I really admire you. It is not easy to maintain a balance in the country so clearly divided between the Serbian and Montenegrin nationalists. I know you've been busy in the north of the country last weekend, and thank you for having me at such short notice.'

President Tomović sighed sharply. I knew he wasn't happy: he liked to be considered a visionary, not a balancer between two nationalisms.

Elke went on, wishing him success in the upcoming social reforms presented during his recent visit to Brussels. She voiced her support for Montenegro to receive a more recognised international status.

I was translating even though I didn't have to. It was an introduction, a lullaby for the president. Vukas and I were waiting for The Point of that meeting.

On her previous visits, Elke had been quiet, made a lot of notes. She used to come not alone, but as a member of an OSCE or OEBS delegation or another, and she'd let others do the kissing up and the wrapping up. Now, her assistants seemed to be taking minutes. I glanced at the mirror behind their backs. On their paper sheets, they were just doodling childishly. What were they, really? Were they her bodyguards? That was what the men really looked like. What the hell? Elke didn't feel safe with Vukas in his Cabinet?

More compliments were exchanged. Vukas coughed; Elke sighed. We had to move on.

'My concern,' she finally said, 'is the following: the dangerous network of smuggling has, as I've been informed, included Montenegro and here it has, as, again, I've been informed, been used also for the trafficking of humans. I am going to visit Women's Safe House after this meeting.' Vukas was nodding all along. 'Would the President accompany me? I heard there were at least three women there who had been robbed of their documents and made slaves by somebody very important and high ranked in this country.' Her assistants were 'writing this down'. 'By somebody close to the president.'

'But,' I answered directly, without translating anything to Vukas, who had stopped nodding. 'The address of that Safe House is secret, nobody knows where it is. The president...'

'I know where it is,' Elke went on, 'And so does everyone else. Including a Mr Berković, the Head of State Security.'

'Tell me, why did she mention Smeško and me? *Brzo*,' Vukas said, trying to sound unmoved.

I told him. He stole some time. He removed his elbows from the table, crossed his arms over his chest. He lifted his chin up, fixed his gaze on the ceiling. He inhaled briskly.

'Tell Miss Elke,' Vukas said, 'that I've been the President of this country for more than a decade now; I met Bill and Hilary Clinton. I met the current US vice-president. The name escapes me, but you fill it in. I met Tony Blair, Xavier Solana. Kofi Annan. They have all shown immense respect for my democratic reforms and me. They have all understood the implications of being the leader of a country, of a *democratic* country, with a bitter dictator such as Milošević as a next-door enemy, and an even more bitter opposition that's allowed to spread their statements often based on gossip, rumours and wishful thinking without any repercussions. Miss Elke also seemed to understand it last time. I have welcome OSCE in my country and they have produced a favourable, optimistic report. What has happened in the meantime that has made her change her tone during our meetings?'

I translated and Elke pursed her thin lips into the net of wrinkles that spelled 'disdain'.

'I visited the Opposition Party Headquarters this morning before coming here,' she said. 'The person who has informed me about this was extremely trust-worthy. The person also suggested I should try and persuade the president to visit the Safe House himself and meet the victims of sex-trafficking, bought, as they claimed, by Mr Berković personally, during one of his visits to the Bosnian women-slaves market known as *Arizona*.'

'Unheard of!' Vukas cried out before I was finished translating Elke's speech. 'Were that so, I can assure you, it would be the end of my political career! But . . . I will have that rumour investigated. For now, I fail to see the point of my visiting the Safe House. With the complicated task of running the country in transition times, with the plans of visiting my colleagues, politicians from other Socialist Parties from all over the world, including Miss Elke's country, Miss Elke wants me to put my jacket on and - what - hire a taxi for all of us, and spend a day in some shelter because of some hearsay? In the middle of my busy schedule?'

'I would admire such an action from you,' Elke replied.

'I can send somebody from my Cabinet staff,' Vukas said, 'to go with you and investigate this and report back to me. Milena, would you volunteer?' Vukas looked at me innocently. I translated and eagerly accepted to accompany Ms Konelke.

'I'll take that as a 'no' from you, Mr. President. No offense, Milena,' Elke said, getting up. 'We have to go, I'm afraid. Some unhappy women there need our help.' She turned towards the door and started walking out.

Her personal assistants (or whatever) quickly shook hands with Vukas and me and followed Elke. Before we could escort them, they marched outside the Cabinet and into the office of unsurprised Anka. Vukas used his English again.

'Have happy nice day!' he said.

When he saw them out of the door of Anka's office, he started shouting.

'That ugly lesbian is *what? Blackmailing* me?'

'If only she'd wash her hair *once* when visiting the president . . .' we heard Anka mutter.

Vukas closed the door of his Cabinet, walked across it in three long strides, opened the bar and poured himself a large amount of Chivas into a whiskey glass. Then he turned back to me.

'Such disrespect, unheard of!' he was yelling. 'And I, a moron who agreed to see her because I felt sorry for that opportunist!'

I giggled. Vukas's eyes darkened.

'Stop that giggling! What am I paying you for? If I'm only paying you for your interpreting, then I'm paying you *o-ho-ho - way* too much. There are girls lined-up for that job! But, I trusted you. I gave you a place in the society, a segment to excel in.'

'Sorry, Boss, but what is the problem here?'

'The problem is that you've become arrogant, like everyone else. I thought you were different. I thought you'd make that extra effort. But, you're just an eel, like the rest of them. Slipping through everyone's fingers. Bullying me for the raise, for money. More money, more money.'

'You're doing the bullying now.'

'Oh, am I? Why don't you run off and hide in that Safe House?' Vukas sighed and emptied his glass, then strode to pour more.

'It was probably that little shit Mirko, who talked to this awful woman about this...this *trafficking*. God, I hate that word. What does it *mean*?' he lifted his hands and his glass to heavens, and it was a bit comical, were I not terrified.

'And then you asking me, *What do you mean, Boss? What do you mean?*, like some fourteen-year-old girl. Can't you just use your brain sometimes and connect the dots?' Vukas paused to drink. I was shocked and speechless. 'I proved the cigarette smuggling rumours pointless and boring, but now this! I am so mellow on the Opposition. Opposition! They still don't know about fear. They still don't know what I really think of them. In one sweep I can destroy their sleazy union of blabbermouths! Blah, blah, blah...' another shot of whisky and he went on, '*I* am the leader of this country and everyone that represents *anything* more powerful than the sisterhood of Scandinavian lesbians comes to *me* first and then visits the Opposition on the way back home, like one would visit a hairdresser for the latest gossip. A chatty pastime that makes one look better. And you, you forget what I'm paying you for. I'll remind you: it's not for the lunching and dining with the people that already think the world of me! It's for the social reforms. Social. Reforms. You didn't even notice what every market-seller must have known: that Mirko and his parrots have been carving *trafficking* into another affair, because you never take initiative, you don't see the big picture, you don't care about me, and you're superficial!'

'I need to take a walk,' I whispered and went out.

'Go, take a walk!' Vukas was shouting behind my back. 'Run away from real life. Go and take your walk!'

I held my head high as I passed by the desk of Anka the Unperturbed, who was just doing her job, scanning letters and destroying them. I closed the doors behind me quietly, as if it was just another workingwoman's morning, indeed.

Outside: the grim siege of autumn made more urgent by the endless honking of cars. Outside, the roaming dogs with pieces of garbage in their mouth; my head banging against an invisible wall; my heart beating like a war drum in my throat. People in thin jackets, their hands in empty pockets. They didn't know, did they? They were quickly dying out in history, my nation.

The polluted, terrible town. The polluted, *small* town – what a killer fusion! Was I to cross the same bridge all my life? The swinging bridge over the hysterical river? Meeting people who resembled the river: shifty, crazy, unreliable? They said: 'Hello' and started

the string of questions and they walked on, not waiting for the answers I didn't want to give, moving their
jaws, mumbling curses into their chins, overwhelmed
by worthlessness.

Then up and down this boulevard of rats. All my
youth, at which I wouldn't be given second chance,
spent pacing the same boulevard. It was wasted, maybe
even non-existent. The claustrophobic, autistic theatre of country. When you're born in the West, even as
white trash, there's still a chance you'll make it one day,
at least in reality TV. Or you'll make a psychedelic CD
with the lyrics describing the hanging axes above the
heads of your sleeping parents and you'll find an audience, somebody will buy your drama. Somebody will
even sell pirate copies of it in Montenegro.

But, when you're alone in Montenegro, you're alone
all over the world. Stuck with Serbia, the Great Aggressor, and divided within our tiny republic. The one sure
thing about Vukas was that he was a seasoned politician who had stuck his neck out there, and by now
learnt to see the big picture. And I should stick to my
job; it wasn't a bad cause, after all, for which I'd been
receiving my salary. And with a prospect for the raise
if I . . . How should I put it? Protect the image of the
President? Yeah. Now I knew what he meant by social
reforms. Socialise with the opposition and reform their
views. Use any method. The method...Oh, fuck the
method . . . History would polish the method.

So I dialed Vukas. 'I'm sorry,' I said when he
answered. 'I want to work for you. I will put in an extra
effort, as you say. I'll connect with Mirko.'

92

'That's fine," the President replied. 'Listen to me -'

'Yes?' I was all ears.

'Never ever skip a healthy breakfast is my advice. Vitamins by handfuls, B-complex, magnesium, zinc. It's always stressful, the kick-off of a career in politics. You're no exception. Many couldn't deal with it, became diabetics. Take a couple of days off, a sick leave. Anyway, I'll be busy visiting ordinary people, shaking hands, making promises I intend to keep. No foreign delegations for now. No double-faced foreigners with their own dirty, after-midnight secrets. Smeško shared some info on our M*s* Konelke with me. Why do you think she practically *lives* in that *Safe* House whenever she visits? She likes the girls of course, likes being their Viking savior twenty-four-seven, when there's even no need for it. A *warden*, a sick Scandinavian warden, that's what she is! But that awful woman's visit has helped me focus on my priorities. My back is killing me, I'll have a massage. I'll call you,' said my benefactor.

I was hungry. I'd been walking for an hour. I had my apartment; what the hell was I doing on the street? I went home.

10

Mirko. *The Peaceful one*, his name means.

Mirko must have been in his forties at the time, a big, handsome man who, as myth had it, wrote poetry. Mirko, a poetic soul of eternal opposition in the murky waters of politics.

Could he get any better? Though no one had ever actually read any of *his* poetry, but, with his hypnotic voice, during the Opposition Party's rallies, he quoted beautiful verses written by others, by the greatest bards. He was married, had three children and a martyr's reputation - even the Vukas's pre-election scandal-sniffing dogs never managed to trace a single slip of Mirko's, no shags on the side. So, everyone was *spiritually* in love with Mirko – though it makes me smile to use this description with the Montenegrin kind of love – but, spiritual or not, that kind of love wasn't enough, it seemed, for the majority to divorce Vukas and his Party.

I met on a warm November day in 2001. I was wearing just an easy dress (sleeveless, short & thick with elastine), a leather jacket over it, and I walked to the café where Mirko and I were to have drinks with a young, married couple, our mutual friends whom I'd begged to introduce me to him. They asked why, of course, and I said I had something important to tell him. I knew they thought to themselves that I just wanted to sleep with him. That kind of assumption always stood, but never stood out in Montenegro. There was something for each of us in the introduction – they'd asked me to recommend them for the government's project for young couples to be given cheap flats, and I said I'd do that although I suspected it was one of the blank pre-election shots (there's always an election looming around the corner in Montenegro and the ruling party wins them all) - and everybody accepted.

A table had been reserved – by whom I didn't know - for the four of us in the café's garden. The reservation

94

note said *Mirko Popović* – a little heart drawn next to his name. I was the first to arrive, always, everywhere, and I didn't mind it. I made myself look busy, pretending to write down something important while actually doodling – much like Elke's bodyguards. I was Vukas's negotiator, a sort of mindguard. We were all doodlers.

I knew a lot of people that were sitting around in the garden, almost everyone in fact, and I didn't feel like chatting with them. *She's Vukas's girl now.* I sniffed their scorn in the warm south wind that made the temperature rise and the men sweat and fret. Live commentators from cafés. Their gossipy comments were all they had.

Then Mirko walked in followed by our mutual friends.

The scorn evaporated. People sitting there spontaneously applauded.

'You, legend!' someone cried to him.

Mirko smiled.

'No legends, please,' he said, his palm humbly resting above his heart. 'No Godfathers and Tony Montanas. They totally ruined us here.'

We were introduced.

Every time Mirko pronounced my name, it was with a sweet, crooked smile on his face. He was motioning to our mutual friends not to interrupt me while I was talking, though it was mostly nonsense I said, just flaunting my little, pathetic tricks. Seated down on a small, café chair, he looked huge but comfortable, with elbows relaxed on his thighs and hands hanging between his knees.

'How do you call this drink again?' he asked, pointing at my empty glass.

'Vodka-*pla*tonic,' I said. 'Just a drop of vodka with light tonic. A perfect daytime drink. In some cafés they've even added it to the drink list so, as its - sorry to use the term - *Godmother*, I get it for free.'

He laughed and made a move with his hand as if to rustle my hair, but halted mid-air, above my head, and finally used it to signal to the beaming waitress, who had probably drawn the glittery heart on the table reservation, next to Mirko's name.

'I'll have one,' he said to the waitress. 'I'll have the vodka platonic, please.'

And tic-tic, he jerked his left shoulder and his neck.

I loved those. I loved his tics.

They were another delicious part of his life story. Rumour had it that those were the souvenirs from his judo tournaments from all over the world, and when I asked him whether that was true, he said: 'That sounds great, like a compliment. Couldn't have come from Smeško's factory of lies, that one.'

'My friends told me you had information for me,' he said at one point. 'We can talk in my office if you want. One of my boys will drive us there. Sounds ok?'

Across the street a man in a suit, one of Mirko's guards, was already opening the door of something unmemorable, like a *Passat*.

I felt playful at that moment. I felt as if the real life had let me go and have some fun, but it remained camouflaged, hidden behind a bush, from where it was eyeing me through the binoculars.

96

I crossed the street with Mirko. In the car, he sat next to me on the back seat.

'*Ei*, Jumbo,' he tapped the guard-driver on the shoulder when the man sat behind the wheel. 'Can you move your seat forward? Milena's legs are taking up so much space.'

'Yes, boss,' the Jumbo man said, his eyes smiling in the rearview mirror. 'These Podgorica girls are dangerous.'

'Milena's not dangerous,' Mirko replied. 'She knows dangerous is so last century. Am I right?'

'You're absolutely right, chief. Especially about Milena.' Jumbo turned his head to me and smiled, starting the car and driving forward, in the opposite direction from where he was watching.

'You don't remember me, do you?' Jumbo asked, still looking at me, but driving forward. 'We went to high school together, well, only one year though because I failed and had to repeat the year even though you did some of my tests. She was the best student.'

'Is that so?' Mirko said.

I asked Jumbo to please look ahead while driving. The men laughed.

We arrived at the HQ flat. Mirko and I entered one of the rooms, his office, crowded with tables, lamps, PCs and fax machines. I just stood in the middle of it.

'Something important to tell me?' Mirko was smiling and switching on the lamplights. I shrugged.

'What is it?' he mildly tic-ticked his neck and shoulder.

'Nothing,' I said.

'Are you Vukas's gift for me, is that it?'

In two steps I was next to his big body, which he held charmingly stooped for me. His shirt whispered: the sigh of the starched. It saddened me. Nobody ironed locally produced white shirts with such dedication any more; or, to use Mirko's phrase: it was so last century to do it.

I kissed him on the mouth: he smelled of fruit jam, of the approaching winter and pancakes for breakfasts in dark mornings. He tasted like home, and I was just a girl. Tears rolled down my cheeks.

'O-kay...' he said and placed his hands on my face. 'I was very stupid and rude, wasn't I?'

I kept my eyes closed until my tears stopped.

'Can we start over some other day?' I asked.

'Sure, Milena. Your terms. I'm here for you. I can wait.'

We went outside, where the night had crept in so suddenly, and Mirko motioned to a car, parked with the lights on, and asked me if I needed a ride. I answered that nobody needed a ride in Podgorica. People should walk all the time.

'Well, then . . .' he said. 'Walk back to me this Sunday, same time. If it suits you.'

'It does,' I said.

In my flat I kept the lights off. Winter was coming. It occurred to me that I was too thin to stand and face it alone. My stomach craved warmth. Perhaps if I just called my mother and asked her to make some soup for tomorrow, some thick, creamy soup for me, or *kachamak*, that would be great, and perhaps the coldness in my stomach would be killed? We could have lunch together, Mama and I, and then I could lie on that tortured sofa in my parents' living room, and she'd stroke my hair. Or I hers. In peace, I'd be thinking of Mirko's mouth; his freshly ironed shirt; fantasizing, like I used to, about a man's touch. Remembering the winters of the past with power-cuts, candlelight and early darkness gathering up in the windowpanes. And the old neighbours, who would come and stay during a power-cut, talk the power-cut out, tell the most intimate stories of their lives while their shadows flickered on the walls. Everyone was chain-smoking and laughing, keeping warm. I was pretending to be asleep on the floor. Later, they'd be talking about Miloš, my dead brother. Through my eyelids, I'd peep at their lengthening shadows on the walls. I wanted my brother's ghost to walk by my side; I wanted to see him in my dreams. He never came to me, which disappointed, which still disappointed; I had many questions for him. So what did I do instead? I began avoiding people, my friends, anyone who really knew me. I dived into my new job as if it were a new country, where I could pretend to have always been an only child, spoiled by over-protective parents, sent to the best schools, fed self-confidence till I had self-confidence coming out of my pores.

Through the darkness of my flat, I searched for the sleeping pill, deciding not to walk back to Mirko on any Sunday afternoon. I was doing him a favour.

11
The bitter smell of December in my hometown.

Through the mist of twilight, the howling winter wind pushed the gusts of bitter-smelling smoke from garbage and tyres burning in Old Airport and Konik suburbs of Podgorica. Under the slim soles of my shoes, cold pavements creaked. I had a feeling I was walking on pressed coal. My winter wardrobe consisted of several pairs of thin and tight shoes and two leather jackets. Why? Open up, girl, I said to myself, and I obeyed myself – on my way home, I stopped by my clothes-selling cousin Viki's hub, and bought a fur coat. Viki said her price was eight hundred Deutcshe Marks, but I could pay her what I had on me, and the rest in monthly installments for as long as I worked.

The next day, as if she sensed I was moving up into her league, buying fur coats and all, Darinka called and ask me to meet her for a late lunch, without Bella.

'Please,' she added and I said yes, of course, great, no problem. I suspected she wanted to discuss her brother losing his sanity over me, so Bella didn't need to be there.

The three of us Charity ladies had been working hard, visiting orphanages, children hospitals, talking to nurses, carers and doctors. It felt like a campaign. I was exhausted. Darinka spent most of the visits keeping her fur coat on, looking around for a chair to sit down. I knew that her plan was to just give money to Bella and go back to her people-watching while seated in much nicer, less sad places. That was exactly the plan Bella had in mind as well. All our visits conveniently ended in time for lunch, but Darinka, for once, wanted to avoid Bella.

In the Blue Club, again, and she apologised for it, while sipping her new favourite drink – vodka platonic.

'I know that this Blue Club must be boring for you,' she said, 'but whenever I go anywhere else I end up being kissed by women and children I don't *know*, which is fine, I can appreciate it, but my skin is so sensitive, it gets this awful rush I can't get rid of, for days,' she touched her face and looked at her empty glass. 'People patronize me all the time,' she went on. 'Vukas is such a giant figure for people here. So when they see me, they sympathise with me because they're in awe. It's hard to explain. And of course everyone knows about these other so-called c*oordinators*, don't think I don't know about Vukas and them. I do nothing. I look the other way. Those women are all older than me, or sometimes even him, his old flames, from the times when we were just a pair of poor outsiders. *Now* they want him.' She almost had me there. Was Darinka an interesting young woman, once, when she was a poor outsider? Nah, I decided, she was living the unbelievable dream now, as the First Lady, and her complaints shouldn't reach my heart, hidden beneath my new fur coat. 'And I guess they can have him,' she was still on the subject of 'other coordinators'. 'He'll use them until the day, or the night, when their plastic surgeries don't help. Oh, don't I sound bitter? You're gold though. You're so open that I bet everyone feels they can be themselves around you, and you wouldn't judge them. So I wanted us to meet and have a normal conversation, without Bella and her preaching.'

'Bella is a blessing in disguise,' I said. 'She's so layered. I wouldn't be surprised to find out about drugs and orgies in her past. But she seems unstoppable. We should learn from her. '

'Yes,' Darinka said. 'Aren't we all layered?' *Did I know who she really was*? *What she was really like*? She closed her eyes and for a moment I thought she was going to cry.

Well, what was I supposed to say? No need to say anything, apparently. She went on to answer those questions for me.

She was Vukas's main adviser. In their bedroom, who did I think helped him with making his decisions? *She* could see through people. Perhaps she didn't speak foreign languages, and she never read the doomstering, dirty newspapers, but she read body language and had inherited good old common sense from her parents. She was always spot-on on everything, from decorating to the unthreatening sizing-down of economy. I only interrupted her monologue to order a lean protein for both of us. She was drunk and didn't touch the food.

'Don't give up on Bella,' I managed to tell her. 'Let's use her. Bella works hard. All you have to do is smile while she's marketing your project. I'll translate what needs to be translated.'

'You're gold,' Darinka repeated. 'And so perfect for Branko. You know, I can easily see the two of you replacing Vukas and me one day, when our mission here is fulfilled. Oh, would you please come and celebrate the New Year's Eve with us? The party will be here, but please don't be put off by that. You will meet everybody you should meet. And I need you.'

* * *

Darinka must have given Branko my phone number. He kept calling and I tried to be polite but when
he said: 'Enough of the fooling around. I find you really attractive. Don't make me wait for the New Year's
party,' I had to complain to Vukas.

Vukas told me not to worry; he'd be sending Branko
to the US soon after the New Year. 'But you're celebrating with us, aren't you?' he asked. 'I want you to meet
Chris, now that you've sorted his wife out. I want you
to tell me if you sniff a rat there.'

12

On the New Year's Eve I made myself feel moder-
ately happy for wearing a dress that Viki, my clothes-
selling cousin, had lent me. In her barrack-type house,
half-turned boutique, as I was counting some more
cash to give for the fur, she promptly put the plastic
bag containing the dress and the matching pair of shoes
into my arms.

'It's a very expensive Escada mermaid dress,' she
informed me, 'and I'm just the middle hand in this
transaction, so you'll have to return it after holidays,
odourless and in perfect condition. The shoes you can
keep longer. Have fun, advertise my merchandise well,
now get out, I have Darinka coming in a minute. She
needs complete styling from me.'

On the night of the party one of the president's bulletproof Audi's was parked in front of my building. The
heavy car window slid down and I saw the face of the
bodyguard I knew.

'Hi handsome,' I said to the young man. 'I'm glad it's you and not Branko driving me there. Would you please drive me back home, too?'

He stepped out of the car and opened a back door for me. 'Unless you fall in love with the prince,' he said and we both laughed. I'd hyped myself up pretty well with the shoes, the dress and the coat, so the small bag of coke remained unopened in my purse.

Sometime, not so long ago, along the simple frame of the past New Years' parties, I'd wondered what it would feel like to be driven to a club in a limousine wearing an evening gown and a pair of expensive stilettos. This was close enough. I was going to celebrate with men who didn't sweat beer through their teenage outfits but wore Italian suits and were responsible for the important decisions they made in this world. What did it feel like? I sent a message back in time to the younger Milena: it still felt wrong, girlfriend.

Because, all I wanted was to be with Mirko. No dress, shoes, bulletproof cars, drivers, nothing compared to the stuffy but cold (there was only one butane gas heater that got moved around, wherever necessary) HQ flat and our Sunday afternoons. I did go back to him, of course. We'd had several 'dates' by then, our Sunday afternoons. Mirko, always in his white, well-ironed shirts. Such an obvious *opposition leader*: basic, clean, stainless, with everything around him coated grey. We made tea, made love, smoked and talked. During love-making Mirko always said: 'You like this, don't you, you like this so much,' and I wanted to scream: 'I didn't know I liked it! I just found out!'

I was quiet though, under the sounds of the TV. In the living room, where we sat, talked and made love, he always switched the TV on, to foil the recording bugs that we knew had to be planted there. Some awful music was always on, loud and liberating, like an old, good but ugly friend, who let us be ourselves.

I kissed him first, that was our silent agreement – that I would start things between us. The couch there was small, and the man was too big, so we slid down on the floor, onto a rough rug. I was out of my simple clothes in a second. There was no protection from anything. The rug scratched my back as Mirko entered me, inch by inch, until I came with a mixture of surprise, pain and pleasure. It was cold in the living room, in the bedroom-offices, in the hallways, the kitchen, everywhere in that HQ-apartment, but nowhere as bad as in the bathroom. I never took a shower there, only peed, and quickly came back to the living room, where Mirko handed me a cigarette and we smoked and watched TV, sitting on that cruel rug.

'It's a gift from the Swedish government,' he said about the rug. 'Supposed to be ecological. Or anti-bacterial, or something.'

'Misers,' I said. 'They could at least have given you a sauna.'

Later, Mirko would talk to me with the snugness of an idealist older brother coming back from a victorious battle. 'Look,' he'd say, 'you have to trust me: they are falling apart. Did you watch the interview/press conference last night? Did you read about the miners' strike/anti-mafia rally? Ha ha. They are finished.'

I knew he wasn't saying those things to me so that I would feed Vukas with Mirko's 'state of mind'. He *believed*. He was forty-something and, with a fucking sparkle in his eye, he believed the evil government was going to be voted out. He didn't know about the wealth they'd accumulated, the power of their connections, the hypocrisy of the Foreigners Who Lunched. Mirko only knew that *Vukas Unlimited's* were the crooked and lying sons of bitches. And yes, that way he could believe they were as good as finished, as all the crooked, lying sons of bitches would be, eventually. I didn't argue. If I argued I would lose my Sundays with Mirko. But who did he think I was? What story did he think I came from? He never asked *me* about me. Surely he'd asked around and heard a perception of me that was handily summed up, as most of the local perceptions were, in an adjective, a noun and a verb phrase: *a manipulative bitch who sleeps around*; or: *a clever nympho who polishes Vukas's shit*. In any case, I'd lived in a small town long enough to know that a provincial perception of a person *was* that person, and one should just stick it up her ass and carry on with her dreams. And, one summary or another, what Mirko must have found out had probably only proved to him that I was a deluded servant of the imploding regime, but interesting enough to . . . To what? Fuck? Convert? Shake up, wake up?

Mirko was old school: he didn't want his girl to embarrass herself by having to lie, or admit an unpleasant truth.

Oh, Mirko . . . I was still thinking about him when I

106

entered the Blue Club. I hoped I'd be the first guest to arrive, so that I could have a drink in peace with more thoughts of the Peaceful one.

The Blue Club's salon had been a meat eatery for far too long. As the most spacious salon of the biggest and oldest hotel in the centre of Podgorica, it had been used as *the* hotspot to devour the most admired food product in Montenegro – the mixed meat plate. The poignant vapour of the grilled and burnt animals' intestines, tongues, livers and muscles was still present. Many things (the menu, the curtains, the make-up) were upgraded since this hotel's *kafana* had been turned into the Blue *Club* first, then the half of it became the Blue Salon. Now the walls were covered with boiserie, and bookshelves for an ad hoc library, in front of which several leather armchairs were placed. Relax and read, dear member, the ghosts of grilled animals guard over you.

For the special party the shiny oval table was brought in, laid with embroidered damask cover with heavy ribbons hanging on its sides, the silver and golden *pashada* on, the paraphernalia for the *uber*-slick feasts of the Vukasids. Above the table – two monster chandeliers. And finally, the only blue item in the Blue salon – a dance floor, which shone with an electric blue madness. The heavy, black-leather-and-metal doors were wide open and for the first time I realized that there was yet another room adjoining the eatery, and I saw the roulette and Black Jack tables in there, surrounded by more books and sofas.

But I wasn't the very first person to appear. Bella and

Chris were already there, champagne glasses in their hands as they hugged each other on the dance floor. That couple, their second youth . . . I wondered if that happened only to Western lovers. Only to the rich people? What was their secret, what?

Bella spotted me, beamed a wide smile and waved. Such a lady. She knew when and how to show love to every human, however unlikeable to her. She put her arm on her husband's shoulder and led him towards me, whispering the brief summary of my social status into Chris's ear, I'm sure, while Chris smiled approvingly, as if she was telling him that I wasn't really a social climber, but an influential member of the emerging elite. She probably didn't have to tell him anything – Chris being the omni-connected, Washington D.C.-born maverick – if *he* didn't have the jigsaw puzzle of human comedy neatly put together in his head, who did?

'Sweetheart!' Bella approached me and unleashed her no-nonsense velvet voice. 'This is my wonderful husband Chris. But, you can call him *Ambassador*. Makes him feel more comfortable.'

Chris extended his arm to me. He seemed to wear his size proudly as if he'd been given the opportunity, during Creation, to choose his future height and he ticked the box that said: SHORT, and he added – *please*. His eyes were kind, looked sagacious under the contrast of his white hair, dense with tiny curls. His nose was flattened as if he'd had it done a bit. Or did he used to be a boxer, I wondered. But I let it pass.

'Mila,' I introduced myself, wanting to adjust my

name for a foreigner.

'Mila,' Chris repeated. 'I like the name. Sounds silky. And it goes well with your dress. '

Bella scanned her husband with her clever eyes; she scanned me.

'Well,' she said, 'The band is here, the champagne. The young and the beautiful,' she raised her champagne glass at me. 'And the damned,' she gestured to Chris, laughed and, tilting her head back, she emptied the glass. 'To the best of times!'

Then she danced her way back to the dance floor and the waiter sneaked toward us with the tray full of flutes with bubbles.

'Do you have vodka?' I whispered into the waiter's ear.

'Yes, Milena,' he replied.

'Please,' I said, 'put a bottle of best vodka and some cranberry juice here on the table and never approach me with those champagne filled condoms ever again.'

'Ha!' Chris laughed standing next to me. Of course. Hadn't Vukas told me that Chris could speak our language?

'I'll take some of them . . . condoms,' he said.

'I think maybe this size too small for you, Ambassador,' the waiter said. He obviously already knew Chris.

'Very good, young man, very good,' Chris said, reached into the inside pocket of his jacket and tipped the young waiter with some folded dollar bills. Then he took a thin flute anyway.

Enter other couples. Vukas and Darinka. Accompanied by Branko! Who wasn't accompanied by anyone, damn it.

I forced myself to smile. We were not friends. They were the nouveaux riches of Montenegro; I was still on the waiting list *and* arrived solo for the party.

Vukas looked classically elegant in a more relaxed version of black tie, ie – the jacket was midnight blue and there was no tie. Darinka, compliments to my cousin Viki, never looked more attractive: with bedroom-styled hair and an almost too playful black moiré dress, to which the quality of seriousness was added with three long sets of pearls, she looked as if she'd had great sex just before arriving to the party, and therefore couldn't really be bothered to try and impress – yet impress she did, as much as she could. They were both so imperious, so tall as they stood close to the entrance door to welcome other guests.

The band was playing a set of welcoming domestic and foreign festive pop ballads, not too loudly, its members sweating on a stage tucked in the corner by the fireplace. The arriving guests were exchanging hugs, kisses and compliments.

It was the first time I saw the infamous duo: Smeško Berković and his *intimus* - as I was to discover they called each other - Lazar Perić. I recognized the grin I'd heard about when Smeško entered the Club, followed by Perić, addressed to by his last name by Vukas and Darinka. Perić looked like a wild singleton, hunk-ing his thirties coolly, clad in a tuxedo, with the rock-n-roll touch to it. But, as Darinka quickly informed me, Perić was at least fifty-five. That night he came with

110

one of his escorts, a tanned, Caribbean-looking but local, young girl, dressed in near-nudity. Her chestnut nipples peeked out of her . . . corset? Bikini top? Why did I care?

Perić walked in long strides, pulling the girlfriend along. Smeško slithered in behind the two of them. Perić kissed Vukas and Darinka on the cheeks. Smeško and the girl didn't; they more like bowed to the First Couple.

'I wanted to come to your place first for a drink,' Perić explained flashing his blindingly white, even teeth. His bleached smile made me think of a sacrificed toilet seat, broken into pieces for Perić. 'But Saša here wasn't ready.'

'Who's Saša?' Vukas asked.

'That would be me,' the almost-naked girlfriend answered, 'Perić calls me Saša.'

'Well, I hate *Stanka*,' Perić explained. 'It means *tired* in Italian. *Tired*. Who wants tired?'

A young man burst into the Club carrying a big wooden box in his hands. The bodyguards followed closely behind him, ready to floor him down, their jaws set. But Smeško and Perić laughed.

'Ahh, let him, let him, he works for me, he's my new butler,' Perić said.

The young man placed the box on the oval table around whose elliptical end we were all standing, drinks in hands, acting out amazement.

'He's bringing us cigars and Chivas from my seaside hut.' Perić winked to make sure we all understood he was being humble about the 'hut'. 'I didn't want to drain the state reserves,' he went on. '*But*, Vukas, look at this humidor! It's my New Year present to you. That and whatever's left of the Opus X's after the party. But, the humidor, take a look at that piece of art. Made by Castro's brother himself. The guy has this wood-carving hobby. He carved the family's histoire into it. I'll decipher the details for you later. Mistresses, murders, revolution. Mind-blowing!'

Vukas and Smeško regarded Perić with eyes full of adoration. Chris listened with his mouth open, probably only managing to catch the international, reliable terminology. I wondered what he made of that.

'How on earth did you get a hold of it?' Vukas asked Perić.

'A lady friend of course, how else?' Smeško said.

'I'll drink to that!' Chris cut in.

'Ah,' Perić said, 'of course you will, my friend.' It seemed that he and Chris had already met.

'And who are *you*?' Perić asked, sizing me up.

Smeško raised his eyebrows at me as well, as if for him, too, I were an enigma, which was almost comical because we all knew that it was Smeško's job to know everything about everyone in Montenegro. People said *that* was the reason he'd never got married. He'd fancy a girl, but, even before making the first move, he'd tap her phone and discover, again and again, that all girls had secrets and thus couldn't be trusted.

I opened my mouth.

'Milena is the best interpreter in Montenegro,' Darinka jumped in.

'Interpreter, dentist, plumber...' Perić replied. 'What's

your *talent*? You have nice pecs. Were you a ballerina? A swimmer? I love swimmers and ballerinas. They make me happy.'

Everybody laughed. Smeško's grin slid more to his left ear. I felt uncomfortable. I didn't really want the intimus duo to notice or discuss me. I could *hear* darkness beneath the cracks in their laughter. Well. I was the president's coordinator. I was going to be ok.

'Perić, if I didn't know you better . . .' Darinka purred. 'How can somebody's *swimming* make somebody else happy?'

'Ahh, Dasha, Dasha, how much I love you, the blushing Dasha. Vukas, you lucky monkey. Saša, come on love, let's dance. Wow, Chris, is that your lady twisting on the dance floor?'

'Yes, that's my Bella.'

'See,' Perić hugged his Stanka-Saša's bare midriff, 'that means 'beautiful' in Italian. Well, more like 'pretty'. That's a cool name. I want to meet Bella. Bella Bellissima.' And off Perić went to the dance floor with his girlfriend.

Darinka sat down. She'd been standing for an unusually long time, after all.

Chris raised his glass at the rest of us. I looked at Vukas. He looked back. I lifted my eyebrows a little. He nodded.

Smeško recorded our short exchange of grimaces with the only grimace he was capable of making: his scary, eternal grin. Smeško probably understood Vukas's body language better than I did. Smeško was a scheming grave, no question about that. Odourless, silent and probably constipated. Behind a Joker's façade, no wit resided. I shuddered and scanned the club for more drink and a safe spot.

There were some more people there whose names were not mentioned. *Kumovi* – was their joint title. The parents of Vukas's numerous godchildren. They all sat down, lined like dominoes next to Darinka, and they started gossiping, palms over their quickly moving mouths. The superyawn of it! I directed myself to the ladies' room to powder my nose.

The ladies' room, velvet and golden-hue marble. The mirrors of the most expensive kind, lit to make the visiting ladies look younger and slimmer. I put my handbag on the marble counter and took out my pressed pack of coke I'd bought from the owner of the grocery shop under my flat. I sprinkled the coke on the hand-mirror, framed in sterling silver. I snorted and cheered myself up. Toughen up, girl, 'cause thereby hangs a plan. Play on with Vukas and the crowd. Save enough money and open something – maybe a spa for women to feel safe in, and beautiful, with the smell of eucalyptus and the anesthetic sounds of Chinese music lingering from there to insanity. Oops – *eternity*, I meant. Someone with Mirko's face should be with me in a long-term plan of mine, someday. Someone with his smell. Someone that could make me feel the pang of joy in my stomach, in my breasts, like a small, secret pregnancy.

I whispered his name, snorted another line and held my chest as if hugging him.

The door flew open. Smeško.

114

'What an interesting scene,' he said, drink and cigar in his hand. His voice sounded like some old-fashioned, noisy mill. It must have been a drain on his throat. No wonder he talked so little.

'This is the ladies' room,' I informed him, tidying up around me.

He placed his drink on the marble counter, next to the mirror with my coke on it.

'Don't be afraid of me,' he said.

I tried to produce my most convincing laugh. 'Why would I be afraid of you, Smeško? We both work for Vukas.'

He dipped his forefinger into my coke and licked it.

'This is good stuff,' he said. 'Where do you get it? From your grocer downstairs?'

I didn't react. Smeško wasn't stupid, but his downfall welled in the fact that he actually believed that people of Montenegro thought him human, friendly, well-intentioned. At least during holidays. No, Smeško. Never.

'Can I have some? Don't worry, I'm off duty.' He spread his arms and lifted his brows. 'Ah, too much stress at work. A man's got to relax don't you think?'

'Whatever you say, Smeško,' I said to him. 'Help yourself. I need to use the loo, if I may, please.'

Inside the cubicle, I covered the toilet seat with toilet paper. I intended to sit and wait for the sound of Smeško leaving. Being alone with him inside a small space made me nauseaus with fear. I shouldn't show it. He should know that I was protected by my title, by the President. But my bladder reacted. I couldn't pee. I was only sweating.

I flushed and stepped out of the cubicle. Smeško was gone. My stuff was unused, the silver-framed mirror still covered in coke, and surrounded by the pile of warm hand towels, neatly folded, absorbing the pleasant smell of the Angelica scented candles. On the high, slim table there were several bottles of perfume and a shell-shaped plate filled with mints made from *organic* Swiss herbs. Next to them stood a study lamp with a smart, green shade, a writing block and a Mont Blanc pen under it. Gentle tunes, volume low, were continuously played out of the discreet speakers in the bathroom. *Return to innocence.* Who got paid to think about those details? Probably a coordinator for detail reforms, and she'd done a great job. I could tell she'd enjoyed it. I snorted more of the coke, and ran the taps to cool my wrists, my neck and my armpits.

Back in the salon, I spotted Branko, drinking champagne like water. I knew he was waiting for me. It seemed that in his spoiled-little-brother mind, the guy had decided we were a couple.

The food had arrived, the South Balkan's meze, salty and spicy, to numb the premature alcohol boost: lots of old cheese, pumpkin seed bread-loafs, cured beef and olives, prosciutto with figs, vine leaves stuffed with minced meat and rice, octopus and red onion salad, cheese and spinach pies and *ajvar*, the Club's own, a souvenir from the meatery era.

I was seated next to Bella, both of us glistening with sweat, but from different reasons. Her sweat was from dancing, I assumed.

'*Who* is *Perić*?' Bella wondered aloud, still breathing

116

heavily and fanning herself with a napkin folded in the shape of a swan. 'I *love* that guy. He's got the Travolta moves, doesn't he?'

Darinka looked at me for translation.

'Bella was talking about Perić and his dancing moves,' I said to Darinka. 'Compared him to Travolta.'

'Perić is quite something,' Darinka replied, widening her eyes at Bella. 'He can fly his own plane, also like Travolta.'

Bella gasped and nodded.

'In fact, we met Travolta one summer, in St. Tropez,' Darinka added and Bella clutched the root of her throat; so impressed she was. 'Travolta is okay, but by my standards, Perić is even more successful. He was born, well, nowhere, really. Raised by a grandmother who died when he was a teenager. And now he's very . . .' Darinka smiled and rubbed her fingertips together in the air in front of my face. 'He's loaded,' she whispered. 'Done it all himself. Worked hard.'

'I can see that our charity project is in no financial jeopardy then,' Bella concluded. Darinka squinted at me and I translated.

'Hm, I wouldn't be pushy about that,' Darinka replied. 'Perić is into a much larger charity which concerns all of us. His business and his money hold this whole country together in the times of crisis. This is a small country and from time to time he alone, with his funds and his good will, provides . . .'

Bella seemed to have understood and she smiled, elegantly lifting her knife and her fork to start eating but I asked: 'What? Provides – what?'

Darinka waved her hand. 'Ah,' she said. 'Salaries, pensions, *ovo – ono . . .*' 'And what is his business?' I wanted to know.

'The government business of course,' Darinka answered.

'Really?' I said. 'What's the government business?'

'He hates publicity,' Darinka went on, ignoring my question. 'But he's very clever. The best economic adviser Vukas has ever had. He reads International Herald Tribune every day and Economist and Financial Times and then some German newspapers and he cuts out the articles and has them translated for Vukas. I never read the newspapers, you know.'

Yes, everybody knew that. 'Of course,' I said.

'He's married. These girlfriends he parades with, you know who they are? They are *professionals*,' she made a pause there, looked at me. 'They are *prostitutes*,' she continued as if I needed more explanation. I was unimoressed, but she probably thought I was shocked. 'Seka provides them for him. You know who Seka is?' Darinka posted another question. I shook my head 'No'.

'Oh, you *must* know her,' she went on. 'She drives the golden Range Rover non-stop, up and down the town, with her golden hair extensions and nails' extensions. She's my generation, you know, but looks older when you really take a good look if you can ever catch her without make-up and giant sun-glasses on. But, I'll tell you this, she was gorgeous when she was younger. Like an actress! Not even stupid, like, she did well in school, I mean I've heard this from someone, we were never friends or anything. But now, that's what she does. She keeps the girls, you understand? For the men you would never tell. She keeps the best girls for Perić because Perić *adores* prostitutes. And he calls prostitution *the talent*. But, he will never leave his wife. They were both *Gastarbeiters* in Frankfurt once, and made their initial money together. Perić says they were in food industry. But to me he confessed that he'd worked in a pig abattoir near Frankfurt. He says he has nightmares now about Frankfurters sucked up his nose, suffocating him during sleep. He's crazy', Darinka smiled gently, as if Perić were on of her godchildren. 'Vukas and I both adore the guy because he's a good business partner and so much fun – a rare combination. Well, bon appetite, Mila.'

I tried to enjoy the meze, but soon discovered that even the sight of it, piled up on my plate, gave me heartburn, so I grabbed my vodka glass again.

'Well,' Bella spoke. 'Can I at least hear the most abridged version of Ms D's monologue?'

'Doesn't she bore you', I replied, craving for some British venom from Bella's bloodstream, 'our First Lady? After all the interesting political and business wives you must have met?'

'Of course she doesn't,' Bella replied. 'She's merely a non-showy type. Humble is not boring, you know?'

Did *I* know? Of all the party participants – did *I* know?

'Besides,' Bella was saying, 'the charity I'm mentoring her for is a win-win situation. Those poor children get the chance for better care and she gets respect. Respect from others would open her up; she needs to fall in love with personal achievement. You do see the point, don't you? You just don't like to merely be an interpreter in the process. I see your angle; after all, you're more educated than she is. But, from my rather considerable experience, I draw the conclusion that one is never too young to learn the simple skill of prioritising. Let's look at you: young, pretty, educated, and with a good job. So, do you want to fight the social injustices, or do you want to keep that job? Prioritize. Work ethics is more important than education. Education alone, with no work ethics, could as well be the sociological cul-de-sac. You understand cul-de-sac?'

'Sounds like French for asshole,' I said.

'Figuratively,' Bella replied without a blink. 'That's one way to translate it. Bon appetite.'

I got up to dance. *Some dance to remember, some dance to forget.* Dancing was my win-win situation. I'd forgotten Branko, losing myself on the blue-marine dance floor. Everyone was in the phase of old-fashioned, tacky dance moves that resembled swimming and snorkeling, to the sounds of *Hotel California*, *Brown Girl in the Ring* (sha-la-la-la-laa), *Bye Bye Miss American Pie*, and the such. I didn't mind. Then it was midnight and we all kissed and hugged and looked into each other's drunk eyes. Branko made the most of the 'Happy-New-Year' opportunity.

'From this moment on if I can't have you,' he proclaimed, pulling me onto his half-unbuttoned shirt, 'only God can! Dance with me.'

I could dance with anyone, why not? But Branko's way of dancing was an illustration of his previous threat. His penis, like a stuffed python, bore into my

120

stomach as he held me tightly. His hand rested on my ass, squeezing and un-squeezing it in tune with music. A rape without proof. Branko really had a way of insulting a woman's IQ by acting and looking beyond stupid himself. He was so unlikeable that I even felt sorry for him, not for myself.

'I need space when I dance,' I told him and backed away. He remained a bitter-faced, solitary statue with a massive erection on the blue dance floor. His lips were moving with insults audible over music. His sister overheard. She went to him.

'You drunk fool!' Darinka said to Branko. 'Get going at once. Walk home. You know you shouldn't drink like that.'

Branko obeyed and strode to the exit door coatless, his head and limbs loose.

'He's such a baby,' Darinka said to me.

I smiled and she gave me a short hug.

'I'm a secret feminist,' the First Lady went on. 'Don't think I don't know how women are humiliated even when it seems they are privileged. Take me for example: Vukas is so universally adored and I practically don't exist except as a wife. Nobody cares. Only Perić, believe it or not. He's the only one who seems to care about how I feel. We have these conversations . . . That's why I like him.' She smiled at Perić, dancing across the Club. He sent her a kiss from the tips of his fingers and swirled his hips into 'eights' quite expertly. Darinka laughed.

Behind us, Smeško was shouting: 'Come on band, move on to *cardio*!'

I turned around and saw him hitting his chest with his fist.

The music changed to trumpets and hardships-of-life lyrics. A good moment to leave any party, according to my mother.

But, I stayed, afraid that Branko might be waiting around the corner, angry and cold on the street.

Others were still arriving. At half past midnight a group of women rolled in, like special delivery. One of them, the oldest and the tallest one, raised her arms and squealed and all the men replied in the same way. Her hair had been burdened with differently dyed extensions throughout it, from tennis-ball yellow to chocolate-brown, and fell down to her waist. She had a tight, black leather dress on. Her large mouth had dramatic-red lipstic on. It was Seka. Even Vukas approached her and kissed her on the cheek. I looked around to see Darinka's reaction, but Darinka was not there. Had she gone to the ladies' room or left the building in a hurry, upon the arrival of someone like Seka?

Two of the girls that had arrived with Seka positioned themselves immediately on the dance floor and began to shake their hips, but another two sat down at the table to eat, not taking off their camouflage-coloured overcoats. They were cleaning up everyone's plates, stuffing food into their mouth with fingers.

Smeško popped the bottle of champagne open and sprayed the drink directly from the bottle onto girls' coats. 'Take the coats off,' he ordered.

'Oh, mamma mia,' Seka shrieked. 'I swear to god…

122

Nobody would tell from looking at the two of you how expensive it is to feed you. That's enough now. Sonja, Enisa, that table is for dancing, not for eating! Up on it, now!'

The girls stood up and removed their coats. They were both wearing something like transparent, extended t-shirts. Underneath those, their slight thongs were showing. They climbed on the table in their stilettos and started moving hips and shoulders slowly.

'They look tired,' Smeško observed, adding, 'I hate tired,' obviously sharing the motto of his *intimus*, Perić. Then he popped open another bottle of champagne and poured that one on the girls. 'Wake up!' he yelled.

'Relax, Smeško,' Seka told him. 'I know you're hungry for Sonja. But it gets better. The night is still young.'

'Don't anyone tell me to relax,' Smeško replied. 'I get nervous when I relax.'

Perić heard that and, walking to us with his Saša, he cried at Smeško:

'That's right, my friend, *re-lax*. You're such a control freak – if you don't take it easy sometimes, *you* will be the end of you. Like Napoleon and other great men!'

I just stood there, mesmerised and sickend at the same time. Chris came closer.

'Balkan parties,' I said to him as if apologising.

'You don't have to translate them for me,' Chris said.

'Where's Bella?' I asked.

'I don't know. I'm surprised she's not up on the table.'

'Excuse me,' I said and went to the toilet again. I had to throw up some acid. I stayed a while, convincing myself that, basically, that was what all parties turned into – sexhunt. And only the levels differed, depending on the power. The higher the power, the darker the hunt. Because we were a dark species, but not all of us could afford to show it.

When I came out, the band had disappeared and music was coming from the speakers: a hard-rock version of *Katyusha.* One of the girls, Sonja – some people seated around the table shouted out her name - was still up on the oval table. The damask silk cover had been removed from it. Sonja now had only her thongs and stilettos on and, holding a microphone in her hand, her eyes closed and her slender, bony hips swinging, she was lip-synching to the song. *Oy, ti pesmya pesenyka devichnya, ti leti za yasnim soncem vsled* – her breathy whispers were audible over the singer's voice. She started kicking the table's lacquered surface with the needle-thin heel of her shoe. She did the *Kassatchok* squats like a member of Bolshoi. She was no local. Opa, opa, she spiraled with gazelle-like leaps to the triumphant climax of *Katyusha*. I could see how the men could persuade themselves that she was really enjoying the party.

Smeško sat at the table, his gaze full of adoration and fixed on Sonja, his hand stroking his groin. Maybe Sonja was his ideal girlfriend: enslaved, kept in the darkness of some basement, without identity, without a *phone*. Perić was part of the mesmerized audience, too, observing the dance while stroking Saša's naked breast, round and hard like a melon. The headache struck me, the kind only the fresh air could cure. I decided to walk home; the idea of it didn't seem unsafe, only a bit too athletic at the moment. When I turned to leave, I met Chris's generous hug. He held on to me like onto a million dollar cheque.

'What are you doing? Where is Bella?' I asked, gently parting from his embrace.

'She and your First Lady are hosting the New Year's Charity Cabaret at the National Theatre,' Chris said. 'I understood you were invited to go with them, but you decided to stay here because of – me?' he added, blinking. 'Anyway, that's why I stayed.'

What the hell? Who told Chris I'd stayed because of him? Vukas, who else?

I ran off to the gaming room, to look for the President. He was in there, playing roulette with Seka and the other girl that Smeško had previously sprayed with champagne. The table was covered with pink chips and alcohol drinks. The girl was stark naked as she spun the roulette ball.

'Twenty-four,' the little girl whispered after the ball had tucked itself in on a number.

'Enisa, little bitch, you lose,' Seka cried at her. Enisa twitched. 'We don't have that one covered. That's a bad number and you have no more clothes on, so *kneel*!'

Enisa went down on her hands and knees.

'Yelp!' Seka ordered. Enisa tried to bark. It came out long and thin, like a fire alarm in the Land of Elves. The little girl's stomach was bloated. Was she pregnant? I hated the thought; as if it were fine if she'd been simply stripped bare and made to act like a puppy, but not pregnant. Vukas was laughing. Surely, if *he* didn't see there was something unacceptable in that . . . If he didn't see little Enisa as a slave . . . then she must have been doing that for money, like that was her role for the big party. And I'd better excuse myself.

'You know,' Seka turned to the president. 'Chinese people think number twenty-four brings death to a house.' She crossed herself thrice. 'And who's this?' She thrust her chin at me. Vukas aired me a kiss.

'Sorry to interrupt,' I said to Vukas. 'You don't need me anymore and I don't feel well. I'm going home.'

'Are you sure?' Vukas said. *Was I sure?* I looked at Enisa, still kneeling under the roulette table, avoiding any eye contact, like an abused little animal.

I nodded at Vukas's chest. His shirt was completely unbuttoned.

'Well, then . . .' he said. 'Ask one of the drivers to take you home.'

'Who's that bitch?' I heard Seka wondering behind my back. 'I thought she was foreign. Can't place her anywhere.'

Outside, the guns were fired into the Balkan skies. The same bodyguard who had brought me to the party last year (it really seemed like a year had gone by) was driving me back home.

'You're one lucky lady,' he said in the car. 'Going home early. I'll have to stay till early morning and search the rooms for the collapsed girls. Fucking parties and fucking Smeško. I left the police squad because of him.'

'He likes to beat them?' I dared. 'He beats those girls?'

'Yes,' the guard replied quickly. 'Beats, burns, cuts

126

them. Especially that poor Sonja. I don't like Smeško, that creepy bastard.'

'Yeah, and you have to tidy up after him,' I said.

'That's another story,' he replied. 'I do it for Vukas. I'd tidy up any place he's been to. Got to protect the country and its President, right?'

'Makes sense,' I said. 'But will you really miss Vukas when he's gone?'

The driver-guard stopped the car in front of my building. He looked at me. 'You mean like everyone missed Tito when he died?' he whispered.

'Yes.'

'First cut is the deepest, I guess,' he said with a sigh and we both stared ahead. 'No further comments.'

My cosy street was quiet, no signs of celebration there. I checked the car clock. One thirty in the morning. The winter's deaf hour. Stuck in the no man's time between night and dawn. Silently active, like frost invading soil. I felt the northern wind picking up with its characteristic howl from the mountains around my town.

On my street, there was only one window lit now and I knew whom it belonged to: the insomniac teenager who went to school on his skateboard. Sometimes, if I smoked on my balcony, I could see into his room. He sat in his chequered armchair, reading, biting his nails. He would look up from his book and see me across the narrow street. Before his father would enter his room like a man from a weather clock - in warmer seasons the dad wore a wife-beater, while during winter he put on a navy-blue fleece – and turn the lights off in the boy's room, the two of us made sure to send goodnight kisses to each other from our windows.

I got out of the car and went into my building. Vukas's driver-guard slowly drove off behind my back. As I entered the building's dark hall, my teenage neighbour cried 'Happy New Year, Mila!' from his window. I went for the doorknob again to reply to him, but at that moment a silhouette of a man jumped at my side, dragged me further in and pushed me onto the stair railing.

'I'll have you tonight. *I* will have you tonight!' I heard a familiar threat and shivered.

Branko and his smelly breath, like a rotten tonsil on a grill. *Was this night ever going to end?*

'Branko, darling,' I whispered into his ear, too tired to swear at him, 'I have my period tonight. But as soon as...'

'Don't try to fool me, bitch.'

'I'm not lying.'

'*You*'re not lying? The bitch that fucks *the* crazy Mirko Popović is not lying? Sooo disappointing, how you underestimate me. Let's see your menstrual blood. Nothing wrong with blood. It's all Mother Nature.'

Branko was breathing heavily, mumbling 'Mother Nature, Mother Nature,' and sliding something cold and hard over my thighs. Not his python, a gun! How unexpected, frightening and – disappointing, yes: to die with that sick man next to me, in a dull, cold building's hall.

'Let's see your menstrual blood, foxy lady,' *groan*, 'or your brains scattered on this staircase!'

128

His gun was pressing into my pubic bone.

'I want you. I want all of you. I'm an all or nothing kind of man.'

Maybe he was not going to kill me but what if the gun accidentally went off, disconnecting me forever from my female parts? I decided to shower Branko in my most generous kisses. But then someone cried out my name. I recognised the mutating shriek of my teen-age neighbour, the skater-knight, who must have been waiting either for my Happy-New-Year-to-you-too reply or the light in my flat to be switched on, but when none of those happened he decided to act.

'Meee-laaah!' he hurled his pubescent pitch over the quiet street. 'Are you okay?'

Branko's quest for Mother Nature's gift of menstru-al blood was interrupted by my young saviour. I yelled something completely non-human as a response to the boy and – as brutally as I yelled - I pushed Branko away from me. Forgetting he had climbed up a stair to press me onto the handrail, Branko lost his balance and fell back, dropping his gun. Still screaming (having quick-ly realised that bestial screaming *worked*) I jumped on Branko, kicked his balls with the spiky tops of my left *and* right shoe, and snatched his gun – a short scene that can still make me laugh. A bouncy witch. I ran two stairs at the time, thanking God and my-previ-ous-self for having bought a first-floor apartment. I quickly unlocked and entered it, locked the door well behind me and hurried to my bathroom where I threw Branko's gun into the barrel of the washing machine.

Then, I swallowed a handful of tranquillizers and

painkillers without water and went to my window to smoke another one before sleep and wait for the pills to start working. The boy was still there, standing in his window. He saw me, waved and I smiled, raising my hand to my lips.

'Happy New Year,' I whispered in his direction. 'Go to bed now.'

It still wasn't too late to call Mirko. I knew that Smeško mercilessly tapped his mobile phone; mine too, probably. I could imagine Smeško's toady face grinning at Vukas as he placed the listings of our phone calls on the President's king-size desk. 'Our lovers calling each other on New Year's Eve,' he'd comment. 'Too sweet. Let's bitter it down for them.' But I wasn't going to be frightened by that Smeško monster; nor by the imbecile brother with the mighty name of Branko, the Defender. Vukas was different, and wasn't Vukas on my side? Vukas could be broad-minded enough to see my point, to laugh at characters like Smeško and Branko. He needed his Smeškos, his in-laws and the ever-multiplying godchildren, but he knew when they overreacted under the excuse of duty to protect their Boss, their tribal chief.

So I called Mirko on his mobile phone from my landline, the number he couldn't recognise. He answered.

'Happy New Year,' I said. 'I want you to have a winning one.'

'Do you now?' Mirko said. 'Well, Happy New Year to you too.'

People were singing around him, or addressing him

from such a small distance that I felt directly involved into yet another New Year party. I heard the voice of his wife. 'Ah, you're on the phone,' she said. 'You've got a man waiting to talk to you on your office line.'

'Sorry,' I whispered. 'You're too busy.'

'I'm not busy tomorrow around six in the afternoon,' he said. 'Want to meet me in the HQ?'

'Sure, love, sure,' I said.

13

The next day - or the same day, but in the bright new sunlight, enforced by that Northern wind which had cleared the sky - the New Year Party seemed less ugly.

I called my parents. I was hoping that somehow I could pay them a visit without spending much time with Father. I wanted to give Mama some of the money I had saved. In the past, Mama had to report to Father whatever income she'd made cooking or sewing for other people, yet, sometimes, she managed to put some of it into my hand or my pocket as I, always rushing to go outside, brushed against her. It was payback time, and Mama deserved it.

She answered the phone.

'Happy New Year,' I said.

'Thank you, Mila,' Mama said. 'We didn't want to call you and wake you up. Have a wonderful New Year. How was the party?'

'Oh, it was...' I was unable to say anything, least of all that it was a lovely party.

'Mi-la?' my mother said.

'Mama,' I said, 'I would really love to see you now. I'm not in the mood to see *tata*. Only you. Is it doable?'

'Come have lunch with us. Don't complicate like that. He'll behave.'

Kisses rained on me as soon as I stepped into my parents' flat. It was obvious that my mother had asked my father to behave as if they were blessed with a perfect daughter, in response to which he'd probably swallowed a handful of Lexilium pills. They were both instructed by their doctor to avoid red meat, so, instead of pork, Mother decided on roasting lamb. I could smell it. They were never going to learn that *red meat* didn't mean just *pork*. I'd pass on that lamb, I thought.

'Don't you worry about that,' Mother said when she saw me wrinkle my nose at the smell coming from the oven. 'We have *sarma* and Russian salad for you. Oh, and cod salad. And Mila's cake.'

Her menu made me hungry. Mila's cake was my favourite dessert, caramel rolled into a biscuit crust. When I was a little girl, I'd had whooping cough. Mama cured it with sugar caramelised in boiling milk and gradually the cake was born. Other families referred to it as *oblande*, but in our house it was called Mila's cake.

'You cooked all this since I called?'

Mother smiled one of her tender smiles I hadn't seen for a while; a smile that beamed like a new moon. 'No darling,' she said. 'I always cook the meals you like, just in case you walk through that door.'

My beautiful, lonely mother, who found some comfort in cooking for an erratic daughter, seemed radiant but distant as if careful not to overwhelm me by showing her happiness for finally having me there too open-ly. I leaned on the kitchen desk and chewed the crust peeled off a freshly baked loaf of bread.

'*Ajde, ajde*', Mama said. 'Ruining my homemade bread as usual. And let's not stand up while eating today. That's one habit you inherited from your father.'

'Yes, right,' Father replied from the living room where he had already positioned himself for the holi-day's TV marathon. 'Same old, same old. And every-thing good came from your mother and her folks. But, that probably is so. Your mother is an angel. The best woman I've met. And I was not born yesterday.' Father's voice was so festive that it was actually scary for me.

In the past, whenever he was under the influence of alcohol or other factors he couldn't control, his behav-ior would accelerate with odd jolliness.

'You're my *everything*, the two of you,' he'd say to us while kissing and hugging us a bit too eagerly. We accepted his gust of emotion, and returned it with smiles. But we knew that the thread of his love was tightening, becoming thinner, easier to rupture. A minute alteration in the plans he'd made switched his mood. And something always went wrong; went *not* according to his perfect plan. We were so stupid and clumsy, the two of us. Why did we have to spoil every-thing? He gave his life to us, bought us everything we needed: a dishwasher, the coats from Yugoexport, cured legs of pork, the best home-made sausages; he'd put me all the way through University; why were we so ungrateful then, seeing him only as our slave, and he was so tired, so overworked?

I rolled my eyes at Mama in the kitchen and whispered: 'I don't like it when he's bubbly like that.'

'He's growing old, Mila,' she slid her palm over my hair, while the voices of the hosts for *Srbija Slavi* TV show, too loud, too librettoed, were heard from the living room. 'You'll notice the changes.'

We ate lunch in the living room, in front of TV. The table was dominated by the old-fashioned pump and scale for measuring blood pressure. I had to smile: some things were never going to change. The thought made me soften towards my father and his unfulfilled ambitions: first he'd failed to become a doctor, then he failed to keep alive a gifted son he'd been blessed with, and now, he was stuck with a strange daughter and obviously no grandchild on the horizon to fulfill his doctor-in-the-family dream.

I knew that Mama had given it her best to render the old flat spotless, but it was evident that an older, retired couple lived there. Even the aroma of the roasting lamb capitulated before the smell of their tired, over-used peignoirs, slippers, carpets, furniture and skins. I was born when they were both in their thirties, which now placed them on the wrong side of middle-aged, not old, but old-fashioned, destined to expire cashless and flummoxed by change.

'So how are you, Mama?' I asked.

'I'm fine. Your father...'

'You're NOT fine, Mother!' My father snapped. Here we go, I thought. He had drunk a glass of red wine with us, claiming it was bad luck not to drink on the first day of New Year. Red wine always wound his head anti-clockwise. 'Don't spoil your daughter. She can take some bad news. She's a grown up, a politician, paid to love and admire the most powerful men in this country. Go on, tell her how not fine you are.'

'That's enough,' Mother said.

'Nobody tells me it's enough in my own house!'

'Don't raise your voice in front of our child,' Mother said.

'Go on, blame it all on me,' Father was shouting.

Mama smiled looking at me. I knew that we both wanted to cry. But I smiled back even though I felt sick: my own father almost called me a whore. I was nothing special to any man in the world. I smiled at Mama again, wider. I wanted to tell her that I wasn't offended at all, to share with her the small joy that fluttered in my stomach: soon I would see a man I loved. She didn't have to know it was Mirko Popović. I was going to let her believe I might be dating a professor, or a doctor.

'Woman, you are sick,' Father went on. 'What's so funny about you being sick? You never smile about it with me.'

'Mila brings out my smiling side,' Mother replied. 'I have just realised it's the best thing to do: ignore my sickness.'

'Difficult to ignore the price of medication,' Father was determined not to let us stay in the happy moment for too long.

Mother got up from the sofa. 'You've had enough of food and drink,' she said with unprecedented authority. 'Time for your afternoon nap. Mila and I will tidy up.'

I got up and followed her into the kitchen, to put the

dishes into the famous dishwasher, the pillar of father's fading glory, of his supreme command in the household.

As I was placing the plates into the washer, I heard a loud crash of knives and forks hitting the kitchen tiles. I turned and saw my mother collapsed on the kitchen counter. She was bent backwards unnaturally, knees on the floor. Her arms were raised above her head and, jerking from elbows up, they looked like lightning bolts. She let out a horrible moan, accompanied by face twitching. In one step I was by her side, and I tried to hug her. She pushed my arms away with a groan and fell flat on the floor.

'Daddy!' I cried. 'Come here, quick!'

My father ran into the kitchen.

'Don't touch her now,' he said.

'What's this?' I asked. 'What's happening? Is it a heart-attack?'

'No. It's an epileptic seizure. She won't die. It will be over soon.' Dad held Mama's mouth open.

A thin line of spit ran out of it. A pool of urine spread from underneath her.

'When soon? How soon? Are you sure?'

'There. There,' Father whispered.

Mother opened her eyes. Her body loosened up. She looked at us, kneeling beside her. She knew what happened; she smiled with her eyes. I stroke her arm.

'Epilepsy!' I said.

'Yes, bless her,' Mama mumbled. 'At least not cancer. I feel jumbled. And wet.' She still tried to smile. 'I have to go and change. Sorry for this, Mila.'

136

Father helped her get up. He led her towards the bedroom. I followed them.

'Mama. I had no idea.'

'Really, it's nothing,' she said, and Father closed the bedroom door in front of me.

I went to the living room. Father joined me in there.

'So for how long -' I started.

'For some time now,' Father replied. 'It began when she, you know, stopped having her female monthly visitors.'

'It's called 'menoapuse'. So, what do you do when this happens?'

'I wait. The first time she fainted I thought she died. She wasn't breathing, only lying on the floor all crumpled and . . . lifeless. When she came back she said she felt very tired and had muscle pain. We saw a neurologist. She had an MRI. Epilepsy, they said, and now she takes pills twice a day. If she skips them, she gets seizures. Like this or lighter, when only her arm jerks and her eyes go glassy, but she remains conscious.'

'I want to help. I want to buy her medicine.'

'Help yourself. She has me. I'm going to clean up the kitchen floor.'

Mama walked into the room, her step unstable. I got up to help her lie down on the sofa that faced the TV. She took the remote control, changed the channel. If I wanted to stay, it seemed, I was to simply sit there by her, keep quiet and watch whatever programme she chose. I felt useless. I got up, fetched my bag from the hallway, walked back to the sofa and opened my bag.

'I have money,' I whispered. 'Look, Vukas gave me a

bonus. I wanted to bring you some. Well, I'll give you for your medicine and MRI, but don't tell Dad.'

'How much?' Mama whispered back.

'Around 2000 Deutcshe Marks.'

'Put them in that jar over there, on the glass shelf,' Mama said and smiled in conspiracy. 'I'll keep them there for you, Mila. You can't save if your life depended on it. And God knows you'll need it.'

I walked to the glass shelf and stuffed the money into a jar placed by the photograph of my dead brother. Now Mama had something from both of us above that TV.

'Promise, you won't skip the pills,' I said, as if the action of stuffing some of my cash into her jar had giv en me the right.

'You don't know what they do to me, those pills.' Mama replied.

'Tell me.'

She told me that, every time, half-an-hour after she took her pills, hell rose in her head and her body. Even drinking a glass of water made her feel bloated and boneless, like a jellyfish. That bloatness turned into arresting sadness when no tears came, only numbness and impotence, strange urges to burn her hair, gnaw on her cuticles, or jump off a roof. 'You could use my mood swings as a stopwatch: they are regular, every ten minutes, for several hours,' she said. 'When neigh-bours come and talk, my brain boils, I want them to go, to leave me alone. When they leave, sadness grips me. I think I'll give up on the pills. These small seizures don't happen daily. And the big one is rare.'

138

I didn't want to undermine her decision. I wanted her to be the one to decide at how to deal with her own illness, at least that. She swallowed so much steam from my father's rages that it had to erupt somewhere, like a geyser. Poor humans. When we keep our misery in, trying not to upset the world, a heart bursts like a garbage bag, a colon mushrooms with poisonous cells, a face twitches into grotesque expression of smirk, a liver runs like a cheap stocking, lungs hole like emmental cheese. But, most often, a brain decides to take a long nap filled with darkness, not dreams.

'You and I were not born lucky, Mila,' Mama whispered. 'You'll have to learn to rely only on yourself.'

I wanted to get out of my parents' home where I felt like a little girl again, raised to unquestionably accept her fate and limitations. Also, it was time to go to the Opposition Party's HQ. Mirko was waiting for me there. I kissed Mama and promised I'd come back and visit soon.

14

As I ran under the icy drizzle, in order to meet Mirko as soon as possible, I was shivering with cold sweat. I took a shorter route to the HQ building, not along the main boulevard, the straight line of it, but through the small backyards and potholed basketball courts. The soles of my shoes gave up and let in water. The wine I'd drunk with my parents (they never had any vodka and I didn't have the nerve to bring a bottle with me when visiting them) had turned solid inside my head and stood there like a brick. The reappearing image of my mother's seizure wasn't helping, either. I needed Mirko, and a strong drink.

No bodyguards were standing in front of the building, nobody smoking under the plane tree by the entrance. Clothes hung half-frozen over the washing-lines on the balconies, as if forgotten. Abandoned bulldozers, heads down under the drizzle, were waiting for the holidays to end, the builders to sober up and return to them, so, together, they could root out some more plane and wild almond trees, to make way for more predatory-looking shopping malls and urban villas, in which only two flats per villa would actually be occupied by tenants. The unkind architecture of money laundering.

I entered the building and my phone rang. It was Vukas. I sat down on the cold steps and answered that call.

'How are you today, my favourite coordinator?' he asked. 'Last night I had no chance to properly wish you a good year. And you looked like a star. Can you meet me now in my office?'

What? 'Um, no,' I said. 'I'm at my parents' flat. My mother had an epileptic seizure.'

'Oh, I'm sorry,' Vukas said. 'Bad timing. I mean bad timing for me to call you.'

'I...They need me here.'

'Sure. Sooner or later, there comes payback time when our parents start needing us. Go on now, make yourself useful. I only wanted to ask about, you know, your latest assignment, sort of.' He hung up and again I was sure his words were woven in codes, but I decided to decipher them later.

140

Mirko opened the door for me in his overcoat and with a cigarette hanging in the corner of his lip.

'Hi there, James Dean!' I told him.

'Milena,' he smiled and hugged my shoulders and we entered the HQ flat together. 'I have just arrived myself. Sorry it's so cold in here.'

The Opposition Party Headquarters was on the mezzanine floor, and I noticed that, since I was last here, metal bars had been erected on its windows facing the main boulevard. Mirko saw me looking at the bars and he waved his hand, mumbling something like 'damned bars helping shit-all when they really want to kill you.'

His mobile phone rang. He paused in the hallway to take the call and I went to the back of the flat and into the kitchen, the usual route. I opened the cupboards and found a bottle of grappa. I drank from the bottle. The door to the back terrace was opened an inch and the sweet smell of baked horn-peppers and a whiff of fried garlic came in.

'I missed you,' Mirko said behind my back.

I turned to him, bottle in my hand.

'What happened?' he asked, taking the bottle and placing it on the kitchen counter.

'Too much reality,' I said. 'Parents growing old, sick, even epileptic.'

Mirko hugged me, for a moment. Then he closed the balcony door and drew the thick curtains together, with his head bowed. The voters from the neighbouring flats were always watching.

'Epileptic?'

We went to the usual living room spot and sat on the cruel rug. I told him about my mother. Mirko looked tired and worried. I didn't want that atmosphere again, with him. I undressed myself, sat in his lap and hugged him. It was so cold. Obviously, nobody had bought gas for the good old *Butanka* heater on holidays.

We kissed, cuddled and did everything quietly. Afterwards, my eyes welled up. He lit two cigarettes and gave me one.

'Can I live here?' I asked him.

'In the HQs?'

'Just here, on this awful rug, next to you.'

'But you always cry when we meet,' Mirko said. 'Why's that?'

At that moment, on that rug, I had a feeling he couldn't have ever been closer to any other woman.

'I become overwhelmed. There are too many emotions.'

'Too many emotions,' he repeated and grabbed an ashtray from the coffee table behind his back.

'And...' he went on and watched me exhale the smoke.

'And I love you,' I said.

'Milena,' he said. 'I care about you so much. So tell me what I'm waiting to hear from you.'

It had been a long day. And a completely new year. I wanted to start it fresh, to get rid of the dirtiest of clutter.

'You know I work for Vukas,' I said.

'It's not exactly headline material,' Mirko smiled.

142

'But what do you *want* from *me*? Tell me, perhaps I can give it to you and we can all carry on happily ever after.'

'Ah, it's not fair,' I said. He waited. 'And, anyway, I have failed.'

'Failed at what?'

'Failed at everything. Failed at convincing you to quit politics. Failed at refusing to work for Vukas. But, then, how else would I come this close to you? I love you, everyone loves you, people love you, Mirko. But people will make *you* fail, too.'

'Love here, love there. Love's everywhere, isn't it? You're so young.' He

touched my face.

I wasn't *so* young. I realised he didn't even know my age, my birthday, and he never asked.

'People know you're not a thief,' I went on. 'People must adore your perseverance. They try to do what they can, but Vukas has the machinery that keeps this dwarf country easily governable. People will be given some small change before any election, and so they'll be forever voting for Vukas and only Vukas to lead them. You have opened the bag of shit and, with each new affair uncovered, everyone was shocked for a week or so. After that – nothing.'

'So you're saying...'

'I know that you are not an ego maniac like the rest of them,' I said. 'So, I don't know, but perhaps – oh, fuck it . . . let him be. People have been accepting Vukas all these years. Mafia or no Mafia, you know? The thing that scares all of us is this mysterious democracy, where we'd have to make changes and deal with the consequences. No big daddy to tell us what to do. No big daddy to take the blame. And Vukas did keep Montenegro out of the war -'

'Surely,' Mirko interrupted me, 'you must know that we have all been made the prisoners of an on-going, invisible war. Don't tell me you can't feel it? Or maybe I was completely wrong about you? Don't tell me you don't see that the secret police has the last word here. Oh, there are laws, the laughable laws, totally inessential, as in every war. We are in a war, Milena, the most dangerous kind because we can't believe we are our own enemy. Think of all the lost generations, of all the premature deaths -'

Mirko stopped and looked at me. I looked down and fiddled with ashtray.

'So,' he went on, 'you were saying?'

I didn't reply.

'Were you saying that I should find a soft spot for our domestic war-criminals, our Mafia-bosses?' he asked.

'No, never,' I said, fighting back my tears.

'Good. Because for a moment I thought you were suggesting just that. *Twice* I went against my instincts and my beliefs. I saved Vukas, twice, gave him my support and my voters. I despise myself for that. And now he's sending you. Will you be talking about us to him? Will you blackmail me? You'd only hurt yourself.'

We kept smoking.

'Soften that clever forehead of yours,' Mirko said, touching me between the eyebrows with his index finger as if ironing the worry wrinkle. He thought for a

144

moment, and then added, with sadness and guilt of a boy: 'You don't know what my family's been through because I wouldn't form a coalition for the upcoming Referendum.'

'What?' I asked.

He told me about his eldest child being too scared of bullying to go to school; his wife vomiting every night for six month because she was unable to stomach the political circus anymore; Smeško's plans to target his family for defamation. 'So I'm sending them abroad,' he said. 'They just wouldn't survive another campaign and Smeško's shit. I have friends, supporters abroad, Italy, mostly.'

'That wouldn't be good for the campaign,' I said. 'You'll be criticising Vukas for his selfish goals with your own family leaving you to live in Italy. Smeško will say they went on a shopping-spree loaded with 'Mirko-sold-us-his-soul' money.'

'Nobody's leaving anybody,' Mirko said. 'And even if Smeško found out about it and it exploded all over the media, I wouldn't care.'

'Mirko, don't you ever want to take their money for all they'd put you through? Everyone would profit. And nobody would blame you.'

'Yes, I do, I'm only human. But I work it off. I'm also not a thief,' he seemed angry for a moment. 'I can't stand thieves,' he went on, his forefinger raised, pointing at the ceiling. 'I can't stand them.' I expected a tirade against our 'criminals and cronies' but Mirko melted and philosophically added something about the next generation paying for their fathers' sins.

'You know,' I said, 'I went to Vukas's party last night?'

'Mhm. The Blue Club orgies.'

'Yeah. Smeško was there and a shadowy business-man called Perić, but also the so-called Ambassador, Chris Bernard.'

'I know Chris,' Mirko said. 'Are you sure it was him?'

'Oh, yes,' I said. 'I was supposed to sleep with him. Vukas doesn't trust him much. Chris is also my assignment, I guess. He's sucking up to Vukas and his wife to Darinka. They want money, deals. But Vukas is not sure.'

Mirko looked surprised. He must have trusted Chris.

'Are you sure it was Chris?' he asked me again. 'Partying with Smeško and Perić? Couldn't be. Shit, the Chris I know was educated in a US military school. One of their dogma-soldiers!'

'Mirko, I'm not lying to you now. Of course I'm sure. Chris and Bella, his wife. For god's sake, he *held* me. I can tell you what he smelled like.'

Mirko waved away the opportunity to learn about Chris's personal fragrance. I told him some of the details from the New Year's party.

'Milena' he said and cupped my head with his hands. 'You don't have to work for Vukas, you know. It will get only worse for you from now on, when he finds out we've become very close, you and me, and . . .You were born here, you're our child. You're so pretty. I could write a whole poem about your left eyebrow only. Snap out of it, why don't you? You can teach English, give private lessons. Don't be afraid.'

146

But I was afraid, even though I nodded at his suggestion. Mirko kissed me and I recognized his wrap-up, 'got-to-go-now' kiss.

'I hope you'll forgive me one day for losing me as your project,' he said. 'But, at least, don't let Chris replace me. I'll call you.' He stood up and walked to his office, leaving me alone to get dressed and go.

Cold and tired, I was crossing the wobbly bridge, swinging with it in the North wind, when my mobile phone rang. I checked it: Private Number, the screen said. I always took those calls, feeling that it was the part of my job, to take the calls of the people who hid their phone numbers.

'Milena, it's me.' It was Smeško. His raspy voice. Why did Smeško have my number?

'What do *you* want?' I asked.

'The Boss told me to invite you to this dinner. To translate. He's busy, couldn't call you himself and the dinner is tomorrow night.'

'Could you tell him I'm coming down with a cold? I need to sleep and rest. My mother...'

'Be in the Club around eight. By the way, we're sending the little brother to Washington, immediately after holidays. Got it? As a favour to a certain good girl.'

Smeško's laughter was cracking up. I shuddered, thinking of the phrase *tectonic disturbances*. I could see his *no-passaran*-black eyes winking in the tree branches around me. It was easy for Mirko to tell me to quit. I couldn't quit. I had to make my employer let me go.

15

On the following evening I woke up, had two lines of coke for dinner (or breakfast?), scrubbed, showered and hydrated my body with the 'uplifting honey-and-ginger body treatment' from the shop below, blow-dried my hair, packed some more coke into my purse, got into my uncomplicated clothes, topped it with a fur coat, and was ready to go to work.

When I arrived at the Club, Chris was sitting next to a young man. He was so excited to see me again that his round face lit up pink, like a cabaret lantern. He waved and motioned to me to sit at his table.

I looked around for Vukas. He wasn't there, of course; otherwise, he'd be the first person I noticed.

I sat down between Chris and the young man, who looked familiar.

'Hello, Ms Social Reforms,' the man said. I recognised Pierson Paterson, that OEBS analyst or some similar kind of envoy from the civilised world.

'What are you doing here?' I asked him.

'Had a meeting with Mr Bernard,' Pierson said. 'I was just about to leave. Please forgive my poor memory. I can't seem to remember your name.'

'It's Milena,' I said and laughed, adding that it was very nice of him to ask for my forgiveness, but that he should relax, really. I was only there as an interpreter for the President, who was about to arrive.

'You're too humble,' Pierson said smiling and looking around. 'So, President Tomović is coming tonight? Maybe I should stick around then. As you know, he hasn't replied to my invitations for another meeting.'

I had no idea. My face must have said so. Pierson looked at Chris, who unglued his palms from the table's surface, turned them upwards and shrugged his shoulders, as if to say: 'Really none of my business.'

The entrance door of the Club opened, but instead of Vukas and his entourage, only Smeško appeared. He walked to our table and seated himself across from me. His scar jerked and I nodded. Music around us was quiet. Out of nowhere, a set dinner was served in front of me. I wasn't tempted.

Chris introduced Pierson to Smeško. The young Paterson asked about Vukas. Smeško said Vukas wasn't coming; but that he, Smeško, was there instead for whoever expected to see the President. Pierson looked at me and I translated. He got up, bowed, kissed my hand and said he was not feeling well, anyway.

'See that little spy off,' Smeško told me.

I ignored him. Chris got up and made sure that Pierson was properly bade goodbye.

Smeško laughed, which was unpleasant, as usual. I wanted to just get up and leave, but I couldn't make myself do it. My knees felt locked in. Chris came back and started talking. I immediately understood that my role was to was to fill in the blanks where Chris didn't understand our language or Smeško didn't understand English. They were openly talking business. Finance, public tenders and percentages – their topics of the night - made them seem more in charge yet more relaxed. They addressed each other with 'my friend', or even, for some elusive reason 'habibi'. *Habibi let me be honest, Habibi, you know how we appreciate honesty . .*

. I think they both really meant it; they both considered themselves honest, clean and masterful businessmen. I edited a lot; it was the rebellion I could still afford. At least I was earning my salary doing such traditional, normal and pleasingly boring job as translating

'What was that young man doing here?' I couldn't help inserting the question about Pierson into my translations for Chris.

Chris managed to say: 'Long story,' before his phone rang. He got up from the table to take the call.

In order not to look at Smeško or talk to him, I started eating the set dinner in front of me. It was a plate of cold, overcooked pasta with black-and-white sauce: Béchamel and black olives together. Now that was a meal that most resembled the mass-made, farewell suppers from the camps for Tito's pioneers. But I was hungry, I realised – the coke-breakfast I'd had wasn't exactly a slow-burner or a stomach-warmer, not at all like *kaša*, my mother's version of porridge.

Chris came back.

'Sorry to interrupt your meal,' he said to me. 'Please just tell Mr Berković that it was Perić on the phone. He apologised and, I don't know if I heard him right, but I think he said he'd had a good *facial*, fell asleep right after it, woke up now but it's too late for him to join us.'

'Translate,' Smeško ordered, looking at me.

'I think he must have said *fellatio*, not facial,' I said to Chris, still ignoring Smeško.

'Oh. Is that so?' Chris said. 'Wow, that's even better.'

'I hope you're smarter than that *fellatio* remark, girl,' Smeško said in our language. 'You're allowing yourself

150

too much space. If you want to improvise, go and write poetry or something.'

I didn't want to respond to anything he said, and, fortunately, I didn't have to, because Seka entered at that moment, followed by three of her girls: Sonja, Enisa and a healthier, local-looking number three.

'I think the meeting is over,' Smeško said and waved at Seka. She waved back and raised her eyebrows at me. 'Go, dance,' Smeško told me. 'You're off.'

'Look, Smeško,' I said. 'Your lucky girlfriend Sonja is here.'

'You're trying to be funny now, but I can tell you that you're not my type. Sonja is worth more than all of you local girls put together.'

'Toilet time,' I said and got up. 'Pardon me,' I said to Chris.

Smeško grabbed my arm, pulled me back and said into my face. 'Listen, *narkomanko*, I know Sonja loves me, even when she pretends to hate me. It's a little game we play.'

'Please don't confide in me.' I shook his hand off me, smiled at wide-eyed Chris, and directed myself toward the bathroom.

'Right. You're here for the old *Go-grin*,' I heard Smeško yell behind my back. He meant 'Gringo', but tried to avoid Chris understanding that much. 'Vukas would've told you the same thing and you would've obeyed, no?'

In the toilet, with the help of more white (courage) powder, I persuaded myself it was perfectly normal and safe to simply go back to the Club, pick up my coat and

151

go home, maybe even call my old girlfriends and tell them that if they thought I'd fallen out of touch because my life had become too fantastic to share – well they were so fucking wrong.

But when I opened the toilet's door, Smeško stormed in, pushing Sonja before him.

'Mila, doll,' he said, closing the door behind his back and locking it. 'That Chris is asking about you. He's dying for your candy. It's making me horny.' He unzipped his trousers. 'Suck me hard,' he said to Sonja.

I went for the door.

'That's right,' Smeško whispered. 'Show me your ass.'

Did he say that to me? My hands fidgeted in vain with the doorknob.

The bathroom door shook suddenly with the urgent, strong thumps; somebody's fists were hitting it hard from the other side.

'What?' Smeško shouted. 'Who's this?'

'Let me in,' I heard the familiar moan of a tortured mind. B-R-A-N-K-O. When did he join the party? Branko's voice made me turn to Smeško as to a saviour.

'Please, don't let him in,' I said. 'Don't let him in.'

I lowered my eyes and they were met by Smeško's soft, dangling penis. Looking at his face seemed a better option.

'Let me in!' Branko was begging from behind the door. 'I want some of that! What are you having? An ass-wiping session? I want that, I want some of that.'

Smeško's scar moved up. I whispered: 'Don't.'

'You owe me,' he said.

'Come on, Smeško,' Branko was saying. 'I deserve it,

152

I do. My ass itches, I need some licking.'

'Next time, little brother,' Smeško said.

'Please,' Branko cried and hit the door with two sharp thumps.

Smeško grabbed his cock again. I pictured Branko doing the same behind the door.

'Come here,' Smeško said.

Sonja approached him.

'You too,' he told me.

'No.'

'You owe me.'

'Anything else,' I said.

'Watch then.'

I watched Sonja in the mirror. With her eyes closed, she was leaning on the bathroom wall, travelling through time and space, like a philosopher-martyr. Her face colour was grey with traces of yellow in it, and her lips were red with traces of blue. She wore a massive, curly, blond wig. A synthetic little dress over her skinny body. Her neck, arms and legs were spaghetti-thin, long and with traces of what seemed like cigarette burns on them. She was sweating and embracing herself.

'I have high temperature,' she whispered.

'Good,' Smeško said. 'So take your dress off.'

In one move she was naked and she lay on the floor tiles. She was humming, looking delirious. Smeško didn't have to say anything else, it seemed that Sonja knew the choreography. She slithered to his shoes and licked them. He kicked her face gently.

Sonja got up on her knees and Smeško lowered his

trousers. She licked his balls and sucked his cock and then he sprayed his cum over her face and into her wig, askew now. She stood up and walked to the sink, to wash herself. She avoided looking at the mirror. Smeško came by to use the sink number two. He pissed into it and washed his cock and then his hands. The sounds of running water softened the moment. It was over for now. For Sonja.

When she opened the door to go out of the bathroom, I saw that Branko wasn't camping there anymore. So I followed her. Smeško pinched my butt.

'I'll take care of Branko,' he whispered. 'You take care of the American scum. I don't trust him. I don't trust anyone until proven innocent.'

I picked up my coat from the Club and simply walked out, started walking home. It was late but the streets of Podgorica were safe. The vampires were indoors, partying, their vitality well fed by business deals and 'other social reforms'. Okay - I was thinking - no big deal. That was all because of Mirko and me. They wanted to show me what happened if I kind of defected. Tomorrow, I'd try to get in touch with Vukas. Tomorrow or after holidays. He'd have to get Smeško off my back. And Branko would soon be sent to Washington D.C. Chris was not dangerous, just stricken by *clientitis* and lusting after a young pussy. In fact, Chris could help me, one day. He was obviously cooperating with the young Pierson Paterson. The thought of applying for a US visa and going away occurred to me for the first time. I was going to stay in touch with Chris. I was going to be all right.

154

16

I called Vukas and for two days only his voice mail picked up. I left messages.

'Could you tell Smeško to get off my back?' I cried into the phone. 'Would you please spare me the Brankos and the Smeškos of this world? I hate those monsters. What about my raise? Vukas? Vukas? What's going on?'

Finally, one day, I received a text from Vukas.

Read today's Voice, moron.

Not very encouraging.

The Voice was an independent weekly. I went to the grocery store downstairs and bought it. There was a big, New Year Interview with Mirko inside. Four pages of Mirko's handsome but non-festive face and his rant-in-print about the alarming levels of corruption in Montenegro and the sad fate awaiting the country in 2002 if people voted Vukas again. 'Boycott him, boycott his every campaign, boycott all elections,' was Mirko's main message.

Also, in the text, and in almost every comment that Mirko made, Chris's full name stood out printed in bold font. The same Chris Bernard, Mirko claimed, a shadow lobbyist, who had paid Mirko's Opposition Party innumerable top secret visits to offer his support - his direct connections to any US Congressman, Democrat, Republican, spin doctor, Albright, Clinton, the Bush administration – the same Chris Bernard was the guest of honour for Vukas's and his entourage's private parties.

The New Year Party at the Blue Salon was mentioned several times; also, the pretense, image-friendly charities that the influential US couple had established with the Montenegrin First Couple; expensive evening gowns, fountains of champagne; while the rest of Montenegro was kept in darkness, unknowingly working for this clan, paying for the Blue Salon's opulent orgies.

I had to re-read it sitting on the toilet. My father's child, after all. Except I had locked myself in the bathroom, terrified. Of course Vukas knew it was I who informed Mirko about the Blue Club Party. Why did Mirko do that to me? Did he want to betray me before I betrayed him? No. Mirko knew I could betray nothing and nobody. He knew I was just an innocent child of Podgorica. But, still, he didn't care about what would happen to me.

My mobile phone vibrated on the bathroom tiles, next to my feet. *Daddy calling*. I picked it up and cleared my throat.

I tried to sound calm. 'Hello?'

'Have you read the interview?' Vukas asked.

'I'm still reading it. He goes on and on and on about the same thing really. Boring gossip.'

'Boring gossip?' Vukas said. 'It's sold out. They're reprinting it. The interview only, in bigger font, as a separate pamphlet. Seems it's anything but boring.'

'Well, maybe I'm not your average reader.'

'You're a silly little tart, that's what you are.'

'Why?' I said. 'Don't tell me you think I had something to do with it.'

'*Please*,' Vukas hissed. 'There are too many facts and descriptions there that only you could have provided.

156

I even heard your voice as I read it.' I gasped to say something but Vukas went on. 'Perhaps you don't like Chris and Bella, but what you did is going to harm *me*. Chris and Bella, they don't care. Chris, unlike me, has a very forgiving job description. And Bella just went off and hired a new girl to help her and Darinka with their charity.'

'Oh, the devious *Ambassadoressa*,' I mocked. 'I never received a cent for that job anyway.'

'What do you think your two-thousand Deutc-she Marks cover every month, you little fool?' Vukas snapped. 'I've been more than generous. I've been tolerant. I'm all you have. *I'm all you all have!*' he was screaming. 'I'm all this damned country has! I'm your only choice!'

'Yes you are,' I was quick to reply.

'*Yes you are*,' he mimicked. 'You don't give a shit, do you? See now how much Mirko cares about you, huh? And all you care is *What about my raise?* Moaning about money every single day into my voice mail. You and everybody else in this country. What do you think, that I shit cash?'

'I'm sorry. But, hey, now you know that Chris has been seeing Mirko and offering him Washington support as well.'

'As if didn't know *that* before,' Vukas said. 'But, okay, I will choose to believe that that had been your master plan. To disclose Chris through Mirko.'

'You told me to.'

'Did I tell you to sleep with the poet? Well, I need more from both of them. And then you'll get your raise.'

'They'll never trust me.'

'Chris will. He doesn't know about you and Mirko. Chris is playing a simultaneous game somewhere, with someone. I can feel it. There's a challenge for you. I'm giving you another chance. I'm too soft with you already. If I were a Mafia Boss as your opposition lover claims you'd be dead by now. Relax. Come and see Anka. She'll give you your money,' Vukas said and hung up.

* * *

It was almost morning when I left the Blue Club once more and started walking to my flat. The mist of winter's hollow hours quickly cooled my sweat.

Metallic days, tin-smelling nights. Empty streets; sad, far-away lights.

I wanted to suppress the fact that I'd just had sex with Chris in the Presidential Suite of the hotel where the Blue Club and Salon were, so I paced the boulevard, following the rhythm of the rhymes in my head. I needed to bring myself home first and then pass out there.

Soon I was throwing up by a lamppost. First from the standing position, then squatting, and then I lost consciousness.

When I opened my eyes, I found myself still squatting while holding onto the lamppost, like a horny dog. A man was standing above me. I recognised my old school-buddy turned Mirko's driver. Jumbo. I couldn't remember the guy's real name. He looked tired, wrinkled down his cheeks, like an old sailor. My generation. He knelt down. He wiped my mouth with a wet wipe.

'Mila,' he said, 'I'm taking you home.'

'Why?'

'In class, you did other pupils' tests after you'd finished your own. I tell this to everyone. Nobody could catch up with you.'

'Ah, that,' I said and started walking. 'So long ago. And in another country.'

'Besides,' he said, 'Mirko asked me to make sure you got home all right.'

'I'll be all right walking. It's safe outside.'

'I should tell you,' Jumbo said, 'that Mirko can't see you anymore. He received a recording of you and him in the HQ.'

'I didn't betray Mirko.'

'Yeah, well, he figured that out. Said they must have planted something in the TV screen.' Jumbo looked at his shoes and kicked an invisible stone. 'Real sorry . . .'

I didn't know what to believe anymore. I felt too dirty for Jumbo's car, and anyway I needed a walk.

Jumbo drove very slowly behind me all the way to my building, making sure I got home safely.

17

Sometimes it happens in Podgorica that the reign of winter is ended overnight, in February. It happened that year, 2002. I mostly slept or sleepwalked through the prematurely warm days. I was working nights, hidden under their dark surface, like a tick under skin, my resources growing. The bosses agreed I deserved my cash and they kept me loaded.

Chris the 'Ambassador', my new work project, had

vampires in his bloodline. Sleeping with me took twenty years off his age. His vitality shot back up. He told me he loved me while inside me and then would follow up on that like he really meant it; he'd text or call the day after. I never answered. The Ambassador didn't love me of course. He loved himself again. After several intimate encounters with me, he relaxed, walked around the Grand Hotel with only a robe on, snorted coke with poise, off his fingertips. He never took too much of coke or alcohol - he had his brakes well oiled, the old bastard, trained to dip only his top corner in the cream, the tortilla soldier, the joy surfer, the virtual adventurer, my Chrissy Bear. But the relaxed surrender into the Balkanoid blokeship convinced Vukas and Smeško that Chris was genuinely on their side and wanted only money and a private pussy, in return to which he would lobby for Montenegro in Washington, and bring them clean business partners for their deals. For me, none of those Montenegro-based makers-and-breakers existed when the job was done; I'd take the money, *thank you, bye now*. I'd take the drugs, drinks and food, too. Fine. I was still young, and surely if I focused on the bigger picture, I'd be given another chance, somewhere else, to become an upgraded version of myself. Focusing on the bigger picture at the moment meant, first, I'd forgive Mirko and stop hurting for him. It also meant I'd spend my time with Chris Bernard, make him find, in his heart, a spot for me soft enough so that he'd be willing to help me go away when I asked for it. But I'd never have a soft spot in my heart for Chris, even if he helped me. Chris had to pay for his sin of being blinded by power. Once he helped me get a US visa, or just relocate, I'd need more money to start a new life. So, yes, I'd squeeze a big cash bonus from Vukas before I leave, by writing a bad report on Chris and voice my suspicion about the American lobbyist's true intentions.

I drank and snorted a bit with Chris in the Pres Suite of the Grand Hotel before we were to go downstairs and join the Montenegrin Health Minister for dinner. It was the beginning of some American holiday weekend, and Chris wanted to make the most of it. To miss the infinite possibilities provided by four days without Bella, to Chris it meant to be old and tired again. I asked him about his wife. Chris told me that Bella had stayed in Belgrade, reveling in her position to manhandle their Serbian employees by snatching their weekends away to help her pack for the resettlement to Montenegro.

'Bella is the perfect wife,' he added. 'All she needs to know when I'm travelling is that I'm going somewhere useful for both of us. And she always jumps at the opportunity to use her organisational skills. She actually teaches these skills. She's a guest lecturer at, I don't know, perhaps five Universities in ex-Yu.'

'When does she find the time for lecturing?' I asked. 'I know she comes down here often to help Darinka run the charity they established.'

'I'll answer that with one of her favourite triad theories: build, develop and let go,' Chris said. 'Much like parenting.' He pulled down my dress. 'Easy dressers,' he licked my breast. 'That's what I like about young women.'

He pushed me up on the bed.

'You're very fit for your age,' I complimented him when he positioned himself behind me, his legs bent, knees apart, his feet turned outwards, like a duck's, and entered me.

'Thank you,' he replied, panting.

In the mirror, I could see him squatting. It made me laugh how he fished for compliments. Chris was mid-push when I giggled out loud and he frowned. He didn't like it when my focus strayed during sex. His mobile phone started ringing from some corner of the Suite. The march-like ringtone startled me and I jumped off from Chris' penis, swooshing forward like an underwater gun and hitting the pillow. Chris growled but went to check who was calling; it was Perić. I could hear his hyped-up chatter as Chris held the phone away from his ear. He said something that sounded like one long sentence and then a female voice was heard from the phone.

'Hello, Suzana,' Chris said. 'Good, very good.'

Who the fuck was Suzana now? A new coordinator-for-whatever?

'I understand,' Chris was saying, 'Now tell your boss that I have found investors, I checked them through and through and I think they're the best men for this transaction. Your boss knows my KYC obsession. KYC – Know Your Client, yes. How-*ever*, I don't do business with those men. I don't have anything from their side. I ask for 2.75% from your boss's bank to be paid on the account of Bella's Umbrella Charity Fund in Switzerland. Is that a deal?'

162

'Yes,' the word jumped from inside the phone.

'Okay,' Chris replied to it. 'I always like to *triple*-check. Tell Perić that his bank's letter of guarantee is good enough for me. Two-point-seventy-five it is. I'll see him later, tonight ...' he paused. 'Okay, okay, just be sure to tell your boss that my side is clean.'

Chris hung up, his mind now far from sex.

'So,' I was interested. 'Business blossoms in Monte with Perić, right?'

'Damn Perić,' Chris said. 'Perić procrastinates till Smeško has checked on the men I'm bringing and then the deal is closed, I'm sure. It's a good deal, clean.'

Naked like a snowball, Chris sat down on a chair in front of a mahogany writing desk and he began muttering some figures to himself, then scribbling them down. When he finished, he seemed satisfied and we could go down to the Club to have dinner. The band was playing in the club. The Health minister was already there, waiting for Chris. Sonja and some other girls were on the dance podium, entertaining whomever showed up, I thought.

During dinner, Chris was using me to translate the conversation between him and the Health Minister. He complimented the Health Minister on his vision to build a modern, more effective and an all-inclusive clinic, and he explained the business plan: a Government's rep should sign an MoU; Chris knew the most powerful health sector developers from Israel; Chris would do it for Montenegro; Perić would take care of his share. I, on the other hand, was very impressed by the 2.75% I now knew Chris was going to receive. What an established amount, un-round yet authoritative! So professional. And it didn't seem hard to achieve it. All it took was the infatuation with cash. Business was easy.

Perić appeared, solo that time, obviously not in the mood for girls. He sat with us and kept staring at Chris with a look of anything but love.

'It's all about who you know, everywhere in the world,' Chris was saying. 'Know-Your-Client. KYC. KYC and the human factor. Human factor *is* the invisible hand of Adam Smith,' Chris smiled and the Health Minister nodded. I was going to translate but Perić stopped me.

'Go and dance, Milli Vanilli,' he said. 'I speak English.'

So I went and joined Sonja, my new friend, on the dance podium. I was still thinking about 2.75%, and how I could learn something from that Chris. I should *communicate* with him more often. If I could. Sonja's face resembled a porcelain Geisha now. Her little bum was one pure muscle. The rest of her body bounced and moved as if she had swallowed the rhythm and it was trying to burst out of her. Every section of her body had its own choreography, what she was doing was not dancing; it was erotic storytelling. She became beautiful when the music played, and she died when the music died. She'd found her survival tool. The beat-a-mobile that could drive her away anywhere she wanted.

When the song finished, Sonja turned to me and looked at me intensely, as if seeing me for the first time.

'*A ti?*' she asked me in Russian. '*A ti tozhe bila ballerina? A gdye? V*

164

Moskvi?'

'I understand Russian,' I replied. *'No, ya Cherno-gorka...*I'm from here. I was never a dancer,' I smiled. 'Maybe only once, as a child . . .'

But Sonja lost interest. She crossed herself three times and danced on,

to the next song, obviously not eager to become an *intimus* of a local amateur entertainer.

Smeško must have sneaked in while I was talking to Sonja.

'What's the point of this pop-music?' he yelled, scaring us all off. His arms spread wide, he was shouting at the invisible DJ. 'Give us some emotions here. Cardio!' He touched his chest.

Perić laughed and turned to Chris. 'Now you'll see what letting go means. Let go or die. L-G-O-D. Now you'll see and you will KYC, and you can talk about us to your shrinks in NYC.'

Chris smiled. Smeško whispered something into Perić's ear and walked away from the table to grab Sonja. Perić laughed again.

'What is it?' Chris asked.

'KYC,' Perić said. 'Know Your Cunt.' He looked at me. 'How sweet is she, Chris?'

'She's special. I think I'm in love,' Chris said.

I knew it was time for me to leave. I decided to try and silently slip out of the hotel after the 'cardio' song.

When I did leave, unaccompanied, I saw a black car on the street in front of hotel, with flashlights on. Jumbo? Vukas? The window slid down. Perić!

'You move like a shadow warrior, Milli Vanilli,' he

said. 'Come in. We need to talk.'

There was no way I could say no so I entered his car, sat in the backseat. His 'butler' drove us, speeding like a maniac, as if we were being chased. It was just an act; in Montenegro, nobody was after Perić. We went to the riverbank and up the little hill past the Old Town, where the driver stopped in front of a villa with no windows, only a massive entrance door. We left the car and Perić unlocked the door of the villa.

'I'll wait in the car,' the butler-driver said.

My ever-optimistic mind concluded that Perić needed my impressions on Chris. I was by then accustomed that all of the ruling-clique people were paranoid. Were they born like that, or did they become it? It's a chicken and egg question of any dictatorship's ruling clique, I suppose. So I was quickly forming descriptions of Chris as I entered the villa: *childish, idealistic and easily played*.

All the windows were placed on the opposite side of the villa that overlooked the river canyon and Podgorica by night. I had a short chance to enjoy the view of my hometown, unrecognizably pretty from that mysterious mansion. The streetlights were on, fireworks exploded in the sky, and I remembered that it was the time of year for Mimosa Festival. How I'd lost touch with the proper circle of celebrations in my country! Then Perić led me through one of the doors. The room was lit by a floor lamp featuring an idiotic abat-jour with embroidered national costumes of ex-Yugoslavia. There was a painting on the wall, maybe even an original: horses that looked like Berber's. On

166

the pitted parquet by the bed, international magazines and books on politics were piled, a pair of reading glasses on the top of one pile. There was nothing personal about the space, which looked like the room of an abandoned motel.

Perić took his trousers off. And his boxer shorts. My first impression was that he had three legs and was a pitiful mutant.

'What are you doing?' I asked.

The middle leg was his penis, with the texture (and vitality) of an anchoring rope. He grabbed my hand and kissed it. I tugged my arm, but he held it firmly and pulled me on the bed. He reached under the duvet and fished out his neat drug equipment from which he snorted a lot of coke.

'I've been dying to taste you,' he said. 'I was going crazy, alone here, in this shithole. And that stupid American gets to fuck you. Selfish little prick.'

'Don't,' I said. 'Why are you doing this?'

'Ah, there are days . . . that only ballerinas can light up. Light up my life,

Milli Vanilli. Want some?' Perić asked me, holding a packet of coke and a vial in his hands.

I did take it; it could do me no harm at the moment. I remembered how Smeško had whispered something into Perić's ear before he left with Sonja. That was it – they were just adding the 'scare Milli Vanilli' factor to their little game. I had to be reminded that I belonged to the real President's men, not to foreigners.

'I'm not a ballerina,' I said, seating myself, fully dressed, next to Perić. 'I only participated in a choreographed dance once, when I was a Tito's pioneer and it was May, that time of the year when his birthday was celebrated even though he'd died. They needed as many girls as they could get so they drafted me and put me in the back rows to tiptoe and fall flat as if shot a rifle.'

'Ah, I love stories. Tell me more stories, Milli.'

'That's it for tonight. Time to go to sleep now.'

'Play with my pet, Millie, put it in your mouth. They were made for each

other, both restless, full of stories.'

'Where's your girlfriend, Staša, or Saša, what was it you named her? Recuperating somewhere?'

'I'm a generous man, love.' Perić made a puppy face, trying to look it. 'I sent her to my friend in Dubai to make him happy for a while. She'll get a new nose job in return. Be a good girl now, and I'll send you too to see the world.'

I sighed. 'You know,' I said. 'I thought you wanted to talk about Chris with me.'

'Why the fuck would I want to do that?'

'Because, I don't know . . . I seem to be the only person on this planet that doesn't realise I became something quite different from the image towards which I was heading myself. Like, diagonally different. You read all these foreign books and newspapers. You tell me: how did that happen? And why? I was so ambitious.'

Perić was snorting and snorting. 'You're an *entertainer*, Millie,' he said. 'A paid professional. Flow with it. It's a lovely vocation, like show biz. And now, excuse me, but when I take coke I'd fuck a tree hole. So, first I'll ask nicely . . .'

I got up. 'Can your driver drive me home now?' I said.

'I asked nicely,' Perić mumbled as he pulled me down to him and pushed his pet into my teeth.

Guessing that it might take less than five minutes, I was going to go along with it, so I let him in, taking my jacket off. He stuffed his penis all the way to my throat and some part of me rebelled, so I gagged over, bathing his cock in an acidic mix of drinks and bad food.

'Ah, you're no good,' Perić roared, changing his mind. He wiped his penis with the hem of my dress, which he then lifted up, higher, at the same time pushing me on the bed where he held me pinned down, beneath him, by the unusual broadness of his shoulders and length of his arms, completely disproportionate with the rest of his body, except for that anchor-rope cock. I could picture him well slaughtering pigs in Frankfurt.

'Pig-slaughterer,' I hissed into his ear. 'I bet you fucked pigs as well, haven't you?'

He threw his head back and laughed.

'Milli Vanilli,' he replied, 'Milli Vanilli.'

His tongue slid through his lips like a surgeon's scalpel from its case. He was trying to kiss me but I kept my mouth shut so he mostly salivated onto my lips and into my nostrils, his breath smelling like steel. He was muttering that I liked it rough, didn't I? I didn't talk back and his erection wasn't happening, but then he slapped me: once, twice, more – till there was the taste of blood in my throat. And then he became properly hard.

'You'll pay for this,' I said to Perić when he rolled himself off me and came into the bed sheet. 'You'll pay one day, one way or another.'

'Oh, yeah?' he said, stretching and yawning. 'What are you going to do? Complain to your big buddy Mirko? Why don't you ask Smeško to show you the transcripts of his phone conversations about you? You're insubstantial.'

He turned on his side and started snoring even before I got out of bed, put my jacket back on and went out, trying to appear normal for the driver. At least I had a ride back home. A clash with Perić was going to happen, sooner or later. Well, it happened, and unpleasant it was, but not just for me, for both of us. Perić might even ignore me from then on. One man down. Focus on the future.

18

But, the memory of that night still simultaneously maddens and saddens me. I also remember the soreness of the following day. My vagina burned, my stomach, my throat. Predictably, tears are rolling down my cheeks now. I don't want to cry. Crying will only make me sleepy. It is better to think of Misha Grishin; of the times when we were all becoming close, not just him and me, but all the Grishins and me.

I started working for the Grishins on the first Monday that followed the interview, just a couple of weeks before the end of the children's school's spring term. That term's name is deceiving. London's constant climate seemed to be that of an early winter, with her

170

crosswinds and her low skies.

I arrived at the Grishins early, accompanied by Yola, who was now *in lieu* of my manager - at least that was how I felt. In the Grishins' spacious reception room, the children were sitting in front of huge, flat TV screen, surrounded by the piles of their school clothes. They were yawning and rubbing their eyes.

'They are probably hungry,' Yola whispered. 'Start easy, cookies and milk. Don't go all super-nanny to make French toast and *poshy* stuff right away.' With that warning, she ran down the staircase and disappeared into the basement.

Dina was not around. I went to the kitchen and opened the fridge (extreme dimensions, like everything else) without communicating with Alex and Nensi. I just didn't know how to start a conversation with children; thought the only way was kissing up to them. And for that activity I needed some preparation time.

I stared at attractive-looking assortment of food items, noticing that they were organized impeccably on the shelves, by colour, by type. Everything in that fridge shone, as if regularly polished. Milk was either goat-milk or almond-unsweetened. Goat or almond for children? Eggs were also divided into categories: small and colourful in the lower shelf of the door; larger, mono-coloured and 'intelligent' ones on the higher shelf. Was I supposed to know why? I held my breath, hesitating to upset that balance even by breathing into it, let alone taking the stuff out. I shook my head and pushed the fridge door to close it. The door travelled to meet the destination at its own, relaxed speed and without a sound. I had to seek help from the little people.

'First of all: good morning, children!' I cried in the direction of the TV screen. No answer.

'Today is my training day,' I went on, 'so forgive me if I make mistakes, okay?' There was some movement on the sofa. Yeah, they would eventually pay attention. 'So, like, what kind of milk -'

'Maa-maa!' I heard a cry. It was Nensi. 'Maaa-maaaa!' Louder now.

'What is it sweetie?' I asked in my nicest voice ever. 'Tell me. I think your mama is sleeping.'

'Alex is hurting me.'

'No, I'm not! I was just touching your arm, you freak.'

'What?' I said. 'We don't use those words around here, Alex!'

'Oh, yes we do-o!' Alex yelled back, with a voice too tinny for a child, I thought. 'And I was just trying to change this stupid program she's watching. Stupid Charlie and Lola. We're both too old for it! Except that she's a retard.'

'Well, I hate your Zack and' –

'Shut up!' Dina's order fell from somewhere upstairs, like an icicle from a roof. 'Is your nanny with you?'

'I'm here, making breakfast!'

'What, now?' Dina cried. 'They're going to be late for school. Late is bad. In their school late is worse than not showing up at all!'

I already saw myself giving up, walking out on my short employment. Free again, after five minutes of reality show. The spring would come, eventually.

172

There were still so many walks waiting to befriend and heal me, show me what I'd been missing. Why was I a *nanny*, a servant with the difficult burden of attempting to love the little alien creatures? Please.

But Yola's face appeared from the basement. She stared at me, daring me, a loser and a quitter, an enemy of all the Tonyrobbinsonians of this world, to give it up and defame her, my manager.

'Dress them,' Yola hissed. 'And get out of house.'

'What about breakfast?' I whispered.

'Starbucks,' Yola hissed going back to her basement kingdom. 'Bring back receipt.'

I switched the TV off. My hands were shaking.

'So sorry,' I said and started dressing up the children, pushing their heads and arms into their school cardigans.

Alex was crying.

'Shh. Shh,' I said.

'She's a violent freak,' Alex said. 'I hate her.'

'You think a bit of shouting from your good old mama is violent? Then you wouldn't survive one day with my father,' I said, trying to make a decent knot on his school tie. Nensi was finishing her dressing up herself. 'My dad is a beast. It was scary to just hear him breathe. He used to come into the room and suck up all air into his lungs so my mother and I would turn blue in our faces and we had to run outside to save our lives.'

Nensi giggled first. 'A beast who steals air,' she said.

'Wow,' Alex joined in. 'I sure hope he doesn't come here looking for you.'

We all laughed. 'There,' I said. 'Nice tie, man. Don't

you dare undo this knot before July 12, ok?'

I let them lead me to their school. It was two blocks away, two easy streets to cross. The children could go there alone, blindfolded. When I was their age . . . Ah, no point comparing. I already knew about London: no unaccompanied children on the streets. Holding Alex and Nensi by their soft and warm hands, I pushed my chest forward and broadened my shoulders. Nobody was going to hurt my little protégés. I would bloody punch the children-snatchers' stinking teeth out, go for their necks and strangle them. But the people we did meet on our way to school seemed friendly, nodded their heads at us, smiled and said 'Good morning'. They weren't going to fool *me*.

'I will protect you from evil force,' I said to the children. Where did that line come from?

'That's Buzz Lightyear,' Alex said as if reading my mind.

Buzz Lightyear? I must have overheard a buzz of it while having coffee with my Montenegrin friends who would sit their children in front of TV and play a film for the little ones, so that we could share an hour of adulthood together.

The Grihin children's school was disappointing for me because it didn't really look like a school at all. It was a house and it had a word 'house' in its name. Well, at least they were honest about it and I should've worked on killing my lame prejudices. A serious-looking man in a suit was standing at the entrance door, shaking hands with every single pupil and saying their names out loud, wishing them a good day.

174

Nensi turned to me, hugged and kissed me. Alex kind of kissed me and off they went.

'Have fun!' I shouted after them. Mothers and nannies, gathered on the pavement in front of the school, grinned at me.

'Hello everyone,' I said, beaming back. 'I'm Millie, the new nanny of Alex and Nensi.'

Nobody said a word, of course. I hated them all: a boring pattern of locals. Well, I was different, and proud of it.

At the entrance door, the serious man only shook hands with my children and didn't say their names. Didn't wish them a good day, either. Perhaps he thought I'd done enough, more than enough and now he was making the children pay for their chaperon's inadequacy. I walked up to him, injuring the system more and more seriously, I guess.

'They are Alex and Nensi Grishin,' I said to the man. 'I am their new nanny, Millie.' I extended my arm to him. He only looked at my hand, as if feeling sorry for it. 'I noticed you didn't say their names so I thought'-

'Thank you,' the man said and finally shook my hand. 'I am Mr Skullie.'

'Oh.'

It was the first English 'Thank you' that made itself clear about its real meaning: gather, you, ill-adjusted *dreamer*. And the man's last name was *Scully*, as I learnt later, and he was the Headmaster.

I walked back to Oakley Gardens, managing to get a bit lost on the way. That bit took half-an-hour of my mindless going in circles through Chelsea during which

I kept passing by a Starbucks – was it the same Starbucks all the time? Shit, the Starbucks! Breakfast! I forgot to feed the children.

I felt guilty and completely incompetent when I finally knocked on the Grishins' door. Yola opened.

'There's something for you in the kitchen,' she told me and I knew she didn't mean coffee. She was so robotic inside that house.

Two keys on a silver keychain in the shape of a lion's head were waiting for me on the kitchen counter. Next to them - the list of to-do things, the every-day schedule of aims and responsibilities; a kind of a contract, I guessed, printed out and signed by Dina. What to buy today and what to buy every day, which books to take back to the library, which food to avoid at all costs, what to sign the children up for, where to take them after school, juice only in the morning, potatoes once a week, milk chocolate – never; more rules to learn by heart as well as the PIN number for the credit card I was to carry with me during the day. I thought how I was probably never going to see Dina or Misha Grishin again in my life, only their children. But I decided to be there for the little ones. The grown-up Grishins didn't seem to like their children much and that was dangerous, infectious. I understood how a nanny could catch the loveless bug and carry it on, dispassionately looking after the little ones. I didn't want to be the one to contribute to Alex and Nensi's developing incompletely, like beautiful flowers in the shade of a selfish tree.

As my loyalty for the job developed, Nensi impressed me first. I fell in love with the freshness of her soul, which cleansed my soul. There seemed to be no traces of despondent Slavonic genome in Nensi. She behaved differently from all the children I'd known till then; here was a 'new' child, for whom words were not sticks to attack or defend herself, but more like Lego bricks, used to build up bright, merry sights around her, a world that contained no violence, no injuries.

I trusted her. She couldn't hurt me. She made me become more efficient, more devoted to my job. I caught myself thinking that one day I'd like to have a daughter like Nensi to avenge me, to avenge me *so*. And suddenly, I knew what my mother must have felt when she had me, why she'd been so convinced that I was destined to be lucky. My mother had probably also dreamed of a daughter – avenger, with brain cells unclogged, talents not stinted, possibilities recognised and realised. In 1975, when I was born in what was still the biggest country we'd ever have – Yugoslavia – it was believed, and believable, that the situation was only going to improve, especially for women. My mother had been receiving special packages *and* her full salary for the whole year she'd spent at home after having me. From that year on, we could enjoy as many as three weeks in July or August, holidaying for free in a seaside retreat in Sutomore, reserved for women, employees of Yugoslavian Post Telephone Telegraph services. It was not an elegant resort, not even a charming, white-and-blue beach hotel. Its rooms were small, furnished with brown beds with plank-sides that felt like lichen against my tender skin. The walls were painted in halves – in emerald the lower half and in turquoise the upper, divided by a horizontal orange line – and heavily stained by dark blood smears, the remains of swarms of mosquitoes slapped into their sudden deaths. But it was lavishly terraced towards the most beautiful sandy beach imaginable and visible through the intermittent groups of cypresses, oleander bushes and tamaris trees where, after lunch, my father played cards with other husbands and extinguished his cigarettes in the watermelon crusts, while, on one of the terraces, my mother drank beer with her bubbly colleagues from all corners of ex-Yugoslavia – Slovenia, Bosnia, Kosovo, Croatia, from anywhere in Yugoslavia - as long as they were female and the employees of the old country's PTT. Surely life looked good, at least every summer, or that is how I remembered it, and a simple woman like Mama could never have predicted the terror of the ninety-nineties and its unavoidable consequences, even for the avenging daughters of a fallen motherland, Yugoslavia,

It took longer for Alex to unwind. He was a worrying child, with a pointy chin of a grown-up cynic and something bitter around his mouth that he shared neither with Dina nor Misha. He was obsessive about the correct order in which his miniature monsters ('They are not monsters,' he warned me. 'They are *Equadonians*') were to be placed on the shelf next to his writing desk on which he never wrote any homework – so as not to, again, make any mess. Slow to get going, aloof and hungry for the most artificial of sweets (in his room he also kept bags of Skittles, Jelly beans and Sour strings hidden from his mother), he seemed to

178

be hibernating, waiting for the awful winter of child-hood to be over and something better to come along. It was easy to give up on a charmless child and, aware of that, I fought the urge to remain detached from Alex. I went along with his ideas to keep everyone out of his room, Yola included, to do homework in the study, to have sweets before 'normal' food. When I helped him with the part of his homework called 'spelling sentenc-es', we took our time until we'd find a perfectly original sentence, which would contain the new word given for homework. Thus for 'ritualistic' we had: *My new nan-ny's ritualistic mornings consist of coffee, biscuits and cigarettes.* Alex enjoyed our odd approaches to home-work, there was a solid sense of humour buried deep under his ginger-ness, and I rejoiced, knowing he had something to pull him through life.

During the big lump of a day both children were in school. But there was always something kids-related to do, like go to Peter Jones and buy the mysteriously lost parts of their school uniform, search for the ingredi-ents for their healthy after-school meal, or look for the bits and bobs they needed for their school projects and their costumes for a play or a 'book character' day.

I brought the children home at about five p.m., help with homework, bathe them and kiss them good night. I liked my Saturdays with Alex and Nensi, when I came to their house around ten a.m. with my A-Z map of London and we'd go anywhere. On our way to anywhere, I'd tell them stories, self-censored of course, from my life. Soon the children were referring to my stories as 'the tales from Millie's Believe-it-or-not museum' after we'd visited the real one on Piccadilly, where I pointed out to them that I should've also been one of the exhibits.

'Why you?' Alex asked. 'What's your record?'

'The most endurable female s-h-i-t eater in the world,' I said and he burst out laughing.

'What did you say, Millie?' Nensi wanted to know. I waved it off. 'What did she mean?' she implied of Alex, but her brother was still laughing. 'Hello-o? I want an answer here.'

'Just something from my life,' I replied. 'From my Believe-it-or-not museum.'

I went north with them, and east to Shoreditch, and deeper south. But once we'd visited the West End and the South Bank, the plays and musicals, all other destinations on my A-Z map blurred. Now that they were big enough, by my books, they could enjoy most of the musicals and Saturday matinees were the perfect show times for us. The older Grishins never complained about the price of the tickets.

'I had a great week with you,' Nensi would whisper and kiss me every Saturday night when I put her to bed. She was all her mama's daughter: unobtrusive, fair features, complete with strawberry blond eyebrows and eyelashes - not yet accentuated by Dina's clever make-up skills.

At home, Alex would immediately turn back into a *mega-gloomer*, as I called his 'home alias'. But he loved *me*, I could tell. They were my tools for making me feel better about myself, but also for discovering the corners of London I'd never otherwise go to.

I didn't want to own a mobile phone ever again in my life, so I called my parents once a week, usually on a Saturday or Sunday evening, before their beloved central news broadcast, from the phone booth on the corner of Oakley Gardens and Chelsea Manor Street. That booth was always empty, whenever I passed by it, and on its walls there were no pictures of monstrous tits on teenage girls to make me sick.

Before I'd call my parents, I'd usually go to the library in the nearby Chelsea Old Town Hall, where I could use a PC, check my mail and borrow a book - all this on Yola's membership card before I became enough of a Londoner to have my own card issued. The emails I received were from Elke. She wrote about her latest project in Montenegro, giving me some advice along the way, about taking up a voluntary job, an action that, in her opinion, would help me acquire the relevant papers for an indefinite leave to remain in the UK.

The conversation with my parents was more or less the same each week.

'Have you met anyone interesting?' my mother asked every time. 'Have you been to any funerals?'

I'd answer that no, I didn't meet anyone who then died on me.

'Pick a good funeral,' she went on. 'Have your hair done up. You'll meet serious men there. Serious men don't go to disco clubs.'

I wanted to tell her that I too never went to disco clubs; that I lived on the top of a tall building, next door to the red sign for deadly high voltage, behind a weakly lit window, beneath the airplanes and the low clouds that, like accursed souls, travelled relentlessly over this island. *Imagine, Mama, how far your daughter had to run away: to foreign skyscrapers with no balconies where people become invisible.*

But I never got to share it with her because every time my father snatched the receiver from her hand so violently I could hear the *swoosh* of it. My father wanted to know my financial situation and fast, without many pounds being wasted on meek phone conversations. On the first of every month my parents used to wire five hundred pounds to my account here. It was the rent that a Greek 'investor' was paying in Euros for living in my little apartment in Montenegro. But when I got into the third week of my nanny job, I told them to stop sending me the five hundred Euros for a while. I'd let them know if or when I needed that money again.

'So do you have enough money for now?' Father asked.

'Yes.'

'Good. Listen, I've been thinking: do not giggle too much with strangers and make sure you say only the nice things about your motherland. Don't try to impress the English with political gossip. Foreign visitors like our country, you know. And always answer a question with another question. People will have more respect for you that way. They'll think you work for Intelligence, you understand?'

And so, the Millie *Poppins* version of me settled down with ease. London seemed agreeable when framed by a routine, locally referred to as *structure*.

182

Contrary to my early expectation, I saw quite a lot of Dina. She moved soundlessly through the house and, once I'd fully mastered my job, she expressed herself mostly by smiles. She had days when she became quite bubbly: she held my hand with her cold fingertips shaped like a drop of water, and she talked about numerology, karma and even female friendships. I'd warm up to her only to find her uncommunicative and distant on the following day.

If Dina and Misha planned to go out, I babysat. That was paid extra, but didn't happen often. Dina didn't care much about going out because on the next morning a migraine would force her to rest in bed in spite of the piles of Dr Reddy's Sumatriptan boxes stored in the cabinets and drawers throughout the house. She claimed she was a 'creature of habit' and she had once informed me that the late nights shattered her aura. But twice a month, Misha would persuade her to buy a new dress and a new pair of stilletos and later he would say: 'Please stay tonight, Millie. We're going to Zafferano and Annabel's.' Always those two places; I guess they were Dina's choice, her part of the bargain.

Misha always got ready surrounded by the sounds of the National Anthem of USSR turned on to the maximum. The ghost of the communist revolution shook the Grishin house, if not the whole of Oakley Gardens. The drums, the trumpets! *Partia Lenina sila narodnaya*, he solo-ed above the voices of the Russian male choir. His gutty singing voice made me picture him standing on the bed, naked, his clenched fist high up in the air.

They never stayed too late and Misha always offered to drive me home. It was a short ride, one traffic light, over the bridge and there we were. At that one traffic light he deliberately slowed down several times, and waited for the red light, even if the green was on and the street was empty. He stopped and watched me sitting there, next to him, with my palms tucked under my thighs. He smiled and once he whispered: 'Relax,' and: 'So, what else is new?' The colours were changing on the windshield: red, yellow, green, red again, yellow, green. Red. I wouldn't return his gaze. Finally, he accelerated and crossed the bridge. In front of my building he kissed me on the cheek, without words, without smiles, with something like sad gravitas. I thought of a butterfly choosing a flower petal to die on. I sensed that Misha was worried, had problems like other people, or even bigger, because he relentlessly forced merriment to surround him.

Yola warned me. *Misha disease*, she called it. He had to be *loved*, she emphasized, by all the women he met. 'He'll try to seduce you, you'll see,' she said. 'But don't get excited. His wife never get excited. Keep your cool and only I will know is actually fear. And keep your cash coming. When you have enough cash, we buy you European passport for better work. Rafi has good connections for European passports.'

19

How London shines with gaiety on its first spring-like day. I remember feeling like anything was possible again, after a long period of darkness.

184

'Where's Dina?' Misha asked Yola and me on one such day, after breakfast, while he was standing by the fireplace and opening his mail.

'She's in the sunroom, with her Pilates teacher,' Yola said.

'Eh, I was hoping she finally went outside, with days becoming longer etcetera. This indoor phase of hers is starting to worry me.'

Misha had come down for late breakfast wearing only his boxer shorts and a white t-shirt and now, as he was talking to us, he lifted his shirt up to scratch himself absent-mindedly on the caramel skin of his stomach, covered by golden hair. I bet that, if I licked it, it would taste like *millefoglie* cream. I almost slapped myself on the face not to stare at the sight of it.

'So I was thinking,' Misha went on, 'I'd make a good old birthday party for my little Dinochka. Nothing crazy, no costumes, no male strippers. Venue – here. Theme – eat, drink and dance.'

'How nice,' Yola said. 'Is her birthday soon?'

'Mhm, very soon, so I need your help. I thought you'd be like an event manager for the night. What do you say? I don't know a better event manager than you.'

'I can be trusted,' Yola said.

Of course. Oh, and also, he had no idea who was going to prepare the canapés, the food in general, or the drinks, because Dina had said something about despising all the catering companies she'd come across, no originality, no imagination, and no taste. Scratch-scratch, he flashed his stomach again.

'I see what you're getting at, Misha,' Yola said quickly. 'You're getting at Isztvan - '

'*Da, da*, Isztvan for food and Rafi for cocktails,' Misha agreed. 'And if you could find another two persons to *serve* the guests? Is it okay to say 'serve'?'

'When you pay I guess it's okay,' Yola replied. 'How much you pay per person? Obviously, the chef gets the most. And the manager.'

'I don't know,' Misha replied. 'A million pounds?'

'No, really,' Yola said.

'It's not a problem, Yola, and you know it,' Misha said. 'I'd pay what you ask for. Isztvan and Rafi are good boys.'

'Your party problem is solved. Tell Dina about it, make her smile. For some reason, I think for her surprise party is bad idea. She needs to prepare.'

'Great,' Misha said and kissed both of us somewhere between our eyes and the bridges of our noses, said: 'Oops, sorry girls, must go brush my teeth!' and ran upstairs.

Later in the day he gave each of us a hundred pounds. 'For making Dina smile,' he said and added that surely I was going to come, too, and take care of Alex and Nensi.

Where else was I going to be?

'Eh, *vsyo harasho*!' Misha concluded.

On the day of the party we'd come to the Grishin house to prepare everything well in time, before the guest started to arrive. Isztvan insisted on cooking on the spot while Rafi was experimenting with his drinks and we were to taste them. Rafi positioned himself between the bar and the sink in the main kitchen. He placed his bottles around him, mixed the drinks, and asked from us to judge them. I liked his Bellinis and the lime-green Margaritas, and especially his cinnamon-vodkas. He brought along two bottles of his grandfather's grappa and Misha almost emptied one of the bottles while still in his bathrobe.

Isztvan roasted, fried, rolled and baked in the smaller but still professional-looking kitchen in the basement. 'Food *by Isztvan*,' the invitation cards said. His pride of the evening was something like warm Mediterranean sushi: asparagus or cherry tomatoes rolled into *risotto alla zafferano*. Then, the Italianised dim sum: zucchini, peppers and *melanzani*, fried with garlic, wrapped in the leaves of Parmesan pasta. The dessert menu was more Mitteleuropean: *Rozentorte*, made on the previous day, left in the basement to spend the night under a baking sheet and a pile of heavy books on top of it, for reasons known only to the chef. But, later in the night, when Dina sliced it and the guests tried it, it was gone in one minute. The dessert was going to be served with cognac, Fernet-Branca or pepper brandy towards the end of the party, after the Astrakhan creamy caviar and the Russian nutty butter and after the main course: caramelized vegetable roast, cut into the gift-like parcels with a bow on every piece.

At the party, I didn't see Dina touch any food, not even caviar, although it was she who'd insisted on the menu being meat-free. There was always a glass of champagne in her hand and the frozen little smile on her face. She looked sensational, almost naked in a powder-coloured wrap dress - Misha referred to it as

'Dina's skimmed dress' - which left no doubts about her serious investment in body toning.

Rafi had borrowed two Italian colleagues from the restaurant where he managed the bar and those boys were swift and smooth as only Italian waiters could be, well dressed and charming, too.

The children's music teacher had been playing on the pink Steinway for a while. I heard Misha say: '*Davay, davay*, why so sad?' to her, and soon she was replaced by the loud music mix: a whip that forced life to go on, go on in glory. I mean: *Rasputin,* to which Misha danced, blasted out of the loud speakers first. Then *Daddy Cool,* to which Misha danced again, carrying Alex (stiff like a toy soldier) and Nensi (squealing with joy and with only one silver shoe on) in his arms. Then *Bella Ciao, Echelon* and *Partisan Songs*! *I've got the Power, Big in Japan*; I guess there was logic somewhere in that crazy music-mix.

Surprisingly, apart from the hosts, there was only one Russian couple there. I would've never guessed they were Russians: they were tanned and lean and polite. Everything about them vibrated in the *coco-choco-rum* rhythm that I believed they were a pair of Caribbean jetsetters before I heard them speak their cuddly Russian language with each other. Yola promptly informed me they were Misha's birthday gift to Dina: the homeopaths from Moscow who were flown to London and settled in a nearby small apartment, so that Ms Grishin could always have them on stand-by. Also, they were the ones who ensured that, from then on, caviar supplies never ran dry in Dina's larder.

I'd persuaded Alex and Nensi to help out the Italian waiters and carry the trays of canapés around the grown-ups clustered throughout the house, but soon I spotted the children's half-closed lids and ear tugging, the symptom of bedtime moment. I packed them both into Nensi's bed and when they fell asleep I returned to the party via top terrace where I first went to have a cigarette and where I found Misha and half a dozen of other guests who also needed a smoke of something.

I loved that roof terrace, where the bushes of lavender, olive and fig trees were kept miraculously thriving by Dina's orders and Yola's labour. When I climbed up there, a crowd of smokers grew silent for a moment but then greeted me. I discerned Misha who called my name and motioned for me to come closer and join them. I did. He drew me next to him and introduced me to others not as a nanny but as Millie *of* Montenegro. By the sweetly puckering light of what looked like inextinguishable sparklers, the others seemed nicely eager to have me around although I doubted they knew on which continent my home country was situated. I was wrong. They knew a lot about it and what they were not sure about, they asked me. Before long, I threw myself into a political semi-argument with one of Misha's friends. Not an argument, really; more like a political rebus with no solution, the game I was tired of playing. It turned out that friend worked for Foreign Office. He disagreed with me that my country was run by criminals and claimed that there was nothing wrong with the sitting government of Montenegro; on the contrary, the opposition was unimaginative and lazy. And by the way, any political institution should appreciate the elected leaders of a country until they no longer represented it.

'Ah such tolerance, guildship, solidarity,' I said. 'A *laissez-faire* approach to dictators. Could I have one of your cigarettes?'

'Actually,' the FO man said, looking guiltily at the slim cigarette between his fingers. 'You should ask Apple here. I keep stealing from her.'

Apple was the nickname of the only other woman on the terrace. She introduced herself politely - 'Gemma . . . or Apple,' she said but Misha added: 'Our Lady Appleby' - and she offered me a cigarette. Apple had a physique of a Norse goddess and the richly curled blonde mane that went with it. She asked me to repeat for her what was it that I did, *again*. I said I was a nanny for Misha's children.

'Dina's a mad woman,' Apple laughed. 'What was she thinking?' Words crackled like sugar in her long teeth. 'Employing a good-looking nanny like you.' She poked Misha in his arm and laughed. 'Don't you think?' she asked the host. Her breasts were enormous and so smooth that I could almost see my reflection in them. She was probably my age, but seemed completely *aware* of herself, at peace with her sexuality, so *beyond* her pornographic tits.

'Our Ronnie,' Apple went on, pointing at the FO guy, 'thinks he can smoke my cigarettes without opening up to me. Come on, Ron, say what's on your mind. Those other governments, the government of Montenegro included, have such bad, bad reputations, but – don't they seem less autocratic, Ron, less ironic and more relaxed than our perverse democracy?'

'Perverse democracy,' Ronnie replied. 'A closeted term. We installed it wherever we could. Montenegro and the Balkans were the regions where we introduced our famous policy of willed ignorance,' Ronnie extinguished the slim cigarette and threw his arms up, gently. 'Democracy is perverse but a dictatorship? A different pitch. Take your pick, Apple.'

Lady Apple rolled her eyes at Ronnie.

'My husband loves your country, Millie,' she then said. 'We have a house there, in Perast. In fact, my husband wanted us to go there for Easter but he's broken his hip so I'm afraid that's off. He's older, you know, my husband is. Poor Pierson, though, stuck in that creepy Bay of Kotor . . .'

She lowered her eyes and sighed, lifting her magnificent bosom. There was a brief image in my mind of the Lady pushing her older hubby down the flight of stairs so that she wouldn't have to spend another discounted and wet Easter in Perast. But then I thought: Pierson?

'Would that be Pierson Paterson?' I asked.

'Well, yes!' Lady Apple exclaimed. 'You have met him?'

'No,' I lied. 'I haven't met him, but I know of him.'

'Ah,' Lady said.

Mishap pulled me closer to him and hugged me.

'You're a star, Millie,' he said as if I was some kind of a political performer, and he my manager. 'You're the real thing for all of them who want to go south to your parts and taste some perverse freedom in all those spooky dictatorships.'

'Just cracks me up,' Lady Appleby said, 'how Misha gets away with saying 'your parts'.

'Grrrr,' Misha said to her.

'Yes,' Ronnie jumped back into the conversation. He looked rather young, with nice features. His upper body seemed strong; I was wondering about him and Apple. 'Speaking about Pierson,' he went on, 'my father and Pierson's father worked together in the Balkans, except that Pierson's father considered it as just another job, while my silly dad fell in love with the Balkans, with local women, with the manageability of it all, the unfixable potholes in civilization as well as in the roads there. The *Balkotics*, he called it. Stay away from the *Balkotics*, he warned me. He had to be brought back to his senses, which left me rather crippled, career-wise."

'I better go inside,' I said, thinking of my mother's principal lifesaver: 'It's never too early to leave a conversation.'

Downstairs, where Isztvan took care of food and Rafi stood behind the bar, the guests were now hugging one another like close family members. Yola informed me that she had already given *her* phone number to most of the guests who had asked for Isztvan's, and that we were (she included me in that moment of happiness) becoming a serious catering-slash-party organizing company. We were soon to roll in cash, according to her mind, easily excited by business plans. Isztvan was called out of the basement kitchen, and cheered. He was too shy for that, so he blushed and smiled and ran back downstairs again, only to resurface a couple of minutes later, looking pale and shocked. Soon after, he went home.

After the party and back in our flat, the three of us -Yola, Rafi and I - found out what had happened 'when Isztvan went downstairs.' In the basement, he saw Misha, his hands on a wall, his *ding* filling the mouth of the crouching woman, half-naked and with big hair and huge breasts, while another lady sat fully dressed on a stool, smoking something and, seemingly, disinterested about the *bluejob* taking place next to her. Isztvan was so shocked that he couldn't move away from the spectacle and when Misha unloaded himself, the big-breasted woman opened her eyes and saw the freckled Hungarian chef standing by the kitchen counter, and she, with her tits still out, shamelessly said something like: 'I'm going to make your little chef famous.'

Misha zipped his trousers. 'Man, your food was perfect.' He said to Isztvan. 'I would marry you if you only had Lady Appleby's tits.'

Lady Appleby laughed and pulled her dress up, over her breasts and her shoulders. Then she cried at the woman sitting on the barstool: 'Matilda, dear, time to go back to the party!'

The Lady's command to her chaperone also worked for Isztvan. It snapped him out of his trance and he ran back upstairs to ask Yola for permission to leave early, before her.

'I don't understand Misha,' Yola concluded when we all heard the story. 'Dina looked so beautiful tonight. I couldn't take my eyes off her. Why doesn't he just do it with her, if he has his urges? Why does he need those married Englishwomen, too tall, too large and too . . . all?'

'But, there is no life in Dina,' Rafi concluded, adding: '*E una donna spenta, lei,*' and he and Isztvan exchanged a smile. Then they both looked at me.

'What?' I asked, opening a bottle of water.

'Your eyes are on fire tonight,' Rafi said. 'Who's lit them?'

'Oh, you lit them, signor *artista*, sure thing,' Yola cut in. 'Tell me, if you're so in love with Millie, why don't you marry her? She could use some proper European papers, you know? But don't charge her any currency, or you have to deal with me.'

Rafi laughed. 'Millie has to ask me first,' he said.

After a moment of almost complete silence, broken only by my gulping down of some Scottish bottled water, the conversation was safely steered to the inevitable success of the London's most sought after catering company the four of us were about to co-found. And then the three of them argued over the company's future name and I went to bed where I buried myself under the duvet and grinned myself into sleep.

All parties basically had the same plot, everywhere. Everything was perverse: democracies and dictatorships. Just a different pitch. Take your pick, Apple, that's right.

20

In Montenegro, during the spring of my night shift employment, I lived in fear, self-hatred, plans and dreams. I was anxious but arrogant, imprisoned in the awful version of myself. One day, on my way to somewhere unimportant and alterable, I passed by Darinka's

194

favourite café.

'Mila, hi!' I heard Bella's voice shout after me.

She probably called just to satisfy her curiosity. When I turned back and nodded at her and Darinka, she motioned to me to join them. I walked back to their table, but I didn't sit down. I just stood there, next to Darinka's chair.

'This is paradise, isn't it?' Bella said, checking me head-to-toe from behind her sunglasses. 'This weather, this youth, this freedom.'

'Rain will fall,' Darinka muttered in English, *in English*, looking away from Bella and me, towards the dark clouds gathering above the mountaintops. The First Lady was pretending I didn't exist, that moment wasn't happening, and only the rainfall was certain. I was staring at the baby-blond highlights on the top of her head.

'The only thing missing,' Bella went on, 'is the Starbucks. Dasha, we must bring Starbucks to Montenegro, don't you think so?'

Darinka said nothing, which didn't stop the businesswoman in Bella to plan aloud.

'Only, they wouldn't go for Montenegro alone, so we'd have to include Serbia. So,' Bella started counting on her perfectly manicured fingers, 'Beograd, Novi Sad, Podgorica, Budva. A goldmine! The epicentres of coffee drinking and socialising. A lot of good-looking, young people. Yummy mummies, too. Perfect Starbucks customers. They're going to *salivate* over this market.'

'No smoking in Starbucks though,' I said.

'We sit outside eight months a year here,' Bella

replied to me as if she was already presenting her business plan to the CEO of Starbucks World.

'Not in Serbia.'

'Ah, don't be a party-pooper,' Bella said. 'First, consider the pluses. And sit down, please, have coffee with us.'

'How's your charity project doing?' I asked, still standing.

'Well, when you left us,' Bella replied, 'it was stalled for a while. We took some time to find another girl as our PA. But, as I always point out: tenacity and perseverance, tenacity and perseverance. And now, I'm sure you've heard about our success with it, if you've been around at all since I've last seen you. New Year, wasn't it?'

'Yes, I've been around, Bella,' I said. 'And I didn't leave you. You dumped me.'

'*I* didn't dump you,' Bella said. She waved her bare, tanned and toned arm, a beautiful bracelet on her wrist clicking against an expensive-looking watch. '*Konobar!*' she called a waiter. 'An espresso for you, right?' she asked me.

Darinka turned her face to me. 'I dump you,' she told me in English, her eyes hidden behind the big black circles of her sunglasses. The effect would have been the same with her eyes visible. Her eyes never revealed anything but the bitter emptiness and all the battles she'd lost fighting it. 'You let me down. I dump you.'

'Cappuccino's good here if you tell them to make it *dry*, like martini,' Bella said to me, I think, and giggled.

'Your English has improved,' I said to Darinka. 'How

196

did I let you down? By refusing to let your brother rape me?'

Darinka switched back to our language. 'Look at you. I'm so embarrassed to be seen with you standing above me, the picture of death.'

The waiter was trying not to smirk.

'Ladies,' I curtseyed, 'thank God you exist. Makes me appreciate drinking coffee with friends.' I walked away.

*

In his Cabinet again. It had been a while. Whatever. His attention was what I needed. My raise never happened.

'I have five minutes for you,' Vukas said when I entered. 'So, how high is the level of misery? You know, the one you're on, now. On a scale from one to ten?' He held his right arm stretched over his neck and his left shoulder. In pain again.

'It's contradictory, your question,' I replied. 'The levels of misery don't go higher. They fall lower. So, mine is on, um, minus ten now, but if you give me my money I'll wind it back to zero.'

'I'll simply fire you. That'll wind you back to zero.'

'Was I invited here to be fired? No. You could have done that on the phone. Or by your epic silence. So, why am I here?'

'Darinka tells me you walk around town like an angry ghost. I know it's because you feel unappreciated. So here we are again. I miss you sometimes, Milena.'

'Are you that desperate?'

Vukas smirked.

'Well, yes, actually, but that's another story,' he said.

'What, with all the Senior Coordinators at your feet, plus a real Madame for the darker of desires?'

'I'll pretend I didn't hear that. It doesn't become you. My coordinators don't get that way. Rude. Unattractive.'

'Well, yes, we do. When you drop us. May I ask you something? Why's that, boss, why the politicians, once they find a country to ride, also have to ride every woman in that country?'

'Because we're in demand,' Vukas said. 'It's that simple. Not PhD thesis material, as you see. It's just because we can.'

'Thanks.' I meant it. 'So, what do you want from me this time, dear boss?'

'First of all I want to thank you. In your unusual manner, you did such a good job on Mirko. I must admit I didn't see it coming. But you squeezed him! Poor man, squeezed like a lemon. I almost miss him as a political opponent.'

'I haven't read the newspapers lately,' I said. 'Why is Mirko squeezed like a lemon?'

'You'll find out. He's made plans to leave the country, move to Italy, of course, where his family is. Of which you failed to inform me. Anyway,' Vukas opened his magic drawer, 'I thought I had your salary here. But I must have given it to Anka already. Anyway, the Euro notes still confuse me. Anka handles them better,' he sighed.

'Your shell is breaking,' I said.

'Says who?' Vukas replied. 'Joining the Euro currency is my latest victory. Now, Chris.'

'Chris, what?'

'Yes, exactly,' he smiled. 'Chris what.'

'You don't trust Chris.'

'He's too agreeable. For a Washingtonian. Work for your money, get me something out of him. Something I don't know.'

On my way out, I stopped by Anka's. I signed the reception of the envelope with my salary in it, without opening it, and avoiding eye contact with Anka.

'Use this cleverly,' she said to me. 'Go on a long holiday.'

21

The birds of Podgorica can be so loud, one wants to scream at them to shut the fuck up. My intention to sleep off another boring hot day was interrupted, but not only by bird-chatter: some voices were repeatedly shouting out my name.

I put my bathrobe on. I couldn't find the slippers, so I slid my feet into the pumps that were neatly placed by my bed. How handy; or, how feety. The black fishnets were cutting into my flesh, but I kept them on and went to the balcony. The night before, I'd celebrated God knows what with the crazy, local crowd plus Seka's imported slaves in the Blue Club, after which I passed out on my bed without taking off the fishnets and the red bra beforehand. I had to justify my latest 2000 Euros from the envelope with the golden-plated logo of the Cabinet, which Anka had so solemnly handed to me after my last meeting with Vukas. I partied hard.

When I looked down from the balcony, I saw my friends. And their offspring.

'Mila, we're coming up,' my friends threatened.

'Okay,' I said.

'We're bringing our children with us, even though you hate them.'

'I said *okay*!'

Before they could climb up with their screaming regiment of minors, I tidied up my nest a bit. I left the balcony doors and windows open because I didn't want their kids to have croup attacks because of the stale cigarette smoke in my flat – too much stress for a single junkie's Sunday morning. I emptied one ashtray, only so that we could re-use it. Ding-dong. Shit, no time to change. Well, who gave a fuck?

I opened the door and they poured in. My three oldest friends and their uncountable children, *what are we, Catholics?*

'Wow,' Vanja said, 'You wild woman! Are we waiting for somebody special in those stockings and *lingerie*?'

'No,' I said, 'What can I get you? Vodka, anyone?'

Well, at least I had friends that looked glamorous and respectful. Tanned, compact, no-nonsense. Anđa was a healthy sex-toy, tits, hips and ass in joyous expansion inside her white shirt and Capri pants. Vanja was a fertility goddess with chocolate-coloured hair, so well cared for that the top of her head shone like a halo and Dana looked worship-worthy in her coldish Catherine Deneuve, high-maintenance beauty. The secret spice to this description was the fact that they were all broke. They lived on their ordinary, three-digit monthly salaries, having no idea and no plan how they were going to put their children through to the level of education I knew they wanted for them.

At the moment, though, those children looked as if they might need something strong to numb them. Vanja ignored my question. Vodka with friends, on a Sunday, while surrounded by her precious children – that would be the end of her, according to her difficult husband. She was trained well enough to know better.

'I would love a drink, actually,' Anđa said, 'but I'm on a diet. Can you tell I lost weight? You haven't seen me in a while.'

'Vodka is a non-caloric-healthy-little drinky-minky,' I pressed on.

'Yeah, but can you tell I lost weight? I've been living on sage tea.'

'No alcohol for me,' Dana declared, 'I may be pregnant again.'

'What?' I couldn't help it; I had to spit some fire out, 'You're so ungrateful, you bitch! You have two kids and they are under five. And your mother is raising them. What do you need more children for? To kill your own mother? Or is it because Vanja has three? But she's had two husbands, so far. What's this – a childbearing competition?'

'Well, the Montenegrins will be extinct soon if we all don't have at least three,' Dana informed coolly. 'The Albanians will take over. They all have at least seven. The shepherd with most sheep owns the mountain. And we need to produce some more to replace the ones you got rid of.'

'You know what?' Anđa said. 'I'll have that drink.'

We were all still standing in the middle of my small

living room, which was quickly turning into a voo-doo nursery. The children were speeding around my apartment, throwing things, writing hieroglyphs on my soothing lavender-coloured walls. I hated myself for airing the flat for them; the cigarette smoke might have deadened them for some time. A couple of them ran from the balcony rail as fast as they could, only to stick themselves with their dirty little claws on my fishnets, clinging onto my legs like those blind and stupid flies caught in the web. I grabbed them and with the adrenaline-induced strength unglued them from my stockings, and threw them away from me.

'Little bastards,' I hissed, 'Go, play in the toilet! Auntie Milena will lock you in there.'

'Maa-maa,' a boy from Vanja's flock screamed. 'She's so mean. She's a witch.'

'No, she's not,' Vanja answered mechanically. 'She's not.'

'Yes. She. Is!' the little devil replied and jumped on his mother, hitting her chest with his little fists. Now, that's a breast cancer guaranteed, and she didn't even react. The motherhood seemed to have dulled their pain receptors, which in turn seemed useful.

'Why don't you beat them?' I asked.

'We do,' they agreed. 'But, they beat us back.'

'I believe only Albanians *should* have children these days,' I said.

'So, what did you make of Mirko's farewell rally last night?' one of them asked. 'Not very many people there, eh? And his message 'Boycott everything' had no power really, what do you say?'

'I don't do rallies anymore,' I answered.

'You're lying,' Anđa said, with an already empty vodka glass in her hand. 'Why? What do you mean you don't do rallies anymore? Where does it leave the rest of us? You must know something. What's going on? Did Mirko really sell himself then? Took five million and went west? It's all back to the one-party system then?'

'More vodka?' I offered, thinking I should've had coffee first, nervous now because the visitors had interrupted my morning ritual.

'What's going on?' Anđa repeated, staring at me, her arms spread apart as if she was about to hug me. The other two were standing around, waiting for my reply, surrounded by their children and my furniture.

'Are these children hungry?' I asked, hoping they weren't. There was no real food in my nest.

'Mila,' somebody said.

'*What*? Mila – what?' I suddenly lost it. 'When was there anything else but a one-party system here? And you really don't know?' I was shouting, 'You don't know I'm a whore employed as Vukas's coordinator? Well, let me be the one to tell you then: I'm A Whore! Happy?'

The children stopped their search-and-destroy activities and stared at me. 'No, you're a witch,' Vanja's boy said.

'Unfortunately, I'm not a witch,' I told him. 'I'm a whore.'

Dana quickly explained to her children: 'Now, that was a silly-billy joke. Auntie Mila is an interpreter.'

Anđa started crying. 'My life sucks,' she was sobbing

Anđa-style: the disgusting facts of life should be *her* privilege. 'It's a subdued life of the lobotomised Janis Joplin. I work for a ninety-year old Hitler clone, my husband is a balding teenager, I'm a wasted talent and my best friend is a whore.'

Vanja's mobile phone rang. She went out on the balcony to take that call. She always had to take the calls from her un-wed second husband, partner, *whatever*. Everyone's life sucked. Her son followed her. She finally kicked him away from her, back into the flat. He met my gaze. He decided to take his rage out on me. I was the one to blame because he failed to own his mother while she was on the phone. He grabbed one of the ashtrays from the table and hurled it at me. I escaped it, but it hit the opposite wall and broke into pieces, the cigarette fags and ash scattered on the parquet.

'That was such a bad thing to do,' Dana told him. 'I'll clean this,' she added, turning to me.

Vanja came back from the balcony. 'Oh, my God!' she yelled.

'Don't worry,' I said, 'That ashtray needed emptying.'

My hands felt heavy with ash; and smelly. Sweat rushed from under my armpits and spread all over me, seeped out from my earlobes. I bit on my dry cuticle and blood rushed out of it. Then I remembered the bag of peanuts I had in the kitchen and wanted it really badly.

'Remember,' I said to my friends, 'remember the crazy witch, Jovanka, the crazy witch woman who lived in Podgorica and we were all scared of her. She looked the same age forever. Where is she now?' They just stared at me. 'Her lipstick was always around her mouth, never on it. She walked the streets of Podgorica, munching peanuts.'

'Oh, yeah,' one of them said. 'Munching peanuts and spitting mouthfuls at people. Oh, my god! What about her?'

'Well, I feel like her now. I need a shower. I need to work. I must work. I'll be fine, I'll get back to you on . . .'

'On political situation?' Anđa said.

'Spot-on, baby, as always.'

After they left, I dialed Vukas, Mirko, Chris. Vukas, Mirko, Chris. Vukas, Mirko Chris. No answer, roaming, roaming, no answer, click – voice mail on, and - I'd be a moron to leave a message. Because, in the first place, I lost track of whose number's voice mail it was.

22

The long weekends of summer. One person's paradise is another person's hell. Chris wanted me to stay with him in the Pres Suite for yet another long weekend. I wasn't sure I'd get paid extra. Vukas wouldn't answer my calls. So I used my mother's illness as an excuse and told Chris I'd accompany him for the meals and afternoons, but I had to be with Mama during the nights. I said my father was away. I turned my father into a travelling businessman.

In the Pres Suite, Chris ordered room service after sex and sat in his bathrobe next to me on a chaise longue. He ignored my vodka-wish and ordered only red wine so I drank it, which was never good for me. I started asking him about business. 'Not your cup of tea,'

Chris kind of warned me.

'But business fascinates me,' I went on. 'Business and politics. Or the business of politics. Or vice versa.'

'Keep going,' Chris said. 'You're getting there.'

'Getting where?' I said and got up with a glass in my hand. '*Where*? I wish I could get anywhere. Oh, I hate this country.'

'Why?' Chris seemed genuinely surprised. And amused. 'You have a lovely homeland. Like an extended family.'

'Yeah, but our dad and uncles are abusing us. I hate them, Chris. And you were supposed to help. You're an *American*!'

'Honey,' he said. 'Don't let the heat make you edgy. It's a weakness. Accept the cycles. Cycles are what this planet is all about. Sit down here with me,' he patted the long chair and moved a little. I sat down. 'I help,' he went on. 'I help your country, don't you know? I love this country. Your country belongs to the belt of future. Our civilization will come back to its cradle again. The Mediterranean. And I want to be here when everything ripens and I can pick some fruit.'

'You sure sound well-Mediterraneanised. Only helping Vukas. And yourself.'

'And why shouldn't I? You people have been voting Vukas for your leader for what? Almost two decades? What makes you think he's a bad leader? Bodyguards, smuggling under sanctions, mistresses, cronies? We have seen it all in every single ex-communist country. Not to mention the countries torn apart by civil wars. Yugoslavia qualified in both categories, so the atrocities

206

were doubled. At least your president kept Montenegro safe and remained a civilised, smiling, co-operative, well-dressed, non-ambitious president. He has no territorial, racial or ethnic pretensions. He's so sensible. So we help him while we help him, right?'

'Whatever.'

'And as for me,' Chris went on, 'I'm here to make sure your country gets just the right amount of help from my country. Trust me, you don't want our intervention. We tend to mess up, but I know our limitations in foreign policy, oh, yes, I do, so I'm making sure you only get the sweetest and the best from the US.'

'Vukas is too loaded,' I said.

'So?' Chris said. 'Good for you! Wealth spreads easily in Montenegro, like influenza. He's the carrier. He touches you, and you all get at least a sneeze of it. Don't you? You have more than you ever had, right? It would be a different story if he committed crimes against humanity. Or if he threw rebels like you off the cliffs.

'Would it really?'

'Some people, and I didn't think you belonged in this group, like to make unnecessary fuss when everything goes well.'

'I want to go,' I said. 'I want to leave this country. I'd even go to Belgrade. Can you help me, write some references?'

'You should have done it when the war broke out,' Chris said. 'But if you're serious about it, I can help you.'

'I'm serious about it.'

'You are?' he asked. I nodded. 'Well, I'm not,' he said and laughed.

I hit him across his smiling cheeks with my open palm. He could fuck me, but he couldn't laugh at my plans, and play with them. The wine in me, my father's little girl, pushed my palm to his cheeks again. But that time Chris was alert. He grabbed my wrist and twisted it behind my back. Then he slapped me, very hard with his other hand. I spat on his face. He pulled my hair, twisting my wrist harder and harder. I tried not to make a sound but I was in a lot of pain. So, to release that pain but still keep the rebel-factor, I shouted: 'I hate you, shorty. You'll end up in jail.'

That made him angrier. He yanked and yanked my head, pulling my hair, so I wanted to hit back with words. I encapsulated all the anger and chemicals stored inside me and I aimed them at Chris. If I lost patches of hair, well, at least I gained more heart muscle.

He was hurting me in silence, with immense determination in his eyes, but when I said: 'Your fucking dead mother is spinning in her grave, ashamed of you,' he roared: 'My mother is *not dead*!' (I knew he had vampires in his bloodline.) 'You spoiled my long weekend, you, worthless person. You made me lose my temper. Are you provoking me? Is that the plan? Whose plan? Answer me! Answer me!' He was shaking me, shaking me like a rubber doll.

I felt blood moving inside my nose. Already, a few bright red drops fell on Chris's thigh.

'Listen,' I said, my voice nasal, creamy. 'I have something to say. Listen to me, please. You were supposed to help.'

'Shut up, you little slut,' Chris cried. 'Shut up and leave now or I'll call the police,' he pushed me away from him. He walked to the door and held it open for me to get out. I grabbed a napkin from the room-service tray table, pressed it to my face and left.

Where was I to go? Home, to cry there alone, again?

On my way to somewhere, I passed by the low houses of downtown. People were sitting outside in the shade, wherever they could find one. They were smoking, taking a nap or eating watermelon. I could hear the pleasant hum of water running from the garden hoses, cooling the patches of cement under people's feet.

I saw Viki, my clothes-seller cousin, sitting in her sun-burnt garden, surrounded by a handful of friends with stomachs swollen from gorging on watermelon. *Les Miserables*: that was what she called the lot of people she usually ate her take-away lunches with, most of them Viki's neighbours and childhood friends, unemployed, hungry. Besides feeding them lunch, Viki found day-to-day work around town for them; when she could, that is. When she couldn't, they had to move her furniture, paint her house, clean her front-yard, listen to her stories and voice their endless respect and adoration for her. Viki had her small village all figured out.

I entered Viki's garden and the squeak of the gate as I opened it interrupted the lot's dreamy hour of silent digestion. The sun moved a little and the twisted *košćela* tree offered more shade. Viki opened her eyes.

'Eh?' she asked me, not sounding too shocked by my swelling face and the bloodstained napkin in my hand.

'Don't ask,' I replied.

'Mm-hmm,' she moved her head from side to side. 'Please grow old already,' she said. 'And slow down.'

Les Mis opened their eyes slowly, one by one, like some toady species waking up in summer's sunset. They nodded at my face and Viki's wise words. She picked something from between her teeth with her long nail.

'Boriseeee!' She shouted without warning, as if dying from a spear in the battle. 'Ivooo!'

Some neighbours, the ones she hadn't invited for lunch, shut their window shades in protest.

'Where are you, sons?' Viki yelled. 'You're never here when I call. Better come running right now. I need toothpicks and Red Bull.' Then she relaxed and closed her eyes again. 'Please grow old,' she repeated and touched her head in pain. 'It's easier.' She was only two years older than me.

Her sons appeared with the items she asked for. 'Here Mama,' they said. 'Do you need anything else?'

'Not right now,' she answered and the boys ran back to kick ball in the burnt ground nearby.

'Smeško?' she asked me and raised her eyebrows at my swelling face.

'What? No. Just my nice American friend.'

'Now, that's what I call an Yves Saint Laurent love life. Not Rive Gauche,' she lit a cigarette meaningfully. '*Haute couture*. Why don't you move in with me for the summer, huh? Let's go spend some time on the coast.'

'Maybe. You have ice?'

'Maybe means you're so deep in it that you want to protect me. Oh, Mila. It's all just an illusion, you know.

No ice,' she added, getting up. 'Come into the kitchen with me.' I followed her. She was talking the whole time. 'Butter is better. I put it on my children all the time. Whenever my sons fall, they fall on the head. Then they go to the fridge and look for butter. Come to think of it, they don't know butter is food. Such is life. Please throw that bloody cloth in the bin. Thank you.'

We were standing in front of her fridge. 'But, I heard you were Mirko's little flame and that he'd left the country before you spread into fire,' she said, spreading butter over my face.

'I loved Mirko,' I said.

'We all loved Mirko,' she said. 'Montenegro is so boring without his hero-actions. But you know, he probably decided it was easier to take cash from Vukas and call it a day, live a little. I don't blame him. Now, you're staying with me for the summer. Go home and get you things before the soup you got yourself into has boiled over. We take a small holiday. Then, I will find a connection for you to go away for a while.'

In my flat there was nothing. There were the tapped phones; there were dirty clothes atop of Branko's gun in the laundry basket, and possibly a tiny camera, a chip, installed in my TV screen – Smeško's favourite device, probably grounded on humans' inclination to switch on the TV when trying to hide their vulnerability from the outside world. Most of my money I kept safe with my mother, so there wasn't even much cash around. Whose life was that anyway? The life of a mole.

Well, I wasn't going to drag Viki down into my hole. What I needed now was to secure another delivery of those crisp Euro notes that smelled so good and felt so warm, fresh from Vukas's bakery.

So I sat down at the dining table and wrote a report for my Boss. I decided to keep it short but strong, decorated with details that Vukas didn't know I knew. I wrote that I'd seen Chris that day, how we drank a bottle of wine each, and he opened up. I wrote that he seemed full of scorn for all of the President's closest partners, above all for Perić and Smeško. He called them 'the traffickers', or the Minister of Death and the Minister of Theft. He made comments about the President, about the country's institutions, which should all be turned into only one type of institution, where we should all be institutionalised, like one big, dysfunctional family, daddy, uncles, wicked stepmothers and all the rest; he seemed ready to leave Montenegro as his project altogether, after he'd finalised some all-inclusive Health clinic deal, from which he'd earn 2.75% of the total transaction sum to be paid on the account of Bella's Umbrella Trust in Switzerland. 'Sincerely yours, Milena.'

I phoned Vukas. No answer. I phoned Smeško. He always answered, good old Smeško.

'I have a report for Vukas,' I said to him. 'It's urgent, it's top secret, and I need at least two salaries. I want to go on a summer holiday.'

'You're always welcome to come aboard Perić's *Queen of Hearts*. She's a beautiful yacht. Such an elegant Mangusta. I think next journey is scheduled for next week. Sardinia.'

'Not what I had in mind.'

'I can come by tonight,' Smeško said. 'With some money.'

'Euros, please. And don't come up. When I see your car, I'll come down.'

23

By November 2002, it was clear: there was nothing left for me in Montenegro. Perhaps, a change of fate could still happen for a slightly different version of me; for a Milena with her diploma, her books, her childhood friends and family; a Milena, who could be allowed to polish the affairs of Vukas, flirt shamelessly, and, when proven worthy of the ruling cock, probably sleep with the President; who could have partied with Smeško, the Chief of State Security, who bought and sold trafficked girls for his side income; who could even have known Mirko in the way I'd known him; and Chris. But, it would have to be a Milena that *hadn't, and couldn't have believed she could sell partly*, keeping a sparkle or two of her spirit intact. I knew I had to leave Montenegro.

Many would have envied me, I knew that; the freedom to pack up and leave on my own, with money! Oh, count your blessings, Mila!

The girls who worked in the grocery shop beneath my flat brought up food to me every day. My mother visited and brought food. My friends sent regards, she told me. I hated all that and never had more food in my kitchen. I'd observe it for some time; then I'd throw it in the bin or flush it down the toilet. Mostly, I ate peanuts, my nails and cuticles. And smoked.

213

One day, I took a shower, put on some despicable autumn clothes, and went out, walked to Montenegro Travels, to leave my passport there for a UK visa. The US one was definitely out of question, with Chris now being my enemy. I wanted to buy a plane ticket to London while I still had some cash.

Years ago, under the UN Sanctions, when Montenegro Travels Agency was founded, a lot of my friends, my school friends, wanted to apply for a job there because that was an ideal way for them to see the world for a bargain. But they mostly only had a high school diploma and were unable to write their own resumes, so I did it for them and I lied, and I lied so beautifully. Oh, if only our motherland in reality had produced so many extraordinarily accomplished people as the accompanying applications, made by me, claimed – South Korea wouldn't stand a chance! They were all hired and I celebrated with them.

Now, when I entered Montenegro Travels, a young receptionist I didn't know, stood tall behind the counter.

'Can I help you?' she asked, looking photoshopped in person, in her cream-of-lilac uniform, its jacket unbuttoned and showing a crisp white shirt underneath, and the girl's perfect, ripe but firm, cleavage.

'I want to see a manager. Any manager, any head of anything. I probably know the person. I probably helped them get their jobs here.'

The girl smiled like a china doll. 'First of all, good morning,' she said, probably raised and educated by Latino telenovelas or American sitcoms, smiling her

214

lipstick wide, flirting with any gender. And beyond that – a new frontier spread, untilled.

'I want to see a manager,' I repeated and I smiled; the young bitch scored, she calmed me down with professional kindness, but that was fine. Who was I to compete with her? She had a nice job and tried to do it with decency. I was an old fool that everyone had taken advantage of.

A man I'd practically hired came to see me. Marso. A dropout from planet Mars. I'd forgotten his real name. He was always Marso. I told him I had to leave, now, tomorrow. Tomorrow if possible. Tomorrow.

'Tomorrow? You're crazy.'

'Yes I am.'

'I can't have your visa ready before our Easter package.'

I was shaking. 'Fuck it, my friend,' I said. 'There are things…I must go soon.'

'All right, after New Year, maybe,' he said. 'The visa alone costs hundred-ten pounds.'

'I'll give you the money. See, with my good reference the only way is up. What are you now, Marso, a boss here?'

Marso glanced at the receptionist-girl sideways; he was not a Marso to her. Also, he'd never graduated from high school, and I forged his *outstanding achievement* post-graduate report from the University of Belgrade. The girl smiled back at him. The ultra youth, pushing her way forward. Impossible to break her and see what was inside. A manual?

'Give me your passport,' Marso said.

I left my passport with Marso, and left Montenegro Travels thinking how the new, haggard look I was flaunting, the look of an ex-beauty-turned-cokefuck, had given me certain freedoms, like the freedom to beg for favours, cry in public, dial Vukas once more, wear sunglasses indoors in November. Liberated, I took the route straight through the heart of the town and the café area devoid of life at that hour. Who cared what I looked like, I, the woman of the world?

I was home again and my phone rang. It was Chris.

'I think I spotted you earlier today, in town,' he said.

'Maybe, baby,' I told him. 'I was the only drag Queen out there today.'

'Don't be so hard on yourself. Would you have lunch with me these days if you're not busy?'

'Why?' I asked.

'Business and politics,' he replied. 'Your favourite subject.'

I said yes, sure.

And so we met in that pizza place, and Sonja fell out of the sky on downtown Podgorica, I took her to the Safe House, left her there, bought a pillow as a donation for the Safe House, went to my place, was ambushed by Smeško, stuffed into an ambulance van and taken to the psychiatry ward of a hospital. But I managed to keep the pillow.

24

In front of the hospital, a doctor and some male nurses, known in Montenegro as 'hospital security', helped me step out of the van, then led me through the main entrance, by the night-guard's little cabin as he grinned at us, trying to hide the lit cigarette in the palm of his hand and I briefly wondered – from whom, who would prohibit smoking in all the surrounding madness? We turned left on the ground floor and walked through the thick door of the adjacent ward with no sign, no name to it. Behind the door, this ward was as quiet as empty, with the sanitiser-smelling corridor of linoleum floor and barren walls, at the end of which was my room. Once inside it, my keepers took off the handcuffs from my wrists and simply locked me up. I didn't resist. I was given the single room. I fleetingly enjoyed the sensation that I was a *political* mental patient, that they were afraid I would've organized a mutiny had they put me in one of the group rooms.

Mine was a tiny room with a narrow window secured by dense metal bars wrapped in wire (electricity-infused?) like in ivy, but I could see the sky, its darkness, and I could hear the large drops of rain hitting a tin roof above me. My rather tall, narrow bed had a mattress on, but no sheets; the mattress with the traces of bodily fluids from couple of generations back, I'd say.

I kissed my pillow and decided to sleep the situation off on it, keeping my clothes on, using my jacket as a small, leather blanket. To sleep, to rest, perhaps dream. While taking the jacket off, I was happy to discover that there was a pack of cigarettes and a lighter still in its pocket, so first of all I wanted to smoke myself to oblivion. As soon as I lit one up, a nurse stormed in. What was this now, Betty Ford's addiction-rehab? But, she couldn't care less about my cigarette; she came to check my blood pressure. I rolled my sleeve up and she tightened the Velcro around my arm and started pumping, while I was smoking. Who was the crazy one now? The ashes fell on the curious floor, wallpaper glued on (presumably) linoleum, a photograph of a Northern Adriatic beach, a shore of colourful, ill-shaped, aborted pebbles. I dropped my cigarette on the floor and it blended in; the slim trail of rising smoke showing where the cigarette's burning head had fallen, and I squashed it with the sole of my shoe.

'Hundred-five over sixty,' the nurse mumbled and wrote it down then looked at me with her eyebrows raised.

'Is it the blood pressure of a lunatic?' I asked.

'There's no such thing,' she said. 'But...' she stopped.

'But in your experience it isn't.'

'To me it only means you can be given your prescribed medication.'

'Which is?'

'Tranquilizers.'

'God is great!' I said. 'And I'm hungry.'

'After we've run some blood tests you can have a banana. Or some bread rolls baked in the hospital, nice and warm. You don't want the *kasha* supper.'

'Maybe I better get used to it now.'

I put her on my side, maybe just a little. I could see that. She clasped her lips together and tenderly blushed. She was no rookie; she'd dealt with all kinds of diagnoses. I didn't fit in.

'I'll make sure your bed is properly covered as soon as possible,' she replied, obviously deciding to help with

218

what she could.

'What's your name?' I asked her.

She gasped, swallowing an invisible ball of hospital air.

'I know who your mother is,' she said. 'They've filed you as unidentified, but you look like your mother. I remember when you were born. In this hospital. I remember. I was a midwife back then. When your mother had you – she was so happy, smiling even though it looked scary, because you popped out of her in the corridor before she could reach the delivery room – you didn't cry for several seconds and I was worried but she said that I shouldn't worry because you were born to be the first lucky one in the family. Later she told me about her firstborn. I will never forget her.' The nurse smiled and continued. 'Marija is my name.'

My eyes welled up. 'I never meant to hurt my mother,' I said to Marija. 'She's so unlucky with her children.'

'Listen to me,' she replied. 'Sleep first. I'll help you sleep long enough. I'll make your bed, cover it in the same bedsheets we nurses use for the night shift. Tomorrow we'll talk more.'

She left.

Five minutes later, here she was again, carrying bedsheets, topped with a banana and unpacked needles and phials.

'Tomorrow,' she said while taking her time with my vain, 'when doctor comes to see you, don't argue with him. Your file says: argumentative and dangerous. They want you to be so. Well, don't be.'

She filled five phials with my blood and put a cotton ball on my vein.

'There,' she went on and put some pills and a banana into my palm. 'Swallow these. See you tomorrow after lunch. I have to go, hope you don't mind making your bed.' But I didn't make my bed. Gobbling up that banana was the last thing I remember before sinking into a deep sleep.

I was woken up by a smell. It was the smell of the cleaning disinfectant and it made me sick; there was too much of it rising off the floors, laced with the fumes of discharges from the stomachs bloated by boiled vegetables, with the un-scrubbed crusts of vintage vomit, bad air, imprisoned among the blocked windows - I remembered that I was in a hospital. The square of grayish-white but crisply ironed bed sheets stood in the corner of my bed.

The cleaning woman moved freely through the rooms of the ward – a sweep here, a brush there; through my little window I could make out the light of matured daytime. Seemed that the cleaner was doing her after-lunch sweep. I'd slept well, on my pillow, under my jacket and in my jeans.

Marija entered my room with indifferent efficiency, smirked briefly, brought the lunch I'd skipped on a tray and disappeared. Clear soup, rice and a chicken leg. I craved chocolate, coffee, cigarettes. The ward sounded like a beehive.

'I deserve to be here!' I wanted to shout after Marija. 'This is no injustice! Don't be nice to me!'

There was much yammering, buzzing and zapping

behind my door, and also noises that sounded like hospital beds and chairs being dragged over the floor in the corridor. It must have been the part of day when the patients were given a bit of playtime. Their language was semi-foreign to me. I understood the words but not the sentences, not the meaning. The food on the tray defeated me.

As if she could sense my desperation, Marija appeared again and handed me two pills and two warm bread rolls filled with ham and cream cheese. I swallowed everything and sank back to sleep.

The doctor woke me up on the following morning, the same face from the ambulance van: 'Dr Novak Novaković,' he finally introduced himself.

'I know you know my name,' I told him. 'So why have you filed me as unidentified?'

'Is that how you feel?' he asked. 'Unidentified?'

His forehead formed two thirds of his face. It shone with a generous layer of moisturizer. Some droplets of sweat were glued onto it, like zircons. His tie made him looked stuffed, like a big game. He might have been good-looking once, but somebody down that family's line had descended directly from Frankenstein and it was going to show more each year.

I remembered Marija's advice not to argue. To Be Nice. I told Dr. Novak I wasn't crazy, just confused was all. And hungry again.

Of course not crazy, he replied. 'There are ways to channel anger. I'll help you learn those ways.'

I told him I was not angry, either. Just confused, and hungry.

'How would you call it?' he asked. 'Passionate, impulsive?'

'Hungry,' I snapped. I couldn't resist. 'What's it you're aiming at, doc?' There was no stopping me now.

He smiled with largesse, trained, his arms opened wide. Where was his degree from? On-line, California?

'Too much of unexpected passion knocks at the door and self-control flies out of the window,' he said.

'Which door?' I cried, ignoring nurse Marija's eye-signs to keep it calm. 'What window? Say it, doc. Say it.'

He looked at me with the 'You're proving my point right now' glance.

'Do you know about cognitive-behavioural therapy?' he asked. 'It helps one learn to build a bridge over troubled...'

'You're helping Smeško,' I cut in. 'I know what your game is. There is a reason out there for me to be declared insane, suicidal, responsible for . . . something.'

'Nobody makes anybody else responsible. Let's consider responsibility as Lesson Number One. No attributive errors from here on. I've also been trained as a reconnection technician. Now, that's a magnificent starting-over, with your cells reinvigorated -'

'Look, you Doctorstein shitface...'

Marija interrupted me. 'Doctor, please,' she said. 'She hasn't eaten anything and she clearly needs a certain period to accept...'

'I agree,' Dr. Novak replied although his face was swelling with livid determination. 'Milena, I'll see you tomorrow in my office for our first session.'

'You know my name!' I yelled after him. 'You know

my name, you pitiful apparatchik, you, *serf* with blood on your hands...'

Doctorstein's face was in my door again. He ignored me and looked at Marija.

'Why is this patient still wearing her clothes?' he asked with an ominous croak. His firlmly knotted tie was going to be the end of him, sooner or later.

Marija mumbled something and Dr Novak disappeared.

'You *are* crazy,' Marija whispered. 'I do hope you eat your next meal somewhere else.'

I sat down on my bed. She suddenly got up from it and left, not locking me up behind her. Was she coming back with food? Food and a couple of loony fashion items for me? Either that or she wanted me to go out of my room. I got up from the bed and went out on the corridor. People in the corridor talked loudly but stood still, leaning on the walls.

It was a small ward; more like a psychiatry wing put up together with the minimum of expenses and pasted, screwed, onto the main building, the town's hospital, like an artificial wing on a huge, sick bird. It was shaped like a wing, too: narrow, slate and long. The patients were put in here temporarily, was my guess, until it would be decided where to place them next: back home or further down the road to oblivion – which would be in the mentaldome by the sea. That mental hospital had been built by the Austro-Hungarians as a military base during their clash with the Ottoman Empire there, in the Bay of Kotor. Its catacombs were more elaborate than the Mensa's toughest crossword puzzle; I believed people could be transported to Siberia underground, through its tunnels. Buried too. But, for the time being I was still in my hometown, *my hometown*, and there was no way I'd let them take me underground.

The inmates seemed an unhappy lot, with bitterness so old that it had hardened their skins, turning them into the armour-plated, unlikeable insects, happy to hide themselves from the unduly judgments of the outside world. How could they be helped? As a psycho-wing rookie I could see why the pills were the only answer.

'Hey, who are *you*?' a youngish man shouted at me.

'I'm filed as unidentified,' I answered.

'But do you know your name?' he pressed on.

'Yes, I think I do,' I said in all honesty.

'Then you don't belong here,' the man concluded with the wisdom of an experienced inmate. His face was partly hidden behind the diesel-coloured, aquarelle-like smudge of hair, which fell down to his long neck, thin and pokey like a freshly sharpened pencil. 'If your name is not acknowledged by the registrar of the bat-house, you're an enemy of the state. You belong in prison. Didn't I tell you this before? But here you are again. Why?'

'You have me mixed up with . . .'

'Does it matter now?'

'So what should I do?' I asked.

'Well, this is good for your karma, but bad for you *en general*,' he said and dragged hard on his cigarette. 'Try to get out of here, woman. For people like you, this is a quicksand bus stop on your way to nowhere. Your

224

destiny lies in the hands of shadow authorities once your name has been deleted from the collective memory. I'm just an ordinary junkie, filed again under my proper name.' He whispered his name and laughed out puffs of smoke.

'I didn't catch that,' I said.

'Vissarion,' he repeated loudly. 'Vissss-arion. As in Josif *Vissss-arionovich* Stalin. It was my father who was crazy, obviously.'

'Vissarion Jovovich?' I asked him.

He nodded and bowed. 'Yours truly. Though I must add I forgave my old man when I discovered another Vissarion: Vissarion Belinsky, the mentor of Dostoevsky, the man who made him.'

I winced. Not because of Belinsky-guy. I was familiar with the name of the famous Professor Vissarion Jovovich, of course. I had no idea he was so young. Perhaps he just looked younger, arrested by his unusual spirit. No; he dyed his hair. A better look revealed its white roots, its cotton-candy texture. I used to devour his articles, his essays on the lonely, depressive genius of Montenegrin and other small, isolated literatures of the world. I stopped following his career after he had turned into a columnist full of praise for Vukas and the government gang, claiming they were liberal democrats who did wonders for the cultural development of Montenegro, but now, I was glad to learn that at least he had the dignity to crack up every so often in the dictatorship of which he too became one of the servants.

'Then you must know what you're talking about,' I said and headed for the entrance door of the psychiatry ward with as much determination to free myself as I could possibly gather. It took a Visarion to convince me I was in danger. It took someone with the journey similar to mine to mirror my progress into insanity or death.

Oh, Marija, where are you now? I just needed her to smugly unlock another door for me, and the rest I could do myself. I could push and hit any guard; I could run through the bullets! I only couldn't walk through the locked monster door, not yet.

But I was thumping my fists against it like a proper mad woman. That made everyone from the ward cluster around me. Someone from the other side was unlocking it. It was Dr. Novak, without a tie, in his white coat.

'Marija! Guards!' he started and, over his shoulder, in the hospital's entrance hall, I saw Vera and Elke standing, both of them holding their mobile phones pressed to their ears, while a couple of men in blue uniforms circled around the two women, without a clue what to do with them. The sight of it made me stronger so I flung myself at the doctor and went for his face and his eyes with my nails, calling him something bad once more. I managed to poke my forefinger deep into his eye socket which made him jump away in pain, and I was out, I was out, thinking how Marija was nowhere to be seen, how she was going to be fired or worse for her ducking out exactly at that right-wrong moment. I ran to the women who I knew were there because of me and it was all so clear – someone, probably Marija, must have informed them.

Vera walked quickly to me and she hugged me tight and yelled at Dr. Novak that it was not going to end there.

'You poor liar!' Vera screamed on. 'Calling yourself a doctor! You better quit your job here and ask your friends in high places to secure you a nice spot on the street to sell the smuggled cigarettes!'

Elke added some of her accusations about blatant, Medieval hammering of human rights by a *soul doctor*! In English.

Doctorstein disappeared behind the safe comfort of his kingdom's entrance door.

'Let's just walk out of here,' Vera whispered to me. 'My car is parked on such a bad spot, I'm afraid they've lifted it.'

Well, Vera's car was a huge, white, classic Landrover jeep-ster, sporting a UN registration plate and of course it was still where she'd left it, in front of the hospital's gate.

She drove us to the Shelter office, speeding, just for the speeding sake, I thought. Nobody was following us through the misty cool of the afternoon. A few people on the streets walked with awkward, involuntary steps, as if they too had just run away from a hospital, with nothing but fear and rheumatism on them. Surprisingly, there were no policemen anywhere.

Elke was sitting next to Vera and I was in the back seat.

I asked if it had been nurse Marija who informed them about me being locked away, and they said no, but that it had been a nurse yesterday who passed by them in the hallway and whispered an instruction to come back today, around lunch, which was perfect for them since they had to take Sonja to the police station that morning. Seka had been arrested and Sonja needed to ID her.

'So who had informed you about me?' I asked.

'Jumbo, your old school friend. Used to be Mirko's driver.'

'He said Mirko had asked him to look after you from time to time and so he was around when they came with Ambulance van.'

Vera then congratulated me on my forceful exit through the door of the mysterious ward and over the living *and big* body of the stunned doctor. She said if I hadn't done it, there would've been no way for Elke and herself to prove I'd been abducted and brought in there. Doctor Novak was one of the Smeško's men, through and through, claiming there was no woman they were looking for locked away behind the door of the psychiatry.

I said that it hadn't been too bad; I'd had a good rest on the psychiatry, slept through two days.

'You're so ready for the Safe House,' Vera said. 'So worn out by the outside world. Hamburger?' she asked and stopped her car by a kiosk downtown.

'Sure,' I said. 'With everything they have on the side.'

While I was eating a hamburger, I remembered the pillow I'd left behind. I felt sorry for it, as if I'd abandoned a comrade in a battle. According to some Montenegrin mouth-to-mouth glossary of fortunetelling, wasn't it a sign I was going to return to that place?

No more fortunetelling. I was going to be the maker of my own fate, from then on. A quiet maker, creator. And maybe the pillow was going to be useful, and lucky, for someone else.

25

We arrived in the Safe House and Sonja was there, sitting in the office, having a bad moment. She was recovering from the visit to the police station where she had to identify Seka, her master, from behind the ghost mirror. She couldn't.

She did try, gave it her best, and pointed at Seka once, identifying her as the woman who'd kept her in the locked up flat above the night club called *Hermitage*, that, yes, also the under-aged girl that everyone had known as Enisa, gone missing in the meantime, had been locked up there as well. But, that wasn't enough, she had to confirm it one more time, repeat it, and then Seka mouthed: 'You're dead' at the direction of the devil wall behind which she knew Sonja was sitting, and Sonja lost it; she lost it spectacularly. She sank into a breakdown.

Before the visit to the police station she had been only thinly recovered by the caring actions of the Safe House volunteers. Seka knew how to make Sonja regress into her slave, and it worked to the point where Sonja even lost her speech. All it took, according to Vera, who was there, was a Jack Nicholson gaze under all those hair extensions and one mouthed threat of *You're dead*. Sonja started mumbling in the mixture of Russian and Moldovan, at the same time scratching her anus through the fleece pants she had on, then rubbing her wrists where she'd been handcuffed by Seka many times; she was also trying to pull her lower teeth out of her gums. When she actually managed to pull one tooth out, Vera decided to take her back to the Shelter.

Vera was sure that Seka was 'arrested' and brought to the police station just for the short demonstration of the government's readiness to cooperate with the institutions that protected human rights. Sensational but short-lived, such cooperation had happened before.

Now, Vera felt guilty for not having listened to Elke's advice to wait until Sonja completely recovered. Vera wanted to strike iron while still hot, which resulted in Sonja's breakdown.

Sonja was sitting at the dining table, her hair raised up into a disarranged bun that looked like a flower losing its petals to gravity. She had an elegant neckline and a lovely, oval forehead above the heart-splitting cheekbones. Her eyes, her real eyes were gone forever; she acquired a pair of new ones that really looked second-hand and shifty, and would never reveal anything. She was talking, fast, mostly in our language. Nobody, not even Vera, could out-talk her. So everyone else in the office let her talk while looking at each other from time to time, wondering what to do to help her pull through once more. It was evident she trusted no one, so I was hoping she wouldn't see me, which might throw her deeper into her pit. But she did, she spotted me, she could see everything, the destructive force of the underworld had been plugged into her brain, and she was like a devil scanning the scenery for signs, even

230

though she was a good person; I could tell she'd been a good kid, a good pupil, the broken film roll of her previous life showed from under the skin on her oval forehead, she used to know the answers and timidly raise her arm in front of the class to please a teacher – those were her triumphs – in a school.

What was she saying? She needed to rest, everyone must let her rest, she was repeating that like a chorus line. In between, she informed us how ignorant, *ignorant* we all were, thinking that we could win, ha ha ha, she laughed.

'You will all be killed,' she said, but *she didn't care*, because nobody would let her rest, gynecologist yesterday, hurting her too, well, she wanted to stay in the hospital to rest, but no, these women wouldn't let her stay, they thought they were so clever, protecting her, and then they shoved her into another taxi and then to the police station today, from one car to another, they were just the same like those other ones and she only wanted to rest. She was scratching herself all over her body, stabbing at her scalp with nails. Her bun fell apart.

Everyone here just needed political points, she claimed, and now she became a political issue - well, *stupid cows*, the Muslims in this country won every single election for your government, all the campaigning – so useless. 'Suicidal,' she called us, 'that's what you are.'

And, no-no-no, she didn't want to go upstairs to the *stupid House* and listen to those silly stories of those women who ran away from their husbands and took their children, their noisy, misbehaving children along, why didn't they leave those children with their fathers who at least wanted them?

'Let her talk,' Vera said to nobody in particular. 'She didn't talk for four years.'

'Do you know what they did?' Sonja was screaming now, hissing through the gap left after she'd pulled her tooth out. 'You want to know what they did? They hypnotized me to kill a man and I don't even remember it, but they have the photographs of me kill him.'

'You didn't do anything,' Vera said. 'They wanted to keep you bound up in guilt. They made it up.'

'No-no-no, listen to me, woman. There's a photograph where I'm standing above this dead man with a gun in my hand. They showed it to me when I was hospitalized in this loony ward for a treatment. They said I was lucky not to end up in prison. Apparently, Smeško still liked me a little bit so the hospital was going to make me feel better about myself . . . I almost believed the doctors. But Seka came to visit and I saw it on her face. She wasn't satisfied. I wasn't earning her money, her clients were disgusted by me, afraid of me, even. I knew she was going to end me, pick me for their game. . . Killed by fucking, this game they planned. And Smeško . . . he stopped loving me too, started looking for someone younger. I saw it in Seka's eyes, her business dilemma: was I to be killed by fucking, or, would it pay more to have me sold to Albania for organs? That's money in an old whore like me. Seka snatched me out of the hospital. Nobody could stop her. She has something on everyone in this country.'

'Not on us, she doesn't,' Vera said.

232

'We must find Enisa,' Sonja whispered. She attempt-ed to get up, but collapsed back on the chair. 'They can do everything. They have doctors, astrologers, fortune-tellers, people from all around the world helping them with energy. They're going to do something bad to lit-tle Enisa. I know it. Nobody needs her now when she's mad and maybe pregnant.' Sonja looked at me. 'They're not gonna let *you* go. You're one hundred percent hos-pital material, and why? You had your passport, you had your freedom, they pay you, why you get involved in this, why you bring me here, why you keep coming? Tell them how much I need rest, tell them, *bitch*.'

I shivered but not because of Sonja's calling me bitch. That was just her channeling Seka. I realized that had I missed the moment when I went for Doctorstein's eyes with my claws, I'd have been hospitalised and treated till I'd become the next trafficked item, prob-ably lobotomised along the way. Or killed by fucking.

'Sonja's not safe in another hospital,' Vera was ada-mant. 'Just like you weren't. She knows too much and is obviously very clever. I don't want to have her on my consciousness. She will be like this for a couple of days.' Vera sighed and sat down next to Sonja and hugged her shoulders.

'How did she manage to escape?' I asked.

Vera told me that after another Chivas-bottle-fucking and cigarette-stubbing party, Madame Seka had brought her girls back to the dungeon she kept them in, locked the doors and grills behind her and left. But Enisa couldn't sleep. She was having a complete breakdown, albeit a cheerful one; claiming she was pregnant with someone she called her Blue Angel, she was torturing other girls, waking them up to tell them about her immaculate conception. The girls yelled at her and some of them beat her up. Enisa, afraid she'd lose her unborn baby, screamed her head off. The security guard of the club *Hermitage*, Seka's employee, Seka's club, situated underneath the room with girls, phoned Seka and soon she re-entered the dungeon, cranky, still drunk, and with the intention to kick some kidneys and handcuff all the girls to the radiators. When she came in, it was loud inside, and chaotic and dense with cigarette smoke and Seka lost it and forgot to close down the grills behind her. And while she was threatening to kill and torture Enisa and the rest of them, Sonja saw the chance and she stood up and ran, pushing Seka violently on her way outside, jumping from the terrace above the Hermitage club, disappearing quickly in the snaky streets of the Old Town.

'I m so proud of her,' Vera said. 'After years of torture and humiliation, to actually recognize a chance for freedom, to see an open door. It's very rare, you know. She's intelligent and brave. She must testify.'

'I'll be honest with you, Milena,' Vera went on. 'I wanted to use you, too, to testify. But *she*,' Vera screwed her eyes in Elke's direction, '- I don't want this translated to her so let's not mention names - *she*'s great but sometimes so easily intimidated by the authorities – she persuaded me you'd be better off sent away, helped in that way, than used as a victim-witness. She thinks you should be trusted to find yourself again without being labeled a victim. Whatever. Perhaps *she*

234

knows something I don't. Anyway, *she* knows about your travel plans -' Vera was constantly rolling her eyes or jerking her head in Elke's direction; it was obvious we were discussing the ever-focused Scandinavian, but Vera couldn't even pretend to pretend. Vera had been so calcified in her crusade that all the lesser aspects of life, like diplomacy and compromise, were a waste of energy.

'*She* knows about my travel plans?' I repeated.

Before Vera could answer, Sonja, as if shattered out of her meditative state by an awful premonition, cried: 'You're dead!' into my face. 'You're talking to a corpse, Vera. You, headless chickens, all of you!'

'Do you have music here?' I asked. 'Any kind of music?'

'We have a radio,' a young woman said.

'Find some music on it and she'll feel better.'

Somebody turned on the radio and the newsreader's voice cut through the office air with the announcement that the Montenegrin Madame had been arrested. Sonja giggled then folded over her knees in pain.

'Seka is still in jail,' Vera said, patting Sonja gently on her back, 'and someone is above Seka in the human trafficking network and that someone must go to jail too. We all know who it is, but Sonja needs to say it. Not now. When she's ready. We'll wait. We have time. We'll keep Sonja alive and take care of her health, and wait.'

Finally, the sounds of music filled the office. Sonja didn't get up to dance, but the line of her shoulders straightened back; she grew quiet and allowed her eyes to close, recuperating in the room filled with music.

One of the Shelter volunteers suggested that Sonja should be given a tranquilizer.

'She refuses to take any pills, even the painkillers,' Vera said.

'But...' the young woman went on, '*Bromazepam* pills, do they work if crushed and mixed into tea?'

'We can try.'

'That never worked with my crazy husband,' another woman added.

'Your husband was conveniently crazy, but actually just a bully,' Vera concluded. 'Sonja needs some respect.'

I had a cup of coffee with some Shelter-made *princess* cream cakes while the radio was playing. With my jacket on, I was still shivering. A warm bath seemed like a lottery jackpot.

'When can I go home?' I asked no one in particular.

Elke turned to me from where she was sitting and writing down her notes. 'You want to go home?' she asked. 'Was that what you said?'

I didn't want to appear ungrateful so I answered that I was just wondering about the plans concerning my situation.

'That's fine,' Elke said as softly as she could. 'But Vera and I don't think it's safe for you out there. You can go to your flat with me, take the things you need. In fact, best we do it now, while there's still big confusion at the top.'

Vera said she would drive us.

'Bye, Sonja,' I said to the pretty girl, lost in music. 'I'll see you soon.'

She opened her eyes and looked at me. 'We're not so good-looking in daylight,' she said.

I bent down and kissed her forehead. 'You're beautiful,' I told her.

In front of my building, Vera kept the car's engine on, in case we had to speed away again. She would've loved that. Elke and I went to check on my flat.

Smeško had been digging around my place, looking for anything dirty to destroy me with, but still the apartment didn't look too bad, too messy; it was not a crowded one to begin with. Elke seemed to be familiar with it; she promptly opened my freezer, took out the *Pushkin Blues* and sat down in my kitchen with the bottle in front of her.

I went to my bedroom and checked if some of my cash was still there. Yes, there it was, in the pocket of an ugly jacket I never wore, a small but meaningful pile of money, compacted into the plastic bag for deep freezing.

In the kitchen, Elke fired another shot down her throat and swiftly got up.

'Ready?'

'Yes.'

'Make sure you pack well. Like, for a longer stay, a trip abroad, UK?'

'How do you know about it?'

'From a mutual friend,' Elke smiled. 'Calls himself Pierson Paterson. Asked me about you just the other day, when we spoke on the phone. You'll get a nice, long visa for the UK.'

26

There were only twelve other passengers on my flight. The direct line Podgorica – London had only recently been introduced and, like with every novelty, it took time for people to start trusting the smaller, local company, and use it for travelling instead of the Serbian, or ex-Yugoslavian one, JAT, whose fame and reputation had been passed on from generation to generation.

Nobody was sitting in my row of seats, so I went across the isle and looked through the window on the right and I was very impressed. I only had to move two seats to the right to see a picture of a completely different country. From the window on the left, Montenegro looked Mediterranean; from the opposite side window, it looked like what I, who had never travelled outside my home-country before that April Fools day, imagined Iceland to be.

While the sun was shining from my left, what I gazed at beneath me on my right was the Skadarsko Lake and the pile of fog descending on it apocalyptically from the surrounding mountains. Framed by the airplane's window, shaped like an icon, the view could have been a one-off masterpiece by an unknown artist before he (probably) committed suicide. The narrow, funky highway fought its way through this oppressive scenery with infinite élan, one branch of it turning to Cetinje, the town locked in the mountain range like a beautiful bride in the grey *kula*. It was raining in Cetinje, of course. I could see the two small, cone-shaped twin hills bulging out of the lake. Some crazy

238

man from Cetinje had christened them 'Sofia Loren's tits' once and they are known by no other name to me.

Tits and ass, tits and ass, and passion and flash and sweat and blood . . . I had to find some peace. Elke had said she didn't want me to seek an asylum in the UK. She wanted me to find my way differently; she knew I could do it. Between chaos and despotism, she thought I should choose chaos that time around. The chaos of freedom. And then she asked me if I had saved any money. How much? I lowered the sum for a couple of thousand of Euros – finally used my father's advice to never share the amount of money I earned with anyone - but still she was impressed.

'You must leave,' she said. 'At least for some time.'

Elke voiced her conviction about my leaving Montenegro one evening in December, in the Safe House, after we'd watched the news together. Not just Elke and I, but all the protégées of the Safe House, plus my mother who came to visit every day and brought food of course – we all watched the 19:30 news together because it was our gather-together hour, a way to sum up the day before going to bed. Although it was December, Elke was still walking around barefoot. While watching the news, she took off her Birkenstocks and popped her doughy, yellowish-greenish feet up on a chair. Often, she fell asleep like that and we woke her up later and she just spread herself on a divan and asked to be covered by a blanket, a coat, whatever. Elke and Vera paid little attention to me, which was fine. They spent most of the time bringing Sonja back to normality, preparing her to testify against Smeško as a victim-witness. Sonja bounced between small ups and deep, deep downs. But, she was getting a bit better every day, sleeping and eating more, and she gradually stopped scratching herself all over and pulling out her hair or her teeth.

On the night when Elke said I should leave my country, the main news broadcast started dramatically. While the panicky theme music was still curling in the background, the speaker cried out the breaking news: 'Earlier today, in Podgorica, a sixty-three-year-old American citizen, Chris Bernard, was found dead in the park near Gorica Hill Road.'

I was glued to the couch, my feet in my mother's lap. She was massaging them, gently.

'Chris?' I mumbled and tried to move but couldn't. Elke put her own feet down from the coffee table and slouched toward the television. She understood bits of our language.

'Tragedy,' Elke said.

'It can't be,' I said.

Chris was labeled as 'a controversial lobbyist and business consultant.' That adjective, *controversial*, was a death sentence when used on the state news. And when a 'controversial' person was already dead, the adjective meant 'he had it coming and who really gives a shit?'

Out of nowhere, a once-smiling Papa Chris's face covered the screen. I dropped a tear. Elke mumbled something.

The police made no official statement; they were searching for the weapon and the motive. However, one member of the police, who wished to remain anonymous, believed that Chris Bernard was supposed to meet up with somebody very close to him who lived in the area. Elke turned to me. I lived in the area.

'Bullshit,' I said, angry now, with Chris, mostly, with dead Chris. What was he doing there, next to my building, a desperate American lobbyist? 'I have an alibi.'

Other women, including my mother, but excluding Elke and Sonja, laughed at what they thought was some crazy kind of joke of mine.

'Good for you,' Elke replied. 'Because that's the park next to your building, right? And you were probably the last person to see him alive.'

'They will say you wanted Chris dead,' Sonja said. 'They never liked you being so friendly with him and now they will use it. Jealousy, passion, drugs. Murder. They probably have the photographs they can scatter around.' The laughter in the room was subsiding.

'Oh, Mila . . .' Mama started.

'But I have an alibi.'

'From us?' Sonja smirked. 'But we don't exist outside. We don't exist.'

The gun, I thought. Stupid Branko's gun! *They were looking for the weapon*. Smeško had it. My fingerprints were all over it. Smeško probably still had the report I'd written for Vukas; and my mobile phone, too. And Smeško could do wonders with mobile phones. Smeško, the unsympathetic reptile, was also a technology-wizard.

From then on, on daily bases, the press was going wild with the titles like: *The foreign affair, Business and pleasure,* or *There was a mysterious Miss of*

Controversial Chris.

Controversial, now it seemed, because he was found out to have been close to the high-ranked members of Serbian KOS (What, KOS still existed?), as well as the undercover agents of 'foreign intelligence'. My name was still not mentioned; only, everyone who'd ever known me could've guessed it from the hints. I was silent. I started having vertigo attacks. Vera wouldn't let me go out because, she said, I was behaving like a guilty person. Well, wasn't I guilty? Didn't I provoke Chris's murder, with my stupid report filled with lies?

Elke came up with a daring plan.

'Get ready,' she said to me one morning. 'We have a meeting with the president and you're translating.'

Both of us were dressed not to impress: Elke in her Birkenstocks, a woolly coat too small for her, and a khaki-coloured, shapeless skirt, and I in my jeans and leather jacket, and trainers. In addition to this – there was no appointment scheduled. Elke had planned an ambush. We let the security men search us, but Anka sure looked ambushed.

'I . . . sorry,' she said getting up from her chair when she saw us, but Elke yanked me forward and in two strides we were by the door of Vukas's Cabinet. She knocked twice and pushed the door open. Vukas was in, on the phone.

When he saw us he smiled and motioned to us to sit down.

'Tell Elke I'll finish this soon,' he whispered to me. In a moment he put the phone down and said: 'Miss Elke, very velcome! Nice surprise, no?'

'Indeed.'

'Milena to translate?'

'Yes, please.'

'What brings you here today, Miss Elke?'

'Mr President, I have immense respect for you. I've gotten used to you being the only one in this country who can solve a problem. In the Safe House, where I'm currently staying and helping with the funds, we have Sonja and now we have this lovely woman, Milena here. A lovely child. If I had a daughter, I'd want her to be like Milena.'

'Of course.'

'Now, she and Sonja . . . They've both been through a lot, don't you think?'

'Go on, please.'

'I know that this foolish plan to point at Milena as the main suspect in the murder of Mr Bernard was not your idea. I've been around long enough to recognise the hand of Mr Berković. Milena needs help, but not with the law. She needs other kind of help and I'm prepared to help her. She should be nurtured and made stronger and then she should go away. Please don't stand in her way.'

'I am the one who always wanted to help Milena, too.'

I was just translating, like a machine. When Vukas said he was the one who always wanted to help me, I just translated it, without a grin, without a beat. That was how much I wanted to leave, I guess, to become someone else.

Vukas promised nobody would stand in my way.

Then he changed the subject to Elke's project she'd informed him about some time ago. Her seminars on Gender studies. He said he knew of a cottage in Ljuta, a coastal village Elke had fallen in love with, that she could have. It was only up to her to refurbish it. Elke's hard eyes softened. Her dream, her Mediterranean dream, smoothly coming true.

'Take good care of yourselves, ladies,' Vukas said in (better than ever) English as Elke and I were walking out of his Cabinet.

'*Dobro, dobro*,' Elke replied, grinning and waving her arm.

I turned around to look at Vukas one more time. He was writing something down in his monogrammed Hermes agenda. One day, someone should steal those leather notebooks of his. But what would someone find written down on the silky, faux-recycled pages? Probably a bunch of plans to: take vitamins and amino acids; schedule more massages; do an MRI; send Anka to the dry cleaners.

Those were our president's real tasks that needed planning. Everything else was pure fun. Power games, the primal kind of fun.

It was a successful meeting. The murder of Chris Bernard and the investigations that followed fell among the side news and then disappeared. Still, every aspect of political life in Montenegro called for serious action, so Vukas took none. For New Year holiday, he travelled somewhere foreign and came back sometime in February, for the Mimosa Festival, the carnival time.

I spent the whole winter in the Safe House where I

made myself useful by helping Sonja out. Working on Sonja's recovery was helping me ease my guilty consciousness. Did my report kill Chris? I stopped wondering about that only when I kept myself busy alleviating other people's tough times. Sonja had to repeat every horrific and miserable detail of her story to so many listeners until there was no other solution for Vukas but to force Smeško into retirement and then to lock him up during investigation. My visa came through and I had to go.

On April Fools' Day I was off to London, the jungle, the mutating city with million upon million of unidentified heads, like layers of human bricks, all of them wanting to take some time off, move South, to Montenegro maybe. Elke warned me that London life was glamorous only for the super-rich, and even they dreamed about escaping for a while to countries like Montenegro, where they could sit on a sunny terrace, drink and smoke, while the voices of neighbours speaking in a foreign language bring no urgency, only help them digest life, like a glass of old cognac.

And here was I, flying north, turning my back on a simple Southern beauty to which I belonged.

27

A couple of weeks after Dina's birthday party, everywhere I went, I saw suitcases: zipped up, placed by front doors and ready to go. It was Easter break and everyone from my small social net was getting ready to go to some European destination. My flat-mates were off to visit their families in Jaworzno, Fregene and

Szogliglet, and my employers took their children and Dina's mother for a three-week holiday in Lake Como, where they had a villa. They'd asked me to come along, but I didn't want to take risks with a glass-legged UK visa in my passport.

Loneliness crept back in. It was like a punishment now. The summer before that Easter, I'd been alone in London; I'd been a confused, mute new arrival, expected to feel like an outcast. So somehow it was justified then, it was fine. Now I noticed different things on my walks: empty bottles of alcohol lined up along the pavements that were blotchy with traces of vomit explosions; a lot of generous portions of well-sculpted dog shit; on a cloudy day, the town smelled of garbage and piss; people howled and spat on the streets. That reminded me of the worst days in my hometown, during the war, when my countrymen became animals. But even then, they had dignity to drink and howl inside their flats or taverns, above the sounds of turbo-folk or the news broadcast, and only a few most despicable of cases allowed themselves the awfulness of being sick on the town streets. Like me, for example, after the night with Chris in the Presidential Suite.

I felt as if my small London community hadn't simply gone away for the holiday, but had abandoned me as a kind of shock therapy, which was supposed to teach me a lesson, or punish me for having entered their lives too easily. I thought about my mother, how she used to say: 'A stranger's hand can't scratch one's hives,' and pull me close to her while smoking above the boiling soup; she was the only person who truly loved me and I found her boring more often than not.

In a moment of clarity, I decided I needed communication, a good purpose to leave the flat. I needed to establish a kind of domesticity here or I'd keep on beautifying the life I so voluntarily had left behind. I remembered Elke's email about the centre for immigrants - conveniently situated in Chelsea Old Town Hall - that asked for helpers. Elke had advised me to apply and volunteer there. She thought it would improve my chances of acquiring a permanent leave to remain in the UK.

But volunteer to do what? My knowledge of the world was limited and twisted. How was that going to prove handy for anyone? I felt awkward and sure that the employers would see me through and consider me lost for humanity. It's not only me; all my countrymen, the south Balkan*oids*, felt like suspects when faced with any kind of authority. Our reputation, bad as it forever had been, was made worse because of the last civil war. To apply for a job or a visa in any country was an ordeal, a thorough investigation where we felt as though we, innocent in particular but guilty in general, had been put on a trial. Yet it cost nothing to enter the Old Town Hall and instead of turning left, to the library, turn right – to the Citizens Advice Bureau (not Centre for Immigrants, Elke!) and offer my time for free. I applied to volunteer, armed with the recommendation letters from Elke and Vera, the Safe House manager.

The next day, I received a phone call from a woman who asked me to come and see her for an interview. I went back to the same office to see her, telling myself: 'You'll be fine; you're coming to give, not to take.'

After the short conversation, the woman, Gloria, her nametag said, sat on, rereading my CV and the two recommendation letters. I knew what they said: lies about me being an invaluable contribution to the humanitarian work concerning women and children of Montenegro. And that I was trained to help them. Maybe so.

Gloria knew Elke, and she knew Montenegro: she had been a guest speaker at one of Elke's already famous seminars on Gender studies in Ljuta, a tiny, panoramic sea-side village in the Bay of Kotor.

Gloria said she could put me down as an exchange volunteer, who came to London on a career leave. A career leave? Yeah, right; I almost patted myself on the back. I had to love London though, where my past was being promptly reshaped to fit the feel-good requirements of the moment.

She also said I'd need at least six months of training to be able to sit in the office. But, I'd make a lovely receptionist. How about that? She'd need me there on Saturdays to just keep the Bureau open and make notes about visitors and queries. And could I start that immediate Saturday, at ten a.m.? Well, of course I, a dream volunteer on a career leave, could! We thanked each other very much, till Saturday, bye-bye! I went to kiss her when we shook hands but she stepped slightly backwards, and my kiss, like a small draft, lingered in the air between us, which smelled of disinfectant and ancient cardboard boxes. Exhausted by too much of starting over, I smiled and left.

So I was to sit in the Citizens Advice Bureau on Saturdays, keep an open door for everyone who had nowhere else to go during the tricky weekend days when it was difficult to find help; for women and men who needed papers to work or not work, who wanted to divorce or marry, had complicated questions about their rights here, had even more complicated debt issues they wanted resolved for free. We couldn't resist, the clients and I, and we talked about things, and yes, I listened and learned. Approximately half an hour later, when all of us felt a bit better, I'd finally admit that I could only schedule them for another appointment with a more relevant Bureau employee. But they seemed to like me, especially since I wasn't itchy to leave the office at twelve-thirty, and Gloria asked if I could do the same thing twice a week, and added a Tuesday, another day when the Bureau was usually closed. I said yes, of course.

28

In the last week of April, my people came back to me.

By that time I already felt like St Millie of London's immigrants. Yola said my volunteering had changed my posture and that she was proud of me.

The Grishins came back from Italy accompanied by Babushka, Dina's mother, who planned to stay in London for a week before flying to Moscow. I had to tell them that I was now busy on Tuesdays and Saturdays and that I'd tried to persuade Yola to replace

me on those days but she was like a rock that couldn't
be moved.

'No work with children,' Yola had said. 'My own
child I left in Poland. I'm becoming tired. I have to pre-
serve myself.'

'What are we to do?' Dina asked me, her eyes widening in panic.

'Perhaps your mother can stay longer, until we find
some additional help,' I suggested.

'No!' Dina pressed her palms together. 'I can't wait
to put Mama on the plane! I hate having her around in
London. Anywhere else she can be a normal woman.
Here she looks and even smells differently. A satyr with
boobs, Misha calls her. He thinks she goes in the basement to drink and not to iron as she says. What is it,
Millie? Do you want more money from us?'

'No,' I said. 'It's not more money I need. I need this
volunteer job for my papers. I'll find somebody to
replace me here twice a week, I promise.'

I understood Dina for not wanting to keep her
mother under her London roof. It was a blessing in
disguise that Babushka didn't speak English. When I
took her out for a walk with children, she pulled faces
at everything: the cars came from the wrong direction,
and almost killed her every time we crossed a street;
people bumped into her and had no respect; muffins,
puddings and cured meat looked sickly, plastic. She
mistrusted the pre-cooked 'designer' soups I bought
for her grandchildren and she'd remove the lid in the
middle of the supermarket, inspect the contents of the
pack, gasp with scorn and say that it was dangerous to

250

buy food where you could not tell the ingredients apart. And food made by strangers at that! She'd take the soups out of the shopping basket when she thought I wasn't looking. Back in Oakley Gardens, she commented on the dogs that walked around, free and proud like generals, and when she saw them, she'd stop in the middle of the street, close her eyes, lift up the bags with food and move her lips in silent prayers or curses until they passed her by. Then she mumbled in Russian how London would have been a small town in Germany had it not been for the Red Army and the partisans. And she would sigh louder than most people shouted, heaving her enormous bosom with arms crossed beneath it.

On the following Saturday, the heavens dropped a young woman into my office. She was like a pill for me, a pill to ease my guilty consciousness.

She walked in just when I thought of sneaking out for a cup of coffee and a cigarette. She looked somehow familiar.

'What's wrong?' I rushed and asked her before she even introduced herself. As Gloria had explained, I was supposed to instruct the clients to sit down first and then take my time while writing down their names, addresses, phone numbers; make them relax, think things over, before helping to schedule them on.

'I did something stupid,' the girl answered, still standing by the door. 'So I have nowhere to sleep tonight. Can I sleep in this office? I can't sleep in any shelter or something like that. I'd rather sleep here on the floor.'

Her accent touched my heart.

'Where are you from?' I asked the girl.

'Macedonia. You heard about it?'

'Of course,' I said. 'I'm from Montenegro.'

'Good,' she said. Her eyes were obtuse, dark and heavy with tears. 'I'm Zorana from Macedonia.' She started to cry.

I got up and hugged her. She smelled like McDonald's cheeseburgers and felt extremely small-boned in my embrace and under a padded jacket, more appropriate for winter. Her heart-shaped face was framed by the frizzy, higlighed corkscrews of hair.

'Please sit down,' I whispered in her ear.

I wrote down her name, Zorana Turpevska, and asked for her address.

'No address,' she said. 'And no phone. Only my passport.' Still shivering, she produced a little blue passport out of the pocket of that jacket she didn't intend to take off.

'I only managed to...' she started but grew quiet and sank into the chair. I pushed an opened box of Kleenex tissues to her side of the table.

'O, Bože,' I said and held my head between my hands. 'Now you'll make me cry as well, before I even find out the reason.'

Zorana Turpevska was young, only twenty-two. She'd been living with her English boyfriend in his flat in Kensington. She had no job and studied part-time to become a TV presenter one day. That meant she'd been busy with her studies in Islington only once a week and on other days she could do whatever she wanted but she never once thought of finding a job. Why? She

252

didn't know why. Her English boyfriend (she never said his name) worked long hours in the city, was actually nice, even paid for her studies and the days just flew by and she'd seen a lot of movies and TV shows and bought a lot of shoes, wore them, returned them and bought more. She was bored.

Her English boyfriend had given her a wonderful phone where she could also check her mail. That was the end of them. She didn't understand technology and so didn't know that her English boyfriend was also the main account holder; he was the real owner of her mail and her phone number. He checked her mails and received all the phone listings. Now she knew.

Unfortunately, Zorana kept a very passionate contact with her Macedonian ex-sweetheart. Sexy emails, full of 'your hot big dick and your hot little pussy'. The Englishman fought demons for a while, but finally had Zorana's correspondence translated and found out she despised him and planned to dump him after completing her TV presenter studies.

'Funny,' Zorana said. 'I didn't plan to dump him. I love him, you know. But, he's *different*. Everything's fine, quiet and calm when we're together, and then we drink before bed and maybe make love, but mostly he is too tired by then. So I wrote all these sexy messages to my ex in Skopje who wanted to know if I was really coming back to give him all that I'd promised...*Oh, as soon as I get my diploma,* I wrote back, thinking: I'm not coming back to you, Macedonian loser . . . But how do you prove a thought when it's not written down?'

I could see that the life of a young, pretty woman

in a small country had not prepared Zorana that busy people from around the world wouldn't accept her whims because they knew her *ancestrally*.

'What happened?' I asked. 'Did he beat you up?'

'Who? Oh, the Englishman? No, never hit me.'

'Then what?'

'He just said I wasn't a nice person and paced the rooms, collecting back all the things he'd given me. I felt like shit and proudly left this morning with only my jacket and my passport on me. I can't go back to him now, not today. And I can't live with the guy anymore. Too much wrong. So I'm asking if I can sleep here tonight until he's a little bit calmer and then I'll go and collect my things and call my parents and go back . . .' she started crying again.

'Without finishing your studies?' I asked.

'Ah, what else?'

'Well . . .' I started. 'There's a lot of *else*. Can you cook?'

'Of course I can cook. I'm from Macedonia, remember?'

'Sometimes, you need to be kicked out of everything you own to find your true self.'

'So what are you saying?' she asked. 'Now I'm a cook?'

'No,' I said. 'You'll be a TV presenter. But, to come to that, you need to cook . . . and clean for a nice, Russian family here, in Chelsea.' I sounded like Yola after a full day of Tony Robbins.

I offered Zorana to sleep in my room until we found a better solution for her.

'Don't look back,' I told her.

Yola didn't like Zorana at first. Zorana slept in my bed so I had to move to Yola's and Isztvan's sofa bed in the living-room. Isztvan moved into a sleeping bag on the floor. It was a short arrangement, for two nights only. For two days Yola kissed her teeth after she'd caught Isztvan and Rafi eyeing Zorana's sweet figure from behind while she was wriggling around the flat. That didn't prevent the little Macedonian, the same size as Yola, to borrow Yola's clothes until she collected her own back from her English boyfriend. But Zorana kept herself busy and Yola respected that.

Zorana was a natural tidy-upper with an easy touch, almost a dance, to it. She thought it fun to replace a bulb, clean and polish the window glass on the top floor of our skyscraper, or make the house pipes more airy, less hairy. It took just one Sunday and our flat appeared to have expanded in its size, with the drawers so clean and well organised that they even smelled differently, pharmaceutical.

Dina, on the other hand, was desperate for more help, and she was ready to employ anyone, especially women with the men-related-problems as parts of their biographies. On Monday, when I presented Zorana to the Grishins, she was immediately given a room, a flat really, in the basement of their mansion.

Yola held her head in disbelief.

'That woman,' she said referring to Dina, 'can't see further than her migraines. Zorana's ass is Misha's next dessert.'

* * *

Babushka was leaving. I caught her hush-hushung and shuffling around the house, the children trailing after her, giggling, smuggling and hiding her old slippers, the authentic ones, with thin rubber soles and the ever-thinning discoloured and shaggy fabric, behind the fireplace. I'd overheard Dina promise herself to get rid of Babushka's worn-out slippers *this* time, after having in vain bought numerous 'healthy and odour-free' pairs for her mother to wear at least when staying with the Grishins. But it was Babushka's belief that by using her old slippers and then hiding them behind the fireplace before she left, the house spirits, *domovye*, would not give up on her, but would instead keep her connected in memory and continuity with the household she was leaving.

Misha was going to drive her to the airport since he as well was supposed to travel to some emerging-market country. It was a Friday afternoon and I'd brought the children back home from school earlier so that they could say goodbye to Babushka.

'Ay, they don't love me,' Babushka complained in Russian and winked at the children, which made Alex and Nensi run into her open arms and her soft bosom, and kiss her all over the face soaked in real tears. 'My children,' she was sobbing. 'My poor, little children.'

'Mama!' Dina yelled out. 'Don't call them that!'

Babushka mumbled something like: '*Ledenyakra-lyevna*!' into her chin. I deciphered it as 'Ice Queen'.

Misha laughed.

'I don't want Babushka to leave,' I whispered to him. 'She's a lot of fun.'

256

'*Gospodi*, you must be really home-sick,' he said. 'Hey, Babushka, Millie doesn't want you to leave!'

Dina, the Ice Queen, cut me in half with her glance.

'Bless you,' Babushka said in Russian and tapped my forehead with her index finger. 'You should come with me and marry a nice Russian officer. I saw how you cared about my poor little children.' Then she kissed me. 'I will come back for you.'

'Goodbye, Mother,' Dina said.

Alex and Nensi cried a little, but soon their attention was turned to Zorana. They took to her immediately. She was young, all touchy-feely and pet-like, and the children loved having her around. I wasn't so big on tight hugging and cuddling; I thought that my routine presence in children's lives and my self-censored anecdotes were enough for them.

In the mornings, before eight o'clock, when I'd arrive at the Grishins to start my workday by preparing Alex and Nensi for school, I'd look for them in the reception, in their rooms or bathrooms, but then I'd hear their voices and laughter rising up from the basement. I'd go down there and find them jumping on Zorana's bed, or lying in it with her tickling them. The basement was warm, the dryer constantly spinning clothes and perfumed tissues. It smelled like summer.

29

One day in July, 2005, I received my first postcard in London. It was written by Alex and Nensi, sent from Lago di Como, Italy. It looked beautiful there, so healthy. It made me wonder when I would breathe some fresh, non-city air again.

'Our dearest Millie,' the children wrote. 'We hope you are well, and Yola, too. You don't have a mobile phone and nobody answers when we call your flat. Mama says we may never come back to London. Can you come here and live with us? We love you! And Babushka loves you!!!' Kisses, hearts and their signatures.

I showed it to Yola. She was immediately on the phone, putting the word out that she was looking for another part-time family, central London, although *Around the World*, the catering company she'd launched with Isztvan and Rafi, had not been completely inactive, mostly due to a couple of favourable reviews in *Tatler* and *Evening Standard* – courtesy of Lady Apple's connections. But Misha had advised them to keep their day-jobs and they listened. Anyway, what they'd received so far were three 'half-damaged orders', as described by Yola: a Star Wars-themed birthday party for a bunch of five-year-olds; a 'Can you do Indian without garlic, coriander or cayenne?' and 'We all need comfort food', a night-in for some spoiled teenage girls.

My parents were going insane because of the terrorist bombings. They couldn't understand why I'd stay in London, the city bound to perish soon. 'It's unsafe! It's unsafe!' they were crying on the phone. I was delighted to discover a London-patriot in me.

And how could I consider it unsafe here when Yola's daughter was coming to visit, accompanied by Yola's mother? Yola wouldn't risk losing money on a pair of bread-rolls, let alone the pair of airplane tickets. So they arrived on July 31ˢᵗ, as planned.

The mother was your average Eastern European mum, forced into growing old, fast: severely cut grey hair, varicose veins, a secret smoker, she remained nameless and silent for the whole stay, except when she attempted to cook, but couldn't make anything edible in this foreign country. I could tell Yola was missing Isztvan who was visiting his sick father, in Hungary.

Yola's daughter was called Kelly. Yola told me she'd been watching too much of Beverly Hills 90210 series while pregnant. She had a baby girl and at the same time realized her husband had disappeared in America forever, so she named her daughter Kelly, after her favourite female character ever to be created for TV, the sensitive, sensuous, brave and *rich* Kelly Something.

Her daughter even looked like a Kelly. Long, blond hair, healthy cheeks, healthy smile, opinionated to the core. She hated London. Yola had made big plans for her, but after a couple of days, spent mostly queuing in the drizzle outside the steeply priced attractions, they ended up visiting Zorana who was enjoying her rest, snugly situated in the Grishins mansion, where little Kelly liked playing in Nensi's playroom. Not only that, but, *I* ended up spending my summer holiday there, too.

'Well,' Zorana, said one day, 'if the Grishins never come back, we can all live in this house. Don't you think so?'

'You really believe they will stay in Italy?' Yola asked. 'You talked to Dina?'

'Yes,' Zorana said. 'Dina is almost happy this happened and now she can stay in her beloved Lake Como where she spends days communicating with flowers and driving around the lake in her convertible. But I talked to Misha, too, and he said: 'Nonsense, the whole world is falling apart, and London will be the safest place to live in from now on.' And Misha is the money-machine, so . . . I guess they'll be coming back after all. Shit. I could see myself enjoying the Chelsea mansion like a proper Chelsea bitch.'

'Zorana,' I said. 'If you lose your warmth, the only good thing we could bring from the Balkans, you are nothing and nobody here.'

'Wrong! Wrong!' Yola chimed. 'You think you're warm, Millie? You're a cold snake, but no poison. You lost warmth, but you also lost bite. And if you lose bite in London, you lose your rights to become somebody. You stay nobody here.'

I didn't argue any further. Yola grinned victoriously and a little insanely, I thought, like Jessica Lang in her crazy roles.

The Grishins came back in September, of course. The children were happy to be back in London, unlike Kelly, who couldn't wait to go back to Jaworzno and made Yola cry by telling her she missed her Grandpa more than she ever missed her mother.

'I don't know why you left me,' Kelly said. 'You are nervous here and talk about money all the time, and your apartment is ugly.'

I discovered that every five weeks or so English schools had holidays. Another holiday was at the end of

October. Two weeks! Alex, Nensi and their little friends that I'd dragged over spent it running and screaming up and down the staircase, all the way from the backyard garden to the roof terrace. I persuaded Dina that it wasn't considered abnormal behavior, not even in England. I had them under control, and nobody was allowed to enter her premises, so she could go on and enjoy an acupuncture treatment or another in the 'sunroom' upstairs.

But the weather wasn't bad at all and so, to kill time, I took children out and we'd end up in a gallery. Visiting galleries was the mission of that half-term break. I didn't take only the Grishin children, but another friend or two of theirs as well. It proved easier that way. The children amused each other and asked me no difficult questions, so I could mutely enjoy my personal interpretations of the messages behind the art works. Sometimes, I'd think of Rafi, my household artist, and of the idea of marrying him for papers. Surely if my EU husband chose to stay in London, I'd be able to stay with him as well?

I'd thought that the Chapman brothers were some kind of cartoonists and the children would love them. I mean DINOS? It even sounded like a child-friendly name, like Barney the Dinosaurus. Well, that exhibition was a miss. The children were too silent, their eyes open wide, hypnotized, terrified.

Then another exhibition in Earl's Court, where I thought the drawings and sculptures looked beautiful, so detailed, until Elvis, the little friend of Alex shouted out: 'This gallery is *so* gay!' and I realized that the eyes of every single visitor, and every single visitor *was* male, were devouring us, the outsiders. I strode for the exit, dragging the children past the drawings of beautiful young men, their bare backs, torsos and thighs wounded by knives or arrows, dripping with blood. Beautiful.

So, I made sure that the following visit was going to be a safe one – Paul Horton, John Wilson; safe location, too: Harrods. Very uplifting. Alex, Nensi, Elvis, Chloe and Cooper Jean were transfixed, but in a different way than by the Chapmans, with loud comments on every detail on the paintings. Then someone cried: 'MEE-LAAAH!' and I'd turned my head only halfway towards the shriek before realising that it belonged to *Bella*! To Bella, as in Chris and Bella! With the corner of my eye I could see her pushing through the crowd to reach me. I pulled the children by their jackets and surrounded myself with them. 'We must run, now,' I announced with an urgent whisper.

I threw a glance towards the repeated shrieks consisting of my previous nickname.

'Is that woman calling you?' Alex asked.

'*Meelaah*! Wait!' Bella was crying. 'We *must* talk!' She had a young man in a dark suit on each side of her. They were not her sons or lovers, that much I knew. They were her bodyguards.

'Talk my shit,' I muttered and the children laughed. Lucky them; everything was an adventure, wasn't it? Not for me though, but for their sake, I had to pretend it wasn't a far cry from an adventure.

'Quick,' I said, 'let's find the nearest lift and lose that mad creature. I'll tell you about her later.'

So I was running followed by children, trying to find a lift, because the Egyptian escalator didn't seem too safe to run down it with the minors. I'd probably be stopped by the store's security staff, which would mean Bella and her guards would definitely catch up with me and . . . the possible scenarios were all bad. I saw myself being handcuffed in front of the children.

'Faster!' I turned and said to them.

I heard Bella's characteristic laughter with bubbles. 'You, silly woman,' I heard her say.

We ran past the antique tables, cupboards and clocks.

'Let's hide in a clock, like the little goat,' a child said, and then I saw the lifts.

Bella wasn't trying to catch up with me anymore, but I knew her: now that she'd seen me nannying people's children in London, i.e. 'being actively employed here', she wasn't going to leave the business of locating me unfinished. And she'd always been the one to use her 'connections'. But, now, according to those openly professional bodyguards, she was also *protected* UK citizen, and that couldn't mean good news for me.

'So what was that story?' Alex asked when we were all sitting on the bus 19.

I made up something unconvincing. The children couldn't care less. The best part, the chase, was over, we won and now they were hungry.

Back home, Zorana was busy crushing a dozen of garlic cloves, chopping up three onions and horn peppers as the base for any meal she prepared. I felt safe only when I inhaled the smells of her cooking.

Misha appeared in the kitchen. 'I love this life,' he said. 'Office-free.'

He had let his hair grow. It almost touched his shoulders now. He changed his dressing style, too. No more ties and grey suits. He wore jeans and jackets and looked good. He never again went to the office in the morning, and informed us that he never would; he'd stopped working in London; was off to a different country every other week; said he was 'digging into the goldmines' of the countries where companies were being privatised. When in London, he'd take a shower in the morning and would proceed wearing his bathrobe, sometimes for the whole day. By then, I unveiled the secret of Misha's bourbon skin colour: almost daily, he was using the solarium, which he'd bought for Dina before she discovered it could turn her silky skin into a dry plum. In there, he'd set the timer on fifteen minutes of sunbathing, and after that, he'd spend another fifteen minutes dozing off until the machine had cooled down completely. He claimed that it was the best half-hour rest one could ever get in a house where the lives of adults were organized around the rule of children. Then he'd try to have conference calls spanning over continents in the middle of that *ribyatocracya*, as he called it. Infantocracy. He ran up and down the stairs in his bathrobe and with a phone glued to his ear. He was never in a bad mood.

Sometimes, in the master bedroom, he could be heard arguing with Dina in quick Russian. I wondered what about. Dina would scream and say *Trusliviy, idi, idi* many times. *Coward, go, go.* Other words I couldn't make out. Then there'd be silence. Five minutes later – loud music blasting, with Misha singing and Dina giggling over it.

On the ground floor, he made us all touch his bare legs; thighs, mostly.

'Touch this iron,' he'd say and flex his muscles. Then he'd be back on the phone with someone. The children laughed.

But, Zorana was too young and too soon she was used up by the quantity of her expected multitasking at the Grishins. I started catching the demented version of her around the house. Armed with a kitchen knife, she stubbed at the packages of minced beef or veal escalopes with the movements of the Muppet chef gone mad. She opened the jars of ready-made salsas with frightening urgency. She thumped on the lids and swirled them open with the broad letting go of another heavy curse in Macedonian; she poured the sauce into a pan, shaking the jar as if choking an arch-enemy, her frizzy curls distressed.

'Zorana!' I interrupted her once, called her name behind her back, unable to ignore her sinking into an obvious breakdown.

She screamed. Then she saw me. 'Oh, it's you,' she said, and continued her ritual that so obviously filled her with misery.

The children were upstairs, behind the closed doors, with their piano teacher. They had to practice a piece on their keyboards upstairs first, before they could come downstairs and present it on the concert piano in the reception, where Dina would join to witness her

265

children's progress. For now, Dina was in the sunroom, doing Pilates with a personal trainer. Misha was in another country.

'What's wrong, love?' I asked Zorana and I went to the cooker, to stand by her. 'I feel responsible. I brought you here. What is it?'

'Don't tell them I give them ready-made food to eat,' Zorana answered, shrugging nervously.

'Who cares about that?' I said. 'What is it, really?'

'What do you mean who cares about food?' Zorana went on. 'Dina would kill me.'

'*Dina* would kill you?'

I was relieved, I must admit. I was convinced that Misha was the problem. Not so much food-and-work-wise, but more like after-Zorana's-ass-wise, as Yola had predicted. Misha had rejuvenated. His bathrobe was now more often unbelted than not, the top of his long hair pushed back from his face and cramped into a ponytail as he stood by the fireplace after a late break-fast, leaning on the marble top in his open robe and ripping the piles of envelopes open, mumbling about 'Just another bill, of course,' and how in London he felt as if he was only making money for EDF and British Telecom. 'At least they could write me a couple of ten-der words,' he'd say to noone in particular, 'or send like an upbeat fortune cookie, you know? Not these threat-ening letters.' He'd look around the room and mostly catch me staring at him. He would stare back, or wink.

'Yes, Dina, Dina,' Zorana confirmed. 'Everybody thinks she's so tolerant, nice and easy. Everybody doesn't *live* here. You don't know how she screams and shouts and breaks things after the children have been put to bed. Especially now, after they came back from their long holiday. She's so full of hatred for everything here. Makes my blood freeze in my arteries.'

She unscrewed a tube of garlic paste with her teeth and squeezed it into a saucepan. 'If you ask me why Dina gets into fits, I can't tell you, which makes it worse, more frightening, like she must be crazy then, capable of killing people.' She sighed and went on: 'I'm exhausted. Dina gives me more and more tasks. Hem a torn uniform shirt for Alexei, a button is loose here, a name tag has washed off – replace it, now she's saying she wants to adopt a huge dog, not a puppy, but a *five-year-old* Rhodesian *something*-back, who's supposed to live with me . . .' Zorana's eyes watered. 'Look at me: I'm that dog's appetiser. And worth less than him, obviously. Why can't Dina *buy* a puppy, a *chiwawa*, like everyone else? Or why can't I, at least, buy food like all normal people: pre-cooked, just heat until boiling? But I have to hide that from Dina. She wants homemade for her family! Homemade! What's homemade? Everything is homemade somewhere!' She stuffed the empty sauce jar deep into the black garbage bag. 'See, I can't even recycle these. Recycle bags are see-through.'

'Aren't you over-reacting, Zorana?' I asked her. 'You must be. Nobody can be that stupid to lose you by ordering homemade meals only. But if that's true, why don't you quit?'

'I will, I will,' Zorana said. 'As soon as I can get out of this prison and look for some other job. I can't even prepare for my TV presenter exam. They need to film me doing a street poll on a subject, but I have no time to prepare anything. Not my topic, not my hair, not my questions. I want to go home -' Zorana started crying into the kitchen sink. I hugged her small shoulders.

She was a good kid. She was raised in Macedonia where people sang while they prepared food, but they sang to each other, they did everything tribally. She had come to London on a dream-ticket. She was going to learn the language and TV skills and go back home to enjoy a semi-celebrity status as a certified TV presenter from a London-based school. No small peas. She was a cleaner now, and a cook, undermined by a crazy Russian woman who screamed at nights and broke things, which Zorana had to tidy up first thing in the morning and then to proceed to scrub their toilets, before she even had her first coffee. Of course she wanted to go home. She was only twenty-three, going on at least forty that morning. I imagined her mother, heart-broken at the sight of her slight and pale daughter on the doorstep. 'Why didn't you come home earlier?' I imagined her mother asking. 'Who cares about a diploma? That cruel, cruel West. They are all mad people there, heartless. Come here.' And Zorana would finally get some rest, falling into her mother's embrace that would smell of freshly baked *priganice*.

'Go home,' I told Zorana. 'I'll lend you some money if you need it for a plane ticket. Don't tell Dina anything. Just buy a ticket and go. If you want, come to my place a couple of days before, to refresh for your family.'

'Ah,' Zorana sobbed. 'They...Ah, never mind. I love my parents, but they...' she looked at me. 'They don't

268

live well. That's why I didn't even visit them this summer. Mama needs help in the house also. If I go back, *I*'ll be that house help. Which is fine, but I was hoping to earn some money, so I can also move on, move out, and leave Mama with a helper, so I wouldn't feel bad. But life is full of shit, isn't it?' she smiled. 'Especially when you're a cleaner.' Zorana removed the saucepan from the cooker's ring. 'There. Done. Super-Bolognese. Better than homemade.'

'But it *is* homemade,' I said and made her smile.

'I'm just very tired,' Zorana repeated. 'And I can't save a penny. Do you know, *I*'m buying this easy food, from *my* salary? I carry two baskets in a supermarket: one is make-up food, which Dina considers healthy, and other is easy food that they actually eat. But I pay my money for making my life more bearable. I drop the secret supplies in front of my door and take the false food up here. Eventually, I bin it when nobody's around.'

'Look, Zorana, this is insane. You'll flip out. Why don't you talk to Misha? Don't you think he'll understand?'

'Think? Don't I think? No I don't think. I have no time. Misha is never here and when he is, he lets *her* do whatever she wants. That's why she screams and throws things at him. He spoiled her.'

I instructed her to slow down with work and pretend. To spend more time downstairs in the laundry room, 'ironing', but actually resting. Or drinking, like Babushka used to do. Dina wouldn't know the difference.

'You're so young,' I said. 'You can afford to go back home, completely mess it up there and then try London again.'

'Is that what you did?' she asked. 'Is that why you never complain now?'

I just smiled.

When Dina came downstairs, everything was back to perfect. Zorana was fine; now she had a plan B if she needed it. The smell of lavender-and-cardamom tea lingered in the reception room. The children had already been bathed, combed, dressed and fed, and now, after having practiced upstairs, they were seated on a stool behind the polished keys, waiting for Mama, so they could show her what they learned.

Nensi, deft with her fingers, passionate about music, such a different child from the one I'd first met not long ago, had started by playing the scales. Then Alex joined in and they played *Doll's Funeral* by Tchaikovsky, four hands. The teacher, Rachel from Hong Kong, was trembling, sitting on the edge of a stool, next to her pupils. Dina didn't want to hire a Russian person for piano lessons, although, as she claimed, they were experienced and full of knowledge, but too arrogant: they could spread their peasant hands over two octaves, and so believed they should all be treated as Rachmaninoffs in disguise.

Doll's Funeral made my skin rise. There was something *uber*-creepy about a doll being buried with a hospitable smile forever on her face. But Alex and Nensi seemed proud of their achievement and perfect harmony, and Dina was glowing. She did shout out a couple of observations though.

'Don't rush it! Pyotr Ilich wanted you to suffer, to learn patience! Crescendo here, crescendo!' and she closed her eyes and tossed her head from side to side.

I averted my eyes from so much drama and spotted Zorana, who was standing on the top stair, hiding her smile behind a pile of Dina's sweat-soaked Pilates shirt and tights that she'd picked up from the sunroom to wash.

'See, I told you,' Zorana mouthed. 'So-o crazy,' and she rolled her eyes at Dina. 'Crazy.'

When the lesson was over I told Dina that I needed to go once more through Nensi's lines for the assembly, and that Alex had to wrap up revising for his exams on the following day. After that, they could go to bed.

'Can you stay longer tonight?' she asked, holding my arm with her cold hand. 'I need to talk to you.'

'Can it wait?' I asked. 'If you don't mind, I had something planned for tonight.'

I hadn't of course, never. It was just the ring of that 'need to talk to you' line. I couldn't stomach it, not yet.

'Oh, I guess it can wait,' Dina said. 'If it must.'

30

Montenegro became an independent state after the referendum held on May 21st 2006. I watched the celebrations of independence on BBC Breakfast, feeling like an amputated limb. Then I walked to the grocery shop and there I leafed through the English newspapers, where I saw the photographs of the Montenegrin people I recognised. They were kissing passionately the resurrected, un-banned red Krstac flag with golden Maltese cross.

Since I couldn't explain my contradictory feelings of defeat and pride to anyone here, when people asked me how I felt about the independence, I shrugged the subject away.

It was on the following Sunday that the Mediterranean spring also came to London. Men and women were strikingly beautiful all of a sudden, as they drove by in their open-top cars. I knew not a single one of them. Everyone else but me seemed to be headed somewhere great and festive, or just to a Sunday lunch with family. I wanted to participate in the little family games they were going to act out, although those games usually turned nasty in the Balkans after too much wine and *loza*. But still.

I was longing for the coziness of my country. With Montenegro's new, independent status, surely there came some additional charm. It was so new now, so beautiful, too, and small that if moved to London, its capital could be re-erected, stage-like, on one of the meadows in Hyde Park.

In my mind, I could see my countrymen speeding on the crazy highway, going to the seaside, for a lunch on the beach. In fact, too many of them, the young ones, died that way, but now it only added romance to the memory. Now their ambitions seemed fantastic, in complete opposition to the times and the geography. To live like crème de la crème of the world. Well at least they tried. They knew not how to behave, loaded with guns and cocaine in the nineties, with the war raging around them, so they tried to unglue themselves and leap up from the country's uncompromising roots. And the country yanked them back, and fed on their young flesh.

Young women blossomed like rhododendron in my hometown every spring. Their beauty and behaviour were spied on and talked about in steamy kitchens where yesterday's queens, now married and forgotten, smoked above the boiling beef bones and vegetables and where the smuggled cigarettes were sold, for some side income. *Oh, the proud little bitches; the years would get them, too, break their pride and make them invisible.*

Older men, hanging around the corners of the downtown's low houses, bulged at the girls, throwing short but elaborate comments.

'May God keep your little meatballs round and juicy forever!' a man shouted after me once. I was maybe sixteen.

'Uncle Drago,' I turned back and replied, 'but don't you recognize me? I am Milena, your niece.'

'Oh, *Milenice, srce*,' the man answered, his voice softened, 'you've grown overnight. Tell your parents I'll come and visit one of these days.' His group of friends clapped their hands and thump on his back in fits of laughter.

In the old parts of town, people spent time in front of their stone cottages, built densely and low off the slanted macadam. They sat around on short, wooden, tripod chairs, *tronozac*, drinking sweet, Turkish coffee, some women in peignoirs grinding the coffee beans with manual, gold-plated mills. They were all taking it easy, fixed askew on the narrow passages, looking only seconds away from slipping off this planet and being launched into the universe, never losing the acquiescent smile, like the warped characters in Chagall's paintings.

My country, independence or no independence, was like the rainless thunder - too much noise but nothing happens - and my countrymen knew no other way to live. Vukas knew that, instinctively, and he took advantage of it; he was going to rule forever. My countrymen accepted it. They stopped asking him for more than simple survival. They didn't miss out on anything, what was there to miss? Another winter gone and my people were happy again to simply share the sunlight and ignore the money they owed to others who owed it further, and to snub diabetes, clogged arteries, alcoholism, cancers and the scorn, swelling like sty, in their children's eyes.

And now London and its heat that never stayed behind once the sun went down but slipped off the skin like a veil removed from shoulders. I was the only person still wearing long sleeves while others walked about in beach outfits.

That Sunday, in Cheyne Walk, a car horn honked a melodic, inviting sound behind my back: two-short-one-long beeps, as if calling me to *turn-a-round*. *Bip-bip-beep*. I did not turn around. But then I heard 'Millie! Millie!' and I recognised Misha's voice, deep and characteristically laced with potential bouts of mirth. He drove by me slowly, top down on a small, bitchy car that I'd never seen before. I knew their family car, a huge Audi, with the plate that said DINA I.

The two-seater of that day sported an Italian registration plate, and the evocative, left-hand drive. Misha stopped by the pavement a bit further in front of me on Cheyne Walk and waited. I walked to his car.

'You're back in London!' I said and bent down to kiss him on the cheek.

'Yes, just flew back in. Hop in here, I'll drive you. Where to?'

'I'm not going anywhere special,' I said. 'It's Sunday. I'm just walking.'

'Great, walk with me then. By car. Come, get in, we'll have some fun, I promise.'

Just what I wanted: driving around in a convertible with a good-looking guy. I ran around the back of his car, opened the passenger door and sat beside him. The leather seat was warm because of the open top. Misha turned to look at me, his eyes not so dark now, caramel-coloured when they were strained against the sun. He smelled of sea-salt and had some stubble. The Seaman Misha. I hugged him and breathed into his hair. Yes, he smelled of home so much that the image of my mother and her bosom, pressed over the window-sill in our old flat, came to me. 'When are you coming *home*?' she'd shout as I walked away from her, towards downtown Podgorica, fast. *Home, home, home* – her voice echoed in my head.

Misha slid his thumb over my collarbone, up my neck till he touched my mouth.

'I think you missed me,' he said and checked the

rearview mirror on my side. 'Let's go.' Slowly, he joined in the traffic.

'I visited Montenegro this weekend,' he went on and looked at me.

Somehow, I wasn't surprised. But, where to start with questions about *that*? Better not start.

'Well,' he went on, '*congratulations*! Free at last, eh?'

I couldn't possibly comment on that, either.

'There's a lot of money now in your little country.'

'If you know the right people,' I said, 'yes, there is.'

'Well, as far as I can tell from your CV, you knew the right people there. So what happened?'

I was just staring ahead thinking how *Misha* of all people had brought back to me the fragrance of Montenegro, of the honey-sand beaches there in May, when the colours are so clear, so immaculate they alone could cure. My Russian employer was channeling the much-missed salty air, still unburdened by the blanket of heat, which would come later in the season, together with the crowds of people that carried their own airs about them. Yeah, the heat in my country, I realized, fell on the skin and stayed glued to it for the night. From my London prospective, Montenegro seemed Tropical. I put my palm on Misha's thigh.

'That's how it is in Montenegro,' I said. 'Everybody knows everybody else. The right, the wrong. But those *right people* are ruining that country. I know it's hard to believe -'

'Come on,' Misha said. 'They wouldn't hurt a fly. They're so open-minded, looking for investment partners, you know, to raise the level of tourism. It may look like tough love at the moment, but a decade from now -'

'Oh,' I said. 'I guess I should look at it through your eyes. Who did you meet with?'

'I met with half the country. My host there is an American lobbyist that knows everyone.'

'*A new* Chris,' I mumbled.

Misha said: 'A new *who*? Chris who?'

'Oh, it was the American I worked with, also a lobbyist. But he died, that one.'

'Well,' Misha said. 'You know what they say: Past is another country. Anyway, my American is called Lenny. He introduced me to half the population. Everybody spoke Russian! People quoted Pushkin, Yesenin, Mayakovsky to me...' Misha laughed. '*You think malaria makes me delirious?*' he recited Mayakovsky's *Cloud in Trousers* in Russian, letting his deep voice fly.

Yes, we were all made to learn *Cloud* by heart in high school. In school corridors, we whispered to one another how Mayakovski had meant *erection* with his Cloud in Trousers, *erection*! Which inspired us to memorise it.

''I'll come at four,' Maria promised. Eight, nine, ten...'' Misha laughed out loud and raised one arm up in the air. 'Oh, I had so much fun! Funny little Montenegro!'

'Don't mention me to your friends if you go there again,' I said.

'Don't worry, Millie,' Misha said. 'I'm not just a pretty face,' he laughed again. 'I'm not going to talk about my private space with my business partners.'

Misha was driving along the river with a charming detachment from all the traffic fuss, letting everybody else cut into the long line of vehicles before us; people smiled and waved at him.

'Where are we going?' I asked.

'For a walk-on-wheels,' Misha said. 'Sightseeing.'

I was looking at the bridges and buildings, now glad I'd come to live in London, in the middle of that systematically built beauty.

Misha turned the music on. After a song or two – a beautiful female voice singing *Cambia, todo cambia*, a man singing *Me and my monkey*, no Russians - I had no idea where I was; I was everywhere. Misha's gentle driving, this town, the temperature – the combination worked better than any other stimulant. I pressed my palm harder on Misha's leg and raised my chest, breathing in the whole beauty of the day.

'I'm starving,' Misha said after a while. 'I had some crab salad *a la* British Airlines, not bad at all, but not a real meal, either.'

'British is flying from Montenegro?' I asked.

'No, from Dubrovnik. But next time I'm flying there with a friend of mine, Uklyeyev -'

'*Uklyeyev*?' I laughed. What a name! *Uklyeva* is a local lake fish in Montenegro, tiny and wickedly tasty.

'I know, can you believe it? I'm crazy about that fish dish. Anyway, my point was that the next time we'll be flying on Uklyeyev's Gulfstream, directly to Podgorica. Want to come along? Just to see your family and friends. You don't have to see your ex-employers or nasty boyfriends. Lord and Lady Appleby will go with us, so you'll have some female company -'

'No, thank you,' I said. 'You go with your fruit-and-fish crowd and bring me back this salty smell.' I leaned closer to his neck and sniffed.

Misha made a U-turn. 'Let's find a place to eat and, um, rest.'

I loved his driving. When did he get to know the labyrinthine streets of London so well? To me, this town still seemed as though it had been built by and for the left-handed people.

'I've never seen you in this car before,' I said to Misha.

'I bought it for Dina,' he said, 'just like I bought Q7 for Dina. Me, I'd be happier on something that whirrs,' he made a whirring sound and skated his right hand through the air. 'A motorbike. But this one I bought for Dina when she claimed she could see us in a car made for lovers. She wanted a convertible. A left-hand drive so she could always pretend she's in Lago di Como while driving. So I bought this sweetie. It matched her requirements, but then she changed her mind. She didn't want it. She wanted to stay at home. That phase is still on, as you know. This car is another symbol of my failure to make Dina happy.' As if that had reminded him of her, Misha reached into his pocket and dug out his mobile phone. It was blinking.

'It's her,' he said to me and pressed the phone to his ear.

'Hallo, *lyuba*, I was just about to call you,' he said to Dina in Russian and then was silent for some time.

'*Ne plachi, ne plachi...*' he started saying. *Don't cry,*

don't cry. 'Please. I have to treat this Montenegrin man a lunch. They were such wonderful hosts.' And then in English he said: 'You know what they say here: 'No news is good news', *Dinochka*.'

He locked his phone and put it back into his pocket. I told him that to Dina happiness probably meant having him spend more time with her and the children.

'*Da*?' he said, smiling at me. '*Ti panyimayesh po Ruski*?'

'Yes, I understood some of it,' I said. 'Enough to connect the dots.'

'You're perfect! *Idyalynyaya dyevushka*!' Misha shouted and kissed my hand. 'Too bad you can't be my assistant and travel with me.'

'Do you have an assistant?'

'No, I don't need anyone. I couldn't read and write for a very long time so I'm kind of trained to remember everything I hear. Who needs an assistant then?'

Misha kept driving slowly, passing by the pretty little square gardens, crescents and mews, full of blossoming trees and flowers, but un-peopled to the bone. Why weren't people sitting in front of their houses, sunbathing? They were probably resting in their backyard gardens, reading Sunday newspapers or books. I wanted them up front, out in the open, on the streets. I wanted to see the beautiful eccentrics of this beautiful city; I wanted them to reclaim their territory, lose the shyness and too much privacy. Birds sang loudly above me.

Misha turned a corner and I recognized Gloucester Road, Kensington.

'There's a hotel here, across from the park,' my King

of London said. 'They have a tiny garden outside where we can eat and smoke. And an excellent Italian chef. Sounds good, no?'

In front of the hotel – *Baglioni*, its name said - Misha went out of the car and gave the keys to a porter who asked: 'What about your bag, signor Grishin?' There was a hand-luggage type bag squeezed behind the passenger seat.

'Leave it there,' Misha replied and put some money into the man's palm. 'We came just for lunch.'

Inside, hotel *Baglioni* was painted and furnished black and gold, very modern, but as if trying too hard to seduce. Like many other things that too much money had brought to this town, the design of *Baglioni* made me want to scream: 'Relax!' into its details and the faces of the staff there. Everybody was dressed in black, looked cosmetically treated, smiled at Misha and spoke in the soft tones. I was wearing a shirt, a pair of jeans and espadrilles and felt like someone who had run after Misha to give him back something valuable, like a wallet, which he had dropped on the street, and then, out of gratitude, I was invited for lunch.

We walked past the full circle bar above which a black chandelier loomed, through the restaurant and out, to the small sunlit terrace with only a couple of tables laid out for lunch, with golden plates, black napkins and black ashtrays. As soon as the waiter, another Italian, Toto – his name-tag said - had approached us, I ordered vodka-cranberry. My voice must have been desperate because the waiter forgot to ask us about water, or to ask Misha if he'd like an aperitif; he ran inside to get me my drink first. I couldn't wait to sink my awkwardness in alcohol.

When my drink was placed in front of me, I prodded my mouth with a straw and slurped. My mouth had been so dry that I still had the straw hanging down from it after I'd the quaffed the drink and put the glass back on the table. The straw remained, glued to my lower lip and dangling in the gentle afternoon. Misha looked at it. It had been a while since I lunched on a terrace, with a man. My London life had been reassuringly barren of hotels, men, events. And now Misha, right by my elbow, staring at the straw. I removed the damn thing from my lip.

'I'm rather underdressed for a lunch in *Baglioni*,' I said. All women eating in the restaurant were wearing black or brightly coloured dresses and high heels.

'No,' Misha said. 'You're just as should be. It's Sunday afternoon. You put something carefree on, hoping you look good. And you do. *Forte forte* for it to appear *leggero leggero*. According to Dina, this is the best advice for being cool and stylish. But you're different, mysterious. To me, at least.'

I liked the way he talked. Music for my ears; crazy lyrics, too.

The waiter came back carrying olive oil and a basket full of Italian variations on bread-baking: rosemary *foccacia*, black olives *ciabatta*, oregano bread sticks . . . Misha cut one *ciabatta* in half and dipped it into the smooth, green oil.

'How do we order some serious food around here?' he asked the waiter.

282

The waiter laughed. 'Ready when you are, Mr Grishin.'

Misha ordered *pasta fagioli* and veal a la Milanese and I skipped the beans – too self-conscious – and said I'd only have a mixed salad and a Milanese, already cancelling the salad as I could not rely on my quavering mouth to deal with it properly. Misha then ordered red wine which was a good moment for me to eye-sign to the waiter to bring me another vodka-cranberry. 'Double,' I mouthed at Toto's direction, with my head turned away from Misha who pushed back his wrought iron chair that screeched over the floor tiles. He got up and said: 'Excuse me, Millie. I've got to use the men's room.'

He left his mobile phone on the table and it was blinking in silence. Dina was calling him non-stop.

Misha came back and his *pasta fagioli* was served. He ate without talking until his hunger was diminished and then he sat back and relaxed. By that time I was nicely drunk. I'd barely touched my food, not wanting it to sober me back into a dry, trembling outsider.

Misha checked his phone and put it into the pocket of his jacket.

'Dina was calling you all the time while you were in the toilet,' I said.

'I know. I have twenty-six missed calls from her. Can you believe that? Twenty-six!'

'Maybe it's something urgent?'

'No,' Misha said and thought for a moment. 'I promised Alexei I'd take him to a game today. Well, it's too late now. Dina wants to make sure I know how bad he feels. Otherwise, she'd just text me, or leave a voice mail.'

'I feel kind of guilty,' I said.

'Enjoy,' Misha said. 'It's always my fault. I don't want to go home now. I want to be with you.'

'Why?' I asked. 'I look like an intruder in the land of lunches and chit-chats.'

'Tell me about yourself,' Misha said and leaned closer to me. 'When you were, you know, *younger*, in Montenegro, what were your ambitions?'

I thought about it for a moment. Where to begin?

'I wanted to be different from my parents,' I said. 'I wanted to be alive. I wanted never to change the real me, but to effortlessly make money with the *uklyevas* and sharks of my country. Then at one point I wanted to be able to lock the door behind me and just feel safe.' I stopped.

'Why?' Misha asked.

But I wasn't going to answer. 'What about your ambitions, when you were *younger*?'

Misha then talked about his boring childhood in Bashkiria, in a village where winters were long but often snowless, and so people watched a lot of TV. Especially on Sundays. There was something called 'Sunday afternoon shows' and they lasted for six or seven hours and Misha dreamed of becoming the host for those shows. 'They were our aristocracy,' Misha said of the 'Sunday afternoon show' hosts. 'Beautifully dressed, sitting royally or walking along a *swimming pool* in the newly-opened hotels.'

'So how did you end up here?' I asked and Misha

284

gestured to the waiter to bring another drink for me.

'I like living by the water, but the Thames is not why I'm here. I'm here for happy family.'

'So what happened? You sort of stopped working on it.'

'I don't think so, Millie,' Misha said and helped himself with one of my cigarettes. 'I never knew my father so I'm not sure what and how much I'm supposed to do as, you know, a *dad*. But I do what I can. I provide for them. I brought them to Chelsea, bought a good house, refurbished it. I pay for safe private schools, a good nanny, basketball, football, music, fencing, chess, anything they say they want and, what's better, when they say they are not interested any longer, I say okay and I pay for the next thing. I don't shout. I don't put pressure, don't humiliate, criticise. I don't even ask for their gratitude. I let them find out what they like. You know, I'm tired. I travel a lot, my mind wanders. I'm a daydreamer. Sometimes I think I should've been an artist. I don't know how to play with kids. And anyway, I think kids should play with other kids, so I try to pay for the other kids to come and play. As you know.' He looked exhausted by his presentation, or perhaps the cigarette had made him slightly sick; but I pressed on.

'You just need to spend a bit more time with them,' I said.

'They look fine to me when they spend time with you,' Misha said. 'Stress-free.'

Before I could say another thing about his family, he added: 'Which reminds me - we have a room here, for the afternoon. Could I please have some of your stress-free treatment?' He put out the cigarette and took a room key out of his jacket. The little plate, hidden under the golden pom-pom, said 209. So Misha had made a very strategic visit to men's room.

'You go first while I settle the bill,' he went on. 'Go towards the ladies room. You'll see the lift on your right. Second floor. Wait for me.' He placed the key by my drink. I covered it with my hand.

'I shouldn't,' I said.

'Only if you don't want to. But if you want to have some well-deserved good time . . . I'm a good choice.'

'I kind-a thought so,' I said.

'Yeah you should treat yourself one selfish after-noon,' Misha said. 'Think of it as a short holiday. Invigorating, but not life-shattering.'

'No, I shouldn't. I like Dina,' I said and it wasn't altogether a lie. But the truth of truths was so banal. I hadn't yet reached the level of selfishness where, if I was to be bad, I was to think of pleasing myself first. No, I still wanted to please a man, and I wasn't pre-pared - trimmed, shaved, unblemished – for the perfor-mance. Only tipsy.

'All right,' Misha said. 'I'm going to have a massage here, in the spa. Would you wait for me in the room anyway?'

In the room 209 there was an unpacked razor in the bathroom. I took a shower and shaved what I could, smiling all the time, also happy to finally, after three years – had it been that long? – be able to take a proper shower, with the battery that moved like a microphone.

I put the bathrobe on and checked the mini-bar.

286

They had vodka. I took the small bottles of Absolute out of the fridge and sat up on a tall bed covered in layers of smooth sheets. I drank and drank, refreshing my spirited-ness, saluting to sex. It was just some sex I was going to get, right? It was like exercise with a climax, hopefully.

Good old vodka played a trick on my mind, and I had the feeling I was waiting for Mirko. The Sunday afternoons we'd spent together. And, after the lovemaking: me, tipsy and smiling like now, sitting on the cruel rug in front of the TV and a shut down window, with the smell of butane from the heater creeping into my pores; Mirko, gone to his office-room, to take a phone call from somebody, never within my view when he was on the phone, oh, how wrong I was to think sometimes that he could've never been closer to any other woman. Why did I think that? A little provincial bitch. Thank God with Misha I knew what it was all about: exercise with a climax, hopefully.

There was a knock on the door and I opened it for Misha, wrapped in a bathrobe, and a porter behind him, who was carrying his clothes.

'Thank you,' Misha said to him, collected his clothes from the man and searched the pockets of his trousers and his jacket for some change to give as a tip. 'Ahh,' he said. 'Sorry, man, cash-dry. Next time, okay?'

'No problem, Mr Grishin, have a nice afternoon,' the porter smiled and his face disappeared behind the closed door.

I sat back down on the tall hotel bed, feeling a little stupid. I knew I could change my mind, but didn't see the point of it. Misha climbed the bed and lay beside me. His hair was tousled and shiny, his eyes two nests clouded by sleep, his stubble had thickened and he smelled of Tiger balm, my father's favourite healing prop. After measuring their blood pressure, my father used to rub Tiger balm on everyone who came to visit. They didn't even have to complain of an ache or anything. I was surprised it existed in London, thought that it was a locally smuggled product, a suspicious ointment of backyard countries, banned in the West. But it seemed that Tiger balm was actually a border-resistant Titan that outlived all scientific progress.

'Your phone again,' I said to Misha whose cell-phone was blinking through the pocket on his bathrobe. He snatched it and cried: '*Da, Dina, skazhi!*'

I heard Dina sobbing.

'*Dinochka, sto sluchilo s*?' Misha asked. '*Shto s toboy?*' and he proceeded to tell her that he'd had a lunch, a massage and that he now intended to take a nap in a hotel room. He didn't lie to her. She must have, through the sobs, asked *why* all of that was necessary, because I heard him explain that he had too much to drink and needed *not* to be at home. She sounded devastated and wailed from inside his phone and he let her. Then she started screaming and he hung up on her and growled, hurling the phone away. It hit the opposite wall and it smashed there, its parts landing on the parquet boards painted black. Misha looked at me.

'Shit, I was so relaxed,' he said. 'It was a good Thai. Ever had a Thai?'

'Not whatsoever.'

'Want one?'

'No,' I said. 'Better not start now. I may become addicted.'

'So what did you do?'

'I took a shower and drank from the mini bar,' I said.

'Did you drink enough?'

'Yes.'

'Can you stand me now?'

'You, humble wizard,' I said. 'Very dangerous, very sexy.'

Misha rolled himself towards me and I arched my back for him to take my bathrobe off. He did. He gave me a long kiss. His mouth was full and firm and his kiss like some ripe fruit with juicy promise that the more you bite into it, the sweeter it becomes.

He removed his robe and there it was: his tanned torso, caramel-coloured stomach covered by golden hair, and strong, hairy thighs, all of him shiny and sleek from the massage oil. He looked so beautiful to me. I spread my legs apart and he leaned over, kissed me again, and pushed two fingers deep inside me. He was good with his fingers, searching and playing.

I begged him to give me his cock.

'I can't, Millie,' he smiled. 'Although I would, I'd fuck you like crazy. I don't have the damned protection.'

'I'm practically a born-again virgin,' I said. 'It's been so long.'

'That's a scary turn-off,' he said. 'Let me take care of you,' and he slid his other hand behind my back, placed it above my buttocks. My hips rose to him.

Misha made me come first, with his fingers. He

didn't stop there, but asked: 'Is everything edible on this candy?' – a question only he could get away with - and without waiting for an answer, he was down on me like a horse, his nostrils taut and wide. His long fingers were everywhere again: some inside me, others pressing on my hip bone, adjusting me slightly to the right, slightly up, a bit down. I threw my head back and closed my eyes, ignoring the slight embarrassment I felt because of my wet inner thighs and the shivers that ran through me. Now and then I attempted to lift my head, to say and do something, sigh, moan, give the man a hand, please him somehow, but he seemed happy to do all the work and my efforts remained only the unrealised plans of a born-again virgin, awarded with another orgasm. He turned me on my stomach and came on my back; he even wiped me clean with one of the bathrobes.

Then he took a nap. I enjoyed watching his chest rise and fall with his snore, so vital and proud that I had the impression he was snoring the National Anthem of USSR in his sleep. I went to kiss him and my hair fell on his face. He jolted out of sleep, patted me on the cheek and said: 'Let's go home.'

As he walked towards the bathroom to take a shower, he laughed out loud and pointed at the core of the broken phone lying on the floor, still blinking and vibrating, refusing to die.

When we were in Chelsea again I asked him to drop me off there. I wanted to walk home, at least over Albert Bridge. I needed to be alone for some time between leaving Misha and meeting my flat-mates.

When I opened the door to leave his car, he produced a credit card from somewhere, told me the pin number, which was his date of birth, he said. '1611, November sixteen,' he confirmed, adding that I should take the card and buy something for me, some nice clothes.

I wasn't offended. 'No,' I said. 'Really, no.'

'Yes, I insist.'

'No, Misha,' I hugged his head and I said into his ear. 'I have plenty of clothes. I just don't wear them. I'm a nanny, remember?'

Looking almost bashful, he nodded. I know what he thought I'd wanted to say. He thought I meant it as in *I'm a nanny, not a prostitute.* But he had no idea how much I didn't give a shit. I was grateful to him and he never asked for gratitude; he had told me so himself. So I just walked away and he honked two short beeps: see-you.

It was the first weekend that I forgot to call my parents.

On Monday, I called them after I'd dropped the children off at the schoolgate. My father picked up the phone.

'Don't do this to us ever again,' he said. 'We're old people and your mother is not well. Don't you know she measures time by your phone calls? She thought something bad had happened to you, and you refuse to have a mobile phone. Everybody has mobile phones! What's your problem? Your mother was vomiting all night long, her arm jerking like a dying dog.' He was breathing from the top of his lungs as if he had to run around the block to take that call. Finally, after asking if I had enough money, he let my mother speak to me. Mama was crying.

'I miss you, my little sunshine,' she said. 'I miss you every day. I didn't know you were capable of taking so much good with you. It's been raining here for days. The town seems empty. I don't even meet the people I know. It's like *everyone* moved away.'

'Mama,' I said, 'I'm fine. I really am.'

'Yes you are,' Mama replied. 'I can now hear it in your voice. Did you meet anyone interesting? A nice, serious man?'

I considered lying to her about 'a serious man' in my life, but I didn't have enough coins for the string of questions she would then ask. I answered that my employers treated me well, with respect. She was glad to hear that.

31

Dina started our lunch meeting with: 'You know, Millie, Misha is a good man.'

'I know,' I replied, completely prepared *and* unprepared for her.

The whole year had gone by since Dina had told me that she needed to talk to me about something and I'd replied by asking her if that could wait. The whole new summer had commenced and ended and things got more complicated and I grew more careful and rehearsed for her, prepared myself. Now she was here, it was a Saturday and she had come to my office where I was in fact unprepared; where I was someone else, someone who worked hard for no salary, only for an indefinite leave to remain in this country. In this country, of which I'd seen almost nothing, of which I thought not much or not at all; where, as I came to realise, I had only one inspiration and that was this woman's husband.

She didn't want to talk about *something* in her house, where we were all reunited after that summer. The Grishins had spent two months away, in their villa on Lake Como. Misha managed to fly back from Milano to London several times to see me and spend a day or two with me. We continued to use Hotel Baglioni. Zorana had stayed on in the basement of their Chelsea mansion – I visited her there often, she was having a good rest - but even if she hadn't, both Misha and I had our limits.

He also took me to Windsor and Eton; it was a shame, he said, I'd never stepped outside London. We visited the school there, its gardens, where we picnicked and kissed surrounded by the bushes of chamomile and rosehip. I didn't smoke for the whole day; I needed to fully enjoy some fresh air.

Next time, I asked him to take me to Brighton or Cornwall; he said Wales was better.

'Dolphin Bay,' he said. 'I like the name.'

So he drove us out to the Ceibwr Bay, near Mwnt. We didn't even have to arrive there; just being with Misha and headed with him for those places whose names sounded as if picked out of a time-machine, was enough for me. We didn't mind the thunderous weekend there and we only once left the slightly sinister-looking room we'd rented in a local bed & breakfast.

Our lovemaking was fierce on the first day of our stay in Mwnt, although you would never tell, by the name of the place, that there could be any kind of lovemaking in Mwnt. Another tall bed, but this one old, screeched and wailed under us, begging for mercy. On the next morning, in the post-thunder, windy air, we drove out west, into the bay, and then walked to the Witches Cauldron. Against the layered, black cliffs beneath us, the ocean waves broke like a madman's head against the wall. I ran down to the half-hidden chasm and found a slim, sandy lagoon that looked untouched by humans. My footsteps took its virginity. There, I soaked my feet into the cold Ocean and felt sad and lonely. Misha came down after me, embraced and kissed me like he loved me. We stayed in the lagoon till the clouds had darkened and then we went back to our room and made love again. He was gentle then, still with an underlying desire to rip me apart. I could come just from sensing his emotional turmoil on me. We didn't talk much. Now and again Misha would say to me: 'Oh, look at you...' Our conversations consisted of compliments to each other or comments about our lives in a foreign country. With Misha, the silences were not obtrusive; they were pleasantly pregnant with the stories we could not tell each other yet; we knew enough for the time being; or so we thought.

'Can we go somewhere else?' I asked Dina. 'For a drink?'

'Let me take you out for lunch,' she replied and turned around to leave my office as quickly as possible. I myself had gotten used to the smell of it – of cheap disinfectant and yellowed paper stored since forever in the rows of cardboard boxes. Dina was obviously almost sickened by it. She was taking me out for lunch? It was fine; my official work hours had ended much earlier, but I liked staying on.

I followed her and locked the door behind me.

It was September and Dina was wearing jeans with a purple top, cut low on her back. Her back . . . Her corn-blond hair combed meticulously and so *lisse*, down that modestly tanned and luxuriantly freckled back, narrow and skinny, and with protruding shoulder blades – it was the back that made me melt in an instant. This woman was unable to do any harm. She could be my age, my generation. I couldn't really guess how old she was; she looked frozen by an expensive cosmetic treatment, something not too invasive, a 'spray-on botox' for example. In spite of her indoor living-style, she would not let life pile up on her. There were always various personal trainers, instructors of latest rejuvenation techniques, coming to stretch or sweat Dina out of the cruel passage of time. If she went out the night before, she'd spend half of the next day in the sauna *and* Turkish bath, adjoined to the *sunroom* – Dina's cult room, basically a glass-covered former top-floor patio which she had re-done as the space for relaxation, massages, afternoon tea or an occasional sex encounter with Misha, I'd say.

Outside my office, in the corridor of Chelsea Town Hall, several people smiled at me and greeted me, approached me with questions; this was normal, but that time I could see it through Dina's eyes and I did see it in her eyes that she was surprised by how much I mattered in there.

'Hey, teacher! Come back for me soon! My Mercedes is double-parked,' one of the regular homeless visitors said when he entered the Old Town Hall building as I was leaving it with Dina.

Dina smiled at him. He bowed.

'I envy you,' I think I heard her say, although it could have been that she only pronounced the name of the restaurant she was taking me to for lunch, which was something Japanese nearby, heavily air-conditioned and where of course there was no smoking, so I decided to keep the meeting short and deny everything.

Over the cold sushi rolls in a cold restaurant, Dina informed me that Misha was a good man. She decided to stand by him, I thought, no matter what. I was going to support her.

'Do you remember,' she went on. 'that, apparently, you told my children more than once how their father loves them very much. Do you remember?'

'Yes,' I said. 'Misha travels a lot and they probably miss him.'

'That was nice of you of course,' Dina said, 'but . . .' She paused there and looked as if she might start crying. She snatched her sunglasses off the table and pushed them onto the bridge of her nose.

'Misha is not their father,' she said.

I was shocked, but said: 'Oh, that's fine,' neutrally, for I was not sure whether I was now the only other person who knew about that.

Dina probably didn't even hear me.

296

'Alex remembers his real father,' she continued. 'Unfortunately. So . . . he thought you meant *that man* loved them very much. Their real father. He got confused. It *is* very confusing. And I shouldn't cry now. Migraine will kill me later. Nensi is different. She only remembers Misha.'

I was beginning to enter her world, to get interested.

'Where is their father?' I asked.

'In Kiev.'

Dina kept her sunglasses on for the rest of the lunch. She ate one and a half sushi rolls. There was a lot of crying and re-crying involved in her confession. Confession? It sounded like a confession from her side; she simply needed a therapist, a confidante, and here was I, who ate all the rest of sushi and tempura as she talked.

Dina had been married in Moscow and soon her husband had to move to Kiev; he was involved in privatisation business, a business-spy employed by the powerful people who could order him around and suddenly they needed him in Ukraine. In there, he was supposed to 'work from home', which actually meant 'sit at home and wait for the scary Muscovites' phone calls'. The phone calls were becoming more and more irregular and sometimes, the months passed in between them. The indoor-rooted husband became violent. He'd always been jealous, then possessive, then obsessive, then violent. Alexei was born and the husband became flaming mad and alcoholic. Paranoid. As Alexei was growing up, the husband, having had turned Dina into a complete housebound slave, had no one else to be jealous of, so he was jealous and abusive of his own toddler son. Nensi was born to throw some light on the grim situation, but she couldn't.

All that time, the unhappy family had no visitors. Dina made no friends in Kiev. The life was sucked out of her. She avoided even the few neighbours she'd met on the building's staircase. She hated their curious stares. They must have overheard her husband's shouting and swearing, but she hated them for giving *her* the stares. Don't stare if you can't help, she wanted to tell them, but she didn't want to provoke new animosities. She wanted to become invisible.

The only person who the husband ever co-worked with in person was – Misha. He was like a supervisor who lived in many places and travelled between them, London and Kiev included. Misha was the light. He came to the unhappy family's apartment once and grasped the whole situation.

'Misha is so good,' Dina repeated. 'He saved us, planned everything, brought us to London. He promised me he'd take care of us. But that first year in London was a torture. I was alone with small children here, in a house under refurbishment, none of us able to communicate in English and Alex terrified by school. I screamed and screamed at my son because *he* couldn't become *happy*. I pulled my hair out, frightened the children. I almost went back to my husband. Later, Misha joined us, persuaded his partners that he'd be more useful operating from here, finding new markets. He's a good organiser. He works hard. But he . . . He doesn't have - how to put it - stable social intelligence. He's like a child. This comes from his background. He

298

was raised in an orphanage – that's why he doesn't want to have any children of his own, says he's not happy to pass on his *unsolicited* genes. Anyway, when he left that orphanage he thought everyone outside it was either good or bad – I was an unprotected woman and therefore good. So he took me under his wing. This is how his mind works. In any case, once out of the orphans' home, Misha did everything to fit in and then some more. He hated the name *Ruslan* he'd been given in that orphanage and he named himself Misha Grishin, like some Soviet cartoon character. He invented his birthday, made himself two years *older*, imagine that! He needed to be eighteen instead of sixteen at the time. So this year he turns forty-five, but only according to his invented date of birth. He plays with life.'

Plays with life? I wanted to cry out. Misha didn't play with life. He was a wizard. He invented lives.

'You're smiling,' Dina continued. 'Yes, I see how this story can sound like a fairy tale. Maybe because of my English. But, I'm worried about him.'

'Why?' I asked. 'Because of your ex-husband?'

'No,' she said. 'That person is by now very much out of the picture. I can finally divorce because my ex-husband wants to remarry. But Misha . . . He has now found these people in your *Cherna Gora*, Montenegro, they make him laugh, he feels at home there, I think he secretly believes they are his lost ancestors and he trusts them too much and I don't trust them at all. Excuse me, but - not at all. They are selling beaches there, and marinas, putting them under the company, which is in Misha's name. Too easy. I tell him: 'Misha, that spells trouble,' and he just waves his hand.'

And so finally we had arrived to that *something* Dina wanted to discuss with me. She wanted me to persuade Misha to drop all the shady 'Montenegro business', to stop visiting my country; she had nightmares of him disappearing, swallowed by Montenegro by night.

For the end of the meeting, she had saved a giggle. If I was going to talk to Misha about Montenegro, and also because of my origin, she was sure Misha would be tempted and he'd try to seduce me. But she knew I was a serious person. She begged me to forgive Misha should that happen. He was like a boy, she repeated perkily, he thought it was expected of him to seduce every woman he talked to for more than five minutes. But so far, he'd been able to find his way back home. He was naughty but good.

Dina asked for the bill.

'I'd love to stay and chat,' she said. 'But I have to rush to Urban Retreat. I got myself booked with Claudio for one of his 'rectify and reacquaint' hair treatments. There's too much ash in my hair.'

Well, I had my rooftop to go back to.

32

What had Misha done to my mind with his 'Think of it as a short holiday' summary of our affair? How nonchalantly he had estimated the rhythm of it! It became my mantra. With the word *holiday* incorporated in one's mantra, things begin to unwind. People become inspired. Misha made me view my employment differently, even as a career. The Nanny of

Chelsea. *Your whole family properly (if not obsessively) looked after*. Millie Poppins with expensive, *less-is-more*, knickers underneath her unattractive clothes. The combination of Ms Poppins and Anka, Vukas's PA, except, where Anka resembled a Mastiff (fleshy and loyal), I was more of a Doberman – shadowy and on my way to insanity, guarding the house of my master from around the corner.

What am I talking about? I'm talking about are the rainy, windy, cold and dump autumn nights, which I spent camping (a wide-rimmed *Hotel Baglioni* umbrella my only camping-gear) under an acacia tree on the corner of Oakley Gardens and Phene Street, from where I could gaze at the windows of Misha's (and Dina's) bedroom and catch the light change from switched on to switched off and back; or a silhouette of Misha's naked torso, fresh out of shower and into the bathrobe. All I needed was an umbrella, my music and earplugs, and a pack of cigarettes. Hours flew by.

He had less time for me once the summer was truly over. I saw him during the day, inside the house, which Dina never left again. Dina, who, after having confided in me, started a pact with me, pointing at Misha from across the table or from the top of the staircase, and giving me a wink. I loved him more for what she'd told me about him. I enjoyed observing him from a new angle: he was a mystery even to himself, having grown up as an orphan. He invented his birthday. He changed his name, *Ruslan*, – a catalogued name he'd been given in an orphanage at the outskirts of Russia, of Europe – so, in a way, also a false name to begin with. Nothing and nobody in this Universe could classify Misha; neither astrology, nor KGB.

Many small things, of life importance to me, were taking place in the Grishins' house, which seemed enchanted from where I stood during the night hours. I heard noises I learnt to decipher: of laughter, of piano, of resentment and cuddle. I even saw Zorana a couple of times take the garbage out. She never spotted me as I was lurking in the dark, just a street corner away from her. I don't know what had made me invisible if not the passion, which takes the most unpredictable and mysterious of forms. I started developing the idea of ringing at their door with an excuse I'd forgotten something in their house (which I would've previously planted somewhere planting-friendly) and staying on for the night. I was becoming insatiable.

But one night, Misha managed to sneak out of the house unnoticed by me. I must have been momentarily drowned into a song and a cigarette because he spotted me before I spotted him, and I only heard the motor of his car when it broke through the stillness of the night. I was illuminated by two streams of blinding white light. Feeling like a rare beast, escaped from the Zoo, now vagrant and at large in the city, I bolted around the corner, but that bitchlet car was fast. And it could get through any obstacle. Misha made an immediate and illegal left turn on the pavement, only *just* missing the board that warned: *Bicycles only!*, or the acacia tree under which I'd made my small stalker's den, so now we were both in Phene Street, where he stopped.

'Were you coming to see us?' he asked me through

the rolled down car window.

'Every night,' I replied.

'Step inside, autumn fairy.'

I sat by him. He smelled like the soul of a home-made cake, and was slickly dressed in a navy blue jacket over a crisp, white shirt. He told me he was going to a meeting. He placed his bourbon-coloured hands on the wheel, and the sleeves of his jacket ran up the shirt sleeves to uncover the beautiful cufflinks – small stones, sapphires I guessed, nested inside the golden whir.

'Egyptian flies,' he said, lifting his wrist lightly off the wheel. 'They bring good luck. Well - money. Dina says.'

Every word he pronounced had the power to remain imprinted in my brain and then analyzed over and over again. To me, what he said about the cufflinks meant he was going to a business meeting, not to a romantic date as I'd briefly suspected because of the smoothness of his suit and smell.

'You see?' he whispered. 'The flies have already brought you and I barely left the house.'

He drove slowly into Margaretta Terraces, the intimate, side street, and there he parked his car in front of someone's sealed garage. Already I'd been familiar with the nighttime quietness of that street, and grateful for it.

He held my head between his palms. 'I missed being alone with you, too,' he said looking at me. 'So, you're here every night?'

'Yes.'

'Thank you,' he replied and gave me one of his signature kisses. 'But the winter is coming.'

The rain had started. Its drops, like the grains of rice, made the pleasant sound against the windshield, and I was safely inside Misha's car. Outside, there was only the weather. No people. I wanted us to be naked and to fall asleep together in there. But Misha had to go.

'I have some guests waiting for me in their hotel,' he said. 'Plus we can end up in prison if we're caught being indecent in public.'

'In public? We're in your car. I just want to feel your skin.'

That was my thing with Misha: an urge to make his skin run into mine. Or, rub into mine and become mine. Often, when around him, I had to scratch myself, poke my nails into my flesh till it hurt, to control myself.

'I've just made love to Dina,' he said. 'Persuaded her to throw me some bones,' he lowered his head. 'It's good to relax before hitting the game table. Especially accompanied by someone as nervous about it as these people I'm meeting tonight.'

Both of us were too big for that car, and then there was my *Hotel Baglioni* umbrella almost the size of Yola or Zorana. He was right: we were not that desperate. Yeah.

'What people?' I asked sensing he wanted to tell me.

But Misha looked puzzled.

'Mm, forgot the names,' he said. 'Your countrymen.'

He was lying: I knew by then that Misha never forgot a name, a date, that kind of information.

'But really nice people, well-informed. Tall and elegant, like all of you, Montenegrins. Anyway, I'm taking them to my club where we're going to play a little.'

'Play what?'

'Roulette, silly. Just for fun. That's why I put on these Egyptian flies. It's nice to leave as a winner. But, these guys take it too seriously. First they said they'd just watch. That's what everyone says before the ball lands on their favourite number. Then they think – I can do this. I can defeat the devil. So your Montenegrins got on the table like they were going to rape it. And lost. They should learn from me. Roulette feeds on un-coolness.'

'And you're so cool.'

'Well, don't you think so?' He kissed me. 'I'm late, Millochka, but it's raining. I should drive you home.'

'No,' I said. 'I'll be fine.'

I was crossing the bridge on my way home, thinking of Misha's mysterious new Monte friends. Tall and elegant. Nice. Who were these guys whose names Misha didn't want me to know? But he wanted me to know he was going to meet them. He didn't have a clue how little I cared about my elegant and nice countrymen. Misha had worked like a pill for me. A sweet pill of oblivion. I gave up many things, I became a bore, and I was fine about it because there was Misha in London, just over the bridge from me. Or was he? Was he? Wasn't he just letting me know he knew about my camping in front of his house, mocking me gently about it, then giving me a couple of quick kisses and driving away in a rush? What did those people tell him about me?

The next morning I came to take children to school, itching to ask Misha about his enigmatic friends from Montenegro, but Misha was still sleeping.

Zorana, smirking, conveyed the latest order from our *ludara*, meaning 'loony', Mistress Dina, and it was to respect and obey the Poppy appeal. I was to pin poppies on children's uniform items that were pin-friendly. Misha's and Dina's overcoats were to be decorated by poppies as well.

'First of all, I should pin one on each of their bathrobes,' Zorana said into my ear. 'That's been their main overcoat these days.'

After the drop-off, and Alex's class Assembly, I had to go search for a store that sold bagatelle items for the school's numerous projects, which I was to help the children with, initially, but really *do*, at the end. I couldn't believe it: Alex was supposed to make a large painting or a collage inspired by the works of Klimt. Of Klimt! How old was I when I first heard about Klimt? Twenty-five? And still I struggled to cut through his layers; my artistic friends used to hold the over-the-wine discussions about the consciously uncontrolled ways in which Klimt's art had given birth to a playfully liberated woman. Here was a bunch of ten-year-olds, asked to copy the master's view of female infatuation with her own body.

'We are observing more closely Klimt at his purest,' the art teacher had informed me. 'We only fleetingly learn about his *portraits*. But Alex wants to do a portrait. And I say – why not? He's got a good eye.'

306

It was I who did it, I wanted to scream. It was my eye!

'You're welcome to accompany us on our daytrip to the National Gallery,' the art teacher went on. 'You'll see: it's amazing how useful early exposure to great art is for the young children.'

'Thank you,' I said. The school knew already that I was the grown-up most often willing to help out when they needed an extra adult for their daytrips. It was a perfect way for me to discover more of London; how else would I visit Wimbledon or St. Paul's Cathedral?

And Nensi's projects! In Power Point! All this before she learnt how to tie her laces properly.

When I came back to the Grishins' house Misha had already woken up and gone out again, for meeting and lunch. Dina was sitting at the long oval dining table, whose surface was furnished by white snakeskin, chewing her breakfast rhythmically at the pace of a sheep. She was barefoot, in her cashmere-padded silk kimono the colour of pink pearl. Her hair had been washed and combed back. The chandelier of crystals - put together densely to form a glaring, black-and-white rectangle on which the two F's for Fendi stood in pose 69 to one another - had been switched on above the table. Its light danced on Dina's ash-free, wet hair and illuminated the well-hydrated skin of her face. She fed herself a slice of kiwi, then a slice of nectarine, a sip of pressed pink grapefruit juice, a spoonful of berries. Healthy and boring, but so rewardingly time-consuming, especially in combination with *Tatler* she was leafing through, her nails as glossy as the magazine's pages. I watched her from the hall. Classical music was playing from all the speakers in the house.

Dina had a peculiar trick in her pack of cards (gaming industry again). She could be as annoying as the next Eastern European woman brought to live in London to wonder what the point of it all was if not the daily visits to Christian Louboutin or the launch of her own fashion label. But, whenever I – and I suspected I wasn't the only victim of Dina's trick – observed her for more than one minute, I would get the feeling that she had to be protected and if I didn't help, I'd have her on my consciousness. It only took for my gaze to rest on her blonde head for thirty seconds longer than intended and my knees would sink and I'd catch the trail of confusion and fear she was born suffering from. That kind of vulnerability was her own miniscule hook in the chromosome chain.

Dina lifted her eyes from the newspapers and saw me. I waved.

'Please, come sit with me,' she said. She called out Zorana's name and rang a small paging bell several times.

I sat down next to her. Zorana appeared from somewhere.

'I'm now ready for my Ayurvedic tea,' Dina informed her. 'What would you like, Millie? The tea I take is very good for one's balance if one feels messed-up by autumn. You want to try it?'

I raised one corner of my mouth to Zorana in a compatriot grin. She ignored it and kept a straight face on, like a seasoned butler-ess. I replied that a cup of

Ayurvedic tea would be great for me.

'Finally we can talk,' Dina started. 'I was dying to thank you. I want to buy a beautiful Chopard bracelet of friendship for you if you don't mind. Or would you rather I gave you a gift card?'

'No need for that.' This sentence, I believed, was the best reaction to whatever Dina had in mind. I knew she had nothing to be grateful for to me. There was some misunderstanding and I sure as *samovar* wasn't going to mess it up for anyone.

'No need to be modest, *I'd* say,' Dina went on, touching my hand. 'I may be lazy with praises but I have noticed how my children have changed for the better since you appeared in our lives. And now...ah, you saved us! I could give you cash of course – after all, Misha claims that cash is the only real motherland for all the émigrés – but it would be too...let me see...too smug, too businesslike for such a human gesture of yours. I can't even begin to tell you how happy it made me feel that he doesn't go to Montenegro anymore. So, I thought, a bracelet of friendship would express my emotion most properly. Do you know how these things look?'

'What things?'

'These bracelets. The ones I have in mind are white gold, with charms, made of pre-ordered birthstones. These charms can be in the shape of anything you pick: heart, seashell, key, or the letters, like M for Millie -'

'Oh, I really...'

'I know your birthstone. It's ruby. Ruby is the keeper of your health and good fortune. Chopard does these perfect rubies, the colour of pink flash of a dragon fruit.'

What the hell was she talking about?

'And I planned to put five charms on the bracelet. Five is your number. It's a good number. In your case, it doesn't come from *twenty-three*, but then, if it did, you would not be a nanny. Which shapes do you want?'

'Are you sure Misha never goes to Montenegro?' I asked, dying to crawl out of the bracelet topic, which made my head spin.

'Why would he lie to me? Do you know something I don't? Thank you, Zorana,' Dina said to the little Macedonian, waving her hand. 'That was enough tea for me. More tea for you, Millie?'

'No, thanks.' That tea tasted like water in which boys' socks were boiled. 'So he doesn't do business in Montenegro?'

Dina wrinkled her nose. 'You suspect,' she said.

'I thought he had too much invested in there.'

'He didn't invest any money, no,' Dina replied. 'Only his name, which of course could cost him his life if he didn't pull out on time. I asked him why he never went to Montenegro again, why he didn't mention it since . . . since this summer, really. He said he was finished there. Now he mostly travels to Singapore, Washington. To the countries with some rules and institutions, if you don't mind my being so straight forward with you.'

'No, that's fine. I just don't think it has anything to do with me being dissuasive about Montenegro.'

'You just don't want to receive a gift. That's not good for your personal development, you know. You must be open to gifts. Only if you're open to gifts, life will give you more.'

I could feel my cheeks blushing and I got up from the table.

'Dina, you are too kind,' I said. 'Excuse me now. I must go to the children's rooms and check on the library books that are due back.'

'I am not too kind,' Dina said. 'Not at all.'

I climbed up the stairs and entered Nensi's room. I sat on her fluffily made bed and gazed at the pink bookshelf, thinking about Misha.

Zorana walked into the room tugging a vacuum cleaner behind her. She moved about swiftly, plugged the thing in and turned it on and left it howling in the corner of the room as she approached me.

'Take the bracelet, silly woman,' Zorana talked fast in a hissing whisper that featured a pitch strong enough to carry itself above the roar of the vacuum cleaner. 'Misha lied about Montenegro to quiet the beast. I told you how she screams at nights. Poor guy had to lie. He keeps connections with Montenegro, I know. Maybe he doesn't go there, but people come here now. One of them wants to meet me! Misha says that one is looking for a nice girl to marry. The man is from Montenegro but lives in Washington. A *diplomat*!' And she turned around and grabbed the vacuum cleaner by the tall handle and pushed it around the room. 'I would marry,' she repeated through her teeth. 'I would. I'd marry a man Misha recommends. He's tall and good-looking, Misha says. And I'd have a diplomatic passport as his wife.'

I stood up and walked to her.

'What is this guy's name?' I asked Zorana, following her around.

'Branko,' she said. 'Branko something. You know maybe. A diplomat in America.'

I felt a blow in my stomach, a sickness.

'Listen,' I spoke into her face, 'if it's *the Branko* I have in mind, the tall one, sent to Washington by the president of Montenegro, then you're better off living here in the basement for ever, cleaning after Dina and listening to her nocturnal screams. Listen to me!'

Zorana kept on vacuuming, avoiding my eyes, clenching her fragile little jaw with the unpronounced words of denial. I turned around to Nensi's bookshelf, determined to sort out my job and my life first, before I spoke into other people's faces again.

'It's probably not that Branko,' I heard Zorana say behind my back. 'In Macedonia, I knew *ten* Brankos.'

I had to get on with my job.

That evening, I was super-patient while helping children with homework, all the time waiting for Misha to walk through the front door. I made them supper. I bathed them. Read them stories. Answered their questions. Stayed on. No sign of Misha; no whirring engine sounds, no wheels crackling the pebbles in front of garage; no steps in the hallway, or the beloved voice laced with mirth.

Dina was waiting for him as well: spread on the corner sofa, huffing and sighing, mumbling in Russian, pretending to read Toni Morrison – because, I thought the book was called *Love* - but mostly, dialing him, of

312

course, whom else, in vain from her phone.

Finally, I said goodnight to everyone and went out to wait for Misha under my acacia tree. We, humans, can't operate any longer without a tool that provides us with information that can answer the questions of the moment, however humiliating. I'd decided against owning a mobile phone, so I ended up being addicted to a tree-spot in order to find out what was going on with Misha.

There was a silhouette of Dina in their bedroom window; she was still dialing, dialing and the night stretched hollow and long ahead of me. After a while, I came to my senses and quickly walked home, over the bridge, to Yola and Isztvan and Rafi, the members of my ideal family: mild-blooded, non-perverse and safe.

In my room, I grew restless again, fearing the return of insomnia, craving the sleeping pills; *craving* their bitter taste as they would, swallowed without water, melt in my throat. Something was creeping into my nicely organised new life. With Branko here, and God knew who the other tall and elegant men were, even London was closing up on me, becoming a claustrophobic village in a crevice among the mountains. Branko was in every sense the minor, the peon, but a contaminant for me on so many levels, like banal smoke for people with respiratory problems. My room here didn't even have a balcony I could go to, breathe my anxiety out. The building's roof, under the reign of the unforgiving late autumn, was too communal for the present emotion. Some books I'd borrowed from the library were piled, unopened, beside my bed. I started to read. I looked for the characters that shared my experience, which could be summed up as having a bunch of undeservedly powerful enemies for such an insignificant fate. According to the books, people were foolish everywhere; they fretted and fretted and then died or were dying. But it was never about deaths. Death is communal, like the rooftop. Was it all about survival then, the individuality of it?

Night hours stretched ahead. I'd managed to put together thirty minutes of spiky sleep here and there, and finally welcomed a new morning, however muggy, still more spacious, less dogmatic than the night.

33

Misha was sleeping. Everyone else was supposed to be quiet. Never before had they cared if Misha was asleep while the morning activities were taking place. But, Dina ordered silence, as Zorana, who'd opened the front door for me before I even rang the doorbell, informed me in the hall. Shhh, with her forefinger pressed on the lips. *He's still sleeping.*

'You should have seen her,' Zorana whispered. 'A cranky, old witch hissing from the top of the staircase. And Misha – God knows when he came back. There will be blood on the kitchen floor, I'm telling you. Do you also say this in Montenegro?'

I laughed, as silently as I could. 'No, no, we don't. It's pure English.'

'I'm going out to dinner with Branko tomorrow night,' Zorana said and kissed me.

That young and ambitious Macedonian woman

believed she had a future with an unmarried, professional Montenegrin man, a diplomat, still young himself. Who was I to interfere?

I took care of children's needs in silence. They were such good kids; they knew respect. I taught them respect. I talked with them a lot, they trusted me and learnt that the adults could be worthy of respect.

On our walk to school, Nensy informed me: 'I wee-weed in my bed last night.'

Alex was picking his nose absent-mindedly – another bad sign.

I stopped short on the pavement and pulled children closer to me under my umbrella. *Welcome to Hotel Baglioni.*

'What's going on?' I asked them.

Alex started to cry and Nensi followed, with pearly tears quietly rolling down her cheeks.

'Mama screamed at me for wee-weeing in bed,' Nensi sobbed. 'I ran into her room to tell her and she kicked me out and said I must sleep in my weewee now . . .'

'I heard it all,' Alex said. 'Before that Misha woke us up with his shouting. Remember, Nensi? You came out of your room and you looked scared.'

'Wow!' I said. 'Sounds like the grown-ups had gone a little stoo-pee-dee last night. It happens in all families.'

'Did it happen in your family when you were a child?'

'Oh, yes it did. That's how I know that your parents will feel guilty today. But you know what? Don't forgive them easily. Torture them a bit. Feel the power!'

'But I'm scared,' Alex said and I hugged them. 'Misha said to Mama that

he would push her down the stairs if she continued to be such a monster. And that nobody would miss her. I'd miss her.'

I laughed and Nensi copied me, full of hope.

'That *so* obviously was a joke,' I said. 'A Misha-kind-of-joke.'

'Yeah,' Nensi agreed. 'Daddy's funny like that.'

'Okay, now,' I said, 'remember: you can tell *me* these things and I'll keep them secret and help with some invisible magic. But don't talk about it in school.'

Every time there was a bit of a shocker in the family, witnessed by Alex and Nensi, Dina warned me on the next day: 'Teach our children not to talk about their family in school,' she'd say. She was convinced that the UK government and social services hated Russians and other Eastern Europeans and waited for our one slip so that they could say: *Aha, the Barbarians, of course*, and punish us. She was convinced they checked on us through everything, through children! 'They want to prove we are trash.' After a blink she once added: 'Perhaps you don't feel it because you live from Friday to Friday and nobody is after your money.'

The children nodded and we kept walking. Every three or four steps we'd all sigh under the drizzle and the roof of my huge umbrella.

Misha was zooming out of my life, I could tell, and it hurt. I strongly associated this town with him, which helped me feel as if I had the right to colonise it minutely by my humble presence. But now, Misha's priorities had obviously shifted.   That afternoon, when I brought the children back home, I found out that Misha had gone out, probably with a plan to gamble again, and Dina was left behind, still hissing with steam, like a forgotten kettle. Alex and Nensi had been hopeful all day in school, expecting their parents to act guiltily, apologise and offer a money-spending visit to Harrods' fourth floor. Instead, the grand gloom of family crisis hovered between the walls of the haunted mansion. Haunted by *Montenegro*, I had to smile. Goliath totally confused by David. The tall and mighty string of paintings that represented the perverted actors in the battle of Borodin may have provoked this inversion of roles. Be careful with images you use to decorate your house.

The children seemed choked by the unshed tears because their mama was treating them like 'the soot-orphans' as they said, which were probably some folklore characters from the tales of their Babushka. Dina was either ignoring them or, in a curt voice, asking them about their piano lessons. And Misha was not there to defend them, like a knight in a shining bathrobe.

I had to be alone with Misha and *talk* to him, talk my doubts out. There was no other way than to wait for the opportunity on the street. It was Friday and if I didn't have some clarifications until Monday, I was to be chained to the weekend of eroding insomnia. I decided to leave my *Hotel Baglioni* umbrella behind, in the mansion; if somebody other than Misha spotted me lurking around the house I'd boldly say I'd forgotten that important item of my daily transport.

So, after work, I went to a nearby cafe where I ate my sandwich, drank tea then coffee then more tea, slowly, by the window, focused on the cars that crawled on King's Road. I was so trained at car-spotting – I'd been trained well back in Montenegro, during the days of civil war when the boys in stolen cars always promised they'd call and they never did, so the girls focused on the boulevard and scanned it for their smart vehicles - that I knew I couldn't miss Misha even if he'd left his tiny beast-car or his huge SUV behind and came home driven either by his club chauffeur or by a cabbie. But he didn't come and I finished my sandwich.

I took another paper cup of warm latte with me, back to Oakley Gardens. I leaned on my tree and listened to some music. Incredible how effortlessly a woman in love can wait for her prey. Waiting becomes foreplay. Autumn becomes spring. I became high. Maybe it was the late latte, or my returning insomnia, or my longing for Misha – probably all of it combined – but I caught myself thinking of Misha taking a nap on my thighs, of his crazy hair and his warm body resting on top of me, like a lean ruler of the steppe would take a moment of rest above his prey.

34

Not too late into the night, a black car, a Bentley, slid into Oakley Gardens, stopping in front of Misha's house. A driver in a dark suit stepped out of the car to open the front door for his passenger and Misha came out, looking amused, hip and proud, like a much-praised, well-earning artist, wrapped in his best Italian coat, the one with the velvet collar, a poppy pinned into it. He stood on the pavement, breathing in the mist, breathing out the steam. I could see he was drunk by the way he leered at his bedroom window, even mumbling at it in Russian. Nobody looked out from that window. The driver stooped towards the back door and opened it. He was handed a huge bouquet of ripe lilies by somebody. The lilies, like me, gaped at the damp night. A long leg in trousers and a long expensive shoe stepped out of the back of the car first, followed by a long arm in a raincoat whose colour – basic beige - reeked of diplomacy. And finally the whole person: my countryman, Branko Dubak, the president's brother-in-law.

He seemed drunk as well, as he was swaying slowly back and forth in his long shoes.

But that wasn't the end of it. The black Bentley spat out two more passengers: a young girl with a wildcat's physique, who seemed to have gone out for the night on the town sometime last June and never went back in to put on some warmer clothes; and a rock-a-billy stallion I'd recognised even before he let out his famous over-the-top laughter ('Ha Ha Ha, Misha, my man, nice house in the heart of London, really, I'm impressed.'). Lazar Perić.

For months my life had been moulded into a fine routine. I almost came to a point where I could hope I'd be happy one day. I'd be proud of some achievement of mine. But, no. These people, these ghosts from my past, were everywhere, arrived everywhere, seeping through borders like an ever-mutating virus. And why wouldn't they? They all had official titles; they were professional members of a society. My knees buckled and I leaned back on the acacia tree. Misha, an orphan, with his senses trained to stay open at all times, looked in my direction. I waved. He spread his arms open for me to run into his chest. He was so drunk, he didn't give a damn. The visitors turned their heads towards me. I walked fast to Misha while Branko was shouting: 'Is this the *girl* you had in mind for me? But *this* is not *Zorana*! I know *this*! I know this woman, do you *hear* me?'

'We can all hear you, man,' Misha said and hugged me so hard that the plastic poppy from his velvet collar poked into my cheek. 'This is my Millie. She's from Pod-gori-tza, like you people.'

'Ciao, Millie!' the young woman squealed and I recognised her: it was Saša, the favourite girlfriend of Perić. Of course, I'd always known that my preposterous Millie-ing around London was working like blood for Perić-the-shark, who had once tasted his Millie Vanilli.

Before Perić could express his reaction to seeing me, the front door opened and Dina stood at the entrance, fully clothed in lovely jeans, high heels, low buttoned shirt. Her face was glowing under some high-quality make-up.

'Come inside, you, party people,' she said. 'My husband's birthday has just started and we're having a party.'

November sixteen! I'd completely forgotten how

320

I wanted to do something special for Misha on his invented – but still – birthday. I freed myself from Misha's embrace and walked to Dina saying: 'I just came back for my umbrella. I left it here.'

She raised the pointy ends of her sharply groomed eyebrows almost imperceptibly, in a non-ironic acknowledgment of my excuse. She was only interested in Misha.

From behind my back I heard him cry out: 'Dinochka! Were you going out somewhere, my love?'

'Fuck off,' she replied, still smiling. 'Who have you brought home this time? And where is *my* Porsche? You left it again in front of your club for some Albanian chauffeur to drive it back here, right?'

The umbrella was still placed by the front door and so was I.

'Dina *bambina*!' Misha said. 'Always full of surprises. I thought you hated that little car. I bought it for you and you drove it once in London. *Once*!' He raised his forefinger.

'You bought it for me when I was still a Russian peasant who didn't know Bentley,' Dina said.

'I'll buy a Bentley, *ljubovna maya*, you just have to inform me about your wishes. Orally.'

'Come inside,' Dina repeated and opened her palms to him. 'Happy birthday.' They kissed on the mouth.

The chauffeur peeked from behind the lilies with a quizzical and amused expression as if wondering whether that unusual exchange of emotions had really happened. He walked in first.

'Flowers for you, Madame,' he said to Dina and

placed the lilies on a chaise longue in the lobby.

Dina's eyes bulged at the bouquet. 'Their stench gives me headache and *Misha* knows that,' she said.

The driver shrugged and nodded at me as he passed me by in the lobby on his way out.

'Well,' he said, 'good night everyone. Take care.' And he was gone, back to the club, to drive other gamblers home.

'I forgot my umbrella here,' I informed Dina again.

Branko was trying to catch my eye and scare me or warn me or curse at me. The rest of the party came in.

'Extremely glad to see you, Millie Vanilli,' Perić whispered as he brushed by me. 'I see you've changed your taste in clothes. Sporty Spice now, is it?'

Inside the house, Misha leaned on the stair railing and shouted out Zorana's name down the steps and into the basement flat.

'Where did you steal these old stinkers from?' Dina asked him, pointing at the lilies, placed flat and desperate on the chaise longue. 'Graveyard?'

Her breath was emitting a fume of something bubbly and friendly. Champagne! I spotted a magnum bottle on the coffee table by the fireplace. I needed some alcohol, badly. I made my way towards the reception room, and the bottle. I sank down into deep leather armchair by the fire at which I gazed, unable to move, to just grab the big umbrella, walk out and keep walking over Albert bridge, home.

Misha was still shouting. 'Zarochka! Girl, I brought your man! Come up here to meet him!'

Dina, dramatically elegant on her high heels, walked

into the reception room to join me.

'You look tired,' she whispered. 'We'll talk tomorrow.'

I decided not to remind her that 'tomorrow' was a Saturday, my day at the Citizen Advice office. She would realise that. She was telling me about her migraine, how she felt it coming, knocking at her temple, in her neck, but that she would have some champagne with me. She opened the filigree cupboard and took out several crystal champagne flutes. She filled one up for me.

The guests were still standing in the hallway, next to Misha: Perić and Saša kissing and hugging, Branko pacing the space nervously, unable to share the same room with me – me, a worthless person who was receiving an incredibly special treatment from this mad, but obviously wealthy Russian family. He must have been painfully confused, and, in addition to being drunk, he was bound to do something vile – that much I knew about him. No Ambassador title could change that. And Perić! For anyone who didn't know him, he seemed such a nice, respectful guest, a poised, middle-aged gentleman, with a younger girlfriend on his shoulder. Yes, I nodded at the fire. The very reason why I despised my own country, the very reason why I never wished to meet my countrymen in London, was now not only in London, but a special guest in the house where my work and love mixed. Misha had plans to marry Branko off from under his roof just to impress Perić. Misha had a Montenegrin deal on his mind, and the deal must have, via Perić, included Vukas, the President, who had to be consulted about anything concerning Montenegro - that small, poor country, which had given enormous wealth and power to the concentrate of evil. *Misha was good*, Dina had persuaded me during our only lunch together, and I'd let her do it, from the bottom of my heart. After all, he was an orphan who'd come a long way. But, I wasn't sure about anything anymore. The mock Borodin Battle on the walls . . . Nothing here was reliable, the painting seemed to say, not even the legendary battle's generals. I looked back at the fireplace and spotted the rubber soles of Babushka's slippers, still hidden behind it. I missed that woman. I missed ordinary, reliable people. I believed that someone like Babushka would have enough of an instinct to scare the unwanted guests away. I refilled my glass.

A loud applause broke out from the lobby. Zorana was coming upstairs from her basement dwelling. Misha whistled.

'Shush, you,' Dina hissed at him. 'The children!'

'Oh, it's *not* fair,' I heard Zorana's shy, flirty voice. 'I wanted to look special when I meet your friend.' Her high heel shoes clicked on the marble stairs. So young. It seemed unfair for anyone so young to fall into a trap of marrying a Branko. I wasn't going to shut up about it.

Misha reassured her that she was beautiful even when woken up. And she did look good, all blushed cheeks and sparkling smile.

'Milena?' she said, surprised to see me.

'Everything is ready for your big night,' Misha said. 'First, meet Branko.' The two of them shook hands.

324

'Flowers are here,' Misha touched the lilies. 'In case you guys decided to get married right away, we have guests *and* the maid of honour, Millie, where are you?' I didn't answer. 'Champagne and caviar as well!' Misha added, rubbing his hands.

'What are you talking about?' Branko cried.

'Just kidding, man,' Misha replied.

By the fireplace, I emptied another glass.

'Oh, come sit here you silly boys,' Dina called from the cosy corner of the black velvet sofa. 'And you too, lovely girls. But please, first take off your coats. I have a feeling, if you don't you're going to go to that awful club again. Zorana, *doraga*, can you bring me one *Immigran* pill from you know where? And while you're at it, bring caviar in the silver caviar dish, please.'

Dina couldn't see Zorana's expression from the corner of the sofa. The little Macedonian was about to burst with hatred.

'It's Zorana's moment,' Misha said to Dina, as they all entered the reception room. 'I arranged a little introduction meeting for her and my friend Branko here, the Ambassador of Montenegro in Washington! Have some heart, my love.'

'Oh,' Dina said. 'Misha hatched a lovely plan for our Zarochka. Nice to meet you, Ambassador . . .'

'Dubak. Branko Dubak,' Branko said.

'How do you find Washington, Ambassador?'

'It's a bit disappointing I guess. Not many good-looking women there.'

'Dina meant *professionally*,' I said from behind my champagne flute.

Branko looked at me. '*Professionally*,' he snapped, 'that fact would be useful for your profession. You know, Washington would be a less competitive place for *prostit* -'

'Millie, baby,' Misha interrupted. 'Can you bring the pills for our pill-lady? And I'll fix the caviar snack.'

I jumped from the armchair while Dina was opening her mouth preparing a killer reply to the *pill-lady*. But Branko was faster.

'What is *Milena* doing in your house?' he spoke behind my back, as I ran up the stairs to Dina's bathroom.

'Millie is our nanny,' Misha said. 'I mean, for our children. I mean – mostly for our children,' he laughed.

Upstairs, I opened the mirrored cupboard in Dina's magnificent bathroom, inside which she kept her secret supplies: appetite-killers, the brochures of romantic retreats, ointments with suspicious-looking labels. I snatched a box of *Immigran* and ran back down. Branko spoke again.

'Why are you a *nanny* in London?' he asked me in English. He used to speak this language stiffly, with an invalid tongue, only two years ago. But, of course, now he lived in Washington D.C. 'London is a perfect city for your real profession,' he went on and turned to Misha. 'She sleeps for money,' he informed Misha pointing at me.

'Really?' Misha said. 'What, like a paid sleeper? I like that job. I bet it's not taxable. Can I sleep for money, too?' Misha asked and, still in his coat, walked to the corner sofa in the reception room and hurled himself onto it. He closed his eyes and snored, pretending to sleep, his hands hidden somewhere inside his coat. Then, a pack of casino money fell out of the coat, followed by another, and another, the fourth one, and the fifth. Fat packs of money rained down on the floor.

'I slept for money!' Misha shouted opening his eyes. 'Wow! Millie, can you sleep for money like that?' he added, jumping from the sofa, staring at the packs of money he had obviously won in his casino.

Perić out-laughed everybody.

'Good joke,' Branko said. 'But you all know what I meant.'

'Come-on, man,' Perić said. 'Relax. Let this striking young woman here see you at your best. Zorana, extremely nice to meet you. My name is Lazar, everyone calls me Perić, and this is my partner, Saša. She's an author.'

Partner? Author?

'So you write . . . what?' Dina asked. 'Literature?'

'Music,' Saša said. 'I write and perform my own songs.'

Dina placed a pill on her tongue and washed it down with champagne. Then, as if the pill had been Speed, not *Immigran*, she sprang to her feet and spoke.

'Well, my Misha surely mingles with the jet-set of Montenegro, doesn't he?'

'Yes, my dear wife, your Misha does. Now, if you're too tired or too anxious, please hit the bed, won't you?'

'Let me explain,' Perić said. 'We all had a little too much to drink because my Saša here has signed a contract with the best music producer in London that

Misha kindly introduced us to. Then, in high spirits, we thought tonight we'd introduce our Ambassador Branko here to this lovely future TV presenter, Zorana. Since, you know, it seems to be a fruitful time introductions-wise. Huh? And now, turns out – it's my good friend Misha's birthday. So modest of him not to tell us. But, if the beautiful hostess doesn't feel well, we'll come by another time.'

'You're not leaving, my friend,' Misha said. 'Not before caviar and champagne. Please, seat yourselves at the table and I'll take care of everything. Please.' And he gently pushed the guests to the white snakeskin dining table and drew the chairs out for them.

Perić grinned at me. He tapped the chair next to him, inviting me to sit there. I remained by the fireplace. Branko sat next to Zorana. Dina circled the room like a vulture. Misha went to the kitchen, the larder, opened the cabinets to set the table and feed the guests. Finally, he sat down on the chair that Perić had planned for me.

'Dina, Millie,' Misha said. 'Come on. Let's celebrate.'

'I just didn't like the way the Ambassador had insulted my Millie in my house,' Dina said.

Branko opened his mouth to say something but Perić cut him.

'I take it the two of them have met before under not-so-diplomatic of circumstances,' he said. 'But tonight, we're all friends here, right, friends?'

I was getting drunk, hoping I'd become invisible, but not absent, not while they were discussing me at least.

'Okay,' Dina agreed, her migraine pill probably starting to work. She stopped circling the table and found herself a chair she wanted to sit on. They were all eating and drinking in silence for some time.

'Can we smoke inside?' Perić asked Dina.

'Not too much, please,' Dina said. 'So . . . Saša, was it? What contract, what kind of singer? I'd love to know.'

'I have completed only several songs so far,' Saša replied after Perić had lit up her cigarette. 'I'm a perfectionist, you see.'

'My girl is too hard on herself. She's got this talent. And we have a demo here. The future number one hit! *Perpetum mobile*, the name of the song.'

'What, you have it on CD?' Dina asked. 'Can we hear it?'

'Why not?' Perić replied.

'Zorana, would you -' Dina started but Misha interrupted her.

'I'll do it.'

Saša opened the little across-the-body bag that hung down to the middle of her thigh, longer than her dress did. She took out the CD and handed it to Misha who got up and went to insert it into a tall music centre by the TV. The music started. It wasn't bad at all, the beginning of the song: drums, violins, beat, her laughter, drums, violins, beat, *Not here for you* – her whisper.

'Stop, stop, stop, stop!' Perić said. Misha paused the song. 'This is not right at all without Saša's dancing to it. Go, baby,' Perić touched Saša's elbow,' show them the whole package.'

'*Daj mi prvo malo kokishke*,' the girl said.

'No, no, no, no,' Perić laughed. 'Remember our little

329

conversation?' He was speaking English. 'Superstars are not on chemicals. They just learn to behave as if they were. Let others fuck themselves up – oops, excuse me – but the superstars stay clean, okay?'

'Whatever,' Saša said, got up and walked towards the mirrored wall of the reception. She snapped her fingers. The music started again.

'*Perpe-chum-mo-bee-leh,*' she was singing, '*my middle name, no other way to shake off the shame,*' and she shook her shoulders, then hips, then knees, in a controlled manner of a well-trained dancer. '*Perpe-chum-mo-bee-leh, you get what you see, but my deepest secret is stuck inside me.*'

As the lyrics went on, it was revealed that the girl in question had lost her true love forever, and now she was perpetum-mobile-ing, aka fucking around as a sort of revenge, and Saša really brought the subject of her song to life. I could swear that by the end of performance she'd reach an orgasm. Misha and Perić exchanged glances and I just knew that Misha had fucked her once or twice, that Perić had let him. I was still hoping I'd become invisible. Zorana was impressed by Saša; it was obvious she wanted to have the singer's lucrative life. Branko held the edge of the table with his fingertips white from pressure, spying from time to time on Zorana and her reaction to Saša, judging the little Macedonian's submission potential. Dina was giggling and giggling, exclaiming: 'Bravo! Bravo!' Now, that was something to be afraid of.

Saša fell on her knees at the end of the song, tossed her long hair on one side and yanked the collar of her dress a bit down, offering her wounded heart to the audience. Under the light texture of her outfit, her nipples stood out like two upturned nosetips. Everyone applauded.

'Yeah,' the future superstar said. 'Now, Perić, give me some coke or I'll fucking die!' she went on, speaking in our language. 'I can't fucking breathe with this damned shit of a nostril.'

'Come here, baby, I'll give you some,' Perić replied. 'Now wasn't that great?' he added in English.

Saša approached Perić and he placed a small bag in the palm of her hand.

'Go to the bathroom and do it there,' he said to her in our language. 'It's enough we're smoking inside their house.'

'Like I know where the bathroom is.'

'Go past the kitchen and you'll find it,' Misha said. It seemed he'd learnt his necessary amount of Montengrin. Saša nodded and winked at him.

'She needs to refresh herself,' Perić said to Dina. 'We must fix her left nostril, you know. It needs enlargement. I paid for the best nose job for her, but they didn't do it right.'

'Really?' Dina said. 'Where did she have it done? Here?'

'No,' I said from my armchair. 'In Dubai.'

'Wow, yeah,' Perić cried and looked at me. 'How did you know that, Millie Vanilli?'

My eruptions were back.

'You told me about it on the night you raped me, remember?' I said.

'Whoa!' Perić clasped his hands. 'You sure had me mixed up with somebody. Darling, *I* don't have to rape women. I mean, everyone, please, between Millie and Saša, we choose Saša, no? And sometimes the Millies of this world don't take it so well.'

'No they don't, my friend' Branko said. 'They don't. In fact, they take it so bad they ambush their lovers and shoot them with stolen guns!'

A born diplomat, Branko. So that was still the plan with me back home. And what home? There was no 'back home'. For all I knew, I might be on the Interpol warrant, the red one. My mother might die soon and would I be able to go and bury her? Probably not. I was an orphan now, like Misha, open to reinvention.

So, gazing at the fire, I went on: 'This Branko-man also tried to rape me but he didn't succeed, even though he threatened me with the gun in question.'

'This happened in London?' Zorana asked. That was all she needed to know: if it happened somewhere certifiable. As a Macedonian, she knew how little it mattered if it had happened in stupid Montenegro: it didn't really count then, but was more like a funny story from abroad, shared in a pub, laughed at, quickly forgotten.

'Not in London,' I said, raising my voice above Branko's insults and threats directed at me in our language.

Saša was back from toilet.

'It happened in Montenegro,' I replied to Zorana. 'But, he's a rapist. That's what I've been trying to tell you. He's this re*tarded* brother of the wife of Montenegrin president. That's why he's a diplomat. They too wanted to get rid of him. He's a burden even for his family. Why do you think not one woman from Montenegro would marry the First brother-in-law, now an Ambassador?'

'Yeah,' Saša, high on coke, was saying. 'Yeah, right. I wouldn't marry Branko, no way.'

'They're all whores there, like you,' Branko said, inhaled violently and turned to Misha.

'Wait till I tell Smeško what I have found in London,' he went on. 'The murdering whore. Working as a nanny! In your family. Ha! Why your family, of all the ten million families with nannies here? It stinks like cowshit. Well, she'll never sleep soundly again with the network Smeško has here.' Then he turned back to me and started counting on his fingers. 'The Russians, the Albanians, the many who owe him a favour . . . Hard people, all of them, in all kinds of packaging. You don't have to be dead. You lose hair, skin, speech, organs. They defeat you, millimeter by millimeter, like cancer.'

Dina threw champagne into his face. 'I felt sick the moment I saw you,' she said.

'No!' Zorana cried. 'I should've stayed in bed!'

Branko wiped his face routinely with a napkin, as if people threw drinks at him every day.

'Branko, my friend, be a man,' Misha said. 'Leave Millie alone. Why do you threaten her with Smeško and his network? What's she got to do with it?'

'Isn't Smeško in jail?' I asked.

'Are you kidding?' It was Perić now who snapped. Nobody was allowed to disrepute his *intimus*. 'Smeško in jail? Why? The man is enjoying his active retirement.'

'What? Is he also an *author* now, writing a memoir?'

'Don't you joke about a man like Smeško, you, crimi-nal,' Branko yelled, stood up and walked towards me. 'He still has evidence against you. The weapon, your meetings and rows with Chris in his hotel suite, every-thing!'

I laughed out loud and he jumped on my armchair, grabbed my head and tried to throw me off, push me into the flames, to burn, like a witch!

Dina and Zorana screamed in unison. Misha ran to us, pulled Branko off me and slapped him twice.

'Saša, sit down,' I heard Perić say.

'Sorry, man' Misha told Branko, 'but you had too much to drink.'

Branko threw his head forward and hit Misha on the nose with his brow. Misha squatted and cupped his bleeding nose with his hands.

Dina screamed again. 'Somebody better get this *sickness* out of my house!' Branko turned to her with a slightly apologetic look on his face and Misha,

smudged blood on his face, used the moment to stand up and push Branko from the back, down on the floor, from where he started throwing his long legs about, trying to kick Misha, but all he succeeded hit-ting with his foot was one of the stone vases filled with white flowers. He yelled out in pain. The vase was over-turned, water spilt on the floor, the bouquet of jasmine and roses too.

Zorana, probably realising that the marriage was off and she'd better kept her cash coming, jumped up and, in her lovely high heels, she ran to clean the mess.

334

Misha seized his guest's arm and pulled him back to his feet. Immediately forgetting the pain, Branko started insulting me again.

'Look what you did, you whore,' he said and spat in my direction. Then he came closer to me to spit directly into my face. There was blood in his spit. 'You're destroying another nice family!' he cried standing above me, preparing his fist to hit me.

'Branko!' Misha roared and Branko twitched and retreated from me. 'Enough now.'

'Let me tell you something, my friend,' Branko replied. 'The family of the man she'd fucked in Montenegro she already destroyed. He had to leave the country and he was an ambitious politician. He is nothing now, a forgotten man! Then she shot an American lobbyist because he wouldn't help her with the visa for the US. I know you fucked her. So watch your back is all I'm saying!'

'Misha!' Dina screamed and threw herself at Branko, her nails, like claws, aiming for his face. 'Get rid of this monster!'

Misha caught her and held her in his arms while smirking at Perić over his wife's shoulder. 'Is Branko talking about Chris?' he asked.

Perić nodded, almost imperceptibly.

'And you framed *Millie*? For my lob-job?'

'She wrote that letter to Vukas,' Perić almost whispered.

'Fuck,' Dina said and covered her mouth. 'What humiliation in my own house. Get rid of this man, Misha.'

'Misha Grishin can't get rid of me,' Branko said. 'He needs me. Only I can make him an honorary consul of Montenegro! He needs Perić more than he needs you, Dina. If Perić says *kaput*, your man's bank account in Perić's bank is nothing but a handful of dust, and that lovely villa in Como which you consider yours . . . It still belongs to Mr Lazar Perić here. Ask your husband.'

'Is this true?' Dina shouted at Misha and wriggled out of his embrace. 'You told me you'd never move our cash!'

'Calm down, Dina,' Misha said.

'Calm down? And I told you if you fucked with the Balkans you'd get a devil for life. What money did you move to Montenegro?'

'Ah, just the small lump of it all, I'm sure,' said Perić, still sitting at the dining table, and lighting up another cigarette. 'No big deal. A business window delightfully opened.'

'Oh, that's really great, Misha. So clever. Anything else? What about that dead *lobbyist*? Your domain? The *lob-job*? You sure know some handymen for a lob-job. Ha. Don't think I don't listen to your phone conversations while the shower is running.'

Zorana, having cleaned the mess, came back from somewhere with a wet cloth for Misha to wipe his face. Misha sunk his head into the cloth and Zorana sat down on the sofa and began to cry. Branko walked to her, tall and proud.

'You don't want to stay here one more day I hope,' he said to the little Macedonian. 'It's not healthy, this family. Come with me to my hotel. I respect nice girls like you, hardworking and -'

'Leave my girls alone,' Misha said. 'They are nice girls. Zorana is too good for you, and Millie . . . Millie couldn't hurt a fly.'

'You didn't know Milena before she became a *nanny*, my friend,' Branko remained adamant about me. 'She killed a guy. She changed her name.'

'She didn't kill anybody,' Misha said. 'She certainly didn't kill Chris.'

'It's easy for you to toy with that incident,' Perić said to Misha, getting up and motioning to Saša to follow him towards the front door. 'Living like this, comfortably in the heart of London, visiting Monte only to see that a job gets done. People were investigating. Fucking *agents*, incorporating into the local society, cooperating with the forensics in Belgrade, in Germany. Then the *man's* wife started freaking out.' Perić put his palms together. 'Thank God for Smeško and his network.'

'This is serious shit!' Saša cried. 'I didn't know that old Chris guy was killed. Wow. He had it coming though. Would never pay for his coke.'

'Shut up, love' Perić said. 'You're shaking. Here,' and he put his coat over her shoulders. His grin was leaking from his mouth, silently, like poisonous gas. 'Can you call us a cab?' he asked Misha.

'I'll drive you,' Misha said. 'Let me get my Audi out.'

Dina threw her head back and laughed. 'It's just getting better and better, isn't it?' she said, looking at me. '*Moy muzh* . . . Doing lob-jobs. Ha. Now he's turning into a chauffeur for the wealthy Montenegrins. Ha! Once an orphan, always an orphan! Such a doomed state of mind.'

'Dina!' Misha roared and slammed the front door behind him.

His wife's laughter was filled with fear. I knew it because I felt it too. Misha, the good man, where had he gone? Not only a chauffeur, but a murderer and a pimp? Why? To pay for a villa in Italy and make Dina happy because she'd provided an instant family for him? That was stupid, but isn't it always a stupid thing – something that looks romantic, cool, wild, brave, *different* in the beginning - that does one in, in the end?

Perić approached Branko and gently yanked his arm to lead him out of the house. 'Come,' he said. 'We'll wait for Misha outside. Thank you, Dina.'

Dina ignored him. He looked at me, looking ready to spit a nail between my eyes. Or just to spit at me.

'I'm not afraid of you,' I said to Perić. 'You're like the dirty froth on the sparkling Adriatic sea. You're nothing but scum to me.'

He opened his mouth in an attempt to produce a reply, but, for once, he produced nothing.

Saša did though. 'Sounds great!' she said. 'Can I use your words in a song?'

'Get out,' I said. 'Just get the fuck out of here.'

Saša waved her fingers at us. 'Ciao, everyone, see you!'

I locked the door after them.

Dina took my hands and squeezed them in hers. 'Millie,' she said, 'can you sleep here tonight?'

I said yes, and she collapsed on the sofa, where she sobbed and pressed her fingers into her left temple as if trying to burst the bubble of migraine pain. Zorana was just sitting around, in her high heels. The parcels of casino money were still scattered around the room. I sighed and looked up and saw Alex and Nensi on the top of the stairs, holding each other in terror. I went to them, wondering how long ago they'd been up.

'So, *will* you stay here tonight?' Alex asked through tears.

'Only if you go to bed now.'

'Why . . .' Nensi started. 'Are mummy and daddy going to be all right?'

'Oh, yeah. Those guests were not good people but they are gone now. Puff.'

'Will you go to bed with us?'

'Yes, let's all go to Nensi's bed.'

It took a while before they fell asleep. I had to read two picture books and tell one story from my childhood before I heard them breathing evenly with sleep.

Dina was pacing the rooms; I recognised her steps. She finally entered Nensi's room. I closed my eyes, pretending to sleep, tucked between her children. I could smell the crisp new, Casino money notes off Dina, could hear them rustling against her shirt as she bent down and kissed all three of us, on the mouth.

'*Laka noch*,' she whispered. Good night.

In the darkness of Nensi's room, I thought about one of the children's books I had read to them before sleep. *The Princess and the Wizard*. The wizard captured the princess on her birthday party by turning all the guests to stone, including the princess's fairy godmother who managed to say: 'The princess may try seven times to escape by changing her colour and changing her shape!'

before she too was calcified. So the princess tried and tried; changed herself into a blue fish, a yellow chick, an orange fox, a purple butterfly, a black cat, but every time the wizard would spy on her plans, and she'd get caught and given worse and worse things to do. Until the last attempt – when she turned herself into a blank page of the wizard's wicked spy book. Blank, blank, blank. Nothing! The wizard found no use of the book anymore and he hurled it into a moat. 'Off with you!' The princess was free. But not before she became a blank page, and useless for the wizard.

I sneaked out of Nensi's bed, put my clothes back on, tiptoed down the stairs and left the Grishin mansion for the last time. I walked home stooping under the rain, this time genuinely forgetting the huge umbrella of Hotel *Baglioni*.

I was almost on the bridge when I spotted a lonely car sliding over it with the soft purr of its engine. It was a big SUV, with the plate that said DINA I. Well, weren't we a perfect illustration for a doomed love, miscarried from its beginning, Misha and I? My sinful brother, an orphan, looking for a home, looking for me, knowing I would sneak out of his house after all. What did he want to tell me that I didn't already know? That there were places on this planet, my motherland included, where nothing mattered, nothing counted as reality and everything could be swallowed and digested? Or was he going to ask me what to do next, where to go? To a desert, I'd say, to a war, what else was left? 'And, oh,' I would add, 'leave the best part of you with Dina and her children. Leave them your cash, their new motherland.'

I didn't want Misha to see me, so I ran down the bridge stairs that led to the quiet river that swallows everything, and waited there to hear his car drive by.

One day, maybe. I'll have to move countries again, Southern Hemisphere sounds good, if I try not to mess it up with the entire establishment, perhaps find a real man, someone like Rafi, and together we could enjoy much nicer Novembers. But for now, I was still being *impaired* when paired.

Misha drove by with his car window rolled down. I could afford another glimpse at his face, at the handsome profile of the man that could blend in anywhere, be it a bridge or a continent away from where I stayed. Well, if he needed me, he could always find me. But now, most of all, I needed a toilet.

Back on the roof

Yola always worries when I'm on the roof. She's sure that, sooner or later, I, or anyone else who doesn't read Tony Robbins, may be tempted to jump off. She'll be glad to know that I won't jump off. I want to use the computer at work today (it is Saturday, my busy day at Citizens Advice Bureau) and send an email to Elke Konelke. Elke is still the biggest expert I know when it comes to relocating women. I'll ask her to relocate me neatly, like she did Sonja, to a third, neutral country, with a new identity, and I'll promise that this time I'll learn not to have problematic relationships with a society and its unwritten laws. At worst, if I have to have problems at all, I'll limit myself to one person, and not necessarily a man. I'll beg her to send me down, somewhere deep in the Southern Hemisphere, where I can call myself Mumba the Mute and experiment with making raw, cooling cocktails.

Yes, everyone will be better off. This doesn't make me sad.

Dina will leave Misha, take his money, buy herself a Bentley, and make peace with the fact that Babushka is the best, the most rooted nanny she'll ever find.

Misha will end up back in Bashkiria or some similar empty vastness, if he wants to live. But perhaps he doesn't really care what kills him – vice or men - once he's lost his dream of creating himself a cosy little family.

Even my parents will be happier with me mixing drinks in the middle of a sub-Saharan revolution, say, than remaining in this town where, in their opinion, and according to the news from the Internet they've been following, the benign Delboys and Rodneys had surrendered to the nameless yet protected terrorists, pedophiles, queers and pervert-nannies that had littered in this bone-eating climate from all around the world.

Zorana should marry Rafi and, together with Yola and Isztvan, convert 'Around-the-World' from a small catering company to a truly international food shrine: cooking courses, TV competitions and all that elbowing.

I'm ready for a CAB Saturday filled with people with no idea what to do next in their lives. They'll be complaining, their voices heavy with suppressed sobs, and I'll be a great listener because I'm in a more bizarre position than they are: I'm a model UK resident, first generation; I can teach humility, the useful craft I had to master after being exiled from my own village; I have

344

no children, no computer and no mobile phone; no car, no property; I use cash and Oyster card – and yet, I have powerful enemies with scary networks all over the world. Money-loaded criminals and their globetrotting debtors. But if they're all over the world, why should I run away from London and be on the run forever? Why should I let them win? I'm not going to let them win.

I'm staying. Another year. Another year is what we all ask for. The hunters, the prey, the good, the bad. We are all the same - only as strong as our last encounter with ourselves.

Author's note
& acknowledgments:

This novel was inspired by a true story of a Moldovan girl trafficked to Montenegro. However, everything has been fictionalised, as must be for novel-writing.

I would like to thank my brilliant London-based writing group, The Unwriteables: Cynthia Medford Wilson, Ginevra White, Thea Bennet, Pippa Griffin, Anna Hope, Martha Close, Matthew Weait, David Savill, Josh Raymond, Philip Makatrewicz and Keith Jarrett – for their support, corrections, patience and encouragement.